The Meluhhan Oracle

I J Roy

First published as *The Pparahan Oracle* in 2014.

This edition published in 2015 by Scorpio Books

Copyright © 2013 I J Roy

All rights reserved.

ISBN: 0692358242
ISBN-13: 978-0692358245

Dedicated to

The loving memories of
My dear father
Late S. B. Roy

And

Father-in-law
Late S. Kitao

ACKNOWLEDGMENTS

First of all, I would like to thank my mother, who was also the first person to read my completed manuscript, and let me know that she had bought and read worse.

Next, I would like to thank my three sisters for all their time and advice, and my nieces and brothers-in-law for bearing with the intrusions. Without their support, I would have never been able to complete The Meluhhan Oracle.

Both my sons will not be able to read this book for a few years. However, the genesis of this book is my elder son's history project on Indus Valley Civilization. And without my younger son's insistence on hearing bedtime stories that were made up by me, instead of being read one from the books, I may not have ever thought of writing a book.

Last and definitely not least, I would like to thank my wife. She not only read my book, but also was the first person to edit it. And throughout the months when I was writing The Meluhhan Oracle, she made sure that nothing interrupted my endeavours.

Voices in the Night

Tiraa woke up with a start. Her parents' voices floated up from the courtyard. At first, she thought it was their voices that had woken her up, but then the stomach cramps returned. Her upper thighs and back continued to throb long after the cramping had stopped, and the pain kept her awake. She wondered how late it was. She could not hear what her parents were saying, but she could make out that her mother was doing most of the talking. This was strange; her father was usually the talkative one. She also could hear her mother sobbing. This, too, was strange; her mother rarely cried. Tiraa knew her mother's crying had something to do with the visit to the Temple Sanctuary earlier that day. *Does it also have something to do with what happened at the Baths*, she wondered.

In the beginning, she thought nothing of the changes that her body was going through, until that day at the Baths. Whenever her mother could find time, they went to the Baths together. Avraa, the woman supervising the Baths, had taken her mother aside that day, and Tiraa had thought nothing of it. This was nothing new, after all Zayaa, her mother, was a striking woman. With her translucent, milk-like complexion, sandy-white hair and pink eyes, which were further highlighted by eyelashes and eyebrows a shade darker than her hair, she turned heads wherever she went. In addition, Zayaa was also taller than most women in Pparaha[1]. Everyone always wanted to be around her. However, when Tiraa heard Avraa mention Tiraa's name, she started paying attention to their conversation.

---

[1]A city in East-Central Meluhha near River Ravi

"Avraa, you don't know what you are talking about. You should stop staying out in the sun all day. The heat is cooking your brains. Tiraa is still a little girl," Zayaa was saying.

"I am still a little girl in my mother's eyes," Avraa said, "that has not stopped me from having five children of my own. Are you sure Tiraa has not started having her monthly visits from Aunt Moon. You know it does not matter who her parents are, she will need to register her dates. And she will not be allowed in the Baths from four days before her dates, until the day after Aunt Moon leaves. If she has not started, yet, she soon will. Look how tall she has suddenly become. And I can make out her breasts from here. Only last week she jumped into the bath from the high steps. I have never seen her behave with more confidence. And when she got scolded for it, she became uncharacteristically sensitive and started crying like a baby. And look at her standing there; all hands and feet. I think …"

"Stop thinking," Zayaa cut in. To Tiraa, her mother seemed to get taller as she lifted up her chin and looked down at Avraa. "I am not any ordinary mother. I am the Dreamer of Truths Yet to Come. I know when my daughter will become a woman."

"My heartfelt apologies, O Dreamer of Truths Yet to Come," Avraa said softly, her eyes downcast with acquiescence. Zayaa's friendly disposition sometimes made others forget the power she wielded over them. "I would never try to disagree with you."

"It is all right. I know you mean well," Zayaa said, calming down.

Tiraa could make out the wistfulness in Zayaa's voice. Tiraa herself was surprised, and not pleasantly, by these changes. Though Tiraa usually took all her problems to her father, Vyaan, her instincts told her that this was a discussion she needed to have with her mother. Tiraa loved both her parents, but she was closer to her father. When she had been a child, Vyaan had chosen to stop travelling and stay at home, to take care of her. Her mother, though, had often left home. Tiraa had, however, completely understood about her mother's absence. She knew well that her mother, being a senior Dasasa, had many duties to perform for the town and its people.

Tiraa also knew that one could not choose to become a Dasasa; rather, one was chosen. The Dasasas were servants to the Gods. While most were chosen when at least three of the six High Priests along with the Chief High Priest received a sign that identified a girl between the ages of five and twelve as destined to be a Dasasa, there were a special few, who were chosen directly by the Gods. In such cases, the Gods sent a message about their choice to the Chief High Priest of the Temple Sanctuary, who would in turn inform the people. Only three Dasasas in Pparaha had been chosen in this way, and Zayaa was the only one who was still alive. In Zayaa's case, she had been above twelve when she was chosen—this had never happened before or again in Pparaha. In addition, Zayaa had already been married when she was chosen. This was unprecedented across Givenland[2]. Though the Dasasas could get married and most of them did, too, but they did so only after becoming a Dasasa. Zayaa had been proclaimed as the Dreamer-of-Truths-Yet-to-Come, and whenever the High Priests needed any guidance about the future, Zayaa would go and stay at the Temple Sanctuary, sometimes for days. She usually came back battered and worn out, both physically and mentally. Tiraa had never asked why, for she knew not to ask her mother that. In the recent years though, Tiraa had observed that Zayaa did not have to stay over at the Temple Sanctuary, as much as she used to. However, except for the few days after the festivals and solstices, her mother still had to spend most of her days there.

Though Tiraa got to spend much more time with Zayaa than before, she felt bashful in discussing her changes with her mother. In the next few weeks, Tiraa found that she was becoming heavier, especially in her arms, thighs and upper back. Her chest was getting harder. Her hips seemed to be growing too, while strangely, her waist was getting narrower. Soon, more bizarre things started to happen. She noticed some hair between her legs, and Tiraa was sure she was turning into an animal. When she lifted her arms, she noticed hair under them, as well. She decided not to wait anymore, and ask her father what she should do next.

"Appi," Tiraa braved herself and approached her father, "I am not sure whether I am supposed to talk to you or Ayei. I seem to be growing hair, under my arms, much like you, and in some other places, as well. I am really worried that I may be turning into an animal—or even worse a man."

Vyaan smiled at his daughter, and at that moment, Tiraa's fears seemed to leave her. Unlike her mother, there was nothing striking about her father's looks. He was of average height, his skin darker than most people, his features a little on the blunt side. Though he did not look too muscular, he was very strong. However, none of these had set him apart from the others, but his smile and eyes captivated people. His eyes not only shone with intelligence, but also seemed to comfort people and tell them that he could be trusted with anything, and his smile always made people forget their worries.

2What the people living in Meluhha called their own land (explanation in Chapter 7: The Akkadian's Tale I)

"Tii, don't you worry about it," Vyaan said reassuringly, although a little uncomfortably, "believe me, this happens to every girl. Your Ayei will explain these changes to you. As you know, she is very busy now, preparing for the Harvest Festival. Talk to her after the festival is over. You only have to wait for a few more days,' he suggested, 'and speaking of the festival, on the day after tomorrow, your Ayei wants us to go to the Temple Sanctuary to see the preparations."

"Are you sure?" Tiraa asked, wondering if her father was joking, "but we have never been there except for the festivals and solstices." Then, realizing her father was serious, she grew excited, "great! I will put on the new dress that you got for me. Not the special one. *That* one I will save for the festival. Can we go tomorrow and surprise her? Please, please say yes," Tiraa pleaded, fluttering her eyelids and smiling impishly at her father. Vyaan had no possible defence against his daughter's charms.

Chapter 1

Apart from the outer enclosures for farms, brick-works and such, Pparaha was built as a perfect square. It had thirty-three[3] streets going northeast to southwest, and another thirty-three streets going northwest to southeast. Though the number of streets differed in the different towns and cities of Givenland, the number of streets was usually a palindrome in binary. The Givenlanders had two numerals, the female and the male. The numbers starting and ending with the female numeral were considered auspicious and lucky. There were some old towns that were not built in this way, though, but since Rahira[4]—which had eighteen[5]—streets, was destroyed by a fire, all the towns have followed this pattern. Some were even expanded to make sure they had the necessary number of streets. The distances between Pparaha's streets were the same, except for the three central streets, which were one-and-a-half-times as long as the others were. All the streets had the same width, too, of thirty-three haths[6]—exactly two haths from each edge. There were one hath-wide paving stones covering the three-quarter hath-wide drains.

In Pparaha, except for the Baths, granaries and a few other communal buildings, all the houses were built on similar-sized plots. Each block created by the streets was divided into twenty-five plots, with narrow lanes leading to the inner houses. The only exceptions were the plots enclosed by the central streets. These plots were two and a quarter times the size of the other plots. A few of them were occupied by the High Priests and Dasasas,

---

[3]100001 in binary
[4]A town in South-Western Meluhha/ Givenland
[5]10010 in binary (equivalent to 010010)
[6]A unit for measuring length, used in Givenland (measuring approximately fourteen inches)

but most of them by young families, who had to keep ready two of their rooms for children whose family had taken ill and had been quarantined.

The Temple Sanctuary was at the centre of the town. It was the square created by the outer two of the three central streets. Zayaa had left home that day for the temple, soon after sunrise, and around noon, Tiraa and Vyaan had started for the temple too, to surprise Zayaa.

Tiraa's family lived on the centre street. Unlike the homes of the other senior Dasasas, their house was far from the Temple Sanctuary. Tiraa had once asked Vyaan the reason for this. He had laughed and said that it was because Zayaa loved eating, and she needed the exercise to maintain her figure. From their house, they had to walk eleven blocks to the Temple Sanctuary. Vyaan was almost as popular with the townsfolk as Zayaa, owing to his good and helpful nature, and therefore their journey took longer than it should have, for they had to stop often and talk to people.

Tiraa and Vyaan finally saw the façade of the Temple Sanctuary. Except for being much taller, its walls looked exactly like those of the other houses. The main entrance of the temple faced the Northeast. The entrance was imposing, but there were no doors or gates, for the temple needed no protection from anything or anyone. On both sides of the doorway, the walls were recessed by about ten haths. At about half the height of the walls, there was an eave running around the boundary wall of the Temple Sanctuary.

When they arrived at the doorway of the Temple Sanctuary, they met one of the other Dasasas, Divitaa.

"What are you doing here? Does Zayaa know that you are coming here today?" Divitaa demanded in an urgent whisper. "Anyway, let us walk back a few blocks. Then, we can talk," she instructed, looking around furtively.

"Well," Vyaan said, a little surprised at Divitaa's frantic demeanour, "she asked us to come tomorrow. We decided to surprise her though. We thought ..."

"Vyaan, you should know better," Divitaa scolded, "if she said tomorrow, she must have had a reason for it. Anyway, let's not stand here," she repeated.

"What is the hurry now, Divitaa? And who are these people?" a voice said from under the left awning of the temple doorway.

The Chief High Priest, Apaan, and two other High Priests, then, emerged from the shadows on one side of the doorway. It was easy to identify the High Priests by their braided beards, as no one else was allowed to braid their beards. This ensured that, wherever they went, the High Priests were treated with respect. Apaan was much taller than the other two. He was, also, very pale, his eyes almost colourless. His hair and beard were coloured red, with the leaves of the henna tree. He wore a metal headband, with a bright sparkling blue stone inlaid on it at the centre. Tiraa had only seen him during the festivals, standing on the Ceremonial Platform, adorned with jewellery, a lion skin cloak draped over his shoulders. Up close, he did not look as imposing, but when she looked at his cold emotionless eyes, like those of a dead fish, she felt a shiver run through her.

"Oh, it is Zayaa's husband, I see," Apaan remarked. Then, he turned to Tiraa. "And, this can't be Zayaa's daughter. The way Zayaa talks about her daughter, you would think she is still a baby. *This*, however, is a lady I see before me," Apaan said, turning towards the other High Priests. There was a twinkle in his eyes as he spoke this, which only made him look even more fiendish.

Before anyone else could speak, Apaan continued, "So, Divitaa, why are you chasing our guests away? As you well know, we all are devotees of you Dasasas. And your families are always welcome at the sanctuary."

"O Chief High Priest, I did not want them to disturb the preparations. As I am in a hurry, I was asking if we could walk and talk," Divitaa said, bowing her head in deference.

"Divitaa, if you are in a hurry, you can very well run along, but leave the visitors with me," Apaan ordered.

Divitaa could not find any excuse to stay behind with the guests. She left, after giving Vyaan a reproachful look.

"So Vyaan, what is the name of your lovely daughter?" Apaan asked.

"Tiraa, O Chief High Priest," Vyaan answered.

"Hello, Tiraa. Please go ahead, walk inside with your father and meet your virtuous mother," Apaan said with a roguish smile.

Vyaan quickly took Tiraa's hand.

"She may not have her mother's skin, but she looks just as delicious. Perhaps, she is also destined to be a Dasasa after all," they heard Apaan tell the other priests as they went inside.

"What does he mean by being delicious, Appi? I thought you were chosen to be a Dasasa," Tiraa asked, turning towards her father.

13

"He was joking, Tii. They mean you will cheer up the Temple Sanctuary and make the atmosphere here tasty," Vyaan answered weakly. He realized that their arriving at the temple early was a mistake. He wanted to go back and confront the Chief High Priest, but stopped himself as that would only make the matters worse. He wanted to get to the inner courtyard as soon as possible, but Tiraa refused to be hurried.

Tiraa had been to the Temple Sanctuary many times before, but those visits had been made during festivals, when the place had been crowded. She had, therefore, never been able to see the whole courtyard; now, as she saw it for the first time, she was captivated by its simplicity and symmetry. The bricks on the floor were of four different shades of brown, and the manner in which they had been latticed together gave an illusion that the floor was not flat, but a myriad of steps going up and down in all directions. There stood seven pillars, each coming up to Tiraa's shoulders in height – running from every corner of the outer walls to the corresponding corners of the inner courtyard. There were five more pillars, erected in a straight line from each of these pillars, leading to the path they were taking. The pillars closest to the path were the shortest, increasing in height with the tallest ones closest to the outer walls. On festival days, these pillars had ropes tied to them, to create a meandering path for the throngs of people going towards the doorway of the inner courtyard. And on the winter and summer solstices, they were used to create spaces for people to sit and stand in, providing them with a clear view of the Ceremonial Platform that was erected for such occasions. Without any of these usual encumbrances or limitations, the open courtyard and its geometric symmetry were mesmerizing.

She was brought out of her daze by a sharp tug from Vyaan.

"Are you all right? Come on, let's go and find your mother," her father's voice, seemed to be floating from far away.

"Can't we stay in this courtyard a little longer?" Tiraa pleaded. "Who knows when I can see this courtyard empty again?"

"Let's run along and find your Ayei," Vyaan insisted.

Tiraa grudgingly followed him, as he moved towards the inner courtyard.

As they entered, they saw Zayaa. "Ayei!"

Zayaa turned quickly on hearing her daughter's voice and dropped the clay tray she was holding the moment she saw Tiraa.

"What is my daughter doing here?" she hissed at Vyaan, not hiding her anger.

"My daughter?" Vyaan chuckled good-naturedly, "I brought *our* daughter along to see the festival preparations, as we had already discussed."

"I think," Zayaa began, her eyes blazing and nose flaring, "no, not think, but I *know* that we clearly talked about you both coming here tomorrow. So why are you here today with my daughter?"

Vyaan noted that she had persisted with *my daughter*, but decided to let it pass for the moment.

"We thought you would be surprised – pleasantly, of course," Vyaan said, regretting about giving in to his daughter's wish. "I have already realized that we have made a mistake. Now that we are here, what do you want us to do?"

"Leave, of course," Zayaa snapped. "I will take you to the back entrance. I will explain later, but for now, just leave. Immediately!"

"Ayei," Tiraa called out in a confused voice, for she had never seen her mother act like this before. "Can't we stay and watch the preparations for a while? Besides, why should we leave from the back? Our house is much closer to the front entrance."

Before Zayaa could answer, Vyaan said, "Your Ayei is worried that we might disturb the High Priests. She does not know that we have already met them on the way in."

When Zayaa heard this, it was almost as if some kind of physical force had hit her, and had hit her hard. She fell to the ground, her hand clutched to her heart.

"Which High Priest did you meet?" Zayaa asked in a weak whisper. "Not Apaan, I hope?" Her voice was anything but hopeful, though. It seemed that she already knew otherwise, but was merely pleading with Vyaan, with the world and the Gods for it not to be true.

"We did meet Apaan and two other High Priests, outside the main doorway, while we were talking to Divitaa," Vyaan said.

"You met Divitaa, and she did not ask you to leave? She let you come in? I thought she was my friend," Zayaa said.

"She was asking us to leave, when Apaan intervened," Vyaan defended Divitaa.

"Please leave now," Zayaa said again. "Darling Tii, please listen to your Ayei, and don't argue. Leave now with your father through the back entrance."

There was something in Zayaa's voice that was beginning to scare Tiraa. She did not argue anymore, as asked of her, and let herself be led to the back door.

At the door, Zayaa turned to Vyaan. "Please leave Tiraa with Divitaa. If I know her, Divitaa will be lurking somewhere close by, between here and our house. She will find you, I'm sure, once you start walking back home. Please go and see Mother Tanaa, and tell her exactly what happened, about Tiraa and you both meeting Apaan. Tell her we need to see her. The festival is in three days. I don't think I can go outside the town gates before that without raising some eyebrows. Ask her if we can meet on the day after the festival," she stopped to take a deep breath and then looked into Vyaan's eyes, "I know you will make everything all right–only you can."

She held onto Tiraa's shoulders and turned her around, to face her. She stroked the girl's hair and cheeks and whispered, almost as if to herself, "Go, my darling and don't worry, even if I cannot save you, your father will. Never doubt his strength. If he wants to stand his ground, a hundred elephants cannot move him."

Chapter 2

Zayaa came back to the inner courtyard. She started picking up the scattered pieces of the tray she had dropped, and thus broken, on hearing Tiraa's voice.

While she was working, Apaan came to her, "I saw that trader and your daughter earlier. Where are they?"

"They had to leave."

"I did not see them leave," Apaan said in a stern voice. "Did you send them out through the back door? You know the back door is not supposed to be used by anyone, but the Dasasas or the High Priests. Not even their guests. Don't tell me you broke the rules."

"Rules," Zayaa scoffed, "do you mean to tell me that the women who are let out through the back door in the mornings, that too from the priests' quarters, are High Priests? Some of them are definitely not Dasasas," she mocked.

"Well, well, well," Apaan said. "I see our Dreamer has started rebelling again. We will have to do something about it, won't we?"

Zayaa immediately grew wary. She knew Apaan for the venomous snake that he was. He was not only unscrupulous and cunning, but also exceptionally intelligent. No one had ever beaten Apaan in a game of Goats and Lion – and it never did matter if he played as Lion or Goats. Zayaa had suffered enough in his hands to know not to antagonize him.

"I am sorry. I did not mean that," Zayaa said quickly, a little demurely.

However, Apaan seemed already distracted. "From the way you talk about her, I would not have guessed Tiraa had grown up so much," he smiled, stroking his beard. "She is a woman now. I must be getting old, failing to keep track of the seasons. Now I understand why you never have your family over, in the privileged enclosure during festivals. What a fool I was to believe it was because Vyaan did not like being differentiated or favoured. It was to make sure I did not see this daughter of yours, wasn't it?"

"You promised that you would do nothing to her. You promised she would not be made into a Dasasa," Zayaa implored.

"I made no such promise," Apaan said, still continuing to stroke his beard. "I said that she would not be singled out. And we are certainly not singling her out. Already, two High Priests and I have seen the signs, now if one more High Priest does see the signs, who are we to get in nature's way?" then bringing his lips close to her ears, he whispered hoarsely, "but you know how it works, don't you? Why even keep this secret from you? Like when it was with you, I felt the signs in my loins." He laughed.

"Stop," Zayaa screamed, covering her ears, "you know she is your daughter."

"She *could* be my daughter," Apaan corrected and gave her a feverish smile, "but most probably, she is not. It is one in seven chances, after all, for I had shared you equally with the six other High Priests. And, considering that the others lack any imagination and know only to enjoy a woman in the traditional way, I think the chances of me being her father are even lower. The only thing that we all can be sure about, however, is that Vyaan is not her father. Tiraa does not know that, does she? Won't it break her poor little heart when she finds out?"

"Please, Apaan," Zayaa pleaded, "I have always done whatever you asked of me. I have debased myself for you. I will burn in hell for the rest of eternity, for the things I have done for you, to myself and to others. All I ask is that my daughter be spared."

"Come on, Zayaa, you are being childish. People call me the Lion of Pparaha. Would a lion let a fawn go just because he has fed on the mother's flesh?" Apaan laughed at his own play of words.

"Curse you," Zayaa hissed, "I will not let this happen. I will destroy you. I will call for a referendum. I will go to the Grand Council of High Priests. I will have you removed from your position. I will tell everyone about what you have done to me, and to the other Dasasas."

"I know you would like to do this," Apaan said with a smile, but continued with steel in his voice, "but haven't you been thinking about it for the last twelve years? Have you been able to do anything? No, you have not. And you will not be able to, either. The very quality that attracted me to you – your pale, pale skin – can be made into your biggest flaw. People fear and hate anything or anybody that is different. I would only have to so much as point in your direction, and they will indeed believe you are a 'witch'. And, before you know it, you will be sat on a stake[7]. Imagine the sharp point going into you, into your entrails, through your anus, tearing your body up over two or three days. The jackals will begin to gnaw at you long before you are dead. No, I don't think you can do anything. I will think about your request, surely. For now, go to my quarters and wait for me. The picture of you on a stake has woken up something inside me. I will be there soon. I think we can put that beautiful body of yours to better use than being sat on a stake. When I get there, I want you to be completely naked. All I want to see on you is that goat collar."

Zayaa knew arguing with him was futile. She quietly went to Apaan's room. Apaan's room was a very large square. It was always brightly lit with four torches along each wall and a huge chandelier mounted with uncountable candles hanging from the centre. The candles were always sweetly scented with musk. There was a wash place in one corner, with many different types of soaps, all of which were again scented with flowers and citrus fruits. Like every time she had been in this room, Zayaa wondered why this room, which was a hell on earth for her, looked and felt exactly opposite of what everyone imagined hell would be like. All utensils in this room were made of clay. There were no sharp objects. The bed, which was higher than normal beds, was made of soft wood and not the usual coir ropes. There was nothing in the room that could be used to end one's life. Even the dishta[8] next to the wash place was made of soft wood. She quickly pushed this thought out. If she was to have any chance of saving Tiraa from a similar fate, she would have to bide her time. She could not allow this room to become Tiraa's hell. Fortunately for her, plenty of dhutura leaves were always available in his room. She chewed some. Once the dhutura got her high, it made what Apaan did less intolerable. She undressed and tied the collar made for goats around her neck. She then walked over to the bed and got down, beside it, on her hands and knees.

She sensed Apaan coming in. She felt the collar tighten around her skin, and found it difficult to breathe. Everything turned hazy and she could feel herself passing out, could not see or feel what Apaan was doing to her.

[7] A heinous form of execution – described in detail Chapter 7: The Akkadian's Tale I
[8] Dishta – grinder usually made of stone

When she came out of her stupor, there was no sign of Apaan. She went to the wash place in the corner of the room and cleaned herself. She realized that she was bleeding, from where Apaan had bitten her. She found the Banyan[9] bark and leaf buds in the usual place near the wash place. Apaan always kept a supply of these along with the turmeric root. Zayaa knew that it was not that Apaan cared whether his victims suffered, but did not want them blemished and also wanted to make sure his playthings recovered quickly. Using the dishta, Zayaa ground some leaves and bark of the Banyan into a paste, and applied it to her cuts. She picked up the turmeric root, without having to think about it. Usually, after one of these sessions with Apaan, she would let her mind wander away. Not this time, though, she told herself. She needed her mind to be undistracted this time, by other thoughts. She needed her pain to feel fresh. She could never let *this* happen to her Tiraa, she decided. She put down the turmeric. The turmeric would ease her pain; she, however, needed the pain.

Zayaa went back to the inner courtyard and continued working on the festival preparations. Some of the other Dasasas were there. She looked around at them, watching, thinking about them. Most of them had become a Dasasa after Zayaa, had come here in the first few weeks after their red river had started flowing. Many a time Zayaa had heard their screams for help, coming from the rooms of the High Priests. She had known what was happening, but had done nothing to help them. Until today, she had always said to herself that trying to do anything would only make a bad situation worse. Now, she was regretting that she had not even tried. Some of these girls had been younger than Tiraa when they had been brought here. She had let them down, she realized. She also knew that none of them would help her, especially if it meant inviting the wrath of the High Priests. She could not discuss her plans with them either, in case word of it got back to the High Priests. "What plans? Do you even have any?" a voice inside her mocked her. "No wonder you are called the Dreamer, Zayaa, for dreaming is all you can do."

Tears started flowing down her cheeks. Crying was not an uncommon occurrence amongst the Dasasas, at least in the privacy of the Temple Sanctuary. Outside, the Dasasas were supposed to act as if they felt privileged on being chosen to serve the Gods, had to create a façade of happiness and joviality for the rest of the town to believe, including their own families. And most of them did indeed have families. However, with all the things they had to bear within the walls of the Temple Sanctuary, they would have found it hard to survive without their moments of crying.

---

[9] The Banyan tree – the leaves and buds of which helps stop bleeding

Zayaa wept now because, as much as she tried, she could not see how she could save Tiraa. She had finally decided not to think about it, until she met Tanaa, the midwife of the town. Tanaa knew many things about plants and trees and about how they could be used in preventing and curing diseases that even the High Priests were unsure about. She could also, supposedly, talk to animals. There were rumours that she did all this through witchcraft. Years ago, the screaming-cow disease had killed almost all the cattle in other towns. However, Tanaa's quick thinking and care made sure that Pparaha had lost only one in ten. Since then, no one had cared whether she was a doctor or a witch. The High Priests realized that Tanaa had become very powerful, and though threatened, remained noncommittal about her, for they were not sure how people would react to any action taken against her. As long as she continued to live outside the town, they had reasoned, and did not visit or interfere with the doings of the Temple Sanctuary, they would tolerate her. None of the Dasasas were supposed to associate with Tanaa. However, this rule was broken more often than followed. Everyone in Pparaha thought that the Dasasas' physical pain and suffering were caused by their severe penances. They assumed that this was a price that they had to pay for being the chosen ones. However, if these penances started causing permanent damage, it would raise unwanted questions, and also might shake peoples' beliefs. And only Tanaa was capable of nursing the younger Dasasas back to health, after their initial, painful sessions with Apaan. Therefore, the Head Priest ignored this transgression, as well.

Zayaa made sure all her duties for the day were complete before she left the Temple Sanctuary. She walked home as slowly as she could. She wanted to delay facing the questions that Tiraa and Vyaan would ask her. When she had almost reached home, she spotted Divitaa sitting at the side of her street.

"You took your time," Divitaa complained, standing up. "I have been waiting here since sunset."

"Sorry," Zayaa said, without trying to explain.

"Don't be. I can imagine what you are going through. I always thank God that I only have sons and not..." she began, but when she saw the look on Zayaa's face, she stopped herself. "Sorry, I should not have said that. Well, I have been waiting, because I wanted to talk to you alone. Vyaan came back as the sun was setting. He informed me that he had gone to see Tanaa. He should not have told me this. You know very well what happens within our so-called sanctuary. Any of us – that includes you and me – can be bought off by promises, of even a few months of respite from it all. I

21

will try to help you, as long as it does not endanger my family or me. But, before you start on anything, think about the consequences it will have, on you, on Vyaan and, of course, on Tiraa. I know that you think you are saving her from a fate worse than death, but don't forget there are worse fates that could come upon her. I know you must hate me for saying this, but someone has to," Divitaa finished, looking directly into Zayaa's eyes.

"Divitaa, I know you are one of the few people whom I can trust, but I will not involve you in my trouble–not unless I am desperate, that is. In any case, first let us get the Harvest Festival out of the way," Zayaa said quietly.

"Are you sure you can afford to wait that long? I know it is only three days, but three days can be a long time."

"Tiraa is not a woman, yet. Her red river has not started flowing, yet. Even Apaan or his lackeys won't dare break that tradition."

"You might be right, but be careful. He is a cunning jackal. He always seems to stay a few steps ahead of everyone else," Divitaa said. "I need to take your leave now. Be strong and remember what I said."

"I will," Zayaa gave Divitaa a hug, leaving the latter shocked, for Zayaa was known for her dislike of physical contact.

When Zayaa entered her home, she found both Vyaan and Tiraa waiting for her in the inner courtyard.

"Please go ahead and wash up. It is quite late, but Tiraa wanted to wait and eat dinner with you. Let us eat, and then Tiraa can go to bed," Vyaan said.

Zayaa translated this for herself: *Let us not talk in front of Tiraa*, her husband was saying.

Zayaa did not feel like eating, but she said, "That is a very good idea. I am ravenous. So whose cooking am I being treated to today?"

"Appi had to go out. So, I cooked," Tiraa replied.

Tiraa had learnt cooking from both her parents. Though many of her friends made fun of the fact that Tiraa's father cooked, she did not care. She suspected that their teasing was rooted in their jealousy, in the fact that Vyaan was not embarrassed or ashamed to do any task, whether at home or outside.

After Zayaa had washed up, they proceeded to their eating room, which also doubled as their kitchen. Three colourful mats, measuring two haths by one-and-a-half hath, were placed in a row, and in front of each one was a clean piece of banana leaf. Vyaan sat down on the rightmost mat and invited Zayaa and Tiraa to sit down with him – this was another oddity limited only to their home. In the other houses of Pparaha, men ate first, then the children, and finally, came the adult women who shared whatever was left over. However, since Tiraa was also old enough to share their food, the three of them ate together. This was done at Vyaan's insistence. During his travels, once, Vyaan had gone to the lands that lay beyond that of the Sumerian people, and, there, his caravan had been attacked by a tribe of desert nomads. Vyaan had somehow managed to escape and had taken shelter with the people who lived in the nearby hills. According to these people's customs, they ate first, and anybody who was visiting them or had taken refuge with them, lived on the leftovers. Needless to say, Vyaan had not liked the experience. He had, as a result of enduring such indignity, decided that he would not have anyone else suffer the same.

Usually, Zayaa served the food, but on the days when Tiraa had done the cooking, the girl served it instead. Zayaa sat down on the left mat, leaving the middle one empty for Tiraa. "So, what have you experimented with today?" Vyaan smiled fondly at Tiraa.

Tiraa liked to be imaginative with her cooking and usually did not follow any set recipes.

"Nothing fancy today. You know I don't like being alone at home," Tiraa explained, washing her hands vigorously with soap, "and I hate baking bread, when no one is around to enjoy the aroma. I decided to cook the barley, rice and lentils, all together along with the vegetables. I did fry some fish though," she said, as she brought the clay pot, in which the hodgepodge had been cooked. The clay at the neck and mouth of the pot was different from the rest of the body and never became too hot to handle. She used a wooden ladle to serve it out of the pot into the right hand side of the banana leaves. She then fetched the fish and served it with her hand, both Vyaan and Zayaa received the fish in their palms.

Tiraa seemed to have some magic in her hands; even the hodgepodge, which had sounded lacklustre, had come out tasty.

"You need to give this a name and teach other people how to cook it. It is delicious," Zayaa complimented.

Vyaan did not have to say anything. His periodic 'mmh' left no one in doubt about how much he was enjoying his meal.

After they had finished, they washed their hands and rinsed their mouths. Vyaan went out to the courtyard and sat on the stairs, while Zayaa helped Tiraa clean up the eating area. Then, they joined Vyaan and sat down next to him.

"Appi, can you tell us a story from your travels? Even one of your made up ones would do," Tiraa pleaded.

"Okay, I will tell you a story," Vyaan said with a chuckle, "but you have to promise to go to sleep immediately after that. Your Ayei is tired and needs to go early to the temple tomorrow."

"I promise," Tiraa said, but then added a condition of her own, "but it has to be a new story. You cannot repeat one you've already told me."

"All right, I will try," Vyaan said shaking his head in mock exasperation and started, "once long time ago there was a young girl called Raati, who lived with her parents."

"Raati? What type of girl's name is that?" Tiraa interrupted, "Which land is she from?"

"Remember, you have to keep your questions for the end," Vyaan admonished. "As I always tell you, do not look at something only from one side. You should study everything from all directions. And, to answer your second question, she is of our people."

"Silly me!" Tiraa exclaimed, "of course, it is my name backwards. Ti Raa – Raa Ti."

"Yes it is," Vyaan agreed, and then warned her, "but remember the rules, if you interrupt me again, no more stories until the next new or full moon, whichever is later."

Tiraa put both her palms on her mouth and sat down.

"Anyway," Vyaan continued, smiling at his daughter's theatrics, "Raati liked to cook."

"Ap..mmmph," Tiraa started, but quickly put her hands over her mouth again.

"Not only did she love cooking," Vyaan continued, "she liked to experiment with new recipes."

"I hope you are telling her a real story and not just about herself." teased Zayaa.

"Have I ever?" Vyaan said in mock anger. "However, any more interruption from either of you, and I will surely stop."

"Sorry, please do continue," Zayaa said, in an apology that was as false as Vyaan's anger.

"Anyway, Raati lived in a farm with many animals," Vyaan began again. "One day, Raati decided to make a pancake, with all the vegetables, fish, meat and spices that were to be found in her kitchen. When she was just completing the pancake – just as she was flipping it for the last time – the pancake came to life and jumped out, onto the floor, and rolled out into the yard. As it rolled itself out, the first animal the pancake saw was a big cow. 'Moo, moo, I am going to eat you,' the cow said to the pancake, but as she came near the pancake, she smelt it and said, 'Yech, you stink of mutton – I can't eat you.' So, the pancake rolled on. Next, a dog saw the pancake. 'Woof, woof, you will disappear into my mouth, poof,' it claimed, but as he came near the pancake, he said, 'yech, you smell of pepper and mustard. I can't eat you.' The next animal to see the pancake was a water buffalo. The water buffalo looked at the pancake and said, 'grunt, grunt, into my tummy you, I will shunt.' However, as she came close to the pancake, she said, 'yech, you smell of fish, and I can't eat you.' The next animal the pancake met was a camel. The camel looked at the pancake and said, 'nuzz, nuzz into my mouth, please buzz.' As he came near the pancake, he again refused to eat it. 'Yech, you smell of pork, I can't eat you,' he said. By this time, the pancake had almost made its way out of the farmyard. Then, it came across a pig. The pig looked at the pancake and, without saying a word, took a bite of it. 'Ouch! That hurt! What are you doing?' The pig was surprised, but unaffected nonetheless. 'Oink, oink, what is this? A talking pancake, is it? Well, I don't care, as long as it tastes good,' the pig said, taking another bite. 'Ouch, but, but, I am made of mutton,' the pancake protested. 'I like mutton,' the pig shrugged, taking another bite. 'Ouch, but, but, I am made of pepper and mustard,' the pancake argued. 'I don't mind, it all just adds to the flavour,' the pig said, taking another bite. 'Ouch, but, but, I am made of fish,' the pancake cried. 'I like the river's smell,' the pig replied, taking another bite. 'Ouch, but, but, I am made of pork – *that* comes from another pig you know,' the pancake reasoned. 'I don't mind that, as long as it is not me,' the pig replied, and it chomped down on the rest of the pancake."

Vyaan, finished his story, asked, "Tiraa, what is the moral of this story?"

"That I am not the first to make the hodgepodge meal, but Raati had done it before me?' Tiraa asked, laughing.

"That too," Vyaan joined in on her laughter, "but it also teaches you not to be choosy with your food. So, now that you have had your story, please get ready to go to sleep."

"That story was really short," Tiraa protested.

"You cannot expect me to make up longer stories. You wanted a new story anyway, remember?" Vyaan replied in a soft but firm voice.

"I am not sleepy," Tiraa tried again.

"You will be, the moment you lie down," Zayaa intervened.

"Ayei, I want to ask you a question before I go to sleep," Tiraa asked, suddenly serious.

"What is it, darling?" Zayaa asked with concern in her voice.

"As you were pushing me out of the temple, you said that even if you cannot save me, Appi would. What did you mean by that, Ayei? Save me from what? And how will Appi do it?" Tiraa asked, looking back and forth between her parents.

Zayaa had been dreading two questions all day. One was the question that her daughter had just asked, and the other was one that, Zayaa knew, her husband would never ask her. And for that very reason, his question had to be answered, she decided. The time had come to tell Vyaan about everything. She had said 'my daughter' twice earlier that day, much to Vyaan's surprise and even annoyance. The only way she could make Vyaan understand about her fears, about why she had addressed Tiraa so, was by finally telling him the truth. For now though, she had to answer her daughter's question, and she had no idea how to do so.

"Well, you see, Tiraa, sometimes we say something, but mean ..."

"Tiraa," Vyaan cut in, strongly, "remember you had another thing to discuss with Ayei, as well, but decided that we would not bother her about it, until the Harvest Festival is over. I know your Ayei would love to talk to you all night about this. However, she does have to go to the temple very early in the morning. So, please, could you let her explain what she meant after the festival is over?"

"She isn't going to sleep, yet. I am. So, if I can stay awake, she can explain, can't she?" Tiraa asked hopefully.

"You know very well that the later you go to sleep, the later Ayei will too," Vyaan said with a smile.

Tiraa knew it was no use arguing anymore. She hugged her parents and went up to her room.

"I know we need to talk, but, first, could I pour us some raajaraas[10]?" Zayaa asked, and then added, "I definitely need some."

"I will join you. But, to be honest, I have already had some of the new brew that Tanaa had prepared. You know her – she never takes 'no' for an answer. Besides, her brews are always tasty, always heady," Vyaan said guiltily.

"How is Mother Tanaa?" Zayaa simply asked, pouring raajaraas into two earthen cups.

"She is fine," Vyaan said sipping his drink, "I think your message got her worried, but she did not ask me anything. She said that she will meet us near the cattle-head shaped hillock about two mahahaths[11] north of here. From there, she wants us to go and meet someone. She thinks this person can help us. Then she said something strange. Her exact words were, 'I think it is time to bring all the pieces together.' But, of course, she did not explain what she had meant."

"She is like that, isn't she?" Zayaa smiled, "I think she knows that everyone is afraid of the mysterious. And her strategy does work. Mother Tanaa is one of the few persons that the High Priests are afraid of. And she has never guided us wrongly. So, if she thinks that *this person* can help, I believe her."

"I agree. If Tanaa thinks we should involve this person, we will," Vyaan said and continued, "she said that she would arrange for one of the cattle herders to cross your path every day, on your way to or back from the Temple Sanctuary. They will come up to you and ask, 'yes or no?' If you say yes, Tanaa will find a way to see you. She also said that the day after the Harvest Festival, just before sunset, we should expect three herders, a man, woman and child, to come to our home. They will enter, as if to make deliveries, and, then, we will take that opportunity to leave our home. They will stay here, in our home, instead of us, until we are back."

"She is becoming melodramatic with age," Zayaa remarked. "Well, we will talk about her plan later. We have more important things to talk about now. I am sure you must be wondering about what all this is about, and I would certainly like to tell you. But, first, I must apologize for having called

---

[10]Givenland/ Meluhha's staple alcohol brewed from Barley
[11]1025 haths – or in binary 10000000001 haths

Tiraa 'my daughter' twice. I refused to correct myself even when you gave me a chance," she repented.

"Let us not worry about that now," Vyaan said, "from what I have observed of your behaviour today, I suspect that we have much bigger things to worry about."

Zayaa could see that Vyaan was hurt by what she had said and done earlier that day. However, now that she had voiced her regret, he did not want to brood over it. He would not forget it, either, she knew. Vyaan seldom forgot anything. Zayaa also knew that Vyaan would bring this incident up again, would remind her of it, if Zayaa ever did make this same mistake again.

"I wanted you to come to the Temple Sanctuary tomorrow, as Apaan would not be there. When, earlier today, I saw Tiraa there, I got really scared. We cannot change what has happened, but what we can do is think about how we can ensure her safety and wellbeing. I have been thinking all day, but have not been able to come up with a solution. I think..."

"Could you slow down a little?" Vyaan interrupted. "I still have no idea what the problem is. I can guess a little, but I need the facts from you, especially if it is Tiraa's safety that is at stake!"

"Of course, the facts," Zayaa agreed. "I don't know where to begin though. We have never really talked about what exactly happened during your last trip to the lands of Sumer. We have also never really talked about any of the unholy things that still go on at our Temple Sanctuary. I think you can guess some of these things," she said awkwardly, "but we have never talked about it. I remember, when you came back, I asked you to hold me. I wanted to tell you everything, but you saw how painful it was for me. You told me to stop, and asked that I only tell you what you needed to know. Everything else could wait, you said, until after the pain was gone," she recounted, her eyes filling up. "The pain was never gone, Vyaan, and we never discussed it again. I think we have to talk about it now. I will tell you everything that happened then, and what has been happening since then. Some of the things you may not be able to forgive me. It does not matter, as I know you will still do whatever it takes to protect Tiraa. And that is the only thing that matters now. I will tell you everything I can remember. Even the secrets I promised my father I will never share with anyone."

Chapter 3

People in Pparaha believed that Zayaa and her father, Riyaansh, had moved to Pparaha from Darromohe[12]. This was not entirely true. Darromohe was where they lived for a short while before coming to Pparaha. They were originally from a town called Kdwar[13], which was located near where the Mother River[14] met the Great Unending Waters[15]. Zayaa's memories of that journey had faded with time. However, she did remember her father and his twin brother, Ridhaan, taking turns to carry her on their shoulders. She also remembered living in a boat and sometimes had nightmares of flooding rivers. Her father had made Zayaa promise that she would never mention the journey or the existence of Ridhaan to anyone. After reaching the outskirts of Pparaha, her uncle had decided to strive out on his own. Zayaa was very good at keeping secrets and had never broken the promise given to her father. Her father had told her that only once she had grown up would he explain everything to her.

In Pparaha, both father and daughter had wanted to lead a normal life. However, Zayaa's skin colour made this impossible. Despite all the unwanted attention, they had somehow managed to create a comfortable life for themselves. They had pleasant and cordial relations with their neighbours. One thing that she remembered clearly was their visits to Tanaa's place outside the city—probably because this was unusual. Other people from the town only met Tanaa when they needed, either for help with childbirth or to cure them of some ailment. However her father and

---

[12]A city in Southern Givenland/ Meluhha on the banks of River Indus
[13]A town in Givenland/ Meluhha, a little upriver from the mouth of the Indus River
[14]The Indus River
[15]The Arabian Sea

Zayaa, not only visited Tanaa often, but also during these visits usually spent a day or two at her house. These visits became less frequent with time and then stopped completely. From time to time, her father would leave her in the care of others and disappear for a couple of days. Zayaa had always suspected that during these absences her father secretly visited Tanaa.

A little over a year after Zayaa and her father had come to Pparaha, Vyaan and his uncle moved into the house next door. Her father had struck up an immediate friendship with Vyaan's uncle. This had struck her as quite odd. Her father was usually very circumspect around people he had newly met. Vyaan's uncle had been the only exception that Zayaa knew of. Within days of meeting each other, Zayaa's father and Vyaan's uncle started sharing a daily drink of raajaraas. Zayaa's father also took an unusually keen interest in Vyaan. At first, this made Zayaa very jealous. Quite a few times she had tried to hit Vyaan with anything that she could lay her hands on. However, Vyaan was growing into a very strong boy for his age, so within a couple of years, such hitting became quite difficult for her to accomplish. When Vyaan was barely thirteen, he joined a caravan on a journey to the faraway land of Sumer. Initially, when Vyaan had suggested this journey, both his uncle and Zayaa's father were against it. However, suddenly, and without any reason, Vyaan was allowed to make the journey. Though Zayaa was surprised by this, she did not really care enough to think too much about it then. Vyaan left for Sumer, and Zayaa went on with her life.

Two and a half years thus passed. One day, Zayaa was out on an errand. As she was walking along the Centre Street, Zayaa saw a strange young man at the head of an even stranger procession. He was darker than most people in Pparaha. He was wearing a strange tunic and an exotic headgear, and was riding an animal that Zayaa had never seen. By the number of laden animals that he was leading, it was clear that, whoever he was, he was coming back from a very successful trip. As they passed through the street, people stopped whatever they were doing and looked at them with awe. Zayaa was not too impressed though and was getting back to her chores, when a boy, not much younger than the dark youth, suddenly stepped into the street. The animal the dark young man was riding, which seemed already nervous by the sight of all the people around it, got startled and started rearing up on its hind legs. He immediately jumped off his mount and then very calmly, but deftly, quieted his mount. After the animal had calmed down, he started walking towards what everyone thought was the boy, who was now cowering behind an older man. But the strange young man stopped in front of a little girl, instead. It was then that everyone realized that the girl had been frightened by the animal and was bawling her heart out.

The young man got down on one knee and said to the girl, in a deep kind voice, "little girl, don't be afraid." Then pointing at his animal continued, "she means you no harm. Would you like to confirm this by riding my ašša[16]?" And then, he smiled at the girl.

The moment she saw the young man smiling, Zayaa started blushing. Looking around she saw that his smile seemed to be affecting everyone. Now, she looked at the young man with new interest. When she saw his soft, but intelligent, kind and confident eyes, still fixed on the little girl, she became irrationally jealous. And it was exactly then that she had fallen in love with him. Unmindful of everyone else, including Zayaa, the young man picked up the little girl and introduced her to his animal. He then handed the girl over to her father and proceeded on foot, towards the Temple Sanctuary, pulling along his animal and the rest of the procession. There were fifteen animals in his procession, Zayaa counted with interest.

"Appi, I just met the person I am going to marry," she announced to her father, when she had returned home. Zayaa still remembered that day's conversation, as if it had only just happened.

"Good," her father had replied with a chuckle. "Have you set a date, yet?"

"No, you silly, Appi," Zayaa laughed, "I am not going to marry him now, but I know it is him I will marry someday. Now, I want you to go and find out who he is."

"Zaa, what is this new mischief," her father had chided her, "you said that you have just met the person you would like to marry, and yet you say that you want me to find him for you. Have you just met this husband of yours in your dreams?"

"Appi, you really are funny," Zayaa teased, "what I mean is that I just saw him come into our town with a procession of animals, and I need you to go out and find out who he is."

Her father had been reluctant to do so and suggested they just wait for someone to come and gossip about it.

Zayaa was obstinate. "I want to know about him now, Appi, not when someone comes and tells us."

"So be it, Zaa," her father agreed, yielding to her wish as usual. "In any case, I need to go out and get something."

Her father came back sooner than Zayaa expected.

---

[16] A horse in Sumerian, as horses were not indigenous to Givenland, they were still quite rare

"Did you forget something?" Zayaa asked, "Why have you come back?"

"Because I live here, silly girl," her father replied with a laugh. "Of course, calling *this* living is truly stretching the truth, as I have to share my house with an overbearing and task-mastering wench." Then he continued in a more serious tone, "I have found out about the man with the procession of animals today. It was our Vyaan, and you cannot marry him."

"Vyaan?" Zayaa cried with disbelief, "That can't be true. The person I saw today wasn't pimply and gangly at all. Perhaps, two different people have returned to Pparaha today."

"I don't know how many people arrived in Pparaha today," her father said, "but it is, indeed, Vyaan and the spectacle of his arrival that everyone is talking about."

"Well, then, it must have been Vyaan," Zayaa accepted, her voice growing fonder. "Come to think of it, I would not care if he was still pimply and gangly. He was so very kind to the little girl he did not even know. You could get lost in those kind eyes, Appi. And when he smiles..."

"Before you dream yourself into something sinful, do not forget that he is like a brother to you," her father warned.

"I hardly knew him before he left for Sumer," Zayaa protested. "So, when did he become my brother?"

"Zaa, please do not make an issue out of this," her father reasoned. "Let us put a cover over these thoughts and visit them later, when we have more information."

"I do have some more information," Zayaa started.

"No, you don't," her father snapped, "Zaa, never forget, I always want what is best for you."

Zayaa agreed with a grudging nod.

"If you really agree, then please stop sulking," her father's face had softened.

"You always tell me that I cannot expect to get everything in life," Zayaa said, "so now that you have my agreement, don't expect more. You have to see this - ."

She stopped her rant, as she heard a knock at the door.

"Well, look who is here?" her father greeted, as he ushered in Vyaan and his uncle, Shubhyaan. "If it is not the all-conquering hero everyone is talking about."

"Uncle Riyaansh, please do not embarrass me," Vyaan protested. "I came here to get away from all those sycophants who are doing this, not to meet someone who is trying to become one. In any case, I don't think sycophancy becomes you. I think we need to …" And, then, his eyes fell on Zayaa. On seeing her, he lost his confidence and his composure. "I am really sorry. I did not know, I mean I did not expect, I... this cannot be Little Zayaa."

"And what exactly do you mean by that?" she retorted. "You are not *Pimply Vyaan* anymore either, are you? So, why then, should I still be *Little* Zayaa?" She realized how silly she sounded and bit her lips.

"Zaa," her father scolded, "is this the way we behave with guests?"

"No, Riyaansh Uncle," Vyaan said, getting back some of his composure. "This is entirely my fault. I should have chosen my words more carefully." Then, turning to Zayaa, he said, "I am really sorry. How do I make up for this?"

"By letting me ride on your ash-something," Zayaa said before she could stop herself. "The animal you were riding earlier," she explained, for Vyaan looked puzzled. "The one you said the little girl could ride."

"Someone has been spying on me."

"Hardly," Zayaa retorted, "I just happened to be there. Besides, with the huge show you were putting on, it would be impossible not to notice, wouldn't it? Was that not what you were trying in the first place, to get people's attention?"

"You are right," Vyaan laughed, "I should have recognized you immediately. You still are the feisty little Zayaa, always ready for a fight. At least, you have not hit me with anything yet. However, I know it is entirely my fault. I provoked you with my bad sense of humour. All my acquaintances in Sumer used to complain about this, as well."

"Everyone in this room already knows that you have been to Sumer," Zayaa said, still not placated. "You don't need to keep mentioning it."

"I think that was the first time that I mentioned Sumer," Vyaan protested, his smile still intact. "But let us not argue." Then, turning to Zayaa's father, he said, "three days from today, Sikkappa[17] and I want you

---

[17] Paternal uncle

both to come to our house and share our lunch and dinner with us. I will be cooking some dishes I learnt during my travels to …" he left his sentence unfinished, while looking pointedly at Zayaa. "Sorry, but I am not allowed to mention the name of the place," he teased.

"We would love to," her father decided, before Zayaa could react, "even though we should be inviting you first, for you are the one who has come back to us. However, I will not argue about this. We will invite you some other time."

"We cannot have these formalities between us," Shubhyaan said. "However, we need to leave now. Vyaan wants to walk around Pparaha to see what has changed. I told him that nothing has changed, but he wants to see for himself."

"I think it has indeed changed. For the better, too, I might add," Vyaan disagreed.

Zayaa quickly turned away to make sure no one could see her blush.

After Vyaan and Shubhyaan left, her father turned to Zayaa.

"Zaa," her father said reproachfully, "you are no longer a little girl. You need to behave better in front of guests."

"Appi," Zayaa protested, "it was Shubhyaan Uncle. Not some stranger."

"Don't start that," her father said, "it does not matter who comes to our home. We always need to make all our guests feel special."

"Shubhyaan Uncle knows he is special to us," Zayaa pouted.

"In any case, I must say that I am not too unhappy with the way things have turned out," her father said, quickly changing the subject. "Seeing how you have taken a dislike for Vyaan, at least I don't have to worry about you marrying him."

"What do you mean?" Zayaa asked in surprise. "I am more positive now than before. And I think he likes me, too. I know many girls of my age who are already married. So, if I am going to marry Vyaan someday, why wait? Why not marry him right away?"

"Hold on there," her father said. "The way you were being overtly rude to the poor boy, I was sure you did not like him. And he must have felt the same way, as well. So before you start getting ahead of yourself, we need to know what Vyaan thinks. And I think Shubhyaan may also have some reservations, especially because you and Vyaan both moved about like siblings during your childhood."

"Appi," Zayaa said gravely, "I really like Vyaan. I want you to help me, not make this more difficult than it already is."

"We will talk after I am back from my trip," her father decided. "I forgot to tell you, but I will need to leave tomorrow morning. I will be back in a day, though."

"Are you going to see Tanaa? I have not seen her for a long time," Zayaa enquired. "You do like her don't you?"

"Yes, I am going to see Tanaa, amongst other things," her father admitted. "And, yes, I do like her, but only as a good friend."

The next day, her father left home at the break of dawn. He came back the following day, after the sun had set.

"How is Tanaa?" Zayaa asked once they had finished their dinner.

"She is fine," her father said plainly, seeming a little distracted. "I have been thinking. If you really are bent on marrying Vyaan, I will try to find out from Shubhyaan about Vyaan's feelings."

"Why the sudden change of heart, Appi?" Zayaa asked, growing suspicious, "Oh, I know, you met Tanaa, and realized how much you love her and regret not getting married to her after Ayei had passed away. So, you don't want to keep Vyaan and me apart."

"You do have a boundless imagination, don't you?" her father broke into a grin. "Well, you have got it all wrong. I was being honest when I said I like Tanaa as a friend, even like a sister, perhaps, but nothing else. Besides, the explanation is much simpler: I had some time to myself on the way to her house, and I got thinking about what you said. I realized how persistent you can be. Like a dog with a bone. So I decided that it would be best if I found out what Shubhyaan thinks, and of course about Vyaan's feelings."

"Thank you, Appi," Zayaa was thrilled, "so, when are you going to ask him? Maybe when you have raajaraas with him tonight?"

"You, young people have forgotten that patience is a virtue," her father chuckled.

After that, everything moved very quickly. Vyaan was initially reluctant about getting married to Zayaa immediately. He was planning to leave for Sumer, on a trip that might take a few years to return. He suggested that they get married once he was back. In case something was to happen to him during the trip. Zayaa, however, felt that as they had already decided on getting married, it would be best that they get it done before he had left. Her father and Uncle Shubhyaan agreed with Zayaa, and, thus, it was decided that Vyaan and Zayaa were to be married before he left for Sumer.

Vyaan wanted to get married the old way, on the riverbanks, having the river and fire as witnesses. He told Zayaa that there were similar rituals in many of the places he had visited outside Givenland. He explained to her that the rivers symbolized the feminine virtues and, also, an auspicious, fulfilling and healthy life, while the fire symbolized the masculine virtues and, also, a life filled with action, passion and resourcefulness. However, Zayaa wanted a grand wedding at the Temple Sanctuary. Her argument was much simpler, although more forceful. She had always dreamt of getting married in the Temple Sanctuary. Finally, it was decided that the wedding would be conducted according to Zayaa's wish and insistence. They would then proceed to the banks of the Airavati[18] River and perform the older wedding rites. Vyaan agreed.

Zayaa was pleased on having won their first serious argument. She had initially felt a little insecure and overawed of Vyaan, considering that he was already well-travelled and successful at his young age; this small victory over him, thus, gave her contentment, a feeling of being equal to him.

On their wedding day, at the Temple Sanctuary, their ceremony was performed by Apaan. Although, initially, one of the other High Priests had been in charge of the ceremony, the Chief High Priest, Apaan, had suddenly come and taken over the proceedings. Zayaa was happy at the turn of events though and even proudly informed Apaan of their plan to go to the banks of Airavati and get married again, in the ancient way. She immediately regretted telling him this, as she thought Apaan might take offense. However Apaan seemed to be taken by the idea. He offered to come to the riverbank and conduct that ceremony for them, as well. Vyaan did not seem very keen on this, but Apaan insisted on his own presence at the second ceremony.

On their wedding night, Vyaan suggested and Zayaa agreed that they would not consummate their marriage until he was back from his trip to Sumer. They spent half the night talking about Vyaan's travels, trying to distract themselves, but their passion eventually got the better of their resolve. And the marriage was duly consummated that night.

In less than a month, Vyaan left for his trip, and two days after Vyaan had left, two High Priests came over to Zayaa's house.

---

[18]The River Ravi

"Praise be to all," one of them shouted from outside the door. "We bring great tidings from the Temple Sanctuary."

"Great tidings, indeed," the other High Priest repeated, and shouted out to the neighbourhood, "the Gods have spoken. The daughter of this house, Zayaa, shall be a Dasasa. Praise be to the Gods. Praise be to Zayaa, our new Dasasa."

Riyaansh quickly opened the door.

"O revered ones, I am sorry to keep you waiting," he said politely. "Please come in."

The High Priests refused Riyaansh's offer. "We have come to take your daughter to the Temple Sanctuary. She has been proclaimed a Dasasa by the Gods themselves."

"However, O Revered One," her father protested, "my daughter is too old to become a Dasasa."

"Who knows the ways of Gods?" the second High Priest said, "and who are we to question them? Our duty is to have trust in their wisdom and do their bidding."

"However, O Revered One," her father continued to protest, "As you may already know, Zayaa is married."

"Gods bless us all," the first High Priest countered, "and mysterious are the ways of Gods. Who amongst us can understand them? All we know is that Pparaha will have a new Dasasa, ordained by the Gods themselves – not by us, their mere servants. You are a lucky father, indeed. The Gods spoke of you, as well, about how their will had moved Riyaansh of Darromohe to Pparaha, as Zayaa was destined to become a Dasasa here."

"They talked about Riyaansh of Darromohe, did they?" her father smiled knowingly. "Can we have a word in private, then?"

"Praise the Gods, they truly are omniscient," the second High Priest shouted with great fervour. "Who can hope to have any privacy from them? Of course, they talked about Zayaa and her father, Riyaansh of Darromohe. Who did you expect them to talk about, Riyaansh of Runaka[19], or Riyaansh of Parroo[20], or maybe Riyaansh of Kdwar?"

At the mention of Kdwar, Her father stepped back, staggering away from the priests in shock, and then fell to the floor grasping the left side of

---

[19]A town in Northern Givenland/ Meluhha on the banks of River Kabul
[20]A town in North-Eastern Givenland/ Meluhha on the banks of River Sutlej

his chest. Zayaa had been listening to the conversation from the kitchen. She was thrilled at hearing about her remarkable fortune and could not understand her father's averseness to this. However, seeing her father collapse to the floor, all these thoughts vanished and she immediately rushed to his side.

"Appi are you all right?" Zayaa enquired with concern. Then, turning towards the High Priests, she said, "Please give us a moment."

"Yes, O Chosen One of the Gods," the first High Priest bowed, "but, please do not take long."

Zayaa quickly brought some water to her father.

"Zaa," her father whispered, growing increasingly breathless, "listen to me. Please find a way to escape from here. Why did Shubhyaan have to be in Parroo when I need him most? I know. Go to Tanaa, she will find a way to get you to–"

"Appi," Zayaa said, "I don't understand. Isn't it an honour to be chosen as a Dasasa? And being chosen despite my age and being married only makes it more special, doesn't it? The Gods themselves have chosen your daughter. Why aren't you proud? Why are you asking that I run away from such honour?"

"Zaa," her father said, "please do not argue with me," he said in a weak voice. "I have a feeling that if you go to the Temple Sanctuary, something really bad will happen."

"Appi," Zayaa said, "I still do not understand, but if you want me to give up this honour, I will. Please..."

The front door of their house was flung open. "Please, O Chosen One," the second High Priest called out, "it's time. You have to come with me now. It is not long before this most auspicious time will be gone. Then, we would have to wait for months." Then turning to the other High Priest, he said, "please take care of her father, while I accompany the Chosen One to the Temple Sanctuary."

The first High Priest sat down next to her father, holding both his hands.

Zayaa protested in vain, as the second High Priest gently, but firmly took her hand and led her out. As she looked back from the doorway, it seemed to her as if the other High Priest was forcibly holding her father down. However, she was sure she must be mistaken.

When they reached the Temple Sanctuary, Zayaa was in a daze. She wanted to find a way to rush back to her father. She was barely aware of her surroundings, as she was escorted to a room and asked to wait.

After a few moments, Apaan walked in and smiled at her.

"O Chief High Priest," Zayaa smiled back at him, "I am really lucky that it is you who has come. I realized even on our wedding day that you are kind and understanding. I am in a dilemma. On one hand, I consider myself truly blessed to be chosen for such an honour, but, on the other, I have given my word to my father that I will not be a Dasasa. I would really appreciate it if you help me to find a way out of this quandary."

"That is very easy, my little dove," Apaan said with a grin, "you will simply have to agree to become my protected woman, and you will not have to become a Dasasa."

"You mean you will give me protection?"

"Amongst other things," Apaan said and then walked up to Zayaa. He took her chin between his thumb and forefingers, lifted up her face and examined it. Then running his forefinger down to her shoulders, and onto arms, he said in a hoarse voice, "but there are things that you will have to do for me in return."

There was something in his touch and his voice that made Zayaa's skin crawl. She was suddenly filled with disgust for him, and fear for herself.

"Please stop," Zayaa cried. "O Chief High Priest, please let me go. My father is unwell, and I need to get back and take care of him."

"Hear me well, my little white dove," Apaan whispered with a wicked gleam in his eyes, "you can take better care of him by being here and doing my bidding. You see, your father has not been entirely honest. You do not come from Darromohe but from a place called Kdwar – a town that, sadly, no longer exists. I have managed to locate one of the few survivors from it, though, and he tells me an interesting story about a father and daughter who had run away from Kdwar. What were their names, I forget... Oh yes, Riyaansh and Zayaa!" he snapped his fingers dramatically, while Zayaa looked on, terrified, understanding dawning on her about her own past. "This father and daughter, escaped just before being sat on a stake for practicing witchcraft. This survivor said that the daughter was white. Whiter than bleached bone, he says. Now when we hear of these people, Riyaansh and his daughter Zayaa, who is supposed to be whiter than bleached bone, it reminds us of some people we know, doesn't it? This survivor also seems to believe that Kdwar was destroyed because it could not prevent the escape of this wizard and his little white witch. I don't put much credence to such things, but people—be it in Kdwar or Pparaha—believe in such things. And if the people of Pparaha hear about this, they would insist that I carry out the punishment sentenced to these people, on behalf of Kdwar's dearly departed citizens and its highly respected Chief High Priest, for, otherwise, Pparaha might face a similar fate. I am sure that no tears will be shed for father and daughter as they are both sat on stakes."

"Why would you do this to us? What harm have we ever done to you? No, you will not do this. You are just testing me, aren't you?" she said hopefully. "I know you are a kind person. Why else would you come to the banks of Airavati to fulfil the whims of a young couple? I am sure that you know that neither my father is a wizard nor am I a witch."

"Of course, I know," Apaan agreed, "I doubt creatures, such as wizards or witches even exist. However, what I know or what I think will not matter the least bit to you, Zayaa, when the stake is entering your body and ripping apart your intestines," he laughed at her. "The way I see it, your choice is very simple: you could either choose to have a stake enter your anus and your father's, giving you both pain beyond your wildest nightmare and, then, certain deaths, or you could, instead, choose to have something smaller and definitely more pleasurable entering your orifices, giving you pleasure beyond your wildest fantasy – a lot more pleasure than your trader husband can ever give you, I promise," he laughed again, as he watched Zayaa cringe. "Oh yes, before I forget, I think it will be safe for me to assume that Vyaan and Shubhyaan helped you and your father conceal your dastardly past. Therefore, I don't see how I can avoid sitting them on stakes, as well."

As Zayaa opened her mouth to revolt, Apaan put his fingers to her lips.

"Please don't speak, yet," Apaan instructed. "Perhaps it will be fair if I tell you a little more about myself. This might help you make the right decision. When I was made the Chief High Priest, I sentenced more people to be sat on stakes in a month than it had been done in the previous fifty years. Since then, I have had to do this only twice. And the less I use this form of punishment, the more people believe that I only do it when I really do have to. There is one more thing you should know about me. The previous Chief High Priest died because he found out about what I had done to one of the young priests. He had to go - the poor old man."

Seeing Zayaa's shock and enjoying it, too, Apaan grinned. "O yes, it is exactly what you think. Sexually speaking, I believe that full equality must be given to men and women," he confirmed. "I should have killed that novice, when I realized he had seen my face, but my negligence to do so did help me in the end. As I was saying, the previous Chief High Priest found out about it. Being a kind old gentleman, he gave me a chance to confess to my sins and come clean in front of him and the other High Priests. He told me that the first step towards absolution is accepting one's wrongdoings. I pretended to accept his terms, but asked that I be allowed to confess to my sins on the next new moon, considering that my sins were indeed very dark. The old fool believed my charade, of course, and I had enough time to poison him to his death. Not only that, I ensured that the poison I gave him had hallucinogenic effects, which also make people very suggestible. And before he died, he kindly gave a decree making me the next Chief High Priest."

Apaan looked directly into Zayaa's eyes. "I know what you are thinking," he offered, "you are thinking that you have heard about worse things. Well, perhaps you have. Did I forget to mention that the previous Chief High Priest had found me abandoned by the riverside? I had been sick and starving then, but he nursed me back to life. Then, he brought me up as his son. In a way, he gave me this life, but then, I did not think twice about taking his life from him. So, it would be foolish of you to expect any kindness from me. Just let me know what you decide to accept as your fate – a night of wild pleasure for you, or a slow and painful death for you and your family."

"I don't believe you," Zayaa said with more hope than conviction, "I will scream for help and the other priests will come. They will help me. I will tell them what you told me about murdering the previous Chief High Priest. It is you who will be sat on the stake for this heinous crime."

Apaan clucked his tongue. "I'm afraid that if you go on like this, Zayaa, we might end up spending this whole night in pointless conversation," Apaan sneered, "I however have a completely different plan for tonight, and I am not willing to waste any more time. So, please go ahead and scream and get it over with."

Zayaa stood there mutely, unsure about what she was to do.

"Okay, if you won't, then I will," Apaan laughed derisively. He let out a feminine scream.

They waited for a while, but nothing happened. Apaan screamed even louder, but no one came to them.

"You see, my little dove," Apaan explained, with mock sadness in his voice, "no one is coming to help you. No one really cares. So, do you want me to repeat your two choices again? I must say I'm getting a little tired of doing so."

Zayaa could not answer. Tears were gushing down her face.

"So you still won't answer me?" Apaan asked, "Fine, I will raise the stakes then, to make this decision easier for you. You don't have to enjoy the night with me. I will give you enough dhutura to make sure that you won't remember anything in the morning. However, if you don't give in to me, I will rape you and then sit the four of you on stakes. So, there, which one will it be?"

Zayaa still could not answer. She could only cry.

"Still no answer," Apaan sighed. "I get it. Perhaps, you have indeed made your decision, the wise girl that you are, but are feeling a little self-conscious to tell me what it is," he grinned. "Fine, this is what we will do then: I will leave the dhutura here with you and come back after some time. As you can see there are no windows in this room and the door will be locked from the outside. So, there is no escape from here. You will also notice that there is absolutely nothing in this room that you might use to put an end to your life. When I come back, I will check if you have chewed the dhutura. If you have, then I will know that you have made the right choice. If not, I will know that you have chosen to kill your father, husband and uncle-in-law. "

Apaan fetched some dhutura leaves. And putting these next to where Zayaa stood, still crying, he left the room.

Zayaa knew what she had to do. She did not really have a choice. She took a few dhutura leaves and started chewing them.

She could not recall Apaan coming back to the room. Nor could she remember what he did to her. The next morning, she was in a lot of pain. There was dried blood on her, she saw, from the scratches and bites that Apaan had left on her. She tried to get up, but fell back again, crying out in pain. She could not walk home, she thought. She somehow managed to sit up in spite of all the pain. She looked around and saw that her clothes were torn. However, next to her was a fresh set of women's clothes and, along with it, some more dhutura leaves, a few roots of turmeric, a piece of banyan bark and some banyan leaf-buds. She chewed some of the dhutura leaves to dull the pain. She lifted herself to her feet and staggered her way to the wash place at the corner of the room. After washing herself, she ground the banyan bark and leaf buds along with the turmeric roots into a paste and applied this to her scratches and bites. She then dressed herself. By this time, the combined effect of the dhutura and turmeric had made the pain more tolerable, but the dhutura had also made her nauseous. She sat next to the wash-place for a while, contemplating how to get home. Soon, a High Priest came and guided her out of the Temple Sanctuary. She somehow stumbled her way home.

When Zayaa reached home, she found her father lying on the floor near the doorway, his body trembling, and his face pale. On hearing Zayaa, he turned to see her. He tried to get up, but when he saw Zayaa's battered body, he fell back again, clutching his heart.

"Appi, are you all right?" Zayaa whimpered, sitting down next to him.

Her father seemed to be in a daze. Zayaa shook him. He looked around the room and then towards the front door.

"Did not even put up a fight," her father whispered.

"Please, Appi," Zayaa wept, "I did put up a fight, but he threatened to kill you, Vyaan and Shubhyaan Uncle. I could not let that happen."

"I have failed," her father whispered, "I could not keep my word."

"Please, Appi," Zayaa begged again, "I don't understand what you are saying."

Her father's eyes got a little focused at Zayaa's words. He looked at her.

"Zayaa, I am not your father …" he began.

"Appi," Zayaa protested, "It was not my fault. I know I could not protect my virtue, but what could I do. I did not have a choice."

"I am not your father …"

Then, clutching his heart he fell back to the floor, his mouth beginning to froth, his body convulsing with spasms. Zayaa screamed for help and tried to hold onto him but, finally, when the spasms did stop, his eyes remained wide open. Zayaa realized her father was no longer breathing. Shocked, Zayaa clambered up to her feet and staggered to the kitchen. She brought out the meat knife, the sharpest in the house, and went back to her father. Then, sitting down next to her father's body, she slit both her wrists.

Chapter 4

When Zayaa regained consciousness, she realized she was not in her house. She recognized that it was Tanaa's place. Then, all the painful thoughts rolled back into her. For a moment, she thought that maybe it was all a dream, that nothing really had happened, but one look at her wrists wiped out any such hope. As she sat up, Shubhyaan came to her.

"Don't get up," Shubhyaan ordered, "You are too weak from losing blood. You would not have survived without Tanaa's care and knowledge. She has given you a new life."

"How did I get here?" Zayaa whispered.

"All in good time," Shubhyaan comforted, "please rest now."

After taking a sip from the cup that Shubhyaan handed her, she drifted back to sleep.

When Zayaa woke up the next time, she did not even have a fleeting moment of hope. She remembered exactly where she was and everything that had happened to her. She saw Tanaa sitting on the floor and grinding some leaves.

"Why did you not let me die?" Zayaa asked angrily. "I have nothing to live for. My body has been defiled. My father disowned me before he died. I will never get the opportunity to explain to him that I did not have a choice. Shubhyaan Uncle is being kind now, but the moment he hears what happened, he will disown me, too. So will my husband. I cannot go on living after losing everyone I love."

"Shhh, my little dove," Tanaa reassured but stopped on hearing Zayaa's screams.

"Please call me anything else but that," Zayaa screamed.

"Okay," Tanaa said, "can I call you Zaa?"

When Zayaa was calm again, Tanaa continued, "Anyone who saw your body after what happened would know that you were not a willing participant. I can tell you this, because it was I who dressed up your body. Zaa, I know your father very well. He might have been many things but unjust he never was. So, I am sure you have misunderstood him. He would never disown you. He couldn't, even if he wanted to. He was bound by the covenant."

"I don't understand what you mean by covenant," Zayaa said, "besides, I heard my father say it with my own ears. He was still alive when I came back. He blamed me for not putting up a fight and told me that he was no longer my father. He also went on calling me Zayaa, instead of Zaa, as he usually does. No, Tanaa, I don't want to live in this world, anymore. You know all the herbs and plants. Don't you? Please give me something that will put me to sleep forever."

"First, please repeat the exact conversation that you had after you got back," Tanaa said in a soothing voice.

Zayaa repeated, amidst more tears, the last conversation she had with her father.

"He meant what he said in a very different way. You've misunderstood that," Tanaa announced after Zayaa was done. Stroking Zayaa's hair, she explained herself to the girl: "He might have said that he was not your father because he had failed to protect you. If he wanted to disown you, he would have said 'you are not my daughter.' That would have made more sense, wouldn't it?"

"I want to believe you, Tanaa," Zayaa said, "but you should have seen the repugnant look on his face as he was pushing me away. And even if he meant something else, I did cause his death. And now that my father is dead and even Vyaan is sure to leave me, what reason do I have to go on living?"

"Why don't we wait and see what Vyaan has to say?" Tanaa said. "And never think that you are alone in this world. You will always have me. And your father has many other friends," she consoled.

"My father had only two friends – Shubhyaan Uncle and you," Zayaa said, "everyone else are mere acquaintances." Then, she grew quiet. "How did I get here?" she asked after a few moments.

"As you may remember, Shubhyaan was not in Pparaha the evening you were summoned to the Temple Sanctuary," Tanaa said. "When he got back next morning, he heard about the previous evenings events. He immediately went to your place, and there, he found that your father had already departed from this world. You were trying to join him, too, he saw. He immediately lifted your arms to make sure your wrists were placed above your heart. Then, instead of wrapping up the cuts, he tightly wrapped both your hands between the wrist and elbow. When he stepped out of your house, fate intervened. He came across a cattle herder who was delivering milk and asked him for help. The herder knew that your father was a good friend of mine, so he rushed here to inform me. The moment I received the message, I sent over a few men to bring you here. We cremated your father later that same day."

"What should I do now?" Zayaa murmured, more to herself than to Tanaa.

"That is something that you will have to decide," Tanaa said, "but if I were you, I would confide in someone."

"I don't have anyone to share my pain with," Zayaa said desolately, "my world was my father, until Vyaan came and became part of it, too. My father is gone, and Vyaan is not here."

"If you would like, you could share with me," Tanaa offered, "you may not feel close to me, but I have always thought of you as the daughter I never had."

Zayaa lay there thinking, without answering. Finally, she sighed, "If you will have the patience to bear with me, I will tell you everything. However, you have to tell me what I could have done differently," she asked of Tanaa. "I must have done something wrong to have caused the death of my father."

Tanaa agreed. Zayaa began her story from when the two High Priests had come knocking on their door and had summoned her to the Temple Sanctuary, and ended it with her waking up from the dhutura-induced stupor the next morning and then returning home, only to witness death and grief. By the time she finished, she was physically drained, but sharing her misfortune with Tanaa seemed to make life a little more bearable.

"Please tell me what I could do. I know I have sinned, but how could I have avoided it?" Zayaa ended with a deep sigh.

"Oh, you poor girl," Tanaa whispered, with tears in her eyes, "that monster," she then hissed, "oh, you poor, poor little girl! You could not have done anything different. The fault lies with the Gods that have put such monsters in this world to prey on the innocent. No, Zaa, you could not have done anything different, I promise. And I will promise you another thing, too – even if the whole world turns against you, I will always be with you. Now we have to decide what needs to be done next. Do we try to forget what has happened? Or do we remember it, so it can help us plan our vengeance? We must not act in haste, though. First, we need to find out how much Shubhyaan knows. Then, we must decide how much more we should tell him. We have to assume that if he knows, Vyaan will know too and…"

"I'd rather die, Tanaa," Zayaa said solemnly, "than live a lie with Vyaan."

"Of course," Tanaa said, as if the thought had not even occurred to her, then realizing how exhausted Zayaa was, gave her a potion to drink. For a moment Tanaa thought of letting Zayaa rest first, but afraid that she may withdraw back to her shell, Tanaa continued. "But I think it is only right that Vyaan hears everything from you, and no one else. And he must hear it at a time that is appropriate to the both of you."

Someone knocked at her door.

"Who is there?" Tanaa called out signalling that Zayaa be quiet, by putting her forefinger to her lips.

"It's Shubhyaan," a voice said. "May I come in?"

"Of course."

When Shubhyaan came in, his wet eyes gave away that he had heard at least some of their discussion.

"Shubhyaan, have you been listening to us?" Tanaa confronted.

"I wish I could lie," Shubhyaan said, "but I had arrived as Zayaa was talking about being summoned to the temple. It was not curiosity, but good manners that kept me from knocking. I wanted to walk away, but as disgusting as the tale was, it was also gripping. I …"

"I knew it," Zayaa wailed, "everyone will be disgusted at me. Tanaa, I cannot …"

Tanaa put her hand over Zayaa's mouth. Then she picked up a thick wooden ladle with her other hand. And in a soft but chilling voice said, "if any man is disgusted with you, especially within my walls, I am going to shove this into their anal hole, to show them how it feels. This I can promise you."

Shubhyaan immediately protested. "I was disgusted by that beast that these people call their Chief High Priest. As far as Zayaa is concerned, I think she did what best could be done in that situation. The only thing I would like to say is that if it might have helped Zayaa, I would have gladly sat on the stake for her. And I know my Vyaan would have, too. Zayaa only needs to look into her heart to know that Riyaansh would have done the same."

Zayaa wanted to say so much, but not a word left her lips. She did not know how to express what she felt, because she realized that Shubhyaan was very serious and meant every word he had said.

Shubhyaan continued. "I promise both of you that Vyaan will never hear anything from me. Zayaa will share her story with him when she sees fit. I wish I could walk to the Temple Sanctuary now and slay that beast with my bare hands."

"Save your strength, good Shubhyaan," Tanaa countered, "I am not saying such transgression should not be avenged, but it has to be Zayaa's decision. She might decide to put this behind her. In that case, she will have to leave Pparaha, and I do know of many places where she can go and live in relative safety. However, if she decides that she wants to wreak vengeance, she will have to stay in Pparaha. She will have to become a Dasasa. In that case, she will have not only to face Apaan again, but might have to go through what she went through at the Temple Sanctuary, not once, not twice, but again and again and again. I suspect that Apaan is giving the other High Priests a share in his dastardly acts to keep them in line, much in the way that foxes are offered a lion's leftovers."

"Stop!" Shubhyaan shouted, "if staying here means enduring more of what she went through, then we know what she must do – she has to leave Pparaha so far behind that she will remember it only as a bad dream. I will ensure that Vyaan follows her wherever she goes. I know of one place that neither Apaan nor his minions will dare follow. I will …"

"No," Zayaa burst in forcing herself out of her lethargic state, "I cannot run away from this. I cannot forgive Apaan for causing my father's death, and I shall not give up on my vengeance. I have already been to hell and back. I am sure I can endure whatever else life and fate conspire to throw at me."

"Zayaa," Shubhyaan protested, "all the High Priests will know that you came back, in spite of what Apaan had done to you. They will only do much worse things to you. Are you sure you want to go through with all that? No one will think less of you, if you were to walk away from this."

"I do not think anyone can do anything worse than what Apaan has already done," Zayaa said, "besides, this time, I shall be more prepared. I will avoid as many of these encounters as I can. The ones I cannot avoid, I shall endure."

"Well, if you are sure about this," Shubhyaan agreed reluctantly, "I will help you in whatever way I can."

"Now that we know which direction we will take," Tanaa said, "we must decide on what we should do next. First, the Temple Sanctuary should know that Zayaa is here, under my care." Then, taking Zayaa's hands in her own, she continued, "listen carefully, Zaa, for this is the story we are going to tell them – one of the herders found you wandering on the streets, and not knowing about your whereabouts, brought you here. When I sent another herder to your home, he found your father's body. The body had already started decomposing, and therefore, keeping in mind the safety of our town, I decided to get him cremated. You are still a little crazy though, from the shock of your father's death and will need time to heal."

Zayaa nodded her agreement. She had started to feel light-headed, partly from her exertions and partly from whatever medicine Tanaa had given her to drink.

"You know we don't have to do this now," Tanaa said gently feeling Zayaa's forehead.

"No, please don't stop," Zayaa said weakly. "I will be fine as long as I don't talk much."

"Apaan may soon put two and two together." Tanaa continued sharing her thoughts, "of course, there is always a chance that he may not. He thinks he is smarter than everyone else is. His pride and confidence, which he thinks are his strengths, can also become his weaknesses. He must be very confident that he has already broken Zayaa's spirits. So, two weeks from now, Zayaa will move to her uncle-in-law's house. Then, when she is feeling a little better, she will present herself at the Temple Sanctuary, to start her duties as a Dasasa. What else is left for her to do anyway? She has been defiled. Her spirit has been crushed, and her family broken. She is unsure about what her uncle-in-law does or does not know and what he will or will not tell his nephew. At least being a Dasasa will bring her some solace."

Then, Tanaa smiled, and it was a very strange smile indeed. If Zayaa had not known that Tanaa was on her side, she might have grown scared of this smile, much more than she had of the evil gleam in Apaan's eyes.

"Yes, this will work. It will work very well, indeed. We will strike when the time is right. Let the weeks, months and years pass on, and then, we shall strike, when the opponents least expect it. By then, they would have assumed that they have already won," she sniggered. "They might have even forgotten there had been a battle in the first place. That is when we will get our vengeance."

"As you say, Tanaa," Shubhyaan sighed, "but how will you ensure that this story of yours even reaches Apaan's ears? At present, he will be suspicious of everything and everybody."

"I will make sure he does. I have started to think in circles" she said mysteriously. "As you know, I am not very popular amongst the High Priests. They tolerate me as a necessary evil. So, once, I had suggested to a very good friend of mine, that it might be quite useful for me to have a spy at the Temple Sanctuary, so I would know what was happening there at all times, especially about things that concerned me. My friend had chided me for thinking such simple thoughts. He told me that if I wanted to stay ahead of my enemies, I would need to start thinking in circles, not straight lines. He had explained that even if I got someone to spy for me, I could never be sure of this person's loyalties. If a person was ready to betray his friends or employers, my friend had reasoned, I could expect this person to betray me too."

On seeing the bemused look on Shubhyaan's face, Tanaa smiled again, but fondly this time. "Reminds you of someone, doesn't it?" she asked and Shubhyaan nodded his understanding. "I did as my friend had suggested. I chose someone, a herder, whom I could trust. Then, I acted according to plan: I accused this herder of stealing milk from my cows, which had been left in his care, and I made it into a very public falling out, of course, with me blaming him for betrayal and with him refusing to apologize. In due course, Apaan came to hear of this. He approached this herder and convinced him, through gifts and privileges, to apologize to me and get back on my good side. Apaan convinced him that the latter could then exact his revenge on me, by spying on me. Since then, whenever Apaan is planning anything that concerns me, he usually confides in this herder. And, in case we ever need to give Apaan some information, true or otherwise, the herder calls for a meeting with Apaan. It is as simple as that. That is how Apaan will hear exactly what we want him to hear."

"One thing, though," Shubhyaan spoke up. "I am planning to get a message across to Vyaan, asking that he come back as soon as possible. I am sorry, but no one can convince me otherwise."

Hearing this, Zayaa felt her heart pounding faster.

"I won't even try," Tanaa said, "his place is in Pparaha now anyway, taking care of Zayaa, not gallivanting around in Sumer. A few more things before you go. You must come here every two days to check on your niece-in-law. If you don't come or come more frequently, people will become suspicious. If you need to see me urgently, send me a message through one of the herders. Now, you should get going. You have no reason to stay here this long." Tanaa thus ushered Shubhyaan out.

The next ten days went by without incident. Tanaa's constant care had almost healed Zayaa's physical wounds. Tanaa never mentioned the Temple Sanctuary incident, unless absolutely required.

Late on the afternoon of the eleventh day, Shubhyaan made an unscheduled appearance.

"Something very interesting happened in the Temple Sanctuary yesterday evening," Shubhyaan said rushing in, breathless, without bothering to greet either of them. "I thought about reaching you, but decided that it could wait, until I came here, for my regular visit tomorrow. And then today ..." Shubhyaan stopped, and took a deep breath. Then, he said, "I think it is best I start from the beginning. As you know, yesterday was Summer Solstice. I usually attend these ceremonies and decided it might look odd if I didn't go this time, too. Anyway, during the ceremony, the Chief High Priest of Parroo suddenly arrived with three of his High Priests. This was indeed very extraordinary, for as you may know, Chief High Priests usually never leave their own Temple Sanctuary on the solstices. Apaan looked surprised, too. As he was getting over his surprise and welcoming these unexpected guests, the Chief High Priest of Parroo declared that though he was glad to make Apaan's acquaintance, he was in Pparaha at the command of the Gods, to seek advice from the new Dasasa, whom the Gods called the 'Dreamer of Truths Yet to Come'. The Chief High Priest of Parroo was speaking in a booming voice. And he was also repeating parts of what Apaan was saying. It appeared as if he wanted everyone to hear both sides of the conversation."

"How were the other people around you taking this?" Tanaa asked.

51

"They were as surprised and confused as I was," Shubhyaan said. "Anyway, Apaan quietly said that there was no such Dasasa in Pparaha. The Chief High Priest of Parroo asked if the Dasasa Zayaa, daughter of Riyaansh and wife of Vyaan, indeed did not exist. Then he berated himself for misinterpreting the commands of the Gods. Before Apaan could answer, however, many of those who were gathered spoke out, and informed the Chief High Priest of Parroo that Zayaa, daughter of Riyaansh, did exist. The Chief High Priest of Parroo looked perplexed. Then he said that it was strange that none of the High Priests in Pparaha had been given any sign about Zayaa being ordained as the Dreamer of Truths Yet to Come. Then he brightened up and said that as the Gods had chosen to inform the Chief High Priest of Parroo, it was definitely a sign that Zayaa should be a Dasasa in Parroo and not Pparaha. Apaan refuted this though, and claimed that it was not true that the High Priests in Pparaha had not been told about Zayaa. The fact, he said, was that Apaan and all six of his high priests had been given these signs much earlier. And the Gods had also sent a messenger to inform Apaan of their choice."

"Was I truly chosen by the Gods then," Zayaa whispered to no one in particular, her eyes focused outside the window into the distance. "No, that cannot be, for if the Gods had indeed chosen me, why would they forsake me when I needed them most."

"Zaa," Tanaa said in a tender voice, and then taking Zayaa's hands in hers continued, "remember what we decided. If we are to make sure that we make the right moves, we have to know all there is to know, first." Then turning to Shubhyaan asked, "What was the explanation for not speaking about this Dasasa earlier?"

"I was coming to that", Shubhyaan continued, "Apaan said that as Zayaa was past the usual age for becoming a Dasasa and also already married, he was planning to take his time to explain the importance of this ordainment to the people of Pparaha, instead of surprising them with the news. He also added that all of Zayaa's neighbours must have surely heard about the summons carried forth to Zayaa by two of his High Priests, only a few days ago. The Chief High Priest of Parroo did insist again that Zayaa should be a Dasasa in Parroo instead of Pparaha, but finally lost out to Apaan's arguments. The Chief High Priest of Parroo then wanted to know when he could seek the advice of the Dreamer of Truths Yet to Come. At this, Apaan promised that he would arrange for it to happen within a week. As I had expected, I had a visit from one of the High Priests this morning. He told me that Apaan expects Zayaa to be at the Temple Sanctuary in four days' time. I protested that it was beyond my control and lay solely in

Tanaa's hands. He then threatened that if I knew what was good for me, I would immediately go and make the necessary arrangements. Or else..."

"Or else, what?" snapped Tanaa.

"Well, if Zayaa is not brought to the Temple Sanctuary in four days' time, Apaan would send his people here on the fifth day, to take her there by force, to attend to my funeral."

"Apaan is getting desperate," Tanaa said, "that can only be good for us. We don't want him to sleep too peacefully, do we?"

"Why did the Gods forsake me after choosing me?" Zayaa asked again numbly.

"Gods do things in mysterious ways," Tanaa answered, "and it is not for us to question their ways." Then smiling a mysterious smile added, "Zayaa, I don't know whether this opportunity was created by the Gods or one of their creations, and though I can't promise you this right now for sure, I think there might just be a way to keep you safe from the other six High Priests. You will still have to handle Apaan by yourself, though, at least for the time being."

"Whatever you have thought of, why would it not work with Apaan?" Shubhyaan wondered.

"The way I see it, the other High Priests have lost their morality," Tanaa declared. "Apaan has thrown his away. So, it is difficult to predict his reactions. And so he might be able to render useless our methods against the other High Priests, as well. Shubhyaan, I think you should go back now. If anyone asks, inform them that Zayaa will be present at the Temple Sanctuary five days from now."

"Okay," Shubhyaan asked, "but, if I may ask, why have her go after five days and not four days as ordered by Apaan?"

"Trust me about this," Tanaa reassured.

Shubhyaan nodded. "I hope it is fine if I go to the Sanctuary and inform them about this myself, instead of waiting for Apaan's messenger to ask me about it."

"I do not see any problem with that," Tanaa agreed, "however, it is important that you leave now."

After Shubhyaan left, Tanaa went out, too.

Zayaa lay dazedly and watched them leave. Her emotions were in turmoil. She knew that she had told the others that she did not care what she had to endure to get her revenge. However, she was actually revolted at the thought of going back to the Temple Sanctuary and facing Apaan. She could barely stop herself from vomiting at the very thought of physical contact with him. She tried to distract herself from these thoughts by again wondering why the Gods were playing this strange game with her. If this was a test of her devotion, she wanted to cry out that she wanted to fail her test and have her father back. However, she knew how helpless she was, and again started thinking whether her life was worth living any longer. As her mind started drifting towards how she would end her life, Tanaa came back with some leaves.

"You see these leaves?" Tanaa asked Zayaa, "Though these look like dhutura, they are actually from a different plant. These leaves are also psychoactive, but are not hallucinogenic" Then, on seeing Zayaa's confused look, she explained, "all hallucinogenic plants are psychoactive, but all psychoactive plants are not hallucinogenic. Anything that alters our perception, mood, consciousness, cognition and behaviour is psychoactive. Hallucinogenic plants do not merely amplify familiar states of mind but also make you hallucinate."

Realizing that she had again lost Zayaa, she further explained, "What I mean is that they induce experiences that are different from what is really happening, or they can sometimes put you in a trance and remove you from reality. Sorry for the lesson on the types of plants; all you need to know is that these leaves will make your body go limp. Therefore, even to a close observer, you will look as if you are in a trance or a dhutura-induced stupor. Everyone believes that when one is in such a stupor, one has no control over one's consciousness. So, whatever one speaks when in this state, the words will be taken as words coming from the subconscious, spoken from the dreams. This, along with the fact that you have been proclaimed the Dreamer of Truths Yet to Come, will make you very powerful indeed."

"How will it keep me safe from the High Priests?" Zayaa asked impatiently.

Tanaa told her. After finishing explaining her plan Tanaa continued, "The first time you use these leaves, it will feel quite eerie. I think it would be best if you chew these leaves a few times, while you are still here. In this way, you will get used to the feeling."

Zayaa had many questions, but Tanaa had an answer to each of these. Zayaa sighed deeply, in admiration of the older and wiser woman. "Tanaa, how do you come up with these things?"

"Sometimes, I have help from unexpected sources," Tanaa laughed cagily, "and a parent does become very productive when protecting their children."

"Tanaa," Zayaa said after a moment's thought, "you said that I was like the daughter you never had. Now that you have given me a new life, may I call you mother?"

"Yes, Zaa, but why don't you call me Mother Tanaa?" Tanaa suggested. "I would not want to interfere with the memories of your actual mother."

Things happened exactly as they had planned them. Zayaa went to the Temple Sanctuary on the fifth day. In a lavish investiture ceremony, Zayaa was declared as one of the main Dasasas, and was also given the name of Dreamer-of-Truths-Yet-to-Come. The ceremony was attended by Apaan, the Chief High Priest of Parroo, all the High Priests of Pparaha and the three visiting High Priests from Parroo, amongst many others from Pparaha. Tanaa stayed away, as she did from all the happenings at the Temple Sanctuary, but Shubhyaan attended the ceremony. As he was leaving, Shubhyaan was informed that Zayaa will be staying at the Temple Sanctuary, until she had gone through two full-moon ceremonies.

Until the Chief High Priest of Parroo had left Pparaha, things were uneventful for Zayaa at the Temple Sanctuary. During his stay, he had tried many times to talk to Zayaa in private, but Apaan or one of his High Priests always foiled such attempts.

The day after the Chief High Priest of Parroo left Pparaha, Apaan came into Zayaa's room.

"How do you know the Chief High Priest of Parroo?" Apaan demanded.

"I had never seen him or even heard of him before the investiture ceremony."

"I wonder what his game was then." Apaan wondered aloud. "Why did he come and tell us those lies about the commands from the Gods?"

"How do you know that he was lying?" Zayaa tried hopefully.

"Well, I must say that I have had the honour of giving the people of Pparaha four different messages from the Gods, including the one about you being a Dasasa," Apaan smiled, "all of these messages were, of course, made up by me. I am sure this is also the case for the messages and commands received by the other Chief High Priests. I wonder, then, if you did not know him already, why did Parroo come here with that tale."

Zayaa made no offer to answer.

"Why are we wasting time on this? I am sure in time I will figure it out and think of an appropriate response for his untimely interruption. Let us, instead, talk about more immediate things. Here are some dhutura leaves, and some Banyan and Turmeric paste too, kindly ground up and made ready by another Dasasa. That was really thoughtful of her, wasn't it? I will be back soon."

As he was about to leave her, Zayaa spoke up. "Are you not afraid that the other Chief High Priest might have been telling the truth? That he did really receive a command from the Gods? And you may be punished, after all, for what you are doing? Are you wondering, Apaan, that if you perhaps stop now, you might be spared your punishment or at least have it reduced? You are a man of God, and you must believe in the afterlife. Doesn't eternal damnation scare you?"

When she was done, Apaan began laughing. Zayaa realized it wasn't merely a mirthless laughter, but that Apaan was actually amused. He laughed at her until tears poured out of his eyes.

"Well, if there is a hell and eternal damnation," Apaan managed to say amidst his laughing, "I don't think I can avoid it. Whatever the highest degree of punishment there is, I think I have already earned it. And that's only more reason to enjoy the present. So, where were we, before you spoke all that nonsense? Oh yes, please be ready for me; I will be back soon. Oh yes, one more thing, this time though, please take off your clothes before you take the dhutura and fall into a stupor. I know there are many depraved people who like to tear clothes off the women. I am not one of them."

For a few moments, Zayaa contemplated going against Tanaa's advice and taking the other leaves, the ones that simply looked like dhutura. However, she knew Tanaa was right. After all, Apaan had just told so himself: he did not believe in prophecies.

She took her dhutura, and did not come out of her stupor until the next morning. The bruises were lesser than the previous time. The Banyan and Turmeric paste also helped as much as they could. This went on for the next three days. Finally, Apaan informed her that sharing every night with him must be getting monotonous, so that night Zayaa should expect one of the other High Priests.

Zayaa hoped Tanaa's plan would work. She was impatient for night to fall, and yet dreaded what it might bring her. She chewed some of the mysterious leaves. Her body went limp, as had happened the few times she chewed these leaves at Tanaa's place. She became extremely aware of her surroundings. The High Priest entered the room and closed the door behind him. He came over to Zayaa, and was not surprised to find her in a dhutura-induced stupor. He gently undressed her and caressed her breasts. As Tanaa had promised, even though she cringed mentally at his touch, her body did not even flinch.

As was planned Zayaa said, "come O Prince of Gods. Come and make me yours. The Gods have ordained that four of the seven shall lose their Rod of Life within three full moons of entering me. Come and take me, and thus fulfil the prophecy." Then after a pause, she continued in a monotone, "the Dreamer has dreamed; the Dreamer has seen the future; the Dreamer has spoken."

After the High Priest had heard Zayaa's prophecy, he first recoiled from her. Then he quickly covered Zayaa's naked body with her own clothes and then sat down, next to her. Zayaa, though seemingly unconscious, knew very well that he was waiting for her, but had no idea why he was doing so. Still wondering but tired, and numb from the chewing of the leaves, she slowly floated into sleep. When she woke up in the morning, the High Priest was still there, next to her. This was unexpected, but Zayaa quickly recovered.

"Oh, you are still here," Zayaa observed sadly. "You want more, don't you?" she sighed. "Before you have your way with me again, please let me chew some dhutura."

"No, No, that is not why I am here," the High Priest protested. "O Dreamer of Truths Yet to Come, I did come here with sinful intentions and even undressed you. Please forgive me for that, but I did nothing else." Then, he surprised Zayaa by saying something that Tanaa had not anticipated. "I would really appreciate it if you could keep this between the two of us. If the others come to know of this, they will perceive this as a weakness of my manhood. I will still have to pretend to claim my time with you and, thus, take turns to have you. However, when I am with you, I will not touch you. I will just sit here for a while and then leave."

"Why are you being so kind to me?" Zayaa asked, pretending innocence.

"Well, there is something truly holy about you that I cannot defile," he offered awkwardly. "Please remember not to mention this to anyone else, though."

"Then, you must do something for me in return," she instructed. "I would like you to fight for more than your share, to come here more often than you are supposed to."

"It will be as you say O Dreamer-of-Truths-Yet-to-Come," the High Priest acceded.

"Now, leave me. I will pray to the Gods to forgive your sins," she offered. The High Priest left her room.

Four of the other High Priests followed in a similar pattern. It was only with one High Priest, the one that came third, that she had to get more descriptive. She explained to him, in detail, about how his Rod would shrivel and burn away, that he would feel the most excruciating pain he has ever known, as it drops away from his body. Soon, all the six High Priests were left terrified at the thought of even touching Zayaa. They all also individually promised to fight for more than their share of her time, thus leaving Zayaa to only worry about and deal with Apaan. With time, Apaan moved on to younger girls. However, unlike the other older Dasasas, from time to time, Apaan did visit Zayaa.

It was only three months after her investiture ceremony that Zayaa was allowed to move back to Shubhyaan's house. She still had to spend most of her days and a few nights a week at the Temple Sanctuary. She was instructed in dancing, flower arrangements, floor paining and other art forms. Initially, Zayaa immersed herself in these activities to take her mind off her plight, but soon she not only got interested in these, but quite good, as well. She became especially accomplished in dancing.

When Shubhyaan informed Zayaa that Vyaan would be arriving within a few days, Zayaa's initial euphoria was soon replaced with apprehension. She did not want to go on living, if Vyaan did not forgive her and accept her back. However, since Tanaa had informed her that she was with child, Zayaa knew death was also not an option.

One day Zayaa came home from the Temple Sanctuary and did not find Shubhyaan at home. Though this had never happened before, she assumed that he must have gone out to procure something that Vyaan liked. When Shubhyaan did not come home by nightfall, she became increasingly uneasy. She started suspecting foul play on Apaan's part. She waited up all night, but there was no sign of Shubhyaan.

Vyaan arrived the next day. He was delighted at seeing Zayaa. He became even happier when he saw that she was with child. Zayaa tearfully asked Vyaan to hold her. Then, she insisted that Vyaan hear everything that had happened since he had left for Sumer. She started her story, but Vyaan could see that his wife was in pain as she spoke. Unable to bear her suffering, he stopped her and said that she should only tell him if, and when, she could narrate it, without feeling pain or if she felt that he absolutely had to know everything. Till such a time, he told her, she should consider the story having already been told to Vyaan. Zayaa insisted that she would like to continue, but Vyaan would have none of it. Vyaan stopped all his travelling after that, and he stayed on in Pparaha. Then, Tiraa was born.

For Zayaa, her first few years at the Temple Sanctuary were still all about getting her vengeance. And she was sure she could sacrifice anything for that cause. However, one day, while she was at the Temple Sanctuary, one of the other Dasasas rushed into the inner courtyard, and informed her that Tiraa had fallen down the steps in the Baths. Zayaa did not stop to take anyone's permission, but left her chores and ran to the Baths. At the Baths, Avraa informed her that Vyaan had taken Tiraa to Tanaa's place. Zayaa started running towards Tanaa's place.

Zayaa had not prayed to the Gods, since the day of her father's death. However, as she ran through the streets of Pparaha, she prayed for Tiraa's safety. She implored the Gods to ensure that Tiraa was safe, and she would not ask for anything else. She would also never complain to them about the misfortunes that she had had to bear. When she reached Tanaa's place, she did not even knock, but just burst in.

Tanaa took her in her arms, and asked her to relax. Tanaa then informed Zayaa that though Tiraa would need some time to recover from her wounds, she was out of harm's way. As she looked up to thank the Gods, she realized that Tiraa's safety and wellbeing had become more important to her than wreaking vengeance on Apaan.

Chapter 5

Tears were streaming down the cheeks of both Zayaa and Vyaan.

"And you had to bear all this by yourself," Vyaan finally said to his wife. "I was selfish in not letting you finish your story after I came back from Sumer. I thought I was sparing you the pain, but instead only forced you to bottle it all up inside you and suffer alone for all these years. I have heard of a saying during my travels: 'most unkind is the act of kindness that leads to pain.' I finally understand what it means."

"Vyaan," Zayaa said between her sobs, "please never apologize to me. Without you, I would not have been able to go on living. Now, I need to ask you two things. First, do you still consider me your wife?"

"Zayaa," Vyaan interrupted before she could ask her second question, "there must have been some failure on my part. If I had been a good husband, you would have never asked me this."

"I am sorry, Vyaan," Zayaa said firmly, "but, please, I do need you to answer my question."

"Remember, when we were trying to decide how we would get married ..." Vyaan started.

"Please Vyaan, an answer!" Zayaa insisted.

"I am giving you the answer, Zayaa," Vyaan explained, "but, at the same time, I also want to make sure that you do not have any lingering doubts about how I feel. Please, let me continue," he asked and Zayaa acceded, though impatiently. "I had married you with the river and fire as my witnesses," Vyaan continued, "and I had made a promise then to protect you from all harm. I failed. I was not there to protect you when you needed me most. So, the question is not whether I still consider you my wife, for that is a given, but whether you still consider me your husband, for it is I who has failed in performing my duties as a husband."

Zayaa smiled lovingly through her tears. "I must have done some good in this life, or perhaps a previous life, to have you as my husband. I have one more question, though. This is about Tiraa," she took a long, uncomfortable breath.

"Stop!" Vyaan held up his hand, "I think you should hear what I have to say, before you insult me with your question, however deserving of that insult I may be. Tiraa is my daughter. I was the first one to hold her after she came out of your womb. I taught her how to talk. I held her finger to teach her how to walk. I will rip out the tongue of anyone who says she is not my daughter!"

"Then, I don't have any more questions," Zayaa finished. "You have always taken good care of me, but today you have made me happier than anyone can ever hope to be and certainly happier than I deserve to be."

"Zayaa," Vyaan said, "You are supposed to be the practical one. Let us keep these emotions aside and talk about what needs to be done next."

"I don't think we can do anything now," Zayaa said. "We will wait until the Harvest Festival is over. Then, we can speak to Tanaa and also meet this mysterious friend of hers. I know how things work at the Temple Sanctuary, Vyaan. They will not do anything before the Harvest Festival. In fact, I am sure nothing will be done before the Winter Solstice."

"That's not what I meant," Vyaan said, "we have to decide on what we are willing to share with Tiraa. She has the right to know something."

"We don't have to tell her anything, yet, do we?" Zayaa grew anxious.

"Yes, we do," Vyaan asserted, "what if we need to do something at a moment's notice? We will not have time to explain things then. No, I think she needs to be told something."

"What can we tell her?" Zayaa protested, "She is still a child. I am supposed to have the first mother-daughter talk with her after the Harvest Festival. How does one explain rape to someone who still does not understand sex?"

"I don't know how," Vyaan snapped, "but I'd rather risk having her grow up faster than let her be exploited." His voice softened on seeing

Zayaa's tensed face. "Let us think about it. But we have to do it soon, after the Harvest Festival at the latest."

"I still don't know–" Zayaa began, but stopped, as they heard footsteps coming down the stairs.

"Ayei, Appi," Tiraa called out. "You both are still up? Appi, you said that I needed to go to sleep so that Ayei could go to sleep early, too."

"Well, why are you not sleeping then?" Vyaan asked.

"I was sleeping," Tiraa protested, "but, then, I got up because my stomach was hurting. Then, I heard voices and came down."

"Come, Tii," Zayaa called, "I will go and lie down with you." Zayaa thus left to put her daughter to sleep, but not before giving Vyaan a meaningful look: they would have to wait to speak in private again; she seemed to say to him.

The next few days passed quickly. Nothing untoward happened, just as Zayaa had predicted. On the day of the Harvest Festival, Zayaa left for the Temple Sanctuary early in the morning, before sunrise. Soon, there was a knock at their house's door. Vyaan opened the door to find a herder with a bundle of clothes. "For tomorrow," the messenger said and then left.

When Vyaan examined the bundle, he realized there were three sets of clothes, and of the type that was usually worn by herders. By the sizes, these were clearly meant for Zayaa, Tiraa and himself. The clothes that had been chosen for Zayaa were those worn by the animal singers, who always covered themselves head to toe. Vyaan realized this would completely hide Zayaa's skin colour. Tanaa's attention to details pleased Vyaan. *We are in good hands*, he thought to himself. Although he did not want to attend the Harvest Festival, he knew he had to. Despite Tiraa's protests, he made her dress in drab and shapeless clothes. They managed to stay away from attention.

Zayaa came back very late. Tiraa was allowed to stay up for her.

"Ayei," Tiraa complained as Zayaa entered the house, "you won't believe what Appi made me wear to the festival."

"Tii," Vyaan said, "you will have a lot of time to complain tomorrow. But first, let me talk about an interesting trip I have planned for us. Tomorrow after sunset, we will dress up as herders and leave the city. We'll go to see how the farm animals spend their nights."

"But, Appi," Tiraa pouted, "farm animals give out a bad stink."

"Let us find out why then?" Vyaan countered.

"I don't want to wear clothes made for herders," Tiraa continued to protest.

"Let us do as Appi says," Zayaa intervened, mediating between the two, "but you get to choose what we do in our next trip."

Tiraa seemed somewhat placated at this.

After Tiraa had gone to sleep, Vyaan asked Zayaa, "When are they expecting you back at the sanctuary?"

"Not for a week."

"Good. Let us hope whatever Tanaa is planning is done by then."

The next morning, Zayaa woke up early and, after finishing her bath, woke Tiraa up. She asked Tiraa to take her bath, too. Then, Zayaa sat down with Tiraa and had the talk all mothers dread, but then overcome their embarrassment and bashfulness, knowing how important it is for their daughters to have this knowledge, as they proceed towards womanhood.

Tiraa had many questions, some that were easy for her to ask and for Zayaa to answer. And there were other questions, awkward ones, which Tiraa took time to overcome her shyness to ask, and Zayaa, her bashfulness to answer. It was noon by the time they had finished their discussion. Tiraa felt at peace about herself, about the changes that were happening to her. Not only did she realize that everything she had been worrying about was nothing unusual, that it happens to all girls, but also realized that if any such worry came up again, she could always go to her mother.

Late in the afternoon, a little before sunset, three herders arrived at their home, carrying three baskets. They quickly emptied their day-to-day living things from the baskets and handed the empty baskets to Vyaan.

"Please feel free to use anything you want from our kitchen," Zayaa said to them. 'I hope there is enough food here for you."

"Please do not worry," the woman-herder said. "The herders who deliver meat will come here regularly to ensure we have everything. Tanaa does not want us to leave this house until you are back. We will only be using the kitchen. We will sleep there, as well. No other part of your house will be polluted."

"You will do no such thing," Vyaan said. "Please feel free to use the whole house like your own. I know there are people who eat the meat of the animals you have touched and killed, and yet do not want to get touched by you. I can, humbly, tell you that we try not to be like them."

"Sorry," the woman-herder apologized, "we should not have expected anything different from Tanaa's friends. We will make sure that when you come back, you will find everything as clean as you are leaving them. Please go in peace now. Tanaa is waiting."

The three of them, already dressed as herders, left immediately with the baskets. It was dark when they came to the cattle-head-shaped hillock. Tanaa stepped out of the shadows as they reached. There was another man with her, who was leading five asses. Zayaa recognized this person as someone she had seen before at the Temple Sanctuary. But before she could give voice to her concerns, Tanaa chuckled.

"You are surprised to see Sanj," Tanaa guessed, and took Zayaa away from Vyaan and Tiraa, "and why not? You must have seen him in the Temple Sanctuary with Apaan. Do you remember what I had told you years ago? About how I've made sure that Apaan hears what I need him to hear?"

Zayaa remembered, and she sighed with relief.

"This you will not remember, though, but Sanj was the first person you met when you came to Pparaha. But, let us hurry now, as this is a night full of surprises," Tanaa said mysteriously, and then turned to her spy. "Sanj, please help everyone onto their asses. I will lead, followed by Zayaa, then Tiraa, and lastly, Vyaan. Sanj, you will act as the rear guard. I don't want anyone to follow us. And if anyone does, I don't want them to live to tell anyone where we are going."

Zayaa, Vyaan and Tiraa dutifully laughed at Tanaa's poor attempt at humour.

Even though it was dark, Tanaa seemed to know the way very well. After travelling north for about five mahahaths, they came to a stream. Tanaa rode her ass into the stream, and the others followed her. They thus rode, sometimes along and sometimes into the streambed itself, for another five mahahaths. Then, Tanaa rode her ass out of the stream and came to a stop outside a small hut. Upon a closer look, Vyaan realized that the hut was much bigger than it looked to them. After they had dismounted from their asses, Tanaa went to Sanj.

"Sanj," Tanaa called to him, "until our visitors go back to Pparaha, please ensure that there is no one nosing around anywhere near here, or near the path we took. And as I have warned you, don't take any unnecessary risks. If they do not have a reason to be here, then make sure they don't live to tell anyone about what they've seen. I will let you know when we are ready to leave."

Zayaa and Tiraa laughed again. But Vyaan did not join them this time, for he realized that Tanaa was not joking.

Tanaa knocked on the door of the hut and then pushed it open to go inside. Zayaa followed her, but stopped halfway. She fell, shaking, into the arms of Vyaan who was behind her.

"But how can it be?" Zayaa muttered, steadying herself and then walking towards the elderly man who was standing inside. "Appi, is it really you? But you died in my arms." Then, Zayaa began beating her fists into the chest of the elderly man and sobbed, "Appi, you have to tell me now! Do you really think I was at fault? Please tell me what I could have done differently. Please tell me, what I should have done?" Then, she stopped and looked up at the elderly man's face. "And what has happened to you?" then tracing her forefinger across the scar, which started from the right of the elderly person's right eye, going through his cheeks and ending on the left side of his chin, she continued, "What happened to you Appi? Who cut up your face?"

Before the elderly man could answer, Vyaan walked up to them and pulled Zayaa away. "This cannot be your father," Vyaan said. "This is not Riyaansh Uncle. I have seen that scar before, Zayaa. I don't remember where, but I am sure I have."

Zayaa turned angrily to Vyaan. "What are you saying?" she demanded. "This is my father. Can't you see that?" Then, she turned back towards the elderly man in front of her, who looked like her Appi, and she observed his face. It finally dawned on her. "But of course, it is I who momentarily lost my mind. Please excuse my foolishness," she said to Vyaan. "You are not Appi," she admitted to the elderly man, "you are my Sikkappa, my father's brother, Ridhaan, are you not?"

"But if he is your Sikkappa," Vyaan asked, "why do I know about that scar? How do I know him?"

"If either of you could stop talking for even a moment," the elderly man burst in, "then I could perhaps try to answer your questions."

"Please tell us if you are my Sikkappa," Zayaa asked.

"And how I know that scar?" Vyaan added.

"I will tell you everything," the elderly man smiled. "But first, I, too, need to ask some questions and lay down some conditions."

Ignoring his requests, Zayaa and Vyaan tried to speak again, and a frustrated Tanaa let out a shrill scream in an unearthly high-pitched tone. Everyone else in the room pressed their palms to their ears to shut out the sudden sound.

"Now that I have everyone's attention," Tanaa said with a sneer, "I would like to suggest we stop scaring Tiraa here." Then, turning to Tiraa she asked, "would you like to join this madhouse, or would you like to join me in getting us something to eat? I'm starving!"

"Tanaa," the elderly man said, "you definitely are the most practical person in this mad world. I am sorry for forgetting my duties as a host. Please let us go and eat now. I have a long tale to narrate. And I don't think we can go on without food for that long." As Tanaa led Tiraa further into the house, the elderly man held Zayaa and Vyaan back. When Tiraa was out of earshot, he said, "I think Tiraa has every right to know about everything. I don't think there is any part of the tale I am about to narrate that is inappropriate for her age. However, as her parents, if you decide that Tiraa should not hear the tale I am about to relate, I will bow to your decision."

Zayaa looked at Vyaan.

"No, you are right," Vyaan said to the elderly gentleman, "we do want to guard her from this world. Yet, we realize that knowledge is the greatest shield she will have. I am sure you will keep the language and descriptions suitable to her age, as well."

The elderly man seemed satisfied. "However, when we do come to your story, Zayaa, you will have to decide how much you want to tell her. But please remember there are bigger things at stake here than your feelings or Tiraa's," he added without explanation and ushered them into the kitchen.

After they had sat down to eat, the elderly man started without ceremony, "my first condition is that all introductions are deferred, until I finish my tale. My second condition is that no one asks questions or discusses anything, while I am narrating my tale. Even without your questions, the narration will take a long time," he sighed. "If you disturb me, I will never get done. I am getting old, and will have to refer to these parchments from time to time. Use this time to take care of your bodily functions. Also, we will need our rest and sleep. I will start now, but will stop after dinner. Tanaa will show Zayaa and Tiraa where they will sleep.

Vyaan, you will sleep in the room you found me when you came here. If you all are in agreement I will begin." He waited for their response.

"I agree," Zayaa said, "but could you please confirm that you are indeed my Sikkappa?"

"But, my dear, that would be violating my first condition," the elderly man's eyes twinkled. "Wouldn't it?"

Chapter 6

Riyaansh and Ridhaan were the identical twin sons of the official town-scribe of Kdwar. Their mother had died during childbirth. Even though most identical twins are usually distinguishable by a birthmark or some other feature, Riyaansh and Ridhaan had no such visible distinction.

Even though identical in looks and mannerisms, their characters were very different. Riyaansh was the hard worker. He started learning the art of writing at a very young age. Ridhaan was naturally talented. Though better of the two at character recognition, Ridhaan refused to learn this trade. Instead, he became a trader's apprentice. Riyaansh took the position of the town's scribe after his father. Soon after that, Riyaansh dutifully married the girl their father had chosen for him. But Ridhaan refused to get married. A few years after Riyaansh's marriage, their father died. None of this had any adverse effect on their relationship. The twins only grew closer to each other as they grew older.

A year later, a daughter was born to Riyaansh's wife. The baby was very fair, her skin almost white. Her hair was white, as well, and her eyes pink. The midwife immediately declared that some devilry was at work. She suggested that they get rid of the baby. Ridhaan threw the midwife out of the house. It was Ridhaan who then chose her name: Zayaa, he called her. After Zayaa's birth, Ridhaan's visits to Riyaansh's house became more frequent.

When Zayaa was about four years of age, her mother went to the sea, to collect mussels, as she did once or twice every week. But on this particular day, she was bitten by something poisonous and, as the venom spread through her body, she fainted. By dusk, she was burning with high fever. And though Riyaansh, who had a good knowledge of healing herbs and roots, tried his best, he could not save her. She died the next morning.

Riyaansh was consumed with grief, as he blamed himself for not being able to save his wife. That evening, when Ridhaan came to their home, he found Zayaa's mother lying dead in the courtyard, and Riyaansh lying next to her, staring into the dark sky. His niece was sitting next to her father, simply staring at him. He found out from Zayaa that she and her father had not eaten since the previous evening.

Ridhaan took control of the situation. He sent one of the neighbours to the Temple Sanctuary to fetch a priest, and asked if anyone could feed Zayaa. After inquiring Zayaa's age, the priest declared as Zayaa was still young; her mother would be cremated and not buried.

Zayaa's mother was thus dressed up by the women of the neighbourhood in her best clothes and jewellery. That same night, she was taken to the cremation area of the burial ground and duly cremated. Her ashes were collected in an earthen urn and taken to the Temple Sanctuary, to be kept there for fifteen days[21], by that time it was believed that her spirit would be cleansed of all its sins. On the sixteenth day, the urn would be returned to the family, to be kept in a place of respect within their house.

As Riyaansh was in mourning and in no shape to take care of himself, let alone his little girl, Ridhaan continued to stay on at their place. He knew it would take some time for Riyaansh to reconcile with the situation, and therefore, in the meanwhile, he wanted to ensure that both Riyaansh and Zayaa got properly cooked meals and the house was kept reasonably clean. By the third day, the child had started to become her usual cheerful self. However, she also started asking questions, about where her mother was and when she would be able to see her again. The more Ridhaan tried to answer her questions, the more difficult the following set of questions became for him. He tried explaining to Zayaa that her mother had gone off to live in another place, but, to this, Zayaa wanted to know when she would be back and whether Zayaa was allowed to visit her. Ridhaan knew this was only natural and that it would take time for Zayaa to adjust to a life without her mother. He was more worried about his brother.

Eleven days had passed since his sister-in-law had passed away, but Ridhaan still could not see any change in his brother's demeanour. He wondered if consuming some raajaraas might help Riyaansh sleep better. He thus went to the Raakanaa[22] to fetch some. While he waited for his

---

[21] 1111 in binary

order of raajaraas, he thought he heard Riyaansh and Zayaa's name being mentioned by someone, so he turned and looked in the direction of the voices. He immediately noticed a conspicuous silence at one of the tables, while the occupants of that same table – five of them, Riyaansh counted – looked away awkwardly, unwilling to meet his eyes. Ridhaan knew that nothing would be gained by hanging around, so he collected his earthen jug of raajaraas and left.

However, he did not go to his brother's house. Instead, he went to his own home and fetched one of his most-prized possessions, a curved dagger that he had won in a game of chance from a sailor from some western land. He then went back to the Raakanaa and hunched down in the shadows across the street. He was pleased to see that the particular table was still occupied by the five people, like before. Ridhaan waited patiently.

When the men left the table and began walking out of the Raakanaa, Ridhaan could see them more clearly. He recognized one of them immediately—Tikoo. Tikoo's son had once been bitten by a snake. Riyaansh had managed to save the boy, by sucking out the poison and applying some herbs onto the bite wound. Riyaansh had fallen sick in turn, Ridhaan recalled now, having ingested a little of the poison. After waiting for some time, Ridhaan set off in the direction of Tikoo's house. He walked as fast as possible, yet trying not to draw any undue attention to himself. Finally, when, he came to a deserted place he quickened his pace.

"Tikoo?" he called out to the man. "Please could I speak with you for a moment?" Ridhaan asked, catching up with him.

When Tikoo turned and saw Ridhaan, all blood drained from his face. When Ridhaan saw Tikoo's reaction, any lingering doubts he still had about Tikoo's complicity in some wicked plot, disappeared.

"Tikoo, I just need to talk to you for a moment. What were you discussing about my brother and niece?" Ridhaan asked.

"Oh, it is you Ridhaan. You know I still cannot tell you and your brother apart," Tikoo murmured nervously.

"Yes, it is me. Now, please tell me what you all were discussing. And why did you become so afraid when you saw me?" Ridhaan demanded.

"It does not really concern you. And who do you think you are stopping me in the street and interrogating me?" Tikoo tried to brazen it out.

---

[22]A place where one could buy and drink raajaraas

"Look here, Tikoo, my brother and niece are my concern. And don't forget your son is alive today because of Riyaansh. You owe it to him," Ridhaan appealed. Something in Tikoo's face told him that whatever it was that the man was hiding, it might just be worse than anything Ridhaan could ever imagine.

"I know very well what I owe to whom. Riyaansh saved the life of one of my son's. But I cannot risk the life of my entire family to repay that. I have already said too much," Tikoo said, while avoiding Ridhaan's eyes.

Ridhaan realized that Tikoo was really afraid.

"Look here, you son of a diseased pig," Ridhaan spat out and pulled out his dagger. "I will..."

"Kill me if you have to, but I am not saying another word," Tikoo said with a steely glare.

"I already know what has been planned. I have heard it from one of the others, the one with the scar," remembering that one of Tikoo's companions had a big scar on his face. "I merely assumed that since Riyaansh has saved your son, you would be willing to help us. But now that I know you're useless to my family, I will simply go up to the others and tell them that you have betrayed them, that you've told me everything."

"But I have told you nothing," Tikoo grew alarmed.

"Your friends don't know that, do they? Besides, I will ensure that your stubbornness is repaid with a fate far worse than that of my brother and niece," Ridhaan retorted.

"Ha! And what fate can be worse than being sat on a stake?" Tikoo sneered.

Ridhaan could not believe what he had just heard. Furious, he stepped closer to Tikoo and placed the tip of his dagger's blade on the man's neck, and pressed it into his skin, so it drew blood and a cry of pain from Tikoo. "Tell me everything or I will kill you, I promise, here and now."

Tikoo's indecisiveness could be clearly seen by his shifty eyes and furtive glances. But finally, he seemed to calm down, as if resigning to his fate.

"I am not afraid of you, but I will tell you everything because of the kindness Riyaansh once showed me."

Ridhaan knew that it was fear and not kindness that had helped Tikoo make up his mind. However, he did not say anything, for he instinctively knew that Tikoo would be telling the truth.

Ridhaan eased the blade out of the man's skin, but kept the tip touching his throat, ready to sink it in again if needed. "The Chief High Priest has decided that Riyaansh and Zayaa will be sat on stakes. To achieve this, he will use your sister-in-law's untimely death and Zayaa's strange looks to his advantage."

Ridhaan wondered why the Chief High Priest would wish for such a thing.

"Five of us were summoned to the Temple Sanctuary," Tikoo continued. "All of us have been chosen very carefully. Your brother has done some favour or other, to each one of us. And all of us have some secret that the Chief High Priest already knew, or, as in my case, has gone to the trouble of finding out," Tikoo said with a grimace. "When I was quite young, during a visit to Thallo[23], I lay down with an aunt-by-marriage. This aunt was the wife of the uncle we had gone to visit, a man whose food I had eaten. In my defence, I was young, and the aunt, who was much older, threatened that if I do not lay down with her, she would tell my uncle that I had tried to force myself on her. My cousin caught us in the act. My uncle threw me out of his house, while cursing aloud at his wife and me. So everyone in the neighbourhood found out what had happened as well. This happened many many years ago. However, the Chief High Priest has somehow found out about it. He has also found out that this uncle and aunt of mine had never been formally married, and thus, according to the Chief High Priest, by lying down with my aunt, I had married her. This renders my relationship with my wife as adultery and all my children as bastards. I did counter him with the argument that since my uncle had lain with her much before I had, why that was not considered a marriage. He laughed and told me that, whichever way one looked at it, I had committed adultery and it would be very difficult to argue anything while sitting on a stake and hoping for a quicker death," Tikoo said bitterly.

"So what exactly is supposed to happen to my brother and niece?" Ridhaan asked.

"You have not really spoken to the scarred friend, have you? Or even if you have, he has not told you anything, has he? I should have known. Your brother would never have lied, even to save his life. However, you, on the other hand," Tikoo complained.

---

[23] A port City in South-Eastern Givenland/ Meluhha

"It is too late for you to stop," Ridhaan said without remorse. "I know enough now to convince the others that you have told me everything else."

"It is too late for all of us," Tikoo sighed. "In three days' time, when Riyaansh goes to the Temple Sanctuary to collect his wife's ashes, the five of us will be there. We will accuse him, his wife and little Zayaa, of practicing witchcraft. I am supposed to go first. I will claim that your sister-in-law took the form of a snake and bit my son, as Riyaansh needed to drink my son's blood to make his black magic stronger."

"I suppose that is when the Chief High Priest will announce the sentences on my brother and little Zayaa," Ridhaan said, trying to hurry along the story.

"No, he is too cunning to do that. When I finish, the Chief High Priest will deride me as a liar. He will say that he cannot believe Riyaansh would do something like that. However, then, one by one, the other four will make their accusations. The Chief High Priest will still continue to protest, but, then, will make it seem as if he is slowly being convinced by the severe implications of our accusations. He will then berate himself for not seeing it himself, but he will be thankful that the Gods are omniscient. He will claim that it must have been, at their divine will and bidding, that your sister-in-law has been punished with an untimely and unnatural death. He will then decide that he cannot be blind any longer, that he will need to take action. He will thus declare that Kdwar's safety depends on Riyaansh and little Zayaa being sat on stakes."

"I am going to have to kill the Chief High Priest before he does any such thing," Ridhaan said in a matter-of-fact voice.

Tikoo laughed derisively at this. "The Chief High Priest did say that you might try to make trouble. However, he is not concerned. He knows the people would like to have a wizard's brother being sat on the stake too."

"We will see about that," Ridhaan said, "but for both our sakes, do not tell anyone that we have talked."

"Definitely," Tikoo agreed. "If they find out that I have talked to you, then not only will I lose my own life, but my wife's too, for she will also be put to death for being an adulteress. My children might be killed too, after being branded as bastards. Even though you don't owe me anything, I would appreciate if my name is kept out of whatever you are planning to do."

"You are right in saying I do not owe you anything," Ridhaan hissed. "However, I don't intend to have yours or anybody else's blood on my conscience, unless it is absolutely necessary. So pray that it does not become necessary for me to talk about you. You can be on your way now."

"Before I leave, I would like to offer you some advice. What I am going to say now will benefit me surely, but it will benefit your family, as well. If either or both of Riyaansh and Zayaa are still in Kdwar three days from now, there will be no way for them to get out of this death-trap. Due to the colour of Zayaa's skin, she cannot hide anywhere in Givenland. Right now, the only hope of escape that they have is to find a ship that is leaving for Sumer or even further west, board it, and disappear forever," Tikoo advised.

"We will think about it. Go in peace."

Ridhaan went back to the place where he had hidden the jug of raajaraas and, after retrieving it, he hurried back towards Riyaansh's house.

When Ridhaan reached his brother's house, he found Riyaansh in the same manner that he had left him, lying on his back in his courtyard, looking up into the skies.

"Where is Zayaa?" Ridhaan asked.

"She is upstairs. Sleeping," Riyaansh murmured and then, with a long sigh, he turned to his side.

Since he had left Tikoo, Ridhaan had been thinking about how he might possibly break such horrible news to Riyaansh. Seeing Riyaansh now, lying on the floor listlessly, without a care whether he lived or died, Ridhaan realized that his brother needed to be shocked out of his present state.

"Good," Ridhaan said, trying to keep his voice as normal as possible. "She will be well rested then, for her journey to the other world."

Riyaansh did not react to his spurring, though.

"From what I hear, though, when children as young as her are sat on the stake, they take even longer to die. Something to do with the jackals not being able to reach..." Ridhaan continued.

"By the Holy Mother, what are you talking about?" Riyaansh said sitting up.

"Now that I have your attention, I would like you to have a drink of raajaraas first," Ridhaan said, pouring the drink into two cups.

"No. First, explain yourself, and the sick joke you just made," Riyaansh said, getting up to his feet and walking over to his brother menacingly.

"Calm down, brother," Ridhaan said. "You know I would never jest about such a thing. Please drink up this cup and I will tell you all."

Riyaansh took the cup from his brother's hand and finished the raajaraas in one, furious gulp, "okay, out with it."

Ridhaan told Riyaansh about everything that had happened that evening. After he had finished, Riyaansh sat down to think about it all for a while.

"I will go to the Temple Sanctuary tomorrow and demand that I be heard. I will then challenge the right of the Chief High Priest to continue being in his position, after plotting such a heinous crime," Riyaansh said finally.

"I don't think that will help," Ridhaan explained patiently. "You will not be able to prove anything without corroboration. In spite of the fact that you have done them all a good turn, neither will Tikoo nor the others speak up anything against the Chief High Priest. The only result of such confrontation will be the hastening of your sentences."

"So, what do you suggest? That we just sit and wait for the inevitable," Riyaansh asked with exasperation. Then, he calmed down a little. "I don't care if I live or die anymore, but I cannot let anything happen to Zayaa."

"And we won't," Ridhaan said with determination. He then wondered aloud, "Why don't we take Tikoo's advice and leave this place?"

"I think that is unfair," Riyaansh said. "We have done no wrong. I have always been respectful of the Chief High Priest's wishes. So, I still don't understand why he is doing this to our family. Did Tikoo say anything about why the Chief High Priest wants us dead? Do you know if the other High Priests support this? If it is only the Chief High Priest who wants this, then, perhaps, I can sneak into the Temple Sanctuary and kill him."

"I have already considered killing the Chief High Priest," Ridhaan admitted, "but even if the other High Priests do not agree with what the Chief High Priest has decided, we cannot kill him. If we do, the others will definitely have us killed. They will have to, if for no other reason than to protect themselves from someone else doing the same to them. I have also been thinking about why you have been targeted and have come to the conclusion that it has nothing to do with you or the colour of Zayaa's skin. As you know, last year was very dry and Kdwar, along with most parts of the southern plains, did not produce much grain. You must also remember that the High Priests declared that through careful planning and diligent monitoring, they had been able to provide us with a granary filled with enough grain to last us for three more years. However, what you may not know is that during the last big storm that hit us about a few months ago, the granary roof was severely damaged. Water has thus seeped into the granary, and, despite all efforts to save the supply, the grain is rotting and is covered in black mould. The rains have not ceased yet, and we may very well have the floods upon us soon. You have not gone out in days, but, as of last week, they have started rationing grain. People are getting a tenth of what they are used to. The more the children go hungry, the more anxious their fathers become. They are now demanding answers. They want to know why the Gods are angry with Kdwar. They are questioning whether the Temple Sanctuary has done enough to appease the Gods. The Chief High Priest is caught in a predicament of course, unable to give the people the answers they seek. So, he has decided to find himself a scapegoat, on whom he can focus the anger of the people. Zayaa, who looks different from everyone else, is an easy target. I am sure he will claim that your family's sins have angered the Gods."

"But, you and I know that it is not so. What happens once we are killed and nothing changes for this town? The rains won't stop just because we are dead, and neither will the granary fill up with grains! Then what?" Riyaansh argued.

"I am sure that Zayaa and you will be the first of many. This *witch-hunt* will continue, until the situation improves." Ridhaan saw that his brother was not entirely convinced. "There is actually one more reason why they why Zayaa and you may have been chosen," he offered. "It is common knowledge here that you keep a well-laden kitchen, probably the best one in this town. That is why I have been able to keep this house running without getting impacted by the rationing. I am sure that after you are executed, all your salted meat and fish will end up with the High Priests and all your saved grain will be distributed amongst your accusers. Most probably, your house will also be given to one of them. With these rewards, the High Priests can lure in more accusers. People will start turning against each other. Neighbours will start identifying neighbours who have saved more food than they have. Men will start pointing at men who are competing for the attention of the same woman. Women will point at women whose husbands they might have designs on. And, of course, people will take this opportunity to take long-pending revenge."

"I think you may be right," Riyaansh nodded.

"In any case, let us come back to my question. Why don't we take Tikoo's advice and leave this place? You started giving your reasons on why we shouldn't. Are there any more?"

"Yes, there are," Riyaansh said, "all ships that leave Kdwar have to get their bill of lading approved by the Temple Sanctuary. However handsomely we might pay a captain, he will not give up the opportunity to sell us out, especially as this will get him the blessings of the High Priests."

"You are right," Ridhaan agreed, "but there has to be a way." He started to pace about the courtyard. Riyaansh started doing the same.

"So, we leave by land? We can go to some other town in Givenland?" Ridhaan suggested weakly.

"I cannot hide Zayaa's skin colour, wherever I end up," Riyaansh pointed out without any regret in his voice. "Also, why do you keep saying *we*? You do not have to go anywhere."

"Now, you are just not making any sense. Drunk too much raajaraas, haven't you?" Ridhaan said with a teasing smile, surprised that he could still smile in such a situation. But Riyaansh did not take any offense at this. Since childhood, humour and laughter had been the brother's defence mechanism, and a shared one at that. Ridhaan continued, "I don't have anyone else here to stay back for. Besides, I don't want to live in a town that is ruled by such unscrupulous High Priests. And, most importantly, if both of you are gone, I think they will just make me take your place, especially since we both look identical."

Riyaansh thought about his brother's reasoning for a while. "I think you are right," he eventually agreed. "This will mean that I might end up losing my wife's ashes, but I am sure she would want me to protect our daughter more than she would her ashes. Well, where do we go from here?" Just as soon as he had asked this question, he seemed to have found the answer too, for his eyes grew suddenly bright. "Before I say what I am thinking, please tell me this brother – do you think we could steal a small boat, one that will not be missed for a while?"

"How would that help?" Ridhaan asked gruffly. "We cannot expect to get very far on a small boat, definitely not to Sumer."

"Brother, trust me," Riyaansh said putting his arm around Ridhaan. "Just answer my question."

"There is one," Ridhaan said after some thought. "You know the old man who used to live next door when we were growing up? The one who used to be a good fisherman? He does have a boat, but it has been years since it has been used. When we were young, my friend and I found it in the groves, a little upstream," he said, then flashed his brother an impish smile. "You remember when we were young, how anything you were not willing to share disappeared?" Riyaansh laughed as he remembered. "And no matter how much you searched, you could not find these. Well, I'll let you in on the secret now: all those things are hidden in that small boat. That is why I never told you about it." Ridhaan grew more serious, "but I think even if we patched up the old thing, it would not stay afloat for very long."

"We will discuss later about all the things you have stolen from me," Riyaansh said with a fond smile. "About the boat, we will only need it for a very short journey. We will go around the first upstream bend of the river, cross it and go up the hills. There is a cave on the face opposite Kdwar, which will shelter us from the weather and wild animals. I have enough food stored in this house to last us for more than a year. We can also fish a little upstream or even hunt small animals to further fill our stomachs. We will have to do our cooking after nightfall, as otherwise the smoke will be seen from Kdwar. We can live there for some time, and come back to Kdwar after everything is back to normal. If we climb a little higher from this cave, we will reach a ledge, which wraps around the hill. You can actually see Kdwar from this ledge. What do you think?"

"I don't think coming back is an option," Ridhaan shook his head in disagreement, "but leaving Kdwar is the first step. Once you are convinced we cannot come back here, we will think about what we must do next. I will go tomorrow during the day and clean up the boat, see if any repairs are required. We will also need some weapons and household stuff, and need to figure out how to bring all this food to the boat. We will definitely need something to sleep on too, some cooking utensils, something to store water. We will also need..."

"Most of these are already solved," Riyaansh cut in. "Now, it's my turn to let you in on a secret of my own," he grinned. "As you may recall, since I got married, your sister-in-law and I always went travelling after the harvest season. What you did not know is that we spent only half the time in the towns we said we were visiting. The other half was spent in the cave I just mentioned. Your sister-in-law loved it there. After Zayaa was born, we started taking her along with us. We told her that it was a magical place and would disappear if she ever mentioned it to anyone else. As you did not know about this place, it is safe to assume Zayaa has told no one. Well, we have most of the things already stored in the cave. The only things we have to worry about taking there are the fishing and hunting related things. And, of course, we have to take the food to the cave. I think we should not wait for three days, but leave as soon as possible. Do you think we can go tomorrow night?" He seemed finally excited.

"The hunting-fishing things will not be a problem. I have enough of these," Ridhaan said. "But, how do we take the food outside of our town and all the way to the cave?"

"My wife was loved by everyone in this town. I think ..." Riyaansh started.

"There you go again," Ridhaan cut in, "you know very well that we have to leave Kdwar. I don't think you will get anyone's support if you stay back."

"Brother, please give me a chance to finish. I do agree that we have to leave town. Now please stop interrupting my thoughts," Riyaansh said patiently. "My wife was loved by everyone in this town. She was also known for her love of the outdoors. Before her ashes are brought home, I think I owe it to her memory to host a gathering of all the people who knew and loved her. The gathering can be held outside the town, in the outdoors. And I will have to bring these chests," he said, pointing to the two heavy looking boxes in his home, "to the gathering, for us to display her worldly possessions on. If I have to finish all the preparations in three days, I will have to start tomorrow. And it is always best to start with the most difficult task. Do you see any problems with this?"

"You are as cunning as ever," Ridhaan laughed. "Of course, the chests can be filled with grain. And even the High Priests will not stop the preparations, as the accusations have not been made, yet. This has to work, brother. No, I'm sure that it will definitely work. I will leave early in the morning to ensure we have everything we need for hunting, fishing and protection. By the time I come back, arrange for a cart and make sure it is strong enough to take both these chests – if we take them one by one, it will look suspicious. We must choose a place in the Northwest of the town, so it will make it easier for us to get the boxes to the boat. I think if we plan it right, we can be gone by late tomorrow night."

"You are almost right," Riyaansh said, "but there's one problem though, I think it will be difficult to find us a cart that can bear the weight of these chests, both filled to their brim with grain. I will have to find enough things – light things – for the first run, so that there will be room for only one chest," he pondered. Then, he snapped his fingers. "I know what I will do. I will pack our clothes in bundles. This plan is looking better and better, I must say."

The next day, Ridhaan left his brother's home early in the morning. He first went to his own place and collected all his fishing and hunting things.

He smiled when he realized that all his hunting things could also be used as weapons. As he was leaving, he met one of his neighbours.

"We have not seen you in a while. What are you planning to do with all these things?" the neighbour asked nosily.

"As you know, my sister-in-law has just died. Riyaansh is planning to hold a gathering in her memory. I am going to do some fishing for the event. And in case I don't have much luck with the fishing, I will try to do some hunting," Ridhaan said nonchalantly.

"Be careful with the fishing," the neighbour warned. "Mother River looks very angry these days. And if you get more than you need, let me know. Food is very scarce, and we can come to an arrangement."

Ridhaan heaved a sigh of relief and proceeded to the boat.

When he examined the boat, he was glad to see that it was still usable. He noted that the oars were much sturdier than the boat. He would be able to punch holes into the bottom of the boat, to have it sink easily, once they had crossed over. He did not think they could ever come back to Kdwar. After rechecking everything, he proceeded back to his brother's house.

When he got there, he found Riyaansh waiting impatiently outside his doorway.

Once they were inside, Riyaansh explained, "when they saw me come back with a cart, I had to tell a few of my neighbours about the gathering. They wanted to help me carry the things. I told them that I was waiting for you. But more and more people were coming to offer their help. I was running out of excuses."

Ridhaan then told Riyaansh of the encounter with his own neighbour.

While hoping for the best, the brothers were prepared for the worst. After they had made the two trips, Ridhaan stayed back at the venue of the gathering, to guard chests, while Riyaansh returned home to his daughter.

"Darling Zaa," Riyaansh walked into his child's room, "let us go up to the magical place up in the hills and stay there for a while."

"Yes, let's go!" Zayaa was excited. "Maybe Ayei is waiting there for us."

"But, you remember how the place will disappear if you tell anyone about it, right?" not wanting to give Zayaa any false hope, Riyaansh tactfully changed the subject. "So, we will have to go very quietly. No one should know about our plan. If anyone asks any questions, please leave the talking to me."

"Anything you say, Appi."

They quickly changed their clothes and left the house. Even though Riyaansh had excuses ready, in case someone did see them, luck was indeed on their side that night, and they did not meet anyone on the way out. They soon arrived at the place where Ridhaan was waiting for them, and Zayaa gasped in shock on seeing her uncle.

"What are we going to do now?" she whispered to her father. "Please do not tell Sikkappa about the magical place, or it might disappear. And then, we will never see Ayei again."

"Don't worry," Riyaansh reassured Zayaa, "your Sikkappa already knows about the place now. It turns out that he is allowed to know about it. Your mother and I were mistaken before."

Zayaa looked relieved. Ridhaan greeted his brother and niece.

Taking his brother aside, Riyaansh informed him, "Under the first chest, you will find three sacks, each of which should hold more than one-third of the grain. We can take all the clothes and a third of the grain in our first trip. Then, you will stay in the boat with Zayaa, while I make two more trips with the grain." Ridhaan tried to interrupt, but Riyaansh held up his hand. "Let me finish. Time is of essence. It is best I make those two trips. You see, I plan to wash myself with this raajaraas and pour some of it on my clothes, as well. If I do get caught and am questioned about anything, I will start crying inconsolably about how much I miss my wife, about how I plan to drink my pain away. If required, I will spit and drool on them. So, don't worry about me. But you will have to come back for the last trip. All the salted fish and dried meat is in the small chest. As I am not supposed to partake or touch any fish or meat until my wife's urn comes home, it will seem very strange if I am seen carrying these. So, you will come and fetch those."

Ridhaan realized that Riyaansh had put a lot of thought into this and, thus, decided to go along with his brother's plan.

Again, their luck held. They managed to get everything to the boat without arousing any suspicion or inviting any interruption. Long before dawn, they had slipped out in their boat and were moving upstream, around the bend of the river. Riyaansh knew exactly where to go ashore. After they had reached, Ridhaan stood guard, along with Zayaa, while Riyaansh, who knew the terrain better, carried everything up to the cave.

"I think we will be able to take everything between the two of us in the next trip. Start thinking about how we can hide the boat," Riyaansh instructed, when only three sacks of grains were left. He then left with one of the sacks.

When he came back, there was no trace of the boat.

"Where did you hide the boat?" Riyaansh asked his brother.

"I hid it inside the Mother River," Ridhaan said with a smile. "I scuttled it."

"What have you done?" Riyaansh asked angrily. "How will we ever go back? This was not your decision to make. We should have talked about it."

"Brother, let's not waste our time arguing about this," Ridhaan said, and then offered to explain himself. "While you were planning on how we were to move the food and clothes, I was thinking about this. There is no way one can pull a boat up into these shores. If we tied it, it would be found. In the rare occasion that we have to go back, I do know a way out of here. We will talk about it when the time comes, I promise."

"Fine," Riyaansh grumbled, "but going forward, neither of us should make decisions without discussing it first."

Ridhaan nodded his head. He then picked up one of the oars and a sack of grains. "Lead the way, brother. We all need our sleep."

They fell into a routine soon, only lighting fires after dark, cooking late at night, eating dinner later than they were used to, sleeping until late in the mornings, trying to fish after dark, though without much luck, and discussing where they were to hunt. Zayaa did ask when she would meet her mother, but was too tired and groggy to persist doing so. The twins were busy throughout the day, and exhausted by the time they went to sleep. But sleep still eluded Riyaansh. After making sure that his brother had fallen asleep, he wandered off and sat alone on some rock, and recounted the happenings of the day, as he would to his wife, when she was still alive. Only after this was done, did he go to sleep.

Three days after they had arrived, they were woken up by strange roaring and grinding noises. They climbed up to the ledge, and as they walked on, they found that the roaring got louder. When they looked down, they realized how angry the Mother River was. She had broken free and was ravaging Kdwar.

"O God, forgive my town. Do not punish them for my sins. I should not have left without my wife's ashes. I understand that now," Riyaansh went down on his knees and wailed.

"Riyaansh, get hold of yourself," Ridhaan said grimly, "if the Gods were after you, they would have sent a landslide here, rather than a flood down there. I think the Gods are punishing the town for what they were planning to do to you and Zayaa."

"But, why destroy the whole town? Why punish everyone for the mistakes of a few?" Riyaansh cried.

"All of them are to be blamed," Ridhaan shrugged. "The High Priests are to be blamed for the heinous things they were planning to do, and the accusers, of course, for going along with it. The Gods know that the rest of the town would not have helped you, would have let it all happen. They are all paying for their own sins, not yours."

"How can you be so sure?" Riyaansh asked, wiping away tears.

"I just need to look at Zayaa's innocent face," Ridhaan said, "and then into my heart, to know this to be true. We are lucky, my brother. The High Priests will all be dead by dawn, and no one will be looking for either Zayaa or you after that. So, once the Mother River has quieted down, we shall be able to travel to another town, a new place, and start a new life."

"Which direction shall we take?" Riyaansh asked his brother hopefully, still confused to be able to think of such things.

"North-northeast of course," Ridhaan said, surprising himself, as he said it, for he spoke without having to think about it, "north for the land of Gods, and northeast for luck."

The Mother River raged on for four full days. When the twins woke up on the fifth day, Riyaansh went up to the ledge. He saw that the Mother River was still swollen, and flowing beyond her banks. However, she was no longer furious. Their town was still under water. He could see only debris floating on the water. There were no signs of any life. After a little while, he went back to the cave and described what he saw to Ridhaan.

"I don't think we can cross the river for weeks," Riyaansh sighed, "but if we are to go to another town, it would be best to reach there before the harvest. That way, we can make ourselves useful there and, thereby, receive a warmer welcome from the people of the new town. But that means we have to start now." He was still disturbed, by the sudden destruction of his town, but was slowly regaining control.

"I agree, brother," Ridhaan replied, "but I think we should take a day or two to plan first. We will also have to decide what we will take with us. We should plan on either one of us having to carry Zayaa most of the way there. I have heard of tales from travellers about places where you can walk across the Mother River on ledges that are under the water, but cannot be seen from land. There is supposed to be one such ledge upriver, within a day's walk."

"I have heard of these, as well. However these cannot be used during the rainy season. Also I don't think we should cross the Mother River anywhere near here at all," Riyaansh seemed determined. "We are on the west bank of the river. I know that to travel in a north-northeast direction, we will have to cross the Mother River. However, I think we should travel north first. We can go to Darromohe and spend the Harvest and winter there. Then, from Darromohe, we can travel northeast next spring."

Before Ridhaan could answer, Zayaa, who had been asleep since dawn, awoke suddenly and began talking to them, as if in a trance, her eyes blank as stone.

"Is there a place named Pparaha?" she asked in a dispassionate voice.

"Yes, there is," Ridhaan said, before Riyaansh could reply, "it is in the Northeast. Why do you ask?" he asked uneasily.

"I saw a dream about it," Zayaa said, still speaking dazedly. "It was a very strange dream because I thought I was awake. It was early in the morning and both of you were asleep. But, there was this man. He was wearing something on his head, something yellow and shining. And there was something covering his face, but I could see through it. He was talking into my head. He said we should go to Pparaha. He also said that we should arrive from the North and spend a few days with the woman who talks to the animals. Then, he disappeared."

"That does not make any sense," Ridhaan said, "We will be going towards the northeast to go to Pparaha, and thus, will be approaching it from the southwest. To approach it from the north, we have to go around the town. Does this make any sense to you, brother?"

"I hear your logic, yes," Riyaansh said, "but can both of you keep quiet for a little while. I need to get my thoughts straight. Why don't you stay here with Zayaa, and get yourselves some breakfast. I will be up in the ledge, if you need me."

What Little Zayaa had said was too complicated. She simply could not have made it up. Moreover, Riyaansh was sure that what he had seen happen to Kdwar was not natural at all. Kdwar had survived seasons of far more torrential rain. He remembered that the person Zayaa was describing sounded like someone he had heard about before, from a traveller who had come from the far away land of Sumer. It had been a sunny day one spring, and Zayaa had been playing in the streets. Riyaansh had been keeping an eye on her.

"Who is that girl?" a stranger had suddenly walked up to him, "Why is she so white?"

Riyaansh looked up and saw a very dark man, wearing kaigavas[24] on both hands and fully covered sandals on his feet. As Kdwar never got really cold, this looked indeed strange to Riyaansh.

"She was born this way," Riyaansh answered defensively, for he did not like people pointing out that Zayaa was different. "She is my daughter. And because she is healthy in every way, we have not bothered to find out why she is so white."

"Sorry, if I have offended you," the stranger said, "but she is as white as the Gods from your Great Northern White Mountains[25] are supposed to be. So, I thought she might be a God's child."

"Well, no. She is my child," Riyaansh answered and then joked, "in my younger days, I have been called many things, but never a God."

"This is no joking matter," the stranger said solemnly, "let me show you something."

He then took off his kaigavas and then his sandals; Riyaansh saw that his hands and feet were wrapped in cotton strips. The stranger slowly unrolled the strips from his left hand, and Riyaansh was horrified to see stumps of flesh in the place of some of the fingers.

"I know these White Gods exist," the stranger announced, "or I should say that these Gods exist, as they are not all White. I heard it directly from someone who has been to your Great Northern White Mountains. I am from Kurm[26]. I left home over a year ago, to come to your lands. For almost a year before that, I took care of this Akkadian man, until he passed away. He seemed very eccentric in his ways and everyone thought he was crazy. However, I knew he was not mad, quite the opposite actually. I knew he was the ñizzalkalamma[27] – the most intelligent person in all of Sumer. He had learnt your tongue from my namabba[28] – my grandfather. He told

---

[24]A type of leather glove
[25]Hindu Kush Mountains
[26]A town in central Sumer on the banks of River Euphrates
[27]Pronounced ñizzal-kalam-ma

me about his journey to your northern mountains. Let me tell you his story, or at least as much as I know of it."

"Where are my manners?" Riyaansh had said, then proceeding to introduce himself to the mysterious but seemingly fascinating stranger. "I am called Riyaansh. And I am and always have been from where you have now found me – Kdwar. Let us go inside. My wife will pour us some raajaraas, unless you want something else."

"My name is Ekur. I am from Kurm and have arrived here from Lakho[29]. I don't want to be a bother," the stranger had said, following the norms of proper etiquette, "but if you would have me in your home, I would accept the raajaraas you offer me with great pleasure."

Over the next few days, Ekur had visited Riyaansh every day. Riyaansh looked down to where his house had been and reminisced about the strange tale that Ekur had narrated. As promised to Ekur, Riyaansh had scribed down everything that he had told him. However, these had been washed away by the Mother River, along with everything else he had ever scribed. But everything Ekur had told him had also got inscribed into Riyaansh's mind.

Riyaansh came back to the present with a start and realized that it had already become dark. He rushed down to the cave and saw that Zayaa was already asleep, while Ridhaan was sitting next to the fire, stirring a simmering pot.

"I am very sorry," Riyaansh said. "I got thinking about things. Is everything all right?"

"Everything is fine," Ridhaan said, "when you did not come down for breakfast, Zayaa and I went up to see if you were all right. You seemed to be in a trance. Almost as if you were meditating. I realized that the destruction of Kdwar must have hit you harder than I had thought. So, we let you be. We did check on you before we had our lunch and dinner, and a few times in between. But you had not moved, and were staring blankly at the place where Kdwar used to be. So, I decided that Zayaa should go to sleep. First, eat something, and then we can talk about whatever it is that is bothering you."

"I am fine," Riyaansh said. "I was not thinking about Kdwar, but about what Zayaa had said this morning. Her words stirred up some other memories."

---

[28]Pronounced nam-ab-ba
[29]A town in Northern Givenland/ Meluhha near where River Kabul meets River Indus

"I still think it does not make sense," Ridhaan protested. "I am fine to go to Darromohe and then to Pparaha. I think we should circle around Pparaha, as well, and then when she sees there is no woman who talks to animals, she will come to her senses. You need to teach children to be practical from an early age."

"I agree," Riyaansh said, "let each one of us see what lessons we learn. But as you suggested, first we should take a couple of days to plan our journey. However, I would like to get to a town sooner rather than later. Perhaps, Limak[30], which is south of Lake Keenjhar[31] is a good choice. I need to get a lot of writing material."

"Now, you have totally lost me," Ridhaan said, no longer trying to hide his impatience. "Writing materials are the last thing we need now. I can think of uncountable things that we need more than writing material. Why do you need writing material? Please, do not tell me someone talked directly into your head about it."

"Please be calm, Ridhaan," Riyaansh said, setting his hands on his brother's shoulders to placate him. "I know you have sacrificed everything for us. And in return I am being demanding of you, that too without giving any explanations. Remember the Sumerian, Ekur, whom you met in my house. He had come to Givenland in search of something. After failing in his quest, he went back empty handed. But before he went back, he told me a very strange and implausible tale. Now, I realize that it was fate that had brought him to me, and share with me what he had never shared with anyone else. However, for I was too comfortable to do what fate had wanted me to do, fate decided to jerk me out of my comfort, by snatching away from me my wife and, now, my town. Now, I finally understand, and will start this journey that was always fated to happen. But, I would like to scribe down Ekur's tale. I want you to read it first. Because I am sure that fate wants us both to play our parts. Please listen to me. Let us get the writing material."

"We will get your writing material, but I hope for your sake that Ekur's tale is not boring." Ridhaan conceded, with an exhausted sigh.

"Quite the opposite, my brother," Riyaansh said, "quite the opposite."

Over the next two days, they sorted out all their possessions. They took anything of value that could be traded or bartered and enough clothes to last them until next spring. They also took about two week's supply of grains and as much dried foods as they could carry.

---

[30]A town in Southern Givenland/ Meluhha south of Lake Kalri
[31]Lake Kalri

They started their journey on the third day. They reached Limak on the following evening. As they did not want to enter a strange town in the dark, they camped near the Mother River for the night. Then fate took over again. Just as the sun was rising, they were brought awake with shouts. They realized that the shouting was coming from a near big barge. Riyaansh asked Ridhaan to stay with Zayaa and went to investigate. When he got near, he realized there was an argument going on between what seemed to be the chief of the barge and two workers. Whatever they were arguing about could not be resolved and the two workers walked off in a huff. Riyaansh quickly approached the person who was left standing next to the barge.

"Excuse me," Riyaansh said, "I was camping nearby and was woken up by your argument."

"So, what do you want me to do?" the man snapped at him. "Compensate you for waking you up?"

"No, of course not," Riyaansh said, "but I could not help hearing the mention of Darromohe during your arguments. As we are proceeding there as well, I thought we may be able to help each other out."

"Have you ever loaded or unloaded a barge?" the man asked.

"No, I can't say I have," Riyaansh said, "but did I not hear you tell those two men that you could not imagine a job that was simpler to do."

At this, the man broke out into a grin.

"You are smarter than I thought," the man said, "okay, I will tell you my problem and let's see if we can help each other out. I need to load these crates of vegetables into my barge and then take them to Darromohe, where I need to unload these and get them to a certain trader. If I can get this done within five days, the journey is profitable. If I take longer than that I will have to regret taking up this order. Originally, I had seven days, which would give me ample time. But, my barge sprung a leak, which took two days to fix. Those two realized that I was in a bind and tried to rip me off in the name of renegotiation. But, I told them that they get one part out of five of the profits as usual. As I did not budge they walked away, but the problem is I have a bad back and won't be of much help. And loading and unloading the crates is a two-person job. So unless you can produce a twin brother, I don't see how you can help."

"I can actually produce a twin brother," Riyaansh said with a guffaw. "He is over there, with my daughter. But first, let's see if we can have a slightly different deal. We will only take one part out of seven of profits. But you will have to find us employment in Darromohe."

"If you are any good at this work," the man said, "I will keep you in my own employ. But, even though we will be based in Darromohe, work can have us travel anywhere through Mother River or her daughters."

"Well, in that case, you will have to promise us that early next spring, you will take us to someplace near Pparaha, where our agreement will conclude," Riyaansh said.

"Unless, of course, we come to another agreement at that point," the man said.

"I am sorry, but I want to level with you," Riyaansh said. "I never go back on my words. And I already have an agreement with someone from there on."

"I think we have an agreement," the man said, "my name is Shyaan. I look forward to a fruitful relationship with you and your brother. Now, tell your twin to hurry here and start loading the crates."

"I am Riyaansh," Riyaansh said, "and my twin brother is called Ridhaan. My daughter is Zayaa."

So Riyaansh and Ridhaan spent the next few months loading and unloading Shyaan's barge up and down the Mother River and the River Ashkini[32]. They also made Shyaan's barge their home. During this time Shyaan was always with them, except when they were in Darromohe, which was about half the time. So, whenever they were in Darromohe, Riyaansh spent as much time as possible scribing down Ekur's tale.

On the evening of the Winter Solstice, after Zayaa had gone to sleep, Riyaansh took Ridhaan to the front of the barge.

"Brother," Riyaansh said looking directly into Ridhaan's eyes, "I want to share something with you." Then he brought out a collection of parchments, bound together with thin but firm thread. It was given the title of *The Akkadian's Tale*."

"So, you have finished your scribing," Ridhaan said, and then added jokingly. "Perhaps, from now on, you will start doing your fair share of the work on the barge."

"Even with the scribing, I was doing more than you," Riyaansh retorted with a laugh. "Yes, I am finished with *The Akkadian's Tale*. And yet,

---

[32] The River Chenab

I am not," he said mysteriously. "I want you to read this. And let's not discuss anything about it, including any questions you might have, till you have finished reading."

Ridhaan simply nodded in agreement.

Chapter 7

The Akkadian's Tale I

The Akkadian was six years of age when he had first heard of Meluhha[33]. His father came from a rich trading family in Kurm, and though he had a view about how everything could be done better, he did not like doing any of these things himself. One day, the Akkadian's mother took ill, and the father had wanted one of his servants to take care of their young son. His mother, however, would have none of it. Finally, his father had agreed on letting the Akkadian be with him, but had refused to change his schedule for the boy. And thus, for the first time, the Akkadian was allowed in the Outside Hall after sundown. About fifteen people had gathered there, supposedly to hear his father's monologues, but most probably to drink his wine and eat his food. That day, his father was expressing his views on the Sumerian trade with Meluhha. He felt that these trades were dominated by the traders from Meluhha, and even though the Sumerians were willing to travel, they had not been able to turn it into a profession, as the Meluhhans had. As this was the first time, he was hearing his father talk at length on any subject, the Akkadian got fascinated with the subject. From that day, he lost no opportunity to learn more about Meluhha. The more he learnt, the more enchanted he became. Initially, it was only out of interest, without goal or motive. However, within a few years, he sought such knowledge, in order to help himself, for it became clear even to the young boy, that going by the way his father was spending lavishly, the wealth acquired by his

---

[33]What the Sumerians called Givenland

forefathers and without adding anything to it, the Akkadian would not be left with much of an inheritance. He, therefore, started thinking about becoming a trader– like his forefathers. And he decided to start looking into whether there was any truth in his father's views on the trade with Meluhha.

Once, during a visit to the marketplace, he saw an old Sumerian talking to a Meluhhan trader—in the Meluhhan tongue. Fascinated, he waited patiently until they were done. Then, he approached the Sumerian.

"Excuse me, sir, I am very sorry to disturb you," the Akkadian started.

"Eh, what?" the old man answered. He was clearly startled to be suddenly approached by someone, and especially by a young boy he had never seen before.

"I said I am sorry," the Akkadian persisted, ensuring to never look directly at the old man, but only at his feet, "but were you not talking in the Meluhhan tongue?"

"What if I were?" the old man retorted irritably. "Has somebody called a ban on talking in Meluhhan?"

"No, sir, of course not," the Akkadian said respectfully. "I was only wondering whether it was very difficult for you to learn this tongue."

The old man seemed to relax a little. "Yes it was," the old man said proudly, "I have travelled to their lands seven times – five times by sea and twice by land. And even now, I cannot say that I have perfected speaking their tongue. However, I must say that there is no one else in Kurm who can speak Meluhhan as well as I do."

"Sir, would you teach me their tongue?" the Akkadian blurted out, not being able to control himself any more.

"Why? You, too, want to go in search of the White Gods?" the old man chuckled.

"What? No. I am planning to be a trader and would like to trade with the Meluhhan people," the Akkadian replied.

"In all my travels," the old man said, "I have never come across anyone from Sumer who was involved in successful trade with Meluhha. And there are very good reasons for this."

The Akkadian waited for the old man to explain his words.

When he realized the old man was not going to do so, the Akkadian prompted him, "Why?"

"Why, what?"

"Why are there no Sumerians involved in trade with the Meluhhans?" the Akkadian asked with exasperation.

"The first reason is that most of you youngsters cannot speak in full sentences," the old man said shortly.

The Akkadian realized that the old man must have lost his attention span with age. He had seen how his mother spoke to his father's mother, in slow sentences, repeating as much of the previous parts of the conversation as required for the old one to understand her. It slowly dawned on the Akkadian that this old man might not be able to teach him the Meluhhan tongue, after all. For a moment, he considered walking away, but immediately discarded the idea, as he did not want to be rude. Instead, he decided to try to talk to the old man in the same way that his mother talked to his grandmother.

"You ... were ... saying ... that ... there ... are ... no ... Sumerian ... traders ... involved ... in ... the ... trade ... with ... Meluhhans. I ... wanted ... to ... know ... why ... there ... were ... no ... Sumerians ... involved ... in the ... trade ... with ... Meluhhans," the Akkadian imitated his mother's manner of speaking.

At this, the old man's eyes almost popped out. Then, after a little while, but what seemed like an uncomfortable eternity to the Akkadian, the old man burst out laughing.

"You think I am senile, don't you?" the old man cackled. "Let me assure you, even now, on my slowest day, my heart[34] works better than that of most people in Kurm, and definitely better than you. Senile, indeed," he scoffed, "that is the problem with you youngsters. You are the ones who needed a lesson on communicating," the old man instructed, poking his index finger into the Akkadian's chest. "Here I was trying to teach you – and you went on to conclude that something was wrong with me, instead of realizing your own folly. I will tell you about the Meluhhan trade, my boy, but first analyse for me, what was wrong with your communication. And if you are not sure about how to answer this for me, ask, humbly, and I will let you know!"

"Okay, Abgal[35], I will try," the Akkadian agreed meekly, switching to a more respectful form of address. He was unwilling to answer immediately and stood thinking, wondering what he might have done wrong. In a few

---

[34]In ancient Sumer, it was believed that intelligence came from the heart
[35]Literally meaning 'great elder' – abba gal – also used to address elderly wise men

moments, he was ready to answer the old man's questions. "Let me begin with my most obvious mistake: I should have first introduced myself to you. Then, I should have made it clear to you as to why I was approaching you, and only after that, should I have asked you my question. Also, once I realized that I was not getting the right response from you, I should have done this analysis myself, found out what I was doing wrong and then, dutifully, should have begged your pardon and restarted my conversation. I really hope you will give me another chance."

"You are smarter than you appear to be," the old man smiled. "Well, I have nothing more to add to your analysis, and hence, I, too, shall keep up my end of our bargain. From what I have observed," he explained to the attentive boy, "there are three main reasons why the Meluhhans dominate our trade with them. First, they have taken more time to find out about our needs. Our traders, on the other hand, focus merely on what we need from the Meluhhans. So, our traders send their empty ships and caravans to bring goods from Meluhha. What chances do you think they have, when they are competing against the Meluhhans, whose caravans and ships are laden with Sumerian goods for the Meluhhans and Meluhhan goods for us? Second, the Meluhhans have made agreements with most of the local tribes who live along the caravan routes. They pay for this protection by sharing a very small part of the profits with them, usually by giving them trinket jewellery and salt. This significantly reduces the risk of being attacked by bandits. Moreover, the land route is much more dependable than sea for carrying goods, for the sea involves the risk of uncertain weather. Third, they pay better homage to our énsi[36], our City Lords, than our own traders. So, our City Lords are more disposed to supporting the Meluhhans and wishing them success, rather than impeding them."

"So, in order to compete with the Meluhhans, all three issues would have to be solved," the Akkadian pondered. "Solving only one or two would still leave one at a disadvantage."

"The third is the easiest, of course," the Akkadian began confidently. "Our City Lords can be bought easily, after all. To solve the first is also easy. We will simply have to observe what the Meluhhan are taking back from here, to find out what they do need from us. And I am sure a local Sumerian could get better deals in procuring these goods."

The more the old man listened to this young Akkadian, barely out of his boyhood, the more impressed he became with him.

---

[36] A city's governor or lord originally coming from the term 'lord of the plow land'

"Now, I must admit that the problem lies with the second issue. I am sure that it took a lot of time and effort on the part of the Meluhhans to get these protection agreements in place. And they must have all worked together to achieve this. So, it would be impossible for such agreements to be countered by a handful of Sumerian traders. Unless …," the Akkadian suddenly stopped speaking, gazing into space. Then, after a few moments, he looked at the old man again. "Abgal, what is the relationship between the tribes and the bandits?"

"By Enki[37]!" the old man exclaimed, invoking the god of intelligence and mischief. "I like the way you think. However, in this case, the mischief that your intelligence is prompting you towards will not work. You see, my boy, most of these bandits belong to these tribes that the Meluhhans have forged agreements with, and they still maintain their families in these villages. This is why the Meluhhan agreements work, so well. They are indirectly paying the thieves not to steal from them."

"My grandfather used to say that it is only through worshipping Ea[38]," the Akkadian said, "that one gets Bogu[39] to come and reside in one's home."

"So all this is to get Bogu to come and reside in your home," the old man said with a little disappointment in his voice.

"I would be lying if I said that that was not one of the reasons," the Akkadian said, "but it is definitely not the only reason. You see, Abgal, my grandfather and the generations of fathers before him have been traders and had made a huge fortune. My father, however, is wasting it all away, spending in his one lifetime what took eight generations to build. So, even though I would really like to do something meaningful with my life, I have to be able to afford to do it, as well."

"No, you are right," the old man said, neither being apologetic nor defensive, "it is always easier to do good when one does not have to worry where his own next meal is coming from. Incidentally, this is a saying that I picked up during my travels in Meluhha. That reminds me, you were saying something about learning the Meluhhan tongue."

"I did say that, Abgal, but before that, could you humour me for a little longer," the Akkadian continued in his respectful tone. "When I first mentioned Meluhha, you said something about the White Gods. What are these White Gods?"

---

[37] The Sumerian God of intelligence and mischief amongst other things
[38] The Akkadian name for Enki - God of intelligence and mischief amongst other things
[39] The Sumerian God of wealth

"Ah, you are speaking of the White Gods as *what* instead of *who*—that too in a loud voice," the old man shook his head. "In Meluhha, you would be sat on a stake for even whispering this. You see, even though we call their lands Meluhha, they call their own lands the Givenland. This is because they believe that the land was given to them by the White Gods to live in and prosper. There is much folklore about the White Gods who live in the mountains north of Meluhha. Meluhhans keep things simple, and hence call these the Great Northern White Mountains. We call it the Ní-ñál –kur-gal– the terrifying great mountains. According to the Meluhhans, their Gods live in these mountains. They are supposed to be very tall and their skin is supposed to be very white. That is where the name *White Gods* comes from. As you may know, the Meluhhans do not have City Lords. They are, instead, governed, or rather guided, and controlled by the Chief High Priests, and these Chief High Priests claim that from time to time they receive messages directly from these gods. There are many others who claim to have seen these Gods too," the old man narrated. "Some say they are a head taller than the Meluhhans, but others claim they are two, three or even ten times as tall. There are some designated caves just below where permanent snow starts in these mountains, and in these caves, throughout spring, summer and autumn, the Meluhhans leave out offerings of wheat, barley, vegetables, parts of banyan tree and turmeric, dried fish and meat, and almost all other regular household things. When they go to these caves, in order to leave their next set of offerings, the offerings that had previously left there are usually not there …" the old man stopped. "You seem to have a question."

"I have not one, but many questions," the Akkadian said, "but you must be getting tired. So, if you agree to teach me the Meluhhan tongue, for which I will pay, of course, we can spend our first lesson answering my questions."

"Yes, I am indeed a little tired," the old man said, with a deep sigh, "too much excitement does this to me. Since I'm not entirely sure if I will even have any answers to your questions, your first lesson will be given for free," he smiled warmly, "meet me here tomorrow at noon."

"You mean here, on the street," the Akkadian asked incredulously.

"Yes, it has to be here," the old man said in a sad voice, "my sons and daughters-in-law do not like me bringing over visitors. So, I always meet people here in the marketplace. That is why you found me talking to my Meluhhan friend here."

"I will meet you here then," the Akkadian said and then asked. "Would you like me to walk you home?"

"As I have told you before, I am not that old, yet. I will see you tomorrow," the old man said sharply and then walked away at a good pace. As the Akkadian saw him walk away with a straight back, he silently thanked his Gods. He could not explain why he felt this way, but he was sure he had found the person who would help him get to Meluhha.

The two met again the next day. The Akkadian had brought some fruits for them to share.

"So, you want to show me that you are rich enough to waste good fruits on an old man," the old man teased, without any effort at concealing his pleasure, and then picked up the conversation where they had left off the previous day, "as I was saying, all the offerings the Meluhhans left in the caves were gone the next time they went again, with more offerings. Some are sure that the Gods themselves came to these caves in the night and feasted on these offerings, while others opine that though the Meluhhans themselves are not allowed to keep slaves, or šubur as you know them here, these rules did not apply to the Gods and, therefore, their hordes of slaves came and carried these offerings higher into the mountains, where the gods actually lived. Others would disagree though, pointing out that not having slaves was one of the 108 agreements that were made as part of the covenant between the early Meluhhans and the White Gods, and considering that these rules had been laid down by the Gods themselves, they would not go against such rules," the old man finished, then realized his folly. "I am sorry that I got carried away again. We had stopped discussing this yesterday, didn't we, so I could address your questions."

"Abgal, the first question I have has nothing to do with the White Gods," the Akkadian announced. "I would like to know, though, what you meant by I would be sat on a stake?"

"I am sure you have not seen anyone executed with a saw, but have you ever heard of the act?" the old man asked.

"Isn't this how a person convicted of committing adultery gets punished? From what I have heard, the person is hung upside down and, then, two executioners use a special saw to slowly slice away the condemned, starting from his or her groin. They stop every time the accused faints away or lose consciousness due to the pain, and they begin the torture again only after the condemned has been revived, and repeat this, until the moment when revival becomes impossible, for the accused will be dead. But even then they continue to saw the body into half," the Akkadian explained with disgust and loathing in his voice.

"Yes, that is more or less what happens," the old man said nonchalantly, not sharing the boy's disgust. "Well, this will seem a merciful and easy death, when compared to having one sat on a stake," the old man declared. "Do you know what the Meluhhan stake looks like?" the old man asked the boy, but did not wait for an answer. "The stake is made out of a very flexible type of bamboo. These are cut into slats, wide on one end and tapering into a fine point on the other. The wide ends of the slats are then tied into a circle, about an arm's length wide, and then the narrow tapering ends are brought together, to make the other side pointed. These are then strengthened by tying the wider half with thin coir ropes. This is the Meluhhan stake, and when one is condemned to be sat on a stake, he or she is made to carry one of these stakes to a designated place outside their towns. Here the stake is fixed to holes made into the ground, and are made to stand erect by wedging rocks and stones in the space between the stake and the ground. The condemned is then stripped naked. The executioners, using a double ladder specially made for this purpose, sits the naked man or woman into the stake, making sure the sharp edge of the bamboo enters the anal hole. The stake immediately goes in, about the length of one's palm," the old man measured the distance on his own palm and showed it to the boy. "And then, the bleeding starts. As the stake gets wider, it takes longer for it to penetrate, thus causing the condemned a slow and agonizing death. Sometimes, it takes two to three days for the condemned to die. Usually, jackals come and feed on their legs at night, while they are still alive. Even these beasts can't give them a quicker death, for most of the condemned's body stays out of the reach of these jackals. I see you are shuddering at this, but this punishment is given solely for heinous crimes like rape, violent murder and banditry."

"And this still happens?" the Akkadian asked incredulously.

"Yes, it does, just as sawing still happens here," the old man replied.

"Well," the Akkadian said ponderously, "I think my other questions can wait for a while. Please tell me more about the White Gods."

"There is nothing more to say," the old man answered, "or rather there is not much more that I know about them. During all my travels in and around Meluhha, I have not met anyone who has actually met or seen these Gods. But, they are sure of their existence. They always claim they know someone who has seen these Gods, but, when you question them more, it all turns out to be based on hearsay – they have only heard it from someone who knows someone who had met someone during his travels who used to have a cousin, and so on and so forth. The only other thing I have heard a few times is that travellers have seen such Gods when they were lost; the Gods apparently would come before them, to tell them about how they could get back to the nearest town. But this usually happens at daybreak, when the lost traveller is neither fully awake nor aware of what is happening around him. I assumed that subconsciously they remembered the lay of the land after a good night's sleep. Well, in any case, that is all I have heard and know about the White Gods."

"Abgal, if that is all you know, I will not pester you for more," the Akkadian said but continued hopefully anyway. "If you give your consent, I would still like you to teach me the Meluhhan tongue. I plan to become a trader, a successful one like the Meluhhans."

"Only yesterday you said it was not possible," the old man said with surprise. "You had specifically pointed out that it would be impossible to get protection agreements with the local tribes. What has changed since then?"

"You have convinced me otherwise," the Akkadian said with a twinkle in his eyes. "I am no longer planning to compete with them, but I am counting on becoming included in their agreements."

"And why would the Meluhhans include you and, thus, create a competitor for themselves?" the old man asked, still wondering how he had been instrumental in convincing the young Akkadian.

"Well, they will do it because their Gods will ask them to," the Akkadian said with a broad smile. "Please, hear me out," he requested. "This is my plan. I will learn the Meluhhan tongue from you. I will also learn the lay of their land from you and from others who have travelled to their lands. Once I can speak some of their tongue, I will spend as much time as possible in this marketplace, talking to as many Meluhhans as I can meet, thus being able to learn more. I presume that in six to seven years, I will have acquired enough knowledge to travel to their lands. Then, I will go to these Great Northern White Mountains and seek out these Gods. If they are to be found, I will convince them to look kindly on me and send a message to the Chief High Priest of one of their bigger towns, informing them to include me in their agreements. But, if these Gods do not exist and therefore cannot be found, that is fine, too. I will wait in one of the caves that you mentioned. Once the Meluhhans who take the offerings there, leave the cave, I will inscribe a message onto the walls, that if I am not included in these agreements, the Gods will be very displeased. The Meluhhans will have no choice, but to obey their Gods."

The old man's jaw dropped at the audacity of the boy's plan.

"By Enki, you have been born with an exceptional mind to have come up with such a plan so quickly," the old man whispered in awe. "I know of many who have gone to seek these Gods, but, until you, I did not know of anyone who had thought about what he might do if the Gods are not found. But tell me this, what is stopping you from not seeking the Gods at all, but directly writing this message in the walls?"

"Well, that would be cheating, wouldn't it?" the Akkadian said slyly, much to the old man's amusement. "But more importantly, if the Gods do exist, they could and would countermand whatever I inscribe, and probably condemn me to be sat on these stakes you just described."

"You are a son of a fox," the old man chortled with laughter, looking at the boy with respect. "I will be happy to teach you the Meluhhan tongue. But I have some conditions."

"Anything you want, Abgal," the Akkadian offered.

"Never commit to anything before you know what it is that you are committing to," the old man scolded. "So, hear me out, first. If you ever find the White Gods, you will tell me about it before anyone else, unless I am already dead, of course. And if I am dead though, before I am gone, I would have advised my grandson, Ekur, to seek you out if he ever needs help. I do hope you will take him in. Make him work for you, in return for anything you care to give him, though. He is the only one in my house who cares for me. His parents, his uncle and aunt dislike him because of that, and I assume he might be left without an inheritance."

"I promise to do this. But in that case, should I not be working for you, while you teach me the Meluhhan tongue?" the Akkadian asked.

"Oh yes, you will. For, kù[40] is of no use to me. It will only help get my sons fatter and buy my daughters-in-law more jewellery. So, while I teach you the Meluhhan tongue and their way of life, you will take me to visit any place I want. And bring me any food or drink I want," the old man said, his eyes lighting up at the prospect of doing these things again.

"Okay, I agree. Where should the lessons take place?"

"I don't care," the old man shrugged. "If you feel you cannot learn properly at the marketplace, you will have to arrange for another place."

The Akkadian managed to secure a small reception hall in his house and soon began the lessons. Initially, the old man was keen about visiting

---

[40]Money or wealth in Sumerian

many places. Each day, he requested for different kinds of exotic foods and expensive drinks. But soon he grew tired of these treats.

"Abgal," the Akkadian explained a few days later, "you must be wondering why I have not introduced you to my parents."

"Why should I?" the old man lied fluently, "After all, you never promised me you would."

"Another thing I need to learn from you," the Akkadian grinned, "how to better hide my feelings. My parents spend very little time with each other, and even less with me. They don't care what I do, as long as I keep out of their way." Seeing how embarrassing his pupil was finding to talk about his parent's disinterest in him, the old man quickly changed the subject.

For the next two years, the lessons went on. Finally, one day, the old man asked that the Akkadian to meet him at the marketplace.

When the Akkadian arrived, the old man was already waiting for him.

"Abgal, why did you want to meet here?" the Akkadian asked.

"I would like you to converse with a Meluhhan friend of mine in his tongue. Do you think you are ready?"

The Akkadian instinctively knew the test had already begun and this question was a part of it. He realized that a true Meluhhan would not offer an answer when a direct question is posed by his teacher, and he thus replied with proper etiquette, "Abgal, I am only ready for whatever you think I am ready for."

"Good," the old man appreciated his pupil, unable to hide his smile. "Now, come with me."

The old man led the Akkadian to a person who stood outside one of the shops, busy talking to its owner.

The old man walked up to him and said loudly in Sumerian, "the mangy bitch dog that gave birth to you must have died in shame."

The man turned around in anger, but then gave a broad smile when he saw the old man. "Every time I see you, Ishme, I think about how an ass could have mated with a jackal, for there can be no other way that you were conceived." And then he went on to embrace the old man.

The Akkadian was very surprised, not at the strange way that they greeted each other, but hearing his Abgal being called Ishme. He realized that though by then, he had known the old man for two years, he had not known his name. He had always called his teacher Abgal. And somehow never even had wondered what his name was. "I need to ask you for a favour," the old man said to his friend, as he freed himself from the hug. "I would appreciate it, if you could talk to this boy and find out how bad his understanding of your language is. After that, we could go and have something to eat and drink."

"It will be my pleasure," the Meluhhan agreed, "to talk to your young friend. But, please, forget about the eating and drinking. I am not going to your house – if I did, I am sure one of your daughters-in-law would poison me. Have you forgotten about the time I had to teach one of your sons a lesson, on how they had to speak to their father?"

"No, Vikoo, I have not forgotten," the old man replied in Sumerian and continued in the same tongue, "but please don't shame me by remembering. In any case, we are going now to a different place. It belongs to my student. You can eat or drink anything you want there, without having to worry about interruptions."

"Then, I will accept the invitation. We have lots to catch up on," Vikoo replied, also in Sumerian, then turned to the Akkadian and said in Meluhhan, "come along, boy, let us talk."

Vikoo and the Akkadian sat down outside one of the food shops and started talking. After an initial period of uncertainty, they seemed to be enjoying speaking to each other, the old man observed. Quite some time later, Vikoo came back to where the old man waited for him.

"Is what this boy is telling me true?" Vikoo asked. "He is telling me that it is only two years since he started learning the Meluhhan tongue and way of life. He still needs to work on his accent, but, otherwise, he is perfect."

"Perhaps, he had a great teacher," the old man said with a twinkle in his eye.

"He has already told me that you taught him," Vikoo teased. "But I do have to agree, old man, you have indeed done a great job. Why did he want to learn our language, though?"

The old man was sure that the Akkadian would not have told his reasons to Vikoo. "I think he plans to visit your land."

"I hope he does," Vikoo said simply. "So, shall we go and have our food and drinks?" Vikoo asked. "I assume it is at this boy's place."

"Yes, it is. But if you don't mind, could I speak to my student for a few moments, before we proceed to his place?" the old man asked.

"That might actually be better for me, too," Vikoo offered graciously. "so, shall we meet here around noon?"

The old man nodded and beckoned the Akkadian to come over.

"I think my job is done," he informed, looking proudly at the Akkadian. "I have taught you all I can and know. I would really appreciate it, if you still allow me to entertain my Meluhhan friend at your place," the old man requested.

"Abgal, of course you can. So, you think I am ready to start executing my plan?" the Akkadian asked, feeling a little proud of his achievement. The old man nodded his agreement.

After that evening, the old man and the Akkadian did not see each other as often.

A few months later, the Akkadian's father passed away. The old man came to the funeral and took the Akkadian aside, to make sure he was all right.

"Abgal, please don't tell me how sorry you are. I cannot say I am unhappy," the Akkadian said without any emotion. "If he had lived for another six months, I would have been left with no inheritance to execute my plan. In order to be able to afford his parties, where people came to listen to his monologues, he had started selling off even our household things."

"I will not say how sorry I am then," the old man said. "But, could I at least ask what your plans are now?"

"As you know, I am my father's only son," the Akkadian replied. "Although, by law, my mother is not entitled to the property, I have told her that she can have half of it. I will use the other half to pay for my dreams."

"I wish you all the success," the old man said, "I am really proud of you. I can only wish that my sons had half your self-confidence and tenacity, and even a tenth of your intelligence. Looking at the children I have supposedly produced, I have begun to doubt my wife's fidelity," he chuckled. "Joking apart, I am sure you will succeed in achieving this dream of yours."

"Abgal, thank you very much. Your belief in me means a lot to me," the Akkadian said respectfully, "could I come over to see you, before I leave for Meluhha?"

"I think it's best if we say our goodbyes now," the old man said. "I am getting old, and cannot leave my house so easily anymore. I could not have come here today without my grandson Ekur's help. And speaking of Ekur, do remember your promises, in regard to him. I have to go now. I only wish I was young enough to accompany you."

"You will always be with me, in my thoughts," the Akkadian had tears in his eyes, "and your teachings will always guide me."

The old man left.

Settling his father's affairs took the Akkadian significantly longer than he had anticipated. He converted most of his inheritance to gold nuggets and silver jewellery that could be easily carried and traded. He also procured himself camels, one for riding and two for carrying goods. He thought of taking some other trading items, like leather and woollen goods, but had rejected the thought. Though these would have higher returns, as he wanted to travel as part of a Meluhhan caravan, he did not want to come across as a competitor. After making sure that these preparations were over, he started visiting the marketplace on a regular basis, talking to the Meluhhan traders to buy a passage to Meluhha in their caravan. Most of them rejected the proposal outright, while the others asked for exorbitant fees. He had almost decided that he would try to go by sea, when fate smiled on him again. One day, the Akkadian was sitting in a food shop when he felt a tap on his shoulder. He turned to see the Meluhhan, Vikoo, who had talked to him at the old man's request.

"How are you, boy? Or should I say *young man* now," Vikoo said in his own tongue, "I did not see Ishme during my last visit. Is he in good health?"

The Akkadian knew that luck had decided to favour him finally. He calmed himself down, knowing that one wrong move could ruin things for him.

"Hello, sir," the Akkadian bowed his head, and continued in the Meluhhan tongue. "Hope you are having a profitable visit. The last time I saw Abgal – I mean Ishme, of course – was almost a year ago, at my father's funeral. He did not seem to be in very good health then. I did ask his permission to visit him at his home, but he refused."

Vikoo roared with laughter. "You offered to go to his house?" he snorted. "That could only mean that you have not been there before. Ishme is a very intelligent man, but he did make one mistake. This was before he was leaving for Meluhha, for what turned out to be his last visit. His sons and daughters-in-law convinced him that, as he was gone for long periods and it was uncertain when, or even if, he would return, it would be in everyone's interest if he handed over the property to his sons for the period he was gone. His sons would of course hand it back, when Ishme was back. I was in Kurm at that time. I told him not to go along with this, but he was sure that he could trust his sons. So, he did what they had asked of him. When he came back though, not only did he never get back his own property but they refused to allow him to continue his trips to Meluhha as well. After all this had happened, I had made one visit to their house. Seeing how his sons were treating him and how they allowed their wives to insult him, I decided to teach them a lesson with my hands and fists. Since that day, I have only met him in this marketplace. I had offered to take him on trips to Meluhha, but Ishme was too proud to accept. He would never want you to see him in his house. He was really proud of you, boy. I could see it in his eyes. He probably wished you were his son."

"I am eternally indebted to him for sharing his time and knowledge with me. I really wish I could still see him from time to time. I really miss his advice, especially since I have no one else to ask now," the Akkadian said, hoping to get the response he wanted.

"Why, boy, perhaps, I can help you. In this way, I will be able to partially repay Ishme, for his many favours," Vikoo did not disappoint.

For a moment, the Akkadian almost asked what favours could the old man have done for this wealthy trader, but stopped himself, for he knew that in the Meluhhan way that would be considered a rude question.

Instead, the Akkadian said, "I have learned here whatever I possibly could about your tongue and your ways. The last time I met Ishme, I had promised him that I would make a trip to your lands." This was not exactly a lie, the Akkadian told himself, for what he had said was quite close to this. He, therefore, continued without any guilt, "I have been trying for many days to take a caravan to Meluhha without any luck."

"That can be easily solved," Vikoo said. "I will be going back to Meluhha in ten days on my ship. Come with me. For you are Ishme's student, I will not insult you with charity. You can therefore work as my cabin-boy and pay off the fees for your passage."

The Akkadian was in a fix, for he had already decided that it would be better for him to go by caravan, rather than by sea.

"I would love to come along," the Akkadian said thinking quickly, "but I don't think I will make a good sea traveller. Even when I take river-boats on the Purattu[41], I end up getting really sick," the Akkadian said, remembering the old man describe his first sea trip.

Vikoo laughed again. "What is it with you people from Kurm? I don't know if Ishme told you this, but he felt the same way about sea voyages. Well, in that case, I do have a caravan leaving for Darromohe two days before I do. I will not insult you by making it free for you; you will pay the same cost that any Meluhhan will. You will, of course, have to agree to follow all the instructions that the caravan leader gives you. This rule has no exceptions; even I would have to agree if I were taking a caravan."

"I do not know how to thank you, sir," the Akkadian said, "of course I will pay the cost for the journey. And I promise to follow all the instructions that the leader gives me."

Eight days later, the Akkadian joined the caravan. The first couple of days were tiring and strenuous. Though he had been preparing for the journey for a long time, he realized that nothing could truly prepare one for the daily rigors of a Meluhhan long distance caravan. But, soon, he got into the routine of the travel. Every day, they started soon after dawn and moved on until sunset. Three quarters of the day they travelled, riding on their camels, and for the remainder of the day, they walked, leading their camels. The manner of travel was decided by the Caravan leader, based on either the weather of the place, they were to pass through or the terrain they were crossing. The caravan leader explained to the Akkadian that this kept both the humans and animals in better shape for the long journey. They reached Darromohe without any major incident. By this time, the Akkadian had become much healthier and fitter than he had ever been in his life. His muscles had become toned, and his abdomen lean and hard. And by taking every opportunity to converse with his companions, he further improved his knowledge of the Meluhhan tongue. He also started consciously making sure that he referred to Givenland and Givenlanders, instead of Meluhha and Meluhhans.

[41]The River Euphrates

Chapter 8

The Akkadian's Tale II

The Akkadian stayed in Darromohe for two months. But, again, he did not waste his time resting there. Every day he went to the Raakanaa, and stayed there, from late afternoon until early evening, observing and listening to the people around him, as they drank raajaraas and chatted loudly. Even though he was usually very careful with his spending, he offered to buy drinks for anyone who could tell him tales about the Gods from the Great Northern White Mountains—as long as it was not a tale he had heard before. He spoke with great hope to any new travellers he met, but did not come across anyone who had even gone close to these mountains.

Finally, he met someone who claimed to know more about the Gods. Even though the man's knowledge was second hand, it seemed believable.

"So, what exactly did this person tell you?" the Akkadian asked for the fifth time, pouring the stranger some more raajaraas. He had not got much out of the man during the first four glasses and was beginning to wonder whether the stranger was just trying to get free drinks.

"Well, it was many years ago," the stranger finally began, "my partner and I were prospecting for gold up in the hills near Purawanbhag[42]. In our team, we had a young man, Runggoo, who came from the Swastu[43] valley.

---

[42]A town in North-Eastern Givenland/ Meluhha south of Parroo
[43]The Swat valley

We came across another prospecting team in a valley, which also had a young man from the same region. This person asked for a private audience with my partner and me. My partner thought he may be looking for a job, and thus wanted to refuse, but I suspected otherwise. I had seen him stealing strange looks at Runggoo throughout the evening. So, I convinced my partner to agree to the audience. The young man came into our tent and, bowing low, apologized for being a bearer of bad news. He then informed us that Runggoo had been banished from their lands for stealing from the Gods. Then he went to explain that offerings for the Gods were left in the seven mountain caves near their valleys. All these caves are located just above or just below where the snow never melts, and none of the caves were easily accessible. All the bearers who took up these offerings were expert climbers. Runggoo was one of the bearers, but he had been caught stealing from the offerings and had been banished from their valley for life," he stopped and pointed to his empty glass. "I must be thirsty. My glass is empty again and there is nothing left in the jug, either."

The Akkadian impatiently signalled for another jug and said, "Please continue."

But the stranger did not start until the raajaraas was served. He took a swig of the drink and continued.

"After further questioning, both my partner and I were convinced that this young man was indeed telling the truth. After he had left our tent, my partner opined that we could not have a thief working for us. But I had taken a liking for Runggoo. He really was an exceptional prospector. He was not only a very hard worker but could almost smell out the gold bearing streams. So, I convinced my partner to give Runggoo a chance to clear himself. We summoned him to our tent. When my partner asked whether he was banished from his valley, Runggoo admitted that he was, but did not volunteer any more information. When I asked him the reason, he told us that he had been an exceptional climber since childhood. When he was twelve years old, he was chosen to be one of the bearers to deliver the offerings for the Gods. He had done well, and in five years, he had risen to the role of one of the seven leaders. The deliveries were done from spring to autumn, and never in winter. But ten years ago, during one of the autumn deliveries, there had been an unseasonal snowstorm and his team had to take shelter in a cave for three days. As there was nothing for them to eat or drink, he gave his team permission to use some of the offerings, but only just enough for sustenance. When the snow storm ended, they delivered the offerings to the cave of the Gods."

The stranger again stopped to look at his empty mug. The Akkadian quickly filled it.

The stranger smiled and continued, "As I was saying, when they came back to the valley after delivering the offerings, they did not hide what they had done. The Elders decided that it was sacrilege to have eaten the food meant for the Gods and wanted to banish the entire team from their valleys for five years. Runggoo absolved his team of any responsibility and declared that they were only doing what he had ordered. The Elders then decided that he would then have to bear the punishment for his whole team of twenty and therefore was banished for a hundred years. Runggoo then stated that if my partner and I thought what he had done was wrong, he did not want to work with us anymore". The stranger looked at his empty glass, and then patting his stomach said, "I will tell you the rest some other time, as I am very hungry and will have to go and look for food."

"Please don't stop," the Akkadian said in panic, "do not worry about the food. Let us get something to eat here, along with our drinks, and then you can join me for dinner at my lodgings."

"I will also need my companion to join me for dinner, but seeing your interest in the White Gods, I don't think you will mind having this companion join us," the stranger smiled, without explaining.

He waited until the food was delivered to their table, and then, the stranger continued, "When Runggoo left, my partner still maintained that we could not allow a thief to continue working for us. I suggested that this was a little harsh, especially given the fact that if he had not taken the blame for his team, his banishment would be over by now. My partner insisted that it was too risky, though, for Runggoo had stolen from the Gods. To this, I countered that, as he had not been struck down, yet, the Gods must be more forgiving than some people were. My last statement angered my partner, as he thought I was insulting him. He said that his mind was made up and he would not discuss the Runggoo issue any further. I replied that I understood his stand and that I would look for a replacement. This seemed to placate my partner. He seemed keen that we should check with the other young man, on whether he would like to replace Runggoo."

The stranger reached over and took the Akkadian's untouched raajaraas mug.

Sipping noisily, he gave a big, mischievous smile, "Then, I told him what I had meant was that I would have to look for a new partner. And now that I knew about Runggoo's character, I was planning to offer him the partnership. At first, my partner thought I was joking, and then he assumed that I was giving him an empty threat, that I would not actually do what I had proposed. Once he realized how serious I was though, he changed his stance and backed down, said that he was fine with having Runggoo continuing to work for us. But my mind was made up. That same evening I offered Runggoo the position of partner, but he refused, saying that he would consider taking it only when he had learnt all about our business and could deliver as an equal. This incident happened three years ago."

"So, where is Runggoo now? Is he still working for you?" the Akkadian asked impatiently.

"No, he does not work for me anymore," the stranger said and then grew silent for some time, lost in thought, while he chewed his food slowly and took long sips of raajaraas.

The Akkadian's irritation grew, as he waited impatiently, while the stranger seemed to be unnecessarily prolonging the moment.

"Runggoo spent the next two years learning the prospecting business from me," the stranger finally spoke again. "He works *with* me now as my equal partner. He is the companion I told you about, the one who will be joining us for dinner tonight. I hope you don't object if we fetch him on the way to your lodgings."

The Akkadian could not believe his luck. Finally, he drank some raajaraas, to finish the jug quickly.

"If you want Runggoo to talk about his valley, you will need two more jugs of raajaraas," the stranger informed the Akkadian, after the jug was empty.

"Of course," the Akkadian replied without surprise, for he had expected nothing less from the partner of this man. He quickly ordered two more jugs of raajaraas.

Then, the Akkadian and the stranger proceeded to the place where Runggoo was waiting, and then went on to the Akkadian's lodgings.

The Akkadian informed the keeper that he would need dinner sent over for two more guests. The keeper was not very happy, but as the Akkadian had never brought back guests before, decided to accommodate him.

The Akkadian went to his room, where his two guests had already made themselves comfortable.

"I have told my friend here about your interest in the White Gods from the Great Northern White Mountains," the stranger said.

"Thank you," the Akkadian said and started pouring raajaraas for his guests.

"Stop!" Runggoo said holding up his hand. "Tiraak and you can have your raajaraas. I can't drink alcohol."

The Akkadian took note of the stranger's name, and then looked at him in askance.

"Sorry if I was not very clear before," Tiraak said without any shame or guilt, "what I had meant was that I would need the raajaraas, to keep myself busy while you both spoke to each other."

Runggoo burst out laughing at this. "My partner is quite wealthy, but he believes that the more free things one can get from others, the wealthier one becomes. I am sorry if he has used your thirst for information about the White Gods to fulfil his own insatiable thirst for raajaraas. To compensate for my partner's greed, I will tell you all I know, but only if you tell me truthfully why you seek this information."

The Akkadian studied Runggoo for a while, without replying. Runggoo was shorter than the average Givenlander, and almost a head shorter than his partner was. His features were significantly less sharp than the average Givenlander, as well. He hardly seemed out of his teens, but based on what Tiraak had said earlier, the Akkadian knew that he had to be at least twenty-seven years old.

At the Raakanaa, whenever anyone asked him the reason for his interest in the White Gods, he told them any lie that would move the conversation along. However, even though Runggoo was smiling as he asked this question, there was something about his eyes that made the Akkadian wary of lying. He sensed that Runggoo would immediately know when he was being lied to. The Akkadian decided that even though he may not share everything with Runggoo, he would not lie to the man, either.

"I want to go and meet the White Gods," the Akkadian said. "Please don't ask me why, for that business is between them and me."

"Fair enough," Runggoo said, "I will not ask what business you have with them. But I need to know if you are planning to harm the Gods?"

"Nothing can be further from the truth," the Akkadian objected, "I don't mean them any harm. In any case, if they are Gods, I do not think I could harm them even if I wanted to."

Runggoo seemed convinced. "Will whatever you are planning to do cause any harm to the people in my valley?"

"I do not think so, but I cannot be sure." On seeing a look of suspicion enter Runggoo's eyes, the Akkadian added, "how can one be sure of the consequences of one's actions? Did you even imagine you would be banished for a hundred years, when you decided to let your men eat the food, thus saving their lives?"

Runggoo took this in and said, "I see your point. You can only be sure of your own actions. O stranger to our lands, ask me what you want to know."

"Why do you call me a stranger to your lands?" the Akkadian asked.

"I know you speak like one of us," Runggoo said impatiently, "and your skin could have got darker by spending time under the sun. However, every Givenlander knows, or you may say believe, that you can only go to meet the White Gods, when they summon you. And if you had been summoned you would know how to get there. Whereas I can only describe the valley and mountains to you, as I have no idea where the White Gods' abode exactly is."

"Indeed, you are very perceptive," the Akkadian said with respect. "My question or rather request is very simple: could you take me to the cave where you used to leave out offerings for the White Gods?"

"You call that simple?" Runggoo said incredulously, "Didn't Tiraak tell you I was banished? I cannot go back to the valley even if I wanted to. And even if I could, I would not take you to the caves. By doing so, I would be jeopardizing the future of all my siblings, of all my family who lives there, of basically everyone I know there. And before you ask, I'd rather tell you myself– there is no one from my valley, who would agree to take you to these caves."

"Oh, could you give me directions to the cave? Maybe draw me a map?" the Akkadian asked hopefully.

"Yes, I could do that," Runggoo replied thoughtfully, "do not assume, however, that by drawing you a map, I am trying to betray my people out of resentment. I'm helping you simply because I believe in fate. Since you have found me, I believe that it is fate telling me that I should help you."

"I will be ever grateful if you drew me this map," the Akkadian said.

"I will," Runggoo said, "but, stranger, tell me this, what do you plan to do with this map."

"Go and seek the White Gods, of course."

"I know that many people believe that you get to meet the Gods when you leave this world. If you believe that, then, yes, you have got the right idea," Runggoo said with a devious chuckle, "for, if you try to make this journey without a mountain guide, die you definitely will."

"By Ea!" the Akkadian exclaimed in frustration. "Every time I think I am getting closer to what I seek, I seem to get further away. You say I cannot go there by myself, even with the map you will give me. You also tell me that neither you nor anyone from your valley can take me there. Perhaps, you are right, perhaps my fate is to die and then meet the Gods."

The Akkadian had been so engrossed in his discussions with Runggoo, he had forgotten about Tiraak, until the latter had given out a loud alcoholic belch.

"My Akkadian friend," Tiraak started, and held up his hand when the Akkadian tried to interrupt. "You did swear by Ea, your god of creation, wisdom and learning and, of course, mischief amongst other things – that makes you an Akkadian, doesn't it? Now please do not try to convince me otherwise. The question however is, do you have a problem with your hearing or do you like to make rocks into insurmountable mountains?"

"If you have to say something, spit it out," the Akkadian said irritably. "You have drunk enough of my raajaraas to owe me that."

"I owe you nothing," Tiraak spat. Then, calming down, he continued, "I have already repaid you the raajaraas you bought me, by not only telling you about Runggoo, but also introducing him to you. If I impart anything else, it will be as either gift or charity. By demanding it, you have lost your right to it as gift. But, do go ahead and beg for charity, before I decide that you are not worthy of that either."

A great number of curses and threats rose up the Akkadian's throat, but he swallowed them all down. If it furthered his dream, the Akkadian was ready to take this or any other insult. He calmed himself down before speaking again.

"Please accept my apologies," the Akkadian said bowing his head low. "In my impatience to achieve my dreams, I misspoke. Please, I beg you, but do tell me what you meant."

"That's much better," Tiraak said triumphantly, "you should be paying more attention, for what Runggoo said is that you need a good mountain guide and that no one from his valley would take you to the Gods. But these are not the only mountains that exist, are they? Other mountains have valleys, too, and it, therefore, stands to reason that these valleys will have their own mountain guides too."

"Of course!" the Akkadian exclaimed. "I will travel north and go to a different valley," he thought aloud. "No, of course that will not work. If people from Runggoo's valley will not guide me, I don't think I will find a guide in any of the valleys that lie in the foothills of the Great Northern White Mountains."

"Yes, you will not find a willing mountain guide in the foothills of the Great Northern White Mountains," Tiraak nodded, "but you might find one if you travel west, towards your land. I have heard of a mountain range, which lies north of the route towards Sumer. It is straight north once you have travelled a third of the route. I have never travelled towards west, so I do not know for sure. But, I do know of one place where you will definitely find people capable of guiding you. Whether you will have the patience to convince one of those chiefs to let his men accompany you is, of course, a different matter altogether."

"Would you be kind enough to tell me where this place is," the Akkadian asked. He realized Tiraak treasured the knowledge he had collected, prospecting in territories outside of Givenland, and that Tiraak did not like sharing such knowledge unless people requested or begged him to, for such pleading made him feel important.

"I am doing just that, and I would be able to do it faster, if you stopped interrupting me," Tiraak said with false irritation. "You will have to go to Parroo. Here, you will need to hire a guide to take you to the valleys in the Mountain that Touches the Sky[44]. If you cannot find a guide in Parroo, travel south for less than a day to Purawanbhag. There, seek out my cousin, Viraan."

Then, pointing at Runggoo, he continued, "If you tell him that Runggoo and I have sent you, he will find you a guide and arrange for anything else you might need. He will also make sure you are not cheated. You will have to go to one of the valleys where a dialect of Givenland is spoken. There are four such valleys. It is believed they had travelled east, from the mountains in the north of Givenland, where Runggoo's valley is, and settled here, long before the present towns and cities of Givenland were built. The language spoken there has changed over the centuries, but I do know that they can still understand our tongue. The other five valleys, however, are a different story. These people claim to have travelled south across the Mountain that Touches the Sky. Their language is completely

---

[44]The Himalayan Mountains

different. It is for this reason that there is a lot of distrust between the former four and the latter five valleys. So make sure your guide understands that you want to go to one of the former four valleys."

"I have heard of these mountains," the Akkadian started. "We call it the Sigga-Tuš, which means the home of snow – or maybe the home of ice is more apt a translation. I don't know how to thank you for all this. Please tell me how I can return this favour."

"Well, for a start, you could get me another jug of the raajaraas," Tiraak slurred as he finished the second jug.

"I am your wardum, your slave. Your wish is my command, and I will be back soon," the Akkadian said seriously with a bow.

"I was joking. And as you might know by now, we do not have slaves in Givenland," Tiraak answered. "Thereby, I cannot accept your offer."

"Then, let me do it as a friend," the Akkadian insisted, "it will be my pleasure to fetch the raajaraas. I will join you for a drink of it, as well."

"Well, if you are doing it as a friend, then how can I say no," Tiraak replied, "but if you are going to join me in drinking it, double your pleasure by fetching two jugs."

"I will do so," the Akkadian laughed and left.

He returned with the two jugs of raajaraas, and after they had finished their drinks and dinner, Tiraak and Runggoo took their leave.

As they were leaving, the Akkadian asked again, "If there is anything I can do in return for your favour, please tell me."

"We do not want anything," Runggoo answered.

"Well, there is one thing, my friend," Tiraak said, "I will present you with a challenge. You will not owe us a solution, but if you can find one, we can be of great use to each other."

"Please describe your challenge," the Akkadian said, "and if it is in my power, I will find a solution."

"As I have told you," Tiraak said, "I prospect for gold near Purawanbhag. Every time Runggoo and I make our slow journey upstream, against the flow of the river, we try to think of a way to make our journey faster. If you can come up with a solution, it would more than repay what we have done for you."

The Akkadian's face broke into a big smile. "Well, Tiraak," he said, "I think I already have a solution. So, please tell me, whether you would like to buy me raajaraas at the Raakanaa or would you prefer to meet me here with a few jugs."

"Don't jest with me," Tiraak said.

"I never jest in matters of business," Akkadian said growing serious. "The only joke I did make was about you buying the raajaraas. For what you have done for me, I am more than willing to buy us the food and drinks."

"No. We will see you here tomorrow, before sunset, with the raajaraas, and we look forward to hearing all about the solution you have come up with," Tiraak said and left.

The next day, Runggoo and Tiraak arrived with a big jug of raajaraas, tucked under each arm.

The moment the drinks were poured and first sips had been drunk, Tiraak said to the Akkadian, "we'd like to hear about your solution now."

"We will start in a moment. First, though, I would like to ask you a question," the Akkadian said sternly. "Yesterday, I was told that Runggoo does not drink raajaraas, and yet, now I see him doing just that. Why is that?"

"I had told Tiraak that you would notice it immediately," Runggoo smiled. "I don't drink alcohol with strangers. Yesterday, you were a stranger to me. However, today, you are not anymore. Therefore, I am drinking with friends. It is as simple as that."

The Akkadian shook his head and grinned. "Well, in that case, let us speak about my solution. It is a simple one, of course. All you must do is tie your boat to animals – whatever animal is best suited for the terrain of the riverbank and strong enough to pull the boats against the current. This has been done in our cities for a long time."

"I believe it will work too," Tiraak laughed heartily. "I don't understand why our traders did not bring back this idea. Now, I am in your debt, but I know of a way to start repaying. We will make the necessary changes to our boats, in accordance to your idea. It will take a few days. You can use that time to acquire some leather goods and salt. Those are the best things to trade in the valleys you will be visiting. Then, you can come with us to Purawanbhag. I will personally ensure that my cousin finds you the right guide and means of transportation."

"I will take this favour from you with gratitude and pleasure," the Akkadian answered. "In return, I would like to offer my camels as part of the boat-pulling team."

Tiraak accepted.

The next day, Tiraak and Runggoo took the Akkadian to where their boats were moored. The Akkadian examined the boats and after going over the length of the boat, he jumped into the water to take a good look at the hull.

"You all need to learn to build boats with more draught, as well," the Akkadian observed, coming out of the water. "A boat this size should have the bottom of the hull going at least three times deeper under the waterline."

"We know that," Tiraak said, "but we cannot help it. In a few places on the Mother River and her daughters, there are these underwater ledges, which stretch from bank to bank. For more than half of a year, the water level is only about four haths above these. So, only boats with low draughts can pass these points. We have tried to break these by ramming into them, but without any success. Whatever these are built of seems to be able to withstand anything we throw at it."

"Very interesting," the Akkadian noted, "but never mind, we will make do with what we have then. We will need a lot of bamboo to make the long shafts going forwards from the bow. This will make sure that the boats are not pulled into the banks. We will need a lot of leather strips for the harness and fastenings."

For the next four days, the Akkadian spent the mornings exchanging some of his silver jewellery in return for leather goods and the afternoons with Tiraak and Runggoo's men, helping them make adjustments to their boats. The evenings were spent in Tiraak and Runggoo's company again, regaling each other with stories of their childhood homes.

On the fifth day, they boarded the boats and started upstream. The journey was quite uneventful, except whenever they passed any village or town, people fascinated by this strange sight of boats being pulled by animals, walked next to them on the banks, cheering them on. In a few days, they came to a confluence where a river joined the Mother River from the northeast. The Akkadian was informed that this was the Panj[45]. They followed this tributary. The next day, another large tributary joined from the northeast. Runggoo told him that was the Shatadru[46]. They travelled

---

[45]Panjnad – Beas, Chenab, Jhelum, Ravi and Sutlej coming together before joining the Indus

upstream on this river. After another few days, they came to another confluence, this time the eastern-most river led southeast. They followed this river. Tiraak informed the Akkadian that they were continuing on the Shatadru, while the other river was the Vipasa[47]. Finally, Runggoo informed the Akkadian that the town coming up on the right bank was Parroo.

Tiraak's cousin, Viraan, who had come to meet them in Parroo, was waiting on the banks.

Tiraak and Runggoo introduced the Akkadian to him and informed him all about the latter's quest to reach the valleys in the Mountain that Touches the Sky. Viraan agreed to arrange for two asses and a guide, in order to take the Akkadian to the valleys, but in exchange for the Akkadian's camels. He said he would need seven days to make all the arrangements.

Tiraak and Runggoo were ready to leave on their prospecting trip two days later. By this time, the only person the Akkadian felt closer to, than the two men, was Ishme, or Abgal, as he still remembered him.

"If I fail in achieving what I have set out to, I will still consider this journey to Givenland fruitful, to have been befriended by you both," the Akkadian said with tears in his eyes.

"Now that I know you better, I cannot believe you will not achieve anything that you set out to do," Tiraak replied, trying to hide his tears.

Runggoo had no tears left. Life had already wrung them dry. He looked at the Akkadian and said, "I know you will succeed in getting a guide. Once you do, come back to Parroo, first. Wait for me here. We usually come back every fifteen days or so. I will describe the terrain to your guide, one mountain man to another. In return, when you meet the White Gods, please ask them to give the Elders in my valley the strength and ability to forgive me."

With that, his two new friends bid him farewell. In a few more days, Viraan came with the guide and the two asses he had promised and, along with it, an adequate supply of food and clothing to ensure a safe journey to the valleys in the Mountain that Touches the Sky.

The following day, the Akkadian left Parroo with his guide. They started upriver along the Shatadru. By now, he had total faith in his fate. He was confident now, he believed that if he had made it this far, his fate

---

[46]The River Sutlej
[47]The River Beas

would ensure, that he would make it all the way. It was in his destiny to meet the White Gods of the Great Northern White Mountains.

The journey was quite uneventful. There was no real climbing involved, and most of the journey was done riding on the asses. Only when treading along some of the treacherous paths did the guide ask the Akkadian to dismount and lead his ass up the way. Viraan had chosen a good guide and soon the Akkadian reached one of the four valleys, where they spoke a dialect very close to the tongue of the Givenlanders. According to the guide this valley was called Wacha[48].

---

[48]A valley in the Himalayas somewhere in Western Nepal

Chapter 9

The Akkadian's Tale III

The Akkadian immediately went to pay homage to the Chief of Wacha. He presented the chief with a leather garment, embroidered with seashells. The chief showed this proudly to the people, who had gathered at the chief's courtyard. Introducing the Akkadian to everyone present, the chief then invited the Akkadian to stay at Wacha for a while.

While the chief was doing his introductions, he had mentioned that the Teller of Tales knew more about their history and folktales than anyone else in the village did. The Akkadian, knowing that the Teller would be interesting company, followed this old man to his home, and offered to do all his household chores. In return, the Teller of Tales would let him stay in his house and tell him a story every day.

Over the next many days, the Akkadian showered the chief with many gifts, expecting some sort of an offer in return. However, the Akkadian received none. Soon, he realized that he was running out of gifts to give to the chief.

One evening, while drinking changa[49] with the chief, the Akkadian brought up the subject again.

"O Respected Chief, your people are brave indeed to live in mountains like these. But any person, who has you as a leader, cannot help but be

---

[49] Alcohol brewed in the Himalayan valleys by fermenting barley stuffed inside cucurbits

brave. I was wondering if you had given more thought on when I can hire one of your people as a guide," the Akkadian said with honey in his voice.

"Remind me again, which mountain you wanted to go to?" the chief asked gruffly.

"I want to go to the Great Northern White Mountains. As I have told you before, I will be going there next. If you allow me to hire one of your people, I will make sure he returns with many leather garments and salt for you," the Akkadian politely requested again.

"Yes, yes. I have given it much thought. And I have decided not to send one of my men to guide you," the chief said casually, as if he was refusing to have another refill of his drink. "I do not think anyone can return from the Great Northern White Mountains. They will die there. So no, I cannot ask any of my men to kill themselves, for you."

The Akkadian had not expected this. He had expected, perhaps, more bargaining and negotiations, but not a blunt refusal. When he saw that the success of his quest was at threat again, he forgot both patience and manners.

"So the chief thinks his men are not brave enough to climb the Great Northern White Mountains?" the Akkadian taunted. "Does the chief lead a bunch of old women?"

The moment he said it, the Akkadian knew he had gone too far.

The chief stood up and said, "You do not have my protection any longer. You will leave this valley before winter starts. You are not welcome in my valley anymore."

The Akkadian realized that it was no use talking to the chief anymore. He would have to go back to Parroo and then try another valley. But it would be winter soon, and he would not be able to do anything before the next spring. And he knew he could no longer afford similar gifts as the ones he had brought to Wacha. The Akkadian was desolate. For the first time, he actually considered giving up on his quest, but his fate wasn't ready for him to give up yet.

The Akkadian trudged back to the Teller's house. Dejected as he was, he did not shirk his duties. However, he barely ate the dinner that he had prepared for the Teller and himself. Once the Akkadian had finished cleaning up after dinner, he joined the Teller. As per their agreement, the Teller started telling him a story. The Akkadian's mind and heart were set on other things, though. However, that night fate decided to help him again, for the Akkadian suddenly realized that the Teller was telling him something he had wanted to hear. The Akkadian requested that the Teller repeat himself.

"As I was saying, the Elder felt slighted by the chief and, according to tradition, challenged him to the Fight for the chief's seat," the Teller said.

"Can any Elder challenge the chief for the Fight?" the Akkadian asked, now fully attentive. "And when you say for his seat, you mean if he wins he becomes the new chief?"

"It is not only an Elder," the Teller explained, "but any male adult can challenge the chief to the Fight. And, yes, if he wins, he will become the chief. But if a commoner challenges the chief, then the latter can decide whether he or one of his representatives would fight this person. And if this representative is to lose, the challenger will become the new chief. On the other hand, if one of the five Elders challenged the chief, he would have to fight for himself. He would not be allowed to delegate the Fight."

"Has anyone ever challenged the current chief?"

The Teller laughed and asked, "Have you ever met Pasher? If anyone challenged the chief, Pasher would fight as the chief's representative. And I cannot think of a faster way one might invite one's own death."

He knew that though they were called the Elders, none of them were actually old. They were young, able-bodied commanders. In Wacha, all five of them had been handpicked by the chief, and thus bore him full allegiance. However, the Akkadian remembered something he had heard a few days ago. The youngest of the Elders, Nongru, was attracted to a young woman named Khongrem. And it was well known that she too had feelings for Nongru. Nongru had approached Khongrem's father, and had also agreed on the dowry he would need to pay the latter for her hand in marriage. However, suddenly the chief had decided to make Khongrem his fifth wife. But the chief did not want to come across as someone who would steal the betrothed of another. So, he had asked Nongru to publicly withdraw his proposal so the chief would step in of course and offer to marry the girl, to save her from embarrassment. These details were known only to a few people in Wacha. The reason the Akkadian even knew about this was because a few days earlier, the Medicine Man, who also performed marriages, had come late one night to visit the Teller. As they thought, the Akkadian was asleep; they had discussed this within his earshot. The more the Akkadian thought about this, the more positive he became that he could use this situation and the tradition of the Fight to get his guide.

The next day, he went and placed himself near the entrance of the Changa Hut. It was common for men in Wacha to come to the Changa Hut early in the evening. How long they stayed depended on how much they liked their changa. The Akkadian had also noted that Nongru always came there late, and by this time most of the other men were already quite drunk. As soon as Nongru entered the hut, the Akkadian followed him in and took a seat next to him. After they were both served with changa, the Akkadian turned towards Nongru.

"Respected Nongru," the Akkadian started, "if it is your pleasure, I would like to have a word with you in private."

"I will let you know when I am ready to leave."

After some time, Nongru signalled to the Akkadian that he was ready to leave.

"Respected Nongru," the Akkadian said after making sure that no one was around to overhear them. "What I have to say to you is of a very personal nature. I beg your indulgence. Please hear me out before you react. Believe me, for it is a matter of life and death."

"Go ahead," Nongru said, "but I do know that the chief wants you to leave Wacha. And even if you convince me that the decision is wrong, I will not be able to do anything."

"What I have to say has nothing to do with me," the Akkadian protested. "Khongrem spoke to me yesterday. She has already accepted you as her husband in her heart and soul. So, she has decided that she'd rather give up her life, than marry anyone but you."

"Why should I believe you?" Nongru asked suspiciously. "Even if what you say was true, why would she confide all this in a stranger who comes from outside our valley?"

"I was the only one she could trust," the Akkadian said, "she cannot trust anyone from Wacha, for they would only betray her to the chief."

"She is right in being cautious," Nongru said in a sad voice, "but I cannot do anything. My hands are tied."

"If you don't do anything, Khongrem is already dead," the Akkadian said melodramatically. "Think of the risk she has taken in reaching out to you."

"I have only loved Khongrem from afar." What the Akkadian was saying made sense, but Nongru decided to err on the side of caution. "I don't really know her that well. On the other hand, our chief has always been fair and kind to me. I respect and love our chief. And I think that he loves and respects me in return. So I cannot act against him."

The Akkadian had not expected this line of reasoning from Nongru. "If I were you," he began, thinking quickly, "and I loved the chief as much as you do, I would definitely do something. Not doing anything is doing a disservice to your chief. If Khongrem really takes her own life, and the chief finds out that this happened because he tried to separate her from you, do you think the chief will ever be able to forgive himself?"

Nongru remained pensive for a while. "You may be right. I will go tell the chief that Khongrem plans to kill herself and thus try to convince him that I should marry her."

The Akkadian's plan was back on track. He knew Nongru was talking from bravado rather than confidence. The time had come to give Nongru a way out, which did not involve going up to the chief just yet.

"At present, the chief is blinded by lust," the Akkadian said, looking quickly at Nongru to make sure he was not going too far, "and, therefore, I am not sure how easily he will be convinced by your words. Where I come from, there is a saying that it is easier to beg forgiveness than seek permission from a loved one. Have you heard of an old custom of your people, of taking each other as man and wife in the temple, with God as their witness, and without involving the Medicine Man or the priest? If you are willing to make Khongrem your wife in this way, then three nights from now, halfway between sunset and midnight, be at the temple in the hills. Khongrem will meet you there."

Nongru considered this for a while, "I will be there," he finally decided. "Tell Khongrem not to lose heart."

The Akkadian took his leave of Nongru. It was too late in the evening to do anything else, so the Akkadian went back to the Teller's place. Though the meeting with Nongru had gone according to plan, the Akkadian knew that the next part of his plan was much more difficult and dangerous. He slept well that night, for he understood very well the value of a good rest before any battle.

The next day, the Akkadian went in search of the barber of Wacha. Most men would feel guilty at manipulating people, that too innocent ones, but this was not so for the Akkadian. He kept telling himself that one cannot expect to eat chicken without a hen being killed – ends always justify the means.

The barber had five functions in Wacha. The first three were the normal functions of any barber, which entailed cutting everyone's hair, grooming the nails of the chief and the Elders, keeping clean-shaven the heads of the Medicine Man, Teller and Priest. In addition, the barber acted as the go-between in marriages, taking marriage proposals from one family to another. Lastly, because he visited all the houses in the valley, he was also used by everyone as a messenger. That was the function for which the Akkadian needed him.

He went to the barber's house, not expecting to find him there, but hoping to find out his schedule for the day. He could not believe his luck when he found the barber at home, cutting someone's hair. The Akkadian waited for him to finish, and only spoke when he was sure that the barber had been left alone.

"You may not have heard, but I will be leaving this valley soon," the Akkadian started, knowing very well that the barber was usually one of the first to know everything.

"I did hear something like that," the barber replied warily, "so, would you like another haircut before your journey back?"

"No, my hair is fine. I have come to you for something else. I would like you to have this," and the Akkadian handed the barber one of the last two remaining leather garments he had brought from Darromohe. Before the barber could thank him, he continued, "and I would like a favour. I want you to deliver a message for me."

"Who will I be delivering this message to?" the barber asked even more warily.

"Khongrem," the Akkadian answered casually.

"If you like that woman, I would suggest you forget about it," the barber said, a little surprised, "or you will not have to leave before the winter after all, for you will not be alive to do so," he scoffed.

"I know she belongs to a better man," the Akkadian said, "Nongru is a better man than me." He then paused for a moment, letting the barber think the Akkadian did not know the whole truth, and then completed his sentence by adding, "but I know she will be marrying someone even better – the chief."

"How do you know this?" the barber asked in surprise. The barber knew that the chief was going to marry Khongrem, but he was surprised that the stranger knew about this, too.

"Please don't ask me that," the Akkadian said in a firm voice, "much like how I will never tell anyone about this conversation, I cannot tell you who gave me that information, either."

"Okay, I will not ask you, but I will not do anything against the chief's welfare, either," the barber said.

"No, of course not!" the Akkadian exclaimed, "I will tell you what this is about. I want Khongrem to convince the chief to let me stay on at Wacha. But please do not tell her my purpose. If I can meet her, I know I can convince her. So, if you could tell her to meet me, as I can help her in the situation she finds herself in."

"What situation?" the barber asked, suspicious, but his interest piqued.

"Nothing that I can think of," the Akkadian said with a chuckle. "I know that she will ask you this question. Please inform her that you do not know, either. Being a woman, this will make her curious enough to meet me."

"Once she finds out that you are lying, I think she will not help you. But that is your problem. In any case, I will be taking a huge risk delivering any message to her," the barber grinned, "so maybe you will make it worth my while."

"I will give you a bag of salt," the Akkadian said. Then stretching his hand out to show the size of the bag, he said, "big, bag of salt."

"And something else made of leather, perhaps," the barber said hopefully.

"I have only one more left," the Akkadian said honestly, "whether I am allowed to stay or not, I think I should give it to the chief."

The barber could not argue with this, and thus agreed with the terms reluctantly, "okay, I will take your message to Khongrem in few days. And if she so wishes, she will see you at her convenience."

"I need to see her tomorrow," the Akkadian said, then quickly explained, "I have to leave this valley soon, and unless I can see her very soon, things will not work out according to my plan. If it gets too late, Khongrem will not have enough time left to convince the chief."

"You want me to see her today?" the barber asked incredulously.

"Yes, if possible. If not, by tomorrow morning at the latest," the Akkadian said and quickly added, "I know you are a very busy and important man, but please help me."

"I really want to," the barber said, "but if I have to go so early, I would have to cancel visits to see some important people, I am not sure that I can …"

"To show you how important this is to me," the Akkadian cut in, taking out a silver amulet he had brought along from Kurm, "I will part with this family heirloom, as long as you don't tell anyone that I gave it to you, for the chief may feel he deserves it more."

The last part about the chief deserving it more swayed the barber. "Thank you. As you have begged for my help, I will go to Khongrem now. Wait for me here. It will take a little while, as I will have to spend some time with her father, as well."

The barber left. He came back quite some time later.

"Khongrem will go to the Teller's house tomorrow afternoon. You will have to make sure that the Teller is not around," the barber told the Akkadian, "and please deliver the big bag of salt today."

The Akkadian immediately went and came back with the bag of salt. Then, after thanking the barber profusely, he went back to wait for the Teller. After the Teller had finished his daily story, the Akkadian thanked the Teller for everything he had done for him.

"I do not know with what face I can ask you anything more," the Akkadian started knowing that the Teller could not be bribed like the barber with worldly gifts, "but I do have a big favour to ask of you. Tomorrow is a very auspicious day in my land. I have a strong feeling that if someone whom I respect prays for me to the gods all afternoon tomorrow, my luck will change for the better. Now that I have lost favour with the chief, I really do need my luck to change. But the only person here that I have unreserved respect for is you. So, I would like to beg your indulgence, and ask if you could go to the temple tomorrow before noon and pray for me all afternoon."

"I am not that busy tomorrow," the Teller said warmly. "If you really think this will help you, I will definitely do it for you."

The Akkadian felt a little guilty about deceiving this saintly man, but reminded himself again that one cannot expect to eat chicken without a hen getting killed.

"I will be eternally beholden to you," the Akkadian said.

The next day, the Teller left for the temple sometime before noon, promising the Akkadian that he would pray for him as devoutly as he could.

Khongrem arrived a little after noon. On seeing her, the Akkadian understood why the chief was ready to antagonize one of his trusted lieutenants for her, and why the lieutenant had agreed to risk the chief's wrath.

"Is the Teller home?" Khongrem asked nervously.

"No, he will not be back for some time," the Akkadian said, "thank you for agreeing to see me."

"The barber was very convincing," Khongrem replied, still looking around nervously, "he said you could help me with the situation I find myself in. Please enlighten me, what situation are you talking about?"

"I did not tell the barber the whole truth," the Akkadian confided, but seeing Khongrem get more nervous, he quickly added, "I mean you no harm. I am only a messenger. I was chosen because I am from outside this valley. First, let me ask you this: whom do you love?"

"I love whoever will become my husband," Khongrem answered unhelpfully.

"You are not making this easy," the Akkadian sighed, "okay, let us then assume that you want to marry Nongru. I know that Nongru wants to marry you, too," and raised his hand as Khongrem tried to say something. "It is already a difficult situation for me, so if it is all right, please let me finish. So, yes, let us also assume that though the chief would like to marry you, he does not want to make Nongru unhappy. But having staked his claim, is finding it difficult to step back, without losing face or looking weak. If this were the situation, would you be willing to do something that may allow the situation to resolve itself to everyone's satisfaction."

"If it is for everyone's welfare," Khongrem answered with resolve, "I will, of course, do what it takes," she declared, "but, please tell me, why should I believe you?"

"You don't have to believe me," the Akkadian said, "but ask yourself whether what I am saying is logical. Tomorrow night, Nongru will wait for you at the temple, between sunset and midnight. If you come there, Nongru and you will take each other as man and wife with God as the witness. Then, Nongru will ask for the chief's forgiveness. This will also give the chief a way out. Would you be willing to do go along with this?"

"I will do whatever keeps everyone happy and my family safe," Khongrem said, "but if I go to the temple and do not find Nongru there, I will go and tell the chief and Nongru about this conversation."

"Of course," the Akkadian said. "I would not expect anything else. Please let me know if I can help in any way."

"No," Khongrem said, "I can go there myself. I have to go now. If everything turns out right, thank you. If you are tricking me, beware."

Khongrem left. Now that he had put everything in place, there was nothing to do but wait. But waiting without the ability to influence the outcome was the most difficult thing to do. He started going through his plan in his mind, thinking of things that could go wrong, and what needed to be done if they did.

The plan depended on both Nongru and Khongrem showing up at the temple. The plan would also fall apart if either of them talked about their conversations with the Akkadian before their wedding was solemnized. And even if everything went as planned, there was no way of being sure that Nongru would not get cold feet, or that the chief would do something totally out of character and forgive them. In any case, the Akkadian could not think of anything else he could do at present to change the outcome. Or was there something he was missing?

While the Akkadian was lost in thought, the Teller returned home.

"I have prayed to our gods," the Teller said. "I really hope you will get what you want."

"I am sure I will," the Akkadian answered, head bowed low. "If I don't get it despite your prayers, I will know I did not deserve it."

The next one and a half day was a torture for the Akkadian. Many times, he thought he should go and hide near the temple, to find out what was happening. But he knew that he was a guest at the Teller's house, and it would get noticed if he went missing.

Around mid-morning of the next day, the Medicine Man came to fetch the Teller.

"The chief wants to see you now," the Medicine Man said. "Nongru and Khongrem got married by themselves in the temple last night. The chief is very angry."

Everything has gone according to plan, the Akkadian was relieved.

"Before we go, please tell me everything. How angry was the chief? What did he say?" the Teller said with concern in his voice.

"As I have said, the chief is very angry," the Medicine Man said. "He wants to punish Nongru and still find a way to marry Khongrem."

"Punish Nongru how?" the Teller asked with more concern. "Make him a common man instead of an elder?"

"The chief wants to, at least, banish if not execute Nongru," the Medicine Man said.

"Is there any way we can convince the chief to change his mind and stop at merely making Nongru a common man?" the Teller asked with hope.

"I don't think so," the Medicine Man sighed.

The Akkadian knew he had to speak now. It looked like, in his concern for Nongru, the Teller had forgotten an important tradition of his people.

"My deepest apologies for interfering," the Akkadian said and continued before either of them could stop him, "but did you not tell me in one of the stories that the chief could only marry a woman who has never been married, or who is the widow of an Elder?"

"O Stranger!" the Medicine Man scolded the Akkadian, "please do not talk about things that do not concern you." Then, turning to the Teller, he whispered, "Is what he says true?"

"Sadly, yes," the Teller said, "so, if the chief wants to marry Khongrem, he will have to have Nongru executed while he is an Elder. That means we will have to convene a court and pass the death sentence. If he takes away Nongru's Elder-hood, thereby allowing the chief to sentence his execution without the court, the chief cannot marry Khongrem, as she will become the widow of a commoner."

"Let us not keep the chief waiting," the Medicine-Man said even more concerned, "especially as we will not be giving him the news, which he wants to hear."

Then, both the Teller and the Medicine Man left. The moment the Akkadian was alone he allowed himself to smile. Late afternoon, he went out to find Nongru. As he had expected, Nongru had a collar around his neck and was tied to a tree near the Changa Hut. Usually, when other criminals were tied and displayed in this fashion, there would be many people gathered around them, making fun and throwing stuff at them. There were no signs of such mocking and humiliation, the Akkadian observed and therefore surmised that Nongru was still an Elder. The Akkadian then went back to the Teller's house to wait for the sun to set.

Once it had gone dark, the Akkadian went back again to where Nongru was kept. He found him sitting in the shade of a deserted hut, to avoid being seen by those entering or leaving the Changa Hut.

"Psst."

Nongru thought he heard someone.

"Psst, Psst," the voice persisted.

The sound seemed to be coming from behind the deserted hut.

"Is anyone there?" Nongru whispered.

"How far back can you move?" the voice whispered, "Come away as much from the street as possible."

Nongru obeyed out of curiosity. Then, he said, "What do you want?"

"I am very sorry that my advice has landed you in this situation," the Akkadian whispered again.

"Oh, it is you," Nongru hissed, "you are wise to stay out of my reach, or I might have strangled you with my bare hands."

"I understand your anger," the Akkadian said, "but you should be angry at the chief and yourself."

"Why don't you come closer and explain it to me, you child borne to a diseased she-dog," Nongru said with feeling.

"I am fine where I am," the Akkadian said, "but if I were you, I would hear me out. You said the chief and you loved and respected each other, and my advice was based on that. Could I have really gained something by having you marry Khongrem?"

"Well, you may be right," Nongru said grudgingly. "Khongrem did come to the temple and she did marry me out of her own will. But from what I hear, the only reason I am still alive is because the chief cannot marry a commoner's widow. And an Elder cannot be sentenced without prosecuting him before a properly convened court."

"Well, I have another plan," the Akkadian whispered. "I do not think you have much to lose by hearing me out."

Nongru gave a deep sigh. "But I must admit that I don't expect much out of your plan."

"First, I want you to promise me something," the Akkadian said. "As I am taking a grave risk just by talking to you, I think I deserve at least that."

"What promise do you want?" Nongru asked suspiciously.

"I want you to promise me that if you have it in your power," the Akkadian said, "you will provide a guide to go with me to the Great Northern White Mountains."

"I agree," Nongru said with a chuckle, "for I know that I will never have that power."

"Now that I have your word," the Akkadian said, "let me ask you something. Do you know about your tradition of the Fight? Where you can challenge the chief?"

Nongru gave a wry chuckle and said, "Then, let me ask you something first. Have you ever met Pasher? I would rather take my chances with the court, as I don't think I would survive a fight against Pasher. Even if the court sentences me to death, it will at least be less painful than dying in a fight against Pasher."

"From what I hear, it is not if but when the court sentences you to death," the Akkadian said.

Before the Akkadian could continue Nongru cut in, "Yes, you are most probably right. But my argument still stands."

"In my land, there is a saying: a man is wise who knows what he does not know," the Akkadian said, "you do not know your own traditions, and do not know that you don't know it. According to your tradition, if an Elder challenges the chief, the chief cannot delegate the fight. I have heard this directly from the Teller of Tales. So there cannot be any mistake. So, this is what you should do now. When the court starts its hearing, you will be asked if you want to say anything. Take the opportunity and challenge the chief to the Fight. As the Teller is a part of the court, he will stop any delegation by the chief."

"And you are very sure about this?" Nongru asked doubtfully, wishing he could confirm it with someone else.

"I am sure," the Akkadian answered. "But once you become chief, do not forget your promise."

"If what you say is true," Nongru said doubtfully, but realizing that he did not have anything to lose, "then you could choose any person from Wacha to be your guide."

"One more thing," the Akkadian warned, "at some point, the chief will realize that he has no way out but to fight you. He will then try to make peace with you. However, this will not be a way out for you. The chief will only be waiting for the right time to exact his revenge. I have heard that the Givenlanders have a saying: if you injure a poisonous snake, it is best you kill him, or be prepared to die soon. Remember that."

After saying that, the Akkadian disappeared as quietly as he had come.

The court was convened next morning. The court usually comprised of nine judges, or hearers, as they were called in Wacha. The nine were the five Elders, the Teller of Tales, the Medicine Man, the Priest and the Chief. The Teller was the first to speak. He read out the charges against Nongru. After this was done, the Teller asked Nongru if he would like to make a statement.

Nongru stood up, "Yes, I do. I have been insulted by our chief and would like to challenge him to *The Fight*."

The chief's face lit up in a big smile. "If that is what you want, let someone fetch Pasher."

Hearing this, all blood drained from Nongru's face.

"Chief," the Teller spoke up, but with respect, "As Nongru is an Elder; you cannot ask Pasher to fight for you."

"What?" the chief said incredulously, getting a little nervous for the first time, "Why not?"

"Those are the rules," the Teller said. "If an Elder challenges the chief, the Fight cannot be delegated."

"Is this a conspiracy?" the chief's brows furrowed, "Is that why you advised me not to strip Nongru off his Elder privileges?"

"My chief," the Teller replied with steel in his voice, "even you cannot believe that. You know why Nongru could not become a commoner. I don't want to repeat it here."

"I no longer know what to believe. Your advice yesterday and your interpretations now, all seem to be working in Nongru's favour." the chief said. "I need someone to verify this for me."

"I can verify that the advice given yesterday was based on our traditions," the Medicine Man said.

"You too?" the chief demanded, growing hostile. "I need someone else to verify the rules around the tradition of the Fight." Then, turning to the priest, he said, "O learned one, please go with the Teller and find out what the tradition really is." Then, he pleaded, "Please find a way for me to delegate this fight to Pasher."

The Teller and the priest were gone for quite some time. When they came back, the chief looked at the Priest expectantly.

"Chief," the priest said, "the Teller has interpreted the tradition correctly. If an Elder challenges you, you cannot delegate."

"Okay then," the chief said, "I no longer care whether I marry Khongrem or not. I will strip Nongru of his title. If he is no longer an Elder, I can delegate the fight to Pasher."

"Chief," the Priest said, "the Teller and I checked that as well. Once an Elder has challenged you, you cannot strip him of his rank or title."

"Okay," the chief said in desperation, "In that case this court will strip him of his rank and title."

"Chief," the Teller said, "If an Elder challenges a chief to the Fight, this fight will have to happen before any other business is conducted. The only exception is an abdication by the chief or a withdrawal by the Elder."

The chief sat down crestfallen. He realized he did not have a graceful way out. However, he was still sure that he would be able to extricate himself from the situation and live to fight another day. In any case revenge was like pickle, and would only taste better with age, he consoled himself. He turned to Nongru.

"I have known you since you were born," the chief said to Nongru in a suddenly honeyed voice. "It was I who identified the potential in you and made sure you got all the right training. Again, it was I who made you an Elder. Do you really want to fight me? I have been like a father to you. Why don't we both let bygones be bygones? I will immediately arrange for a wedding feast for Khongrem and you."

The Akkadian's stomach tightened with tension, for this was a very crucial moment, and he did not have any control over it.

"O Chief," Nongru said, "it is true that I owe you for the great amount of good you have done unto me. However, in the last few weeks, you have done a lot of bad unto me too. You decided to steal my betrothed. And you decided that not only did you want her, but also you wanted to paint me as the villain. When you heard that we were already married, you decided that I should be executed, so that you could have her. Do you really think that is the way a father behaves with his son? No!" Nongru said emphatically. "I cannot let bygones be bygones. If for nothing else, then for my wife's honour, I will fight you for the right to be the chief."

The chief was growing really worried. He decided to change tactics.

"Even if you fight me, you can never be sure that you will win," the chief said. "And even if you win, do not forget that the other four Elders have been handpicked by me. So be prepared to be challenged by one of them."

"O Chief," Nongru mocked, "are you so afraid to fight me that you are trying to scare me with such empty threats? Yes, I am sure I can defeat you in a fight. While your last few years have been spent enjoying your food, drinks and your young wives, I have been training to keep fit for most of my day, every day. Besides I do not plan on insulting any of the other Elders or stealing their women," Nongru said with derision, "and, therefore, do not need to be afraid of a challenge of the Fight from any of them."

Things were unravelling fast for the chief.

"I need to confer with the priest and the Medicine-Man," the chief said, ignoring the Teller, for the chief was now sure of the latter's complicity in the whole affair, "I will be back with my decision." As soon as they withdrew from the convening, one of the Elders ordered that the guards take the collar off Nongru. The guard obeyed quickly, apologizing to Nongru.

It was quite some time before the chief came back.

"I have decided that a Fight is not what the valley needs at present," the chief said. "So, for the welfare of all the people in Wacha, I will abdicate as the chief in favour of Nongru. I hope the new chief will spare my life and that of my family and let us continue to live on peacefully in this valley."

Now it was Nongru's time to think. He wondered, both, about the dangers of the chief living on in the valley and posing him threat, and about coming across as vengeful and unforgiving if he did ask the man to leave.

"O Chief," Nongru said, "In that case, I accept. We will not fight. You will stop being chief, thus making me the new chief."

"O Chief," the Elder who had instructed the guard to take off Nongru's collar addressed Nongru, "till such a time that you take a decision on the previous chief, should he be under arrest or be allowed to roam free?"

"Neither," Nongru answered after some thought. "I have deemed it appropriate that he stay confined to his house and not meet anyone in the village, except for his family, until his fate is decided. To ensure this, a couple of guards must be stationed at his house. I would now like to go to the Teller's house to confer with him. This court is suspended, until such a time when we need it again," he said.

When Nongru and the Teller arrived at the latter's house, the Akkadian was already there.

"Greetings stranger from faraway lands," Nongru greeted the Akkadian. "I hope my people are treating you well in our valley."

"Yes, they are, O Chief," the Akkadian said, immediately regretting addressing Nongru as chief, but then realizing with relief that by now this must be common knowledge.

"Please leave us now," the Teller said to the Akkadian, "the new chief needs to talk with me in private."

"I have changed my mind," Nongru said to the Teller, "we will talk later. I have decided that I would like to receive an outsider's point of view. So, please leave us now.

Any doubts the Teller might have had about the Akkadian's complicity in the previous chief's downfall and Nongru's consequential rise had now disappeared. The Teller had determined that it all had something to do with the old chief asking the Akkadian to leave Wacha. The Teller looked at the Akkadian questioningly for a few moments, but, on receiving no answers, he left his own house.

"O Chief ..." the Akkadian started.

"You can continue to call me Nongru," Nongru said quietly.

"Respected Nongru," the Akkadian attempted to start again.

"You can also drop the respected," Nongru said, "I need your honest opinion more than I need your respect. First, let me tell you that you will have your guide. I would recommend Pasher, but you have to be sure you can trust him. Believe it or not, he is even better in climbing and trekking than at fighting. The Pass to Parroo will still be open for at least another three to four weeks. I would like you to defer your departure to as late as possible. I would ask you to stay with us for the winter, but I realize that you have other plans. That reminds me – I needed to ask you something, and you can be honest and tell me the truth without any fear. When you came to see me at the Changa Hut, was it really because Khongrem told you she was planning to give up her life?"

"Respected Nongru," the Akkadian started, and raised his hand, knowing that Nongru was about to object again, "I do respect you, and I can be respectful and truthful at the same time. I will not lie to you. To tell you the truth, I had not even met Khongrem before coming to talk to you. And when I met her, I did tell her that this was your idea, and that I was merely the messenger. I will not hide that I had a personal motive in all this. I had come to this valley with a purpose. Your chief led me on until I was almost out of gifts and time. Then, he refused my request without giving me any reason. If he had expressed his decision earlier, I might have had enough time to go back to Parroo and proceed to another valley and continue looking for a guide. I did manipulate both Khongrem and you, I admit. However, would I have been able to do that, if the previous chief had not wronged the both of you? I know my Gods will forgive me any wrong I might have done, but I have indeed managed to bring together two people who love each other."

"You have a silver tongue," Nongru chuckled, "you do not have to apologize nor explain to me as to why you played this game. But I would really like to use the time you are with us, to learn from you."

"In that case, here is the first lesson, O Chief," the Akkadian said, "you have to make sure that you spend time with the other Elders, the Teller, the Medicine-Man and the priest. You have to talk to them and ask for their guidance. Confer with them about the fate of the chief. Even if you have decided upon his fate, see if you can get someone else to suggest it. Then, tell them that you want to find out about other lands from me, before you send me away. Even better, you could manoeuvre one of the others to suggest this, as well. This way you get what you want, but without alienating any of the others. Remember that the previous chief's biggest weakness was not thinking about consensus, even when it was easy to achieve. That reminds me – if I were you, whatever future I decided for the previous chief, would not involve him staying on in Wacha. Otherwise, your enemies – and you will make many if you want to be a good chief– will know whose support they can count on."

"You are right," Nongru said after some thought. "Are you sure you cannot stay here for the winter? I would really like to have you by my side, as my guide, for the first months of my rule. If you are planning to go to the Great Northern White Mountains, I don't think you can travel before the winter is over. Why don't you stay back, and once the snow melts, I will send you off, and not only with a guide, but also with all the things you will need for your journey. You don't have to stay with the Teller. You can have my place, after I move to the chief's house. I will also find you a wife to keep you warm over the winter months."

"O Chief," the Akkadian considered, "I know I will not be able to go to the Great Northern White Mountains before spring, and I was, indeed, planning to use the winter to prepare for this journey. Also, according to my teacher, it will bode neither of us well if I impart knowledge to you, without you giving me something in return. So, if I agree to stay back through the winter and teach you whatever little I know of the world, I will have to take you up on the offer of providing me with all I need for my journey and also provide me with a house. If you are also serious about providing me with a wife, I would only accept if two conditions are fulfilled. First, I will not marry anyone who is being forced to get married to me. The girl you choose must be given the choice of rejecting me, without fear or prejudice. Second, if there was an offspring from our union, you would raise the child up as your own, in my absence of course."

"Agreed," Nongru said. "I will provide the dowry. Also meet Pasher, and see if you would like to have him as your guide. Take a week to decide upon all this. In the meantime, I will take your advice and spend more time with the Elders, first. This will also give me some time with my new wife."

Saying this, Nongru left. The Teller came to the room soon after.

"I do not know about your culture," the Teller admonished the Akkadian, "but in these mountains, only a snake bites the hand that feeds it."

"This is true for my culture, as well," the Akkadian said, "but I have eaten your food, and I do not remember doing you any harm. And any food or drink that I have had with the chief has already been paid for many times over, with various gifts that he accepted from me."

"Well, as long as you can live with your guilt," the Teller started.

"I can live with it," the Akkadian said firmly. "I only did what I thought was right. I feel sorry that I had to manipulate a few people, but as my teacher has taught me, if you want to eat chicken, a hen has to die. And if you think what I did was wrong, then we must also discuss whether what the chief was doing to Nongru and Khongrem was right – and if you or anyone else in this valley tried to do anything to stop it. How were you all sleeping at night, knowing that you were supporting something that you knew to be wrong?"

"I never thought about it that way," the Teller said, starting to feel a little guilty, "but if you are trying to tell me that you did not have an ulterior motive …"

"I respect your intelligence too much to claim that," the Akkadian admitted, "yes, I did have an ulterior motive. But you are a learned man, so please answer me this: which is worse – to do, the right thing for the wrong reason or to do the wrong thing for the right reason?"

"We have a saying in these mountains," the Teller said with grudging respect, "a man with a smooth tongue can sell you your own goat, and help you eat it too. I assume our new chief will give you what you want and you will leave Wacha soon. And I will be lying if I said that I will be unhappy to see you leave."

"Then I am very sorry to disappoint you," the Akkadian said with feeling. "I will leave only after the winter. But I will not burden you anymore and will move to new lodgings. If you can still bear my company, I would like to visit you in the evenings to continue learning your folklore."

"I hope Wacha will not have to regret you staying through the winter," the Teller mused, "but if you will stay for the winter, I would like that you visit me. But, henceforth, I would like to learn your culture as you have learned mine. I have seen you conquer us without lifting a weapon, and this has made me realize how important it is to know about others."

"I will try," the Akkadian said, "I can only hope God gives me your wisdom and half your eloquence."

In a few days, Nongru decided to spare the previous chief's life, but exiled him to another valley, but only after making sure that the previous chief and his family would have a comfortable sustenance.

The Akkadian stayed back in Wacha for the next five months. Nongru was true to his word and arranged for the Akkadian to move into his old house, after Khongrem and he moved to the chief's house. Nongru then informed the Akkadian that one of Khongrem's cousins was already quite taken by this strange man from stranger lands, and would, therefore, like to get married to him. Also, as Nongru explained to the Akkadian, in case the Akkadian did have an offspring and Nongru did have to bring him or her up, it would be easier for Nongru to have Khongrem accept her cousin's child.

In the meanwhile, the Akkadian met with Pasher and had many long parleys with him. Finally, he was convinced that Pasher was loyal to whoever was the chief of Wacha and was ready to do what Nongru wanted. Pasher also loved climbing hills and mountains and expressed his interest in accompanying the Akkadian on his adventure, if Nongru gave him permission to do so.

Soon, everything fell into routine. Nongru spent most afternoons with the Akkadian, learning all he could, while the Akkadian spent most of his evenings with the Teller. The Teller, in turn, insisted on hearing a story about either Sumer or Givenland for every story or tradition he told about Wacha. Nongru also joined them whenever possible. After a few weeks, Nongru requested the Akkadian and the Teller to have their exchange of stories once a week in the Changa Hut. He wanted the stories that were told during these sessions to have very clear moral lessons.

Soon, the winter was almost over. The Akkadian's wife offered to go on the adventure with him, but was relieved when the Akkadian refused. He did promise to come back to the valley before proceeding to Kurm after finishing his quest. Nongru tried, but unsuccessfully, to talk the Akkadian into staying for another year. The Akkadian promised that if he came down from the Great Northern White Mountains safely, he would come back and stay for a few months before returning to Kurm.

Nongru gave Pasher a free hand to collect whatever the guide deemed necessary for the journey.

The Akkadian was impressed with Pasher's meticulousness and attention to detail in preparing for the trip. He asked him questions only to expand his own knowledge rather than to validate Pasher's decisions.

"Pasher," the Akkadian asked, "I see that you have these thin and thick kaigavas. Why is this? Must they be used at different altitudes on the mountains?"

"No, Master," Pasher started, since Nongru had asked Pasher to look at the Akkadian as his master, no one could dissuade Pasher from addressing the Akkadian thus. "The thin ones are made of a pig's intestine. You pull these over your hands first, and the thicker ones over them. The trick in keeping warm in the mountains is to wear many layers. This is true for every part of the body. We will be using two or more layers to cover every part of our body. The ones made with softer material inside and thick and tough ones outside. The leather garments that you brought to our valley are of better quality than the ones we have here. So we will get these from wherever you got your gifts. We will take the inner layers and lambskin facemasks from here. I have not decided on the headgears yet. Maybe we should take some from here, and then try to get better ones when we get our other leather garments. But, of course, everything will be done with your approval."

"Pasher," the Akkadian said, "on these things, you are the master, and I am a mere student. So, please plan and prepare as you see fit."

"Thank you for your trust, Master," Pasher said, "I am also taking all the climbing gear from here. The things made by Plains People cannot be trusted and will get us killed as surely as the bite of a cobra."

"How soon do you think we will be ready?" the Akkadian asked, "and, also, how soon will it be safe to proceed to Parroo?"

"I will be ready with everything in two weeks," Pasher replied, "snow will melt from the pass to Parroo in about five weeks. But I have been thinking that we should take a few short overnight trips into the mountains starting next week. As the Master has no experience in climbing snow covered mountains, I think we should practice here before we leave the valley."

The Akkadian agreed and over the next three weeks, they made six overnight trips into the nearby mountains. The first trip was a total disaster, and even though they had a rope tied to each other's waist, it was the only because of Pasher's extremely superior climbing expertise that they survived the Akkadian's various falls. However, the Akkadian learned fast and after the sixth trip Pasher was satisfied that the Akkadian was ready.

Soon, it was time for the Akkadian to leave on his quest. Over the winter, and through the many story-telling sessions, the Akkadian had become close to many people and there was a lot of late night eating and drinking. Finally, the Akkadian's wife put her foot down and said that, for the benefit of the Akkadian's well-being during his forthcoming arduous journey, he would have to stop these revelries for the last few days before his trip. What she did not say was that she would like to spend as much time as possible with her husband before he went away. So, for the last few days, the Akkadian stayed home; only Nongru and the Teller were allowed to visit him. Soon enough, the day of his departure dawned. However, it brought heavy unseasonal snowfall. Pasher, Nongru and the Teller arrived at the Akkadian's house early in the morning.

"Master," Pasher said, "we cannot leave today. I did have a feeling that a snowstorm was coming our way, but had hoped it would not hit our valley. Now, we will have to delay our trip by at least three to four days."

"Are you sure you want to embark on this journey?" Nongru asked, "It is clear the gods don't want you to."

At this, the Teller and the Akkadian's wife nodded their agreement, but Pasher did not react.

"Pasher," Nongru urged the guide, "why don't you say something? Don't you agree with me?"

"O Chief," Pasher replied, "you are putting me in a difficult situation. You have told me to follow Master's wishes as if they were your commands. Thus, whenever the Master and you are going to disagree, I think it best for me to keep quiet."

"O Respected Chief," the Akkadian started, "I mean, my dearest friend Nongru, I don't think you are interpreting these signs correctly. I think the Gods just want me to delay the start of my journey by a few days. I don't know why, and I might never find out, but I am sure that this is all they want. So, I will bow to their wishes and start four days from today. I think my wife will agree that I should spend some time with other people as well, and would like to entertain some people here today evening."

And thus the Akkadian and his wife had a gathering at their place that evening, and it went on until late. The Akkadian's wife was ready to share an evening with the others, as the Gods had given her four more days with her husband.

The snow stopped early the next morning, but the skies remained overcast. When the fourth day dawned, it was with bright sunshine. Even though everything had been prepared by Pasher the previous evening, it was almost noon by the time all the farewells were done with. Finally, they were left with only Nongru and the Teller at their house.

The Akkadian first turned to the Teller.

"I know I have not lived up to your high standards," the Akkadian said, "but I hope you will find it in your heart to forget my iniquities and remember the good times we had. I will always remember you as a great teacher and an even better man."

"The silver tongue never stops, does it?" the Teller chuckled, but then grew serious, "you have taught me more than I have taught you. From you, I have learnt that it is much better to do the right thing for the wrong reason than to do the wrong thing for the right reason. And, equally important, I have learnt that people like you, who are ready to compromise with or manipulate any situation or any person in order to reach their goal, will advance this world. I consider myself privileged to have known you and to have got the opportunity to share my roof with you."

On saying this, the Teller left their company, with tears in his eyes.

The Akkadian turned to Nongru, but before he could say anything, Nongru came over and hugged him like a bear.

"Please, my dear friend," Nongru said, "I would like no words of farewell from you. I have learnt from you that one must always have faith in what you believe. And I believe that we will meet again. Also, for the last few weeks, I am having this feeling that you coming to our valley is an important piece of something much bigger – and, by this, I don't mean something as simple as changing the chief. I will leave you with your wife," then looking towards the Akkadian's wife meaningfully said, "and if you are leaving someone else behind, you can go without worry. I will never forget my promise."

After Nongru had left, the Akkadian's wife asked him with a puzzled look, "My lord, what did the chief mean by 'promise'? What has he promised you?"

"My loving wife," the Akkadian said, "Nongru has promised me that if you and I were to have a child, and if something were to happen to me, he will be the guardian and give you any help you might need to bring the child up. He has also promised that our child will be given the same stature as a chief's offspring will."

"My lord," the Akkadian's wife said, "I don't think you are leaving a child in me. A woman knows. But I had a dream that you came back safe and sound from your journey. So, the only thing I will say is that I wish you success in your quest and that I will be waiting here for you, even if it takes forever for you to come back."

The Akkadian took his wife in his arms. He had tears in his eyes. "I will promise you this: if I return from my quest, I will come first to you, before going anywhere else."

"That would be nice. Well, once you are back, after successfully completing your quest, you can tell me all about it."

"Wife," the Akkadian said, "that will have to wait until I have been to Kurm once. You see, before I met you, I had already made a promise to another, about narrating the tale of my quest."

"Oh," the Akkadian's wife said with sadness, "but do not worry, my lord, for I know you are too much of a man for one woman to have as hers. So, I can wait for you to tell your first love about your quest, before you tell me."

The Akkadian burst out laughing. "My Wife," he said still chuckling, "that promise was made to someone at least four times your age. And he was a man. You see, I made this promise to Abgal." The Akkadian could not stop chuckling at the thought of having Ishme as his lover or wife. But then, he added seriously, "no wife, there was none before you, and I am sure there will be none after you."

They held each other close. Soon, there was a knock on their house's door.

"My Master," Pasher called from outside, "if we are to cross the pass tonight we have to leave soon. I would like for us to be deep in the next valley before nightfall."

"Go," the Akkadian's wife said. "Do what you have to do. Be successful in your quest and come back to me, even if for a short while, before you go off to tell your other love," she jested, but with tears in her eyes.

Pasher and the Akkadian thus left, waving back at their well-wishers as they disappeared over the ridge. The journey back to Parroo was as uneventful as the Akkadian's journey to Wacha from Parroo. He could not believe that it was less than a year ago, for it felt like a lifetime. The Akkadian knew he would never have a more settled and peaceful life than the last few months he had spent at the valley, since Nongru became chief of Wacha. But he pushed away these thoughts from his mind. You have to lose something to gain something, he said to himself.

Chapter 10

The Akkadian's Tale IV

When they reached Parroo, the Akkadian took Pasher to the lodgings he had shared with Tiraak and Runggoo. After securing their lodgings, the Akkadian went to the riverside dock where he had arrived the previous year. He recognized one of the persons there.

"Greetings," the Akkadian said, "I am sure you do not remember me, but I ..."

"Remember you?" the person interrupted, "but I have been cursing you for the last many months." Then, he smiled and said, "You were the one who taught my master Viraan, how to use animals to pull the boats upriver. Quite a few people have started doing it too and this has brought forth many problems. First, no one is sure which animals are more suited for doing this and how best to train these animals. Also, these animals are not required in the downstream trip, and, therefore, I have to arrange for these to be sent back and for their herders to come back here. So, as I was saying, you have made my workload four times more than usual. But to be fair, my family has started living better, as my master takes good care of the hard workers."

"I am sorry that I have increased your workload," the Akkadian said, without sincerity, "I am sure we can work together to improve the situation. Where is your master now? Also, do you have any news of his cousin or Runggoo?"

"My master is in Purawanbhag," the person said, "but he will be here in two days' time, as his cousin and Runggoo are arriving here on that day."

The Akkadian gave one of the original silver trinkets he had brought from Kurm to Pasher and ordered him to go and have a good time in Parroo for the next three days.

Two days later, the Akkadian went to the riverside early in the morning. Neither Viraan nor his men were there. He waited there and observed how the boats and animals were being handled and uncovered a few ways that this could be improved. Sometime later, Viraan arrived with a few of his men and, on spotting the Akkadian there, headed straight towards him.

"Hello, stranger from another land," Viraan saluted the Akkadian. "We were worried about you. Before my cousin and Runggoo left for Darromohe, we had decided that if you were not back by spring, we would send a guide back to look for you. I see that you are alone. As I had told you, it is not easy to convince those hill people to come out of their valleys. Many of the prospectors, my cousin included, have tried to hire them, without any success. But if you still want to try, I could ask my guide to take you to one of the other valleys."

"Viraan, thank you for your offer of help," the Akkadian said with a proud smile, "but I have come back with the best mountain-man Wacha had to offer. But, I am really touched at your concern."

"Runggoo was quite sure that you would get your guide," Viraan said, "but to be entirely honest, I did not think you would succeed." Then, looking over the Akkadian's shoulders he added. "Look! There comes our friends' river caravan – as we now call your animal boats. For some reason, only their caravan seems to arrive on schedule."

"Interesting," the Akkadian said thoughtfully. "Are they still using my camels?"

"Indeed, they are," Viraan said. "Do you think that has anything to do with them having a more predictable trip than others? But that cannot be true as they are using many other animals."

"Let us talk about it later," the Akkadian said still in thought.

It was indeed Tiraak and Runggoo who arrived with the caravan. They were overjoyed to see the Akkadian amongst the party waiting for them. They alighted and went straight to the Akkadian and gave him a hug.

"Where is your guide?" Runggoo asked looking around.

"All in good time," the Akkadian laughed. "First, tell me how have you been? I am very glad to see you in good health and making good use of the idea you stole from me."

"Stole from you?" Tiraak said with a chuckle, "Don't you mean bought from you. But it is indeed great to see that you have come back safe. And from your countenance, I can make out that you have been successful in your endeavours."

"When I was still in Kurm," the Akkadian began, "I came to know a Givenlander trader called Vikoo. I do not know if you have noticed that I eat my desserts before, rather than after, the meal. Observing this, Vikoo had told me that, as the dessert was the destination of a meal, a Givenlander would never eat it before the meal. He said that everything is done in a certain order for a reason. So, my Givenlander friends, as you have had a long journey, why don't you freshen up, and over lunch I will tell you about my travels, in the proper sequence and not back to front?"

Both Tiraak and Runggoo agreed. They proceeded to the same lodgings and after freshening up, they decided to have lunch in Tiraak's room.

The Akkadian told Tiraak and Runggoo about his stay in Wacha. He only left out the fact that he had got married and now had a wife in Wacha. He wanted to keep that fact to himself. Tiraak and Runggoo were totally captivated by the Akkadian's story.

"I am glad we have you as a friend," Tiraak said when the Akkadian had finished and shook his head in disbelief, "and I really feel sorry for your enemies. So what is your plan now?"

"I will introduce you to Pasher over dinner tonight," the Akkadian said, and then turning to Runggoo, he continued, "I hope you still remember your offer to explain how to get to the caves to him. Mountain-man to mountain-man was how you had put it. I would also like your advice on the fastest way to get there from here."

"My offer still stands," Runggoo said, "I think it's best if we include Viraan in the discussion on the best way to get to my valley. I think it would be best to talk about a route to Runaka. The fewer people who know of your final destination, the better and safer it will be for you. So, let us think about some other reason, for which you might want to go to Runaka."

"Lapis Lazuli, of course," Tiraak burst in. "Runaka is well-known for its Lapis Lazuli. From here on, until you get to Runaka, procuring good quality Lapis Lazuli should become the reason for going there."

"Thank you," the Akkadian said, "that is good advice indeed. And, I would like to invite Viraan for dinner tonight to discuss this further. I will introduce Pasher to both of you today, but I will ask him to continue enjoying his time in Parroo, until the time I have made the other arrangements. Don't misunderstand me, I could not have hoped for a better mountain-man, but he likes to enjoy life, as well. I think it would be best if I tell the details about our destination to Pasher only the day before I leave on my journey."

"That is a good idea," Runggoo said, "for enjoying life will mean raajaraas, which always leads to a loose tongue. But I think we should give it three days as least. You don't want to be in a situation where your guide sleeps over my directions, and comes up with a few questions, but you are already on your way."

That evening, Pasher came to see the Akkadian, sober as promised. The Akkadian introduced him to Tiraak and Runggoo. Then, the Akkadian informed Pasher that he could continue to do whatever he was doing for the next few days as long as he kept out of trouble. Pasher said that he would come in every morning to check if the Akkadian needed anything from him.

Viraan joined them for dinner in Tiraak's room. After the usual pleasantries were exchanged, Tiraak came straight to the point.

"Cousin, my friend here wants to go to Runaka," Tiraak said indicating towards the Akkadian. "Originally, he had planned to go there from Darromohe. But, as he has come so far north, he was wondering whether there is a better and faster way to get there."

"Cousin," Viraan replied in a sad voice, "it is really hurtful that you all did not trust me enough and found the need to lie to me. When did anyone need a mountain guide to go to Runaka? And if he needed a faster way, why did he waste a year in Wacha?"

"My dear friend," the Akkadian cut in before Tiraak could explain. "It is entirely my fault. It is not that I do not trust you, but I thought it's best for everyone's sake that we do not openly discuss my destination. It was foolish of me to think we could hide it from someone as astute as you."

"I am a trader," Viraan said, pacified by the Akkadian's words, "and, therefore, understand the need for secrecy. If you do not want to share the details, that is fine by me, but please do not lie to me. Rest assured, whatever you tell me will never leave my lips."

"Thank you for being so understanding," the Akkadian continued in his humble tone. "I need to go to the mountains northwest of Runaka. But on the way, I would like to visit some place where I can procure leather garments and headgear of great quality. More than time or distance, I am more concerned about reducing unnecessary risks."

"Before I give you my views," Viraan said, "we will need to talk about what you can afford."

"Don't worry about that," Runggoo said before anyone else. 'I will sponsor him. I think his idea of pulling boats with animals will save us enough."

'Thank you," the Akkadian said, "but I cannot let you do that. As Tiraak pointed out this morning, you have already repaid me for that. However, since this morning, I have found many improvements to the way the animals are being used. Viraan, you can then decide what they are worth. Most of your animals still fear the river. You should start sending them back in flat bottom boats. Make sure they can look outside and see the river during their journey. This will not only reduce the time and energy wasted in the journey home, but also alleviate their fear of the river," he finished. "So, what do you think that knowledge is worth?"

"I think you have more than paid for your trip," Viraan said, unable to hide his admiration and respect.

"In that case, you will have to find some way to arrange for his return trip as well, as I would still like to sponsor at least half his trip," Runggoo said. Turning to the Akkadian, he continued, "Please do not object. I will later remind you about what I had told you the last time we met in Parroo. This is a payment to ensure that."

"I cannot take that," the Akkadian said. "I do remember what you told me, and I will give your message if I ever see them, but I will do that as your friend."

'In that case," Runggoo countered, "I will do this for you, as a friend."

"As there is no changing your mind," the Akkadian said giving in, "I will humbly accept."

"I cannot arrange for a return trip from Runaka," Viraan said thoughtfully. "The nearest place to Runaka that I can arrange this from is Lakho. But, first, we must decide on the route. Considering that the rains are still a few months away, I would personally take the overland route – it would definitely be faster. You will go from here to Pparaha. My trading partner there will help you procure the things you need. From there you will proceed to Lakho. My partner in Pparaha will make sure that his partner in Lakho will also get you anything you need. Runaka is only about a day's journey from Lakho.

"How will he settle these transactions with your partners?" Runggoo asked.

"You will not have to worry about that," Viraan said to the Akkadian. "However, remember that beyond Lakho, I will not be able to help you. So, you will have to make sure that you procure everything you need in either Pparaha or Lakho."

Then Viraan laid out the route that he suggested the Akkadian should take, from Parroo to Runaka, through Pparaha and Lakho.

The Akkadian asked after some thought, "How close or far from the river should we stay while travelling along these?"

"Very good question," Viraan said, "but you will have to judge for yourself. Don't be too close, but make sure you are keeping the river in sight."

After Viraan had answered many more similar questions, the Akkadian said with genuine admiration, "One would think you have planned and executed this journey many times over. I thank the Gods for allowing me to have you as the planner for my journey."

"What are the various risks that he may face?" Tiraak asked, being pragmatic as usual.

"These are of course many," Viraan said, "and over the next few days, I will guide our friend on what these are and how best to avoid them, as well. But now I will have some raajaraas, for my throat is parched."

Over the next seven days, Viraan and the Akkadian went over all the details of the Akkadian's intended journey. Initially, Viraan had suggested that he draw a map for the Akkadian, but the Akkadian insisted that he draw it himself and Viraan check it, as that would ensure there was no misunderstanding.

"I think our friend here now knows the route and all the pitfalls therewith, as well as I do," Viraan said on the eighth day during dinner. "It will take me another three or four days to make sure that I have procured everything from our friend's list. I will also complete my instructions to my partner in Pparaha and his partner in Lakho."

"I cannot mention enough about how lucky I am to have you as my planner," the Akkadian said, pouring Viraan some raajaraas and then topping off the glasses of his other friends.

"This is good news, indeed," Runggoo said, and turning towards the Akkadian continued, "for everyone except Pasher of course," he chuckled. "His fun time is over, the poor man. When he comes to see you tomorrow, please let him know that from the next day, he will have to be here with you and me."

"And tomorrow we will take you to choose your rides," Tiraak said. "This will give my cousin enough time to send them ahead to Ankal[50] to wait for you and Pasher. Have you decided what animals you would like to take on your journey?"

"I will take camels for riding and asses for carrying goods," the Akkadian replied, "Pasher and I will, thus, have had enough time with the asses before we take them into the mountains."

"I think that is a great idea," Viraan agreed. "Asses are temperamental, after all. Also, in this way, you will still be able to replace any of the two in either Pparaha or Lakho. I will make sure to add this in the instructions."

The next day, Viraan chose two camels and two asses for the Akkadian. All four animals were immediately dispatched to Ankal. Viraan then excused himself from dinner for the remaining nights, knowing well that the Akkadian would like privacy when he discussed his final destination with Runggoo and Pasher. Tiraak also quickly took his leave, mentioning that he needed to spend some time with his cousin to discuss business matters.

"Thank you very much," the Akkadian said, and neither cousin objected, as they did not want to insult the Akkadian's intelligence, "but I insist that we have the last two dinners together before I leave. I say two, for on the last day I can only drink in moderation."

Everyone agreed. The next morning, when Pasher came to Runggoo's room, the Akkadian was already there. He had joined Runggoo for breakfast. After confirming that Pasher had eaten, too, Runggoo immediately got to business.

"What do you know about the place that my friend wants to go to?"

"I do not know any details of my master's destination," Pasher said, "but I do not need to know anything either. My chief has commanded that

---

[50]A town in Eastern Givenland/ Meluhha on banks of River Sutlej

I serve my master, as if he were my chief. However, I would like to know everything that will help me bring my master back safe and sound from his destination."

"I personally think that you need to know everything," Runggoo said to Pasher and then turning to the Akkadian continued, "I think, in this journey, you will have many unexpected events and surprises. In such a journey, I would want my companion to be as informed as possible."

"That makes sense," the Akkadian agreed. "Pasher, I want you to know not only what my destination is, but what I expect to find there too. But you can never divulge this to anyone else. You will have to take an oath to that effect."

Pasher promised, repeating his master's words.

"Runggoo will tell us how to get to the cave from Runaka," the Akkadian said.

"As you say, Master," Pasher said. Then, after a little hesitation, he added, "How will we get to Runaka?"

"All arrangements for this have been made," the Akkadian said, "and I will go over the details with you later. For the time being, let us assume we are in Runaka and listen to what Runggoo has to say."

"First, I have a question for Pasher," Runggoo said, turning to Pasher. "I have heard that you are an exceptional mountain climber, while our friend here is a novice. But he tells me that you have given him some lessons. I would like to hear your opinion on his skills. Please be honest, for exaggerating about his skills might become the difference between life and death for both of you."

"Master was a good learner," Pasher said. "If I can assume that this climbing will not be done in winter, I would be willing to climb up to two-hundred-hath tall straight faces. Anything over that will be a problem. If height gained is two-third the length of the face, I think my master can climb any distance. He is actually better at climbing down. He can rappel down as far as the rope will go. And I have very good and strong ropes that I have brought from Wacha. And I have made sure that I not only have smooth ropes to rappel down, but also ropes knotted at every two haths to help in climbing upwards. The knots have been seasoned to make sure they will not give."

"Are you very sure about your master being able to rappel down any distance?" Runggoo asked with interest.

"As you said my exaggeration could mean death of my master, so of course I have given you my honest evaluation," Pasher said.

"Good. The best way to get there will involve rappelling down a straight face of about five-hundred haths," Runggoo told Pasher, and then turning to the Akkadian, he said, "give me the map that you drew under Viraan's instructions, for the journey to Runaka, and I will plot your way from there onwards."

"I don't think that would be a good idea," the Akkadian shook his head, "I may have to show that map to others, while seeking directions. But I think your map should be from Runaka onwards, and should be without mention of any actual place. In this way …"

"You do not have to explain," Runggoo said, "I should have thought of it myself."

Runggoo proceeded to describe the path his ancestor had found to the Cave. His descriptions were detailed and portrayal eloquent, it was as if he had taken his two companions on the actual journey. After he had finished, there was a long silence.

"You mentioned light emitting mosses," Pasher licked his lips nervously, "but in our mountains, most such mosses also poison the air."

"That happens in our mountains, too," Runggoo said, "but you can be sure these mosses will not do that."

Pasher had many other questions, which Runggoo tried to answer as best as he could. But the Akkadian did not speak. He seemed to be in deep thought. Runggoo had noticed that and was glancing towards him, as he talked to Pasher. Finally, the Akkadian looked towards Runggoo.

"My friend," Runggoo said, "you seem to have something in your mind."

"Yes," the Akkadian admitted, "why do you know about this route? And, more importantly who else knows about this?"

"I am a little ashamed of my valley's history," Runggoo said, "but to put your mind at ease, I will share it with you. Many years ago, before even my twentieth forefather was born, my people did not do any farming or herding, but lived as mere parasites, making their livelihood, by stealing from the Plains People. Finally, the people in the plains decided that they had had enough, and when they heard there had been a raid further east, they laid a trap, to the northwest of where Runaka is now situated, where the River Swastu[51] comes out of the mountains. As my people had informers amongst the Plains People, they found this out before walking into the trap. As the waiting contingent was too big to fight, they decided to turn north before reaching Runaka and find a way through the mountains. They found a way, but the journey was so arduous, that they still lost all their loot and half the raiders. It was then that the best trekkers from my valley were sent out to find safer routes into my valley from the plains. My twenty-second forefather was one of these trekkers. He found this particular route, but around this time, something happened to my people – they changed. They suddenly took interest in herding animals and growing crops. And, somehow, within a matter of less than half a generation's time, they became better at it than most of the Plains People. The raids, of course stopped."

"Do you think that this change was caused by the arrival of White Gods?" the Akkadian asked.

"I have no idea," Runggoo said, "but when my twenty-second great grandfather came back, no one took much interest in the route he had found. Yet, he was very proud of his discovery and had described it in great detail to his son, and since then, the same information had been passed down our family. When I was banished from my valley, I tried to retrace my ancestor's route. After some trial and error, I did manage to retrace his steps. I also measured all the important distances. This particular cave will give you some more advantages. This is one of the two farthest caves, which makes the possibility of a surreptitious entry easier. Also, this particular cave has an overhang above it, and when you rappel down you will come to this overhang. And there is a small window-like entrance from the overhang to the cave."

"Fate and Tiraak have been very kind in introducing you to me," the Akkadian said with feeling, and then asked, "Is there anything special about these caves? There must be many more than seven caves near your valley, and yet, why these seven caves in particular?"

"I would not know about that," Runggoo replied. "I have only been to one cave, which also happens to be the one I just described to you. All offering bearers in my valley have also been to only one of the seven caves. Once you have been to one cave, you are never allowed to go to another of these caves. This rule is strictly followed," he said firmly. "Coming back to the cave I have been to, the first thing to note about it is that unless you know where the cave is, you would miss it. There is a rock face behind the entrance, and to go in, you would have to enter and then immediately turn right and then walk along this passage until you cannot see the entrance any longer, before reaching the main cave. Oh, and one more thing – in the back of the cave, there is a circular pool of water. Otherwise, this cave is like any other cave."

"I have one more question: the second entrance to the cave that you spoke about, the small window like one, how high is it?" the Akkadian asked, rubbing his forefinger under his nose, "and how easy would it be to carry things up to this window?"

"Well, I did not actually rappel down to the overhang," Runggoo said a little sheepishly, "I did not want to take the risk alone. And I know this is the weakest part of your plan, as well, for rappelling down a straight face of almost half a mahahaths is one thing, but climbing back up will not be easy. I have seen this entrance from inside the cave, and I don't think it would be easy to carry things out through this entrance. But I cannot be sure."

"Don't worry," the Akkadian said. "It was just a thought. I need to ponder over everything I have just heard. If both of you don't mind, I would like to go for a walk."

After the Akkadian had left, Runggoo started going over the entire route with Pasher.

The Akkadian came back after sundown. As it was already decided that Pasher would not go out any more, the three of them sat down for dinner. The Akkadian asked Pasher to describe the route from Runaka to the cave over dinner. The Akkadian caught on to the two mistakes that Pasher made, even before Runggoo could correct him. Runggoo was impressed by this, but not surprised. He was no longer surprised by what the Akkadian did. However, Pasher was contrite.

"I am very sorry, Master," Pasher told the Akkadian, and continued in an apologetic voice, "I will try to do better."

"Yes, you have to try harder," the Akkadian said, "but do not be sorry. I prefer that you make mistakes now than on the journey. And no one learns everything in a day."

"Except you, of course," Runggoo said with a chuckle.

"That is different," the Akkadian answered in a matter-of-fact voice. "It is natural that I am so unnaturally attentive. We are, after all, so close to achieving the only goal I have had since I was only a boy. I would be concerned, rather than relieved if Pasher was the same. However, such lapses in attention mean that the both of you will have to discuss everything again, all day tomorrow. Runggoo, please bear with my demands for a couple of more days."

155

"Of course," Runggoo answered, "as I also have a vested interest. For I do not think you know how to fail. And if you do not fail, I have a chance at redemption."

They retired early that night, and by the time Pasher came to see Runggoo to continue their discussions, the Akkadian had already gone out. They went over the whole route again and again, getting into more details with every repetition. From time to time, either Runggoo or Pasher would digress though and have a discussion on the people of Wacha or Swastu valley, their culture, their tradition, mountain climbing methods and other things. But they always did come back to the details of the route. The Akkadian came back after sundown and, again, during dinner asked Pasher to walk them through the route from Runaka to the caves. This time there were no mistakes. The Akkadian was both happy and relieved with Pasher's grasp of the route.

"Will we be able to take everything we planned up on this climb?" the Akkadian asked after some thought. "Pasher, the rope that you brought from Wacha is quite heavy. Can we carry it up for such a long climb? I know we have to, but if we take it up with us, we will have to sacrifice something else. And I cannot think of any other thing that we can give up, instead."

"Why don't Pasher and I go through everything tomorrow and come up with some suggestions?" Runggoo said before Pasher could answer.

"Runggoo, how long did it take you to climb to the first cave?"

"I took longer, as I had to be sure of the route. Also, a few landmarks had changed," Runggoo replied, "If Pasher was climbing alone, it would take him four days. However, since both of you will climb together, it should still not take more like six to seven days."

"Good. Pasher and I were thinking the climb would be ten to twelve days. We can definitely reduce some of our supplies."

The Akkadian was again gone by the time Pasher and Runggoo met in the morning to go over the things that would be taken for the climb. In the evening, Tiraak and Viraan joined them for dinner. The Akkadian was the last to join. He apologized profusely to the others for being late.

"I am very sorry that I am late, especially for it was I who insisted on you two joining us today," the Akkadian said, "but I would beg you to bear with me for a little more time before we get to our raajaraas. I know I had set aside today for merriment only, but I need to ask your advice on something first. Has any of you come across anything that glows under water?"

"How strange that you should ask that," Tiraak said, "you will soon have me agreeing with Runggoo that it is the Gods who are guiding your path. A few years back, Runggoo and I were out prospecting. We had set up our camp near a stream. Once, after the sun had set, we were surprised to see the surface of the stream glowing. On closer inspection, we realized that there were these small flat white stones, each a little smaller than my palm, which could glow in the dark. We collected about fifty of these and brought them back with us, to see if they are of any value. We took a few back to Darromohe, but most of these are still with my cousin here."

"All your things are stored in Purawanbhag," Viraan said, and then turning to the Akkadian he continued in a false submissive voice, "and, Master, I know you would like to get hold of these immediately. But if you would be kind enough to let me eat and sleep, I will go to Purawanbhag first thing tomorrow and fetch a few of these stones."

Everyone laughed again.

"Have I really been such a nuisance?" the Akkadian asked, pretending to look offended, but then laughing along with everyone else, "Anyway, I will now not talk about my trip for the rest of the evening. Since the day I met Tiraak at the raajaraas hut in Darromohe, he has been doing all the drinking. Tonight I plan to show him how to really put it away."

"I would advise you not to," Runggoo said, "I have realized a long time ago that Tiraak has hollow legs. If you try to keep up with him, let alone beat him, in drinking raajaraas, Pasher will have to carry you for the first few days of your journey."

Though the Akkadian laughed and smiled, he was feeling very gloomy inside. For outside this room, after all, there were only a few people whom the Akkadian would or could call close – namely his wife, his teacher Ishme, Nongru and perhaps the Teller.

The next morning, except for Viraan, who had woken up early to go to Purawanbhag, all the others slept in late. The Akkadian and Pasher spent the afternoon and early evening going over and over again all the things that they would be taking on their journey, as well as the list of things that they would pick up from Pparaha and Lakho.

"I know I am yet to tell you, about our journey to Pparaha and then on to Lakho," the Akkadian said, as he took final stock of his last few remaining silver jewellery. "We will go through that on our way, after the boat drops us off at Ankal. I want you to concentrate the rest of the time we are in Parroo to clarify everything about the route from Runaka. If we have any problems getting to Lakho or even Runaka, we can get it sorted locally. But except for

Runggoo, we cannot talk about our climb with anyone else. Also, if you would like to send any message back to Wacha, this will be your last chance in a long time."

"Master," Pasher called, looking into the Akkadian's eyes, "you do not have to explain anything to me. You can inform me whenever you deem it necessary. Even though you know that I am at your beck and call, you have never exploited this. I have come to trust you completely. Also, as you know, I do not have a family in Wacha. My father died when I was young, and so did my only brother, who, while on a climb, was attacked to death by a bear. My mother could not recover from this shock and passed away soon after. Even though you have not told me, I can guess that this journey we are going on is special. So, the only message I want to send to Wacha is that you have come back safe from your quest. I will thus wait until I can take that message."

"I have come too far to turn back now. However you should understand our chances of returning from this journey alive is miniscule. At any point in our journey, if you do not want to continue, you may turn back. I will not think any less of you for doing that. As of now, I release you from the promise of service that you had made to Nongru."

"But, Master, that cannot be true," Pasher said unflappably, "for I have promised your wife and my chief that I will bring you back safely. So, wherever we are going, I will bring you back to Wacha, if that is the last thing I do. So, Master, thank you for trusting me and releasing me from the promise, but nothing has changed."

The Akkadian was now regaining his full confidence, "we will come back successful. If fate wanted otherwise, it would not bring you, Nongru, Runggoo, Tiraak, Viraan and everyone else into my life. If you think about it, I have heard there are more than ten times people in Givenland, than there are in my lands, but my fate has ensured that I meet the ones that could help me most."

When they sat down for dinner, all the light banter of the previous evening was missing. Also, Viraan had still not returned from Purawanbhag.

"Those stones that Viraan has gone to fetch might become the difference between the success and failure of my quest," the Akkadian said, "so, in case Viraan cannot make it back, I think I should postpone my start by a day."

"When it comes to a commitment of time, my cousin is usually one of the most dependable," Tiraak said. "Of course, unless it is out of his control, but between here and Purawanbhag, I cannot think of anything that could get outside his control."

Viraan arrived halfway through their dinner.

"I am famished," Viraan said, as he washed his face and hands, "and I am sorry that I got a little late, but as I have been neglecting my work for the last few days, things had really piled up in Purawanbhag."

"No harm done," the Akkadian said, clearly relieved, "you said you would be back within today, you did not say when."

"And even though your voice is calm, I can see the apprehension and impatience in your eyes, so before you ask – I have not forgotten your stones. I have come back with ten of them," Viraan told the Akkadian, "I have also checked them on the way here – they still glow in the dark when you put them underwater."

"Should I pack these up, Master?" Pasher asked, starting to stand up.

"No, finish your dinner first," the Akkadian smiled, "we can take care of it, when we check everything again tomorrow morning."

Unlike the previous day, the Akkadian and Pasher ate and drank with moderation. Tiraak insisted that they all retire to bed early.

The next morning, the Akkadian and Pasher finished all their final packing, including that of the glowing stones. Then, the Akkadian insisted that they check everything again with more care than urgency. After this was done, it was time for farewell. As decided the previous evening, they went to Runggoo's room, where he was waiting with the others.

Viraan wanted to bid farewell and leave first to give the others more privacy. But the Akkadian would have none of it.

"What I have to say, is to all of you," the Akkadian said with a tremor in his voice, "And hopefully, even if I am unable, Pasher will be able to convey these words and feelings to Nongru and my other close ones in Wacha. When I was in ki-en-ĝir[52], or Šumeru[53], as it is called in my tongue, I did not have many close ones. The only person I would call dear to me was Abgal – Ishme – who was my inspiration who taught me about your people and your tongue. The only other person in Kurm, who helped me without expecting something in return was a Givenlander called Vikoo. According to him, he did it for the sake of Ishme's friendship. Until I met you all, I did not understand him, for I never really knew true friendship. Before coming here,

---

[52]Sumer in Sumerian – this was the form used in formal speeches
[53]Sumer in Akkadian

I had never thought my journey would ever become more important than my destination. But now, I realize that it has. If I knew then everything I know now, and was given a choice before I started from Kurm, on whether I would rather have come to know you all or be successful in my quest, I would choose knowing you every day and twice on full moon. I know not whether I will see you all ever again, but my life has become more fulfilling for knowing you. If I ever make it to my goal that is the first thing I will thank them for."

The Akkadian stopped, not for the lack of words, but because he did not want to cry in front of his friends.

Runggoo came to the Akkadian and hugged him, "I would have rather not been born than not to know you. When you see my valley from the cave, I will see it through your eyes. I wish I could go with you, but that would only endanger your journey."

"I don't know what all this fuss is about," Tiraak scoffed heartily. "We won't be rid of our friend this easily. I am sure, he will turn up again when you least expect it, with another of his farfetched idea, which he will convince us can be achieved, and, of course, he will expect us to drop everything, and help him in achieving it. So, instead of goodbye, I say until we meet again."

Then Runggoo went to Pasher and surprised him with a hug and said, "Pasher, I am entrusting you with my friend's life. I am also looking forward to doing some climbing near your Wacha valley once you come back safely with my friend."

"I am a trader," Viraan said, "and so I think in terms of profit and loss. I think knowing you, even without the valuable inputs you have given us for improving things, would be a profitable thing. And I hope my cousin and Runggoo are right and I will see you again. By that time, I would have identified new issues, which you could help me solve. I know all of you are having trouble holding back your tears. But I say, why hold them back, from what I hear crying from time to time cleans up your eyes."

They proceeded to the riverside, where Tiraak asked Viraan to go along with the Akkadian to Ankal and ensure everything was fine with the animals, and also that the loading was done properly. Tiraak and Runggoo stayed on the side of the river for a long time until the boat disappeared into the horizon.

Chapter 11

The Akkadian's Tale V

When they arrived at Ankal, Viraan's men were already waiting for them. All the things were soon unloaded by these men. It was decided that the Akkadian and Pasher would leave for Pparaha the next morning. Viraan informed the Akkadian that he had some other business to take care of. But as he was leaving, the Akkadian overheard him instruct the lodge keeper to ensure that the Akkadian and the Pasher had full privacy and realized why he was leaving. The Akkadian called out to Viraan to stop and went down to join him.

"Viraan," the Akkadian called, "I know you are very busy and need to take care of your affairs here. But, I was planning to go over the route from here to Lakho with Pasher over dinner tonight, and was wondering if you too, could join us."

"What I need to do will take no time at all," Viraan replied. "I will be back momentarily. This lodging does not allow eating in our rooms, so we can have the discussions before dinner."

Viraan came back very soon. The Akkadian then went over the route that would take him from Ankal to Pparaha and then on to Lakho. After he was done, Viraan confirmed that the Akkadian had got everything right. They only talked about the weather, crops and trade during dinner and retired to bed early, and were up early the next morning, rested and ready for their travel.

The loading of the animals was done by Viraan's men. After the loading was completed by his men, Viraan checked everything personally. Then he ensured that the Akkadian had with him the communications he had given for his partner in Pparaha and his partner's partner in Lakho. After ensuring all this, he bid a farewell to the Akkadian and Pasher.

They started westwards towards Pparaha. When they camped that night, the Akkadian finally told Pasher about his destination and all he had heard about the White Gods from Abgal and Runggoo. He, however, did not tell him the purpose for his trip. He had never talked about that to anyone, since his initial discussions with Ishme. Even though they could have reached Pparaha in less than two days, they decided to go slower, in order to reach Pparaha in the morning instead of close to dusk.

As they approached the north-eastern gates of Pparaha, they sighted a few strange pillars on both sides of the path. There were quite a few large birds hovering around or sitting on top these pillars. As they came closer, the Akkadian thought he saw some other movement. It was then that the Akkadian realized that he was finally seeing what his Abgal had described as 'sat on stakes'. But as eloquent as Ishme was, descriptions, however detailed, could not prepare anyone for the real thing. By now the Akkadian could see clearly. There were seven such pillars in all. The one nearest, was the one where he had thought he had seen some movement. It was clearly a man trying to beat away the vultures. His feet were gnawed and bleeding. The Akkadian looked around, but could not see any sign of jackals. *They must only come at night*, he thought. One of his ears had been pecked off. Then coming closer, he saw the blood and excretion rolling down the pillar, seeing this and the other bodies, four of them clearly alive, the Akkadian promptly threw up his breakfast. Pasher, however, seemed totally unperturbed.

"Pasher," the Akkadian asked, "how come you are not disgusted by this?"

"Well, Master," Pasher answered, "as I don't know what their crimes were, I cannot really feel bad for them. I have seen worse done to innocent animals to improve their taste. And I have heard these punishments are reserved for really heinous crimes."

The Akkadian could not help but see Pasher's logic, however bizarre it sounded at first.

Viraan's partner, Divyaan, was very easy to find. And he was a giant of a man, as Viraan had mentioned. He immediately took them to their lodgings.

The Akkadian was very surprised to find that they were already expected and made no secret of it.

"Ho, ho," Divyaan guffawed, "that is exactly like Viraan, isn't it? He sent me a message about five days ago. But in case I did not get the message, his way of managing your expectations was not to tell you about it—no knowledge, no expectations. But where are my manners? You don't look too well. Is everything all right? Did something untoward happen during your journey from Parroo? There I go again, asking too many questions without letting you reply."

"The journey was fine," the Akkadian answered, feeling better in this jovial giant's company, "and once I wash up, I will be fine. I had not expected the sight that greeted us on arrival."

"Of course," Divyaan said, "you arrived from the northeast gate, didn't you? I sincerely apologize. Why don't you wash up? And do any other required ablutions, freshen up, change clothes, or whatever you usually do after your journeys and anything else you need to. Have some refreshments, take a rest. I will be back to take you to my place for dinner."

"We really don't want to be a bother," the Akkadian said, "and you do not have to put yourself out for us. I am sure we can manage dinner by ourselves. But before you leave, could you give me some time to freshen up? I need your help and guidance on a few things."

"Of course," Divyaan said, "I will wait. As for dinner, unless you are tired, or would like privacy, it will not be a bother, but a pleasure. My wife always complains that I do not compliment her cooking enough, so if you come and pay some compliments, it would mean peace for me for a few days. If you have any dietary needs, do not worry. My wife loves a challenge. There I go again, taking up all the time. First, please go ahead and wash up."

The Akkadian returned quickly after washing up. He brought with him the instructions for Divyaan and the one for his partner in Lakho, which needed Divyaan's seal.

"As you will see from Viraan's communications," the Akkadian said, "there are some things that we need to acquire here in Pparaha. If possible, we would like to get started today. The night is long enough for our rest. And if it is really not a bother, we would love to join you for dinner."

"It is no bother. It will be our pleasure," Divyaan said again with a laugh, as he quickly read through the communications and also scanned the list of things a couple of times. "None of these should be a problem. But

Viraan also mentions that if you need anything else, it should be provided, as if it was on his list. So, is there anything that you would like to add, perhaps, a new house and many camels for Divyaan as a present from Viraan? Ho Ho Ho." Divyaan laughed at his own joke.

The Akkadian joined him courteously, "There is only one more thing. I need a small bag made of transparent fish skin. I have seen those used by pearl divers. I am not sure what you call them. It does not have to be made of fish skin, but it has to be transparent and waterproof."

"I will ask the midwife," Divyaan said, contemplating. "She knows all about animal and plant products. The best thing is, she always minds her own business and can be trusted. If this is available in Pparaha, she will find it. For the other items, I don't think both of you need to go out to get them. What I mean is that things are a little delicate here at the moment, and one stranger who looks a little different – no offense to you – going to the marketplace will raise some eyebrows, but two strangers, both looking a little different, and yet not like each other, may not be the best thing. Especially, as these items are not usually purchased in Pparaha by outsiders. So, I may have a better idea. I will get someone to deliver these garments and headgear of different quality to my place. You choose what you need in the comfort of my house, and we will send the rest back. And if you want more than one of any of the things, I will arrange for these to be delivered to my house tomorrow. Let me go and arrange that, and I will be back to take you to my house for the leather inspection and dinner."

After Divyaan left, the Akkadian looked upwards, thanking his fate again for bringing the best people in Givenland to his aid.

Divyaan was back just after dusk and took the Akkadian and Pasher to his place.

"You are a lucky man," Divyaan said, while they were on the way to his house. "I managed to find the transparent bag you wanted, and it is made of the inner skin of a particular fish, though it does not smell of fish at all. As I had said, if anyone could find it, our midwife could. And she always minds her own business and can be trusted."

The first thing that hit them as they entered Divyaan's house was the smell of leather. They saw huge piles of different leather garments and headgear heaped on the floor of the inner courtyard.

"Don't tell my wife that everything has been arranged by Viraan," Divyaan said in a conspiring whisper. "If she knows that you can get anything you want and Viraan will settle for you later – and that is exactly what his letter says – she is going to elope with one of you and go on a shopping spree." He burst out laughing at his own joke.

Pasher took his time in identifying everything he needed. While he was doing this, Divyaan gave the transparent bag to the Akkadian.

"I hope this works," Divyaan said. "I know it is small, but according to the midwife, this is the largest. So, if you needed something larger, I am not sure how I can help. You see …"

"This will work perfectly," the Akkadian said quickly, "it is exactly the size I wanted."

"We will need three more of these leather vests and one more of this leather outer-garment," Pasher finally said, looking from the Akkadian to Divyaan and back. "And this is everything else we need." Saying this, Pasher dropped an assortment of items at the Akkadian's feet.

"Even though it is hard to believe seeing all these piles of stuff," the Akkadian said, "but is there anything that you need that we don't have here."

"If we can get the three vests and the outer-garment, we will have everything we need," Pasher said. The Akkadian nodded appreciatively, and observed with pleasure that Pasher was following his instructions of not referring to him as 'Master' in front of others. Pasher had agreed reluctantly, but was firm that he would still call the Akkadian 'Master' when they were alone.

"Then let us wash the leather smell off our hands and proceed to dinner," Divyaan said.

"I need to talk a little less now," Divyaan again said in his conspiring whisper, as they approached the kitchen, "the wife... she does not like me talking too much. She says I don't give anyone else a chance to talk."

Divyaan introduced his guests to his wife, Kiraa, and poured out some raajaraas for them, including for his wife. Kiraa brought out a platter of different types of spiced vegetables and meat.

"I hope you like this," Kiraa smiled brightly, "but please do not fill yourselves up before dinner. Also my husband says you may start your journey soon, tomorrow, if possible. As I told him, I will give you some packed food when you leave. Some of these will have to be eaten within a couple of days, while some will last for days. I am sure you will get many other interesting and tasty things to eat on your journey. But as I always say, home food is home food."

Both the Akkadian and Pasher were surprised to hear that they were leaving the next day. They were not planning on idling, but they had not told Divyaan that they would be leaving the next day, either.

"I think leaving as early as possible is a good idea," Divyaan said, as if he was agreeing with the Akkadian. "With the situation being a little delicate in Pparaha at present, you never know what to expect."

"Divyaan, this is the second time you have mentioned about the situation being delicate," the Akkadian said carefully. "What situation are you referring to?"

"Our previous Chief High Priest has just passed away," Divyaan said for the first time, weighing his words carefully, "and we have a new Chief High Priest. Our new Chief High Priest believes that our previous Chief High Priest was too kind and that has led to a rot in our society. Thus, he is currently cleansing the town. Many people are being exiled and quite a few are being sat on stakes. That is what you saw as you came in to our town today. We understand that a clean society is very important, but during the twenty-five years of the previous Chief High Priest, we only had three people, two repeat rapists and a murderer, condemned to be sat on stakes. However, forty-six people were sat on stakes in the last twenty days. So, it is taking us a little time getting used to it."

"Nice story," Kiraa said sarcastically. "Why don't you tell our guests the truth? Or are we supposed to be afraid even inside our own houses? Everyone who has been sat on stakes was someone who Apaan, that is our new esteemed Chief High Priest, feels he has been slighted by. Our previous Chief High Priest had thought he had cleaned up the Temple Sanctuary of all its bad elements, but he was too naive to see Apaan for what he was. Apaan waited and kept on acting like a lamb, which convinced the Chief High Priest to announce him as his successor. Now that the Chief High Priest has passed away, he is showing the mix of snake and jackal that he really is. Mark my words: he will cause the destruction of this town."

As Kiraa was saying this, Divyaan looked more and more nervous.

"Wife," Divyaan snapped, "Enough! Please, for the sake of our children do not repeat these things even when you are alone." Then turning to his guests, he said, "I hope I can count on your discretion. You all must have realized that I have a habit of prattling on. So, my wife needs to say things to keep up with me. She does not mean any of these things that she is saying. I am sure she does not even remember what she has said. Women, you know, their thoughts jump about so wildly. I can assure you that she means no harm. And in any case she does not know what she is talking about."

"Of all the gall …" Kiraa started, but the Akkadian raised his hand to stop her.

"If it pleases both my hosts, may I speak first?" the Akkadian asked, and without waiting continued. "Everything I say, I think I say for both Pasher and me. You are very highly thought of by Viraan. And Viraan is someone whom I have come to know quite well and respect a lot. People talk about being able to trust someone with their lives, but in my case, I have honestly trusted him with both my future and my life. Whatever you tell me will never be repeated, and if your wife insists that Apaan is a monster, I am ready to draw big teeth and horns on him. So, there is nothing to explain. To us, Pparaha is whatever you both tell us it is."

"Thank you for your kind words," Kiraa replied before Divyaan could say anything, "my husband is right. In these times, I should not have said what I said in front of people I have just met. I am thankful that what I said is safe with you. I also agree with my husband that you should leave Pparaha as soon as possible. I am sure this is a phase, and if you come back here, in a few weeks or months, everything would become like before. At least, I hope it will."

The Akkadian bowed his head. "We will leave tomorrow, as soon as we can get the leather garments that Pasher has requested of your husband."

"It might look strange if you leave midday, for usually everyone starts their journey early in the morning. Why don't you start first thing tomorrow morning and do some fishing on the banks of Airavati? I will bring the additional garments to you there. In this way, I can also make sure that you get a good boat to cross the Airavati with your animals. By the way, Viraan did mention in his instructions …" Divyaan prattled on about Viraan's many instructions.

The Akkadian smiled, happy to see that the man was jovial and talkative again.

"I like your idea. We will leave tomorrow morning and do some fishing near the Airavati."

They finished their meal. Both the Akkadian and Pasher, without any prompting from the other, drank very little raajaraas. They did not want any mishap in Pparaha, especially if things were even half as bad as Kiraa had said they were. They left Divyaan's place soon after dinner, with both their hosts agreeing that being out late might not be the best idea.

The Akkadian and Pasher left early next morning and came to the banks of Airavati. They took out the fishing rods that Divyaan had given them and after Pasher had dug out some worms, started fishing, with Pasher catching quite a few fish, while the Akkadian, at best, gave swimming lessons to the worms he was using as bait. By the time Divyaan got there with the leather articles, the Akkadian had still not caught any fish and had also managed to lose his fishing rod.

Divyaan had also brought with him the home cooked food that Kiraa had promised. They quickly grilled three of the fishes, and sat down to eat these along with the barley and wheat pancakes and the curried goat that Kiraa had packed separately for their lunch. Divyaan continued his chatter, but the Akkadian stopped listening and started thinking ahead about his journey. When they were done with their lunch, Divyaan took them a little downriver, and arranged for a boat to take them across. After taking leave from Divyaan, the Akkadian and Pasher crossed Airavati and continued westward.

They rode in silence for a while. The Akkadian spent his time thinking about how his quest would end. Would it be as fulfilling as he had foreseen, or would it even surpass his own expectations? Then suddenly, he wondered with apprehension, if fate was leading him on to the greatest of disappointments. He was pondering about all this, when he realized that it was getting close to sunset. As he looked towards Pasher, he realized that Pasher seemed to be in some sort of discomfort. He would first nod his head side to side, his ears almost touching his shoulders. Then he would touch his chest with his chin and rotate his head in full circles. He would then look about in all directions and repeat his previous movements again.

"Pasher, are you all right? Are you feeling sick?" the Akkadian asked, riding his camel parallel to Pasher's.

"Master," Pasher said, "I don't think so, but I am not sure. I think I feel fine, but something seems to be bearing down on me. I cannot really explain it. I am sorry if my movements are bothering you. I will try to control myself."

"I think I know the problem," the Akkadian said with a smile, "first, let me ask you something. Have you ever been outside Wacha for this long?"

"No, Master," Pasher protested, "but please be reassured that I am not feeling homesick."

"That was not what I meant," the Akkadian said. "When I left my home in Kurm for my journey to Givenland, after a few days, I started feeling restless, too. Like you, I was sure I was not homesick. It took me some time before I realized why. I had grown up always having the Purattu River flow in the background, and I was so used to it that, sub-consciously, I was missing not having it around me anymore. For you, the feeling must be even stronger. You have always had mountains to look at in the horizon, actually closer than the horizon. Initially in Wacha, I used to find being surrounded by mountains really overbearing. For you, it is the opposite, for you must be feeling naked and unprotected, without the mountains you've been used to all your life. There is no quick fix for this. Only time will heal it."

"You know, Master," Pasher said with admiration, "I think you are right." He remained silent for a few moments, and then spoke again, hesitantly, "Could I ask you something? I have been thinking about it for some time now."

"Pasher," the Akkadian said reining in his camel and waiting for Pasher to do the same, "let us start looking for a good place to spend the night. I think we should travel only during daylight. After we have settled the animals down, let us address your question."

"Of course, Master," Pasher replied and pointed to a cluster of trees, "I think that place looks as good a spot as I have seen since we crossed Airavati. I cannot see any stream nearby, but I think we have packed enough water. We will fill up the next opportunity we get. If we continue at this pace, we should reach the Ashkini day after tomorrow, sometime in the afternoon. And as Master has told me, the next part of the journey will be done along the banks of Ashkini and Vitasta[54]. Water will, thus, no longer be an issue for a long time."

"You are right," the Akkadian said. "Why don't I give you a hand to take off the loads from the animals, and then you can settle them for the night, while I light a fire."

By the time Pasher had joined him, the Akkadian was almost done with heating up the food.

"Well, Pasher," the Akkadian stirred the goat curry, "we will be together for quite some time. And most of this time, we will not have any other company. I am sure we will find many things that irritate us about the other. The only way we can alleviate this is by being totally open with each

---

[54]The River Jhelum

other. And if we have a question, we should immediately ask the other without waiting. So tell me, what has been bothering you?"

"Master," Pasher protested, "nothing has been bothering me. It is quite the opposite. When you quickly associated me missing my mountain with you missing your river, it reminded me of something I have been observing for some time. And Master, do let me know if you think I am intruding, I have seen that even though you never seem to be homesick, you connect things very quickly to memories from your land. Does that mean you are homesick but are not showing it?"

"We will be spending a great amount of time in each other's company, and intruding will be difficult to avoid. So from now on, don't hesitate. If I don't want to answer, I will let you know." the Akkadian said with a broad smile. "In my land, there is a saying: your house can be where your body is but your home is where your liver[55] is. My liver is with my wife, Nongru, and the others in Wacha. I left a piece of my liver with Runggoo, Tiraak and Viraan, as well. But, if you are asking me whether I miss my house, yes, sometimes I do. Sometimes, I see, hear, smell or taste something that takes me back to my childhood in Kurm. Sometimes, I hear someone talk like Ishme, my beloved teacher and guide, and I remember our time together, as if it were yesterday. He is the only person from Kurm that I really miss sometimes. My father is dead, and even if he was alive, I don't think we would ever miss each other. My mother was still alive when I left Kurm, but again, I am sure she was happy that I left Kurm, for she will not be reminded anymore that she is not a young woman, but a mother of a grown man."

The Akkadian paused on seeing the sadness in Pasher's eyes. Then he continued with a big smile, for Pasher's benefit.

"I may have given you the wrong impression. I am to be blamed equally for the relationship with my parents. How I associate things back to seemingly unrelated things from the past, and yes, it is from the past not from Kurm alone, is something I have to thank Ishme for. Ishme had introduced me to Vikoo, who actually helped me get here. Ishme told me that Vikoo was a very intelligent man, but what made him exceptional was his application of knowledge. It did not matter where he gathered what knowledge, he always knew when and where to apply whatever he knew. I am not a natural like Vikoo, but I realized that if I let my thoughts flow, without consciously looking for an answer, I apply my knowledge better. And over time, I have trained myself to do this. Does this answer your question?"

---

[55] In Ancient Sumer, liver was associated with things related to affection and love

"Yes, Master," Pasher replied, "I will try to keep this last part in mind and see if I can improve myself. And you are right; I should have asked you earlier. Then, I could have started improving myself earlier."

"Now, I want to intrude," the Akkadian asked, "but please, answer only if you want to. The Teller told me that there were two women to every ten men in your valley. He also mentioned that every man in Wacha got married within a couple of years of their Coming of Age ceremony. Except for the Teller and the Priest that is, as they have taken an oath of celibacy. So, why you are not married, yet?"

"The question is much less personal than the answer," Pasher said. After a thoughtful silence, he continued, "but I will tell you. When I was of about ten summers, I had an accident while on a climbing trip. A couple of years later, the Medicine man told the boys who were coming of age about how babies were made. I realized, and the Medicine man confirmed, that because of the accident, I could never be a father. I don't know about your land, but in our valley, if a married couple does not have children, it is the wife who is blamed. So, I decided that it is best if I don't get married."

"I am really sorry," the Akkadian said with genuine grief, "especially for asking you to talk about something that must be indeed painful."

"I know you are," Pasher replied with tears in his eyes. "I knew you would share my grief, rather than make fun of me. Otherwise, I never tell people about this, out of fear, that they will make fun of me. As you have correctly observed, there are very few men who do not marry. People usually distrust them. They make sure to keep their children away from these men for obvious reasons. I like children and I would love to be able to play with them. But, I know I will never have the opportunity to do so."

"That is even sadder," the Akkadian said, now close to tears, "I know it is not much, but I do understand your pain and would like to do something to ease it, but I can't think of anything I can do."

They sat and ate in silence.

For the next two days, they started early each morning, travelling away from the rising sun and ended their day travelling towards the setting sun.

The sun was almost setting on the second day, when the Akkadian made the announcement.

"I think we will be reaching the Ashkini soon," he said, sniffing at the air around him. "The air has that river smell. I think we should camp about a mahahath away from the river."

"I think I see the perfect place," Pasher said pointing towards a clump of trees in the distance, "and, Master, if you don't mind, after seeing to the animals I would like to go to the river and catch some fish. Divyaan was kind enough to leave me one of the rods."

"Let's unload the animals together," the Akkadian said. "Then, I can take care of the others, while you go to the river in one of the camels. I will get a fire ready for you to grill the fish. Take a knife with you, so as to gut and scale the fish near the river. We don't want to attract strange animals."

The Akkadian made the animals comfortable for the night and after making a fire waited for Pasher. Left alone and being tired he dozed off.

"What do you seek in the Great Northern White Mountains?" a voice asked.

"I seek to meet the White Gods fabled to live there," the Akkadian answered.

"How does one meet a fable?" the voice asked.

"I want to find out for myself whether they exist. If they do, I want to meet them," the Akkadian answered and then added, "who are you?"

"I am myself. The question is *who are you*? Why have you travelled to these faraway lands? Why should you be allowed to meet Gods that you are yet to believe in? How does one know what nefarious purpose is hidden in that black heart of yours?" the voice continued.

"You are right. I have sometimes wondered who I am as well," the Akkadian pondered. "However, I am sure that my purpose, though not selfless, is definitely not nefarious. And I cannot believe any God, whether they are Akkadian, Sumerian or Givenlander – would deny a seeker of the truth. And I am seeking the truth in the myth that there exists White Gods who live in the Great Northern White Mountains. I am seeking the truth and not planning to harm anyone, so, my quest should be blessed, not cursed."

"Go in peace on your quest, Akkadian. And the Gods, they are not all White," the voice said.

The Akkadian woke up to find Pasher shaking him.

He jumped up and looked all around, but there was no one else there.

"When did you come back?" the Akkadian asked, "Did you see anyone here?"

"Master," Pasher said, "I have just come back. I did not see anyone here, but you were speaking in your sleep. I have never heard you do that before, that is the reason why I decided to wake you up."

"Are you sure that there was no one here?" the Akkadian insisted.

"I am sure, Master," Pasher replied. "I came back to find you talking to yourself, quite audibly. You were saying something about blessed and cursed."

"Then you must have heard him speak, too? That the Gods were not all white," the Akkadian asked.

"No, Master," Pasher said, "I did not hear anything about Gods. I am sure you must have been dreaming."

"Yes, you are most probably right," the Akkadian replied, without conviction and continuing to look around. "Why don't you start grilling the fish? I think I will go for a short walk to clear my mind."

"Master," Pasher said looking towards his toes, "this time, I had your luck, and have returned empty handed from my fishing."

"That's not a problem," the Akkadian said, still feeling restless. "Please get whatever you would like for dinner ready for both of us, and I will be back soon."

The Akkadian first walked to where the animals lay. None of the animals were sleeping; they looked restless. The Akkadian was not sure whether he was imagining this, or if it was he who had made them restless. He started walking in widening concentric circles around the camp. He was ready to start back towards Pasher when something caught his eye. Under a tree, he could see some strange hoof marks. On closer observation, he also found some footmarks – as if someone had alighted from a mount and gone on to climb the tree. He could not identify the animal by its hoofmarks. It looked similar to the donkeys from Sumer or the asses of Givenland, but the markings were larger and more elongated than either. And the hoofmarks were too small for the Sumerian ašša. He finally gave up and went back to Pasher.

"Master, is everything all right?" Pasher asked, still a little concerned. "Shall we eat now or would you prefer to take some more time?"

"No, let us eat," the Akkadian said, "I am fine now. I think you were right. I might be more tired than I realized I was. Tomorrow, let us start a little later than usual. In any case, we will have to wait for the ferries to start in the morning. I am sure they do not start at sunrise, as we have been doing. That reminds me – when you went by the river, did you see any sign of the ferries and where they ply from?"

"I think I saw some lights downriver," Pasher said, "but I cannot be sure."

"Let us worry about it tomorrow morning then," the Akkadian said.

The next day, they broke camp later than normal. After reaching the Ashkini, they turned left and travelled downriver. Soon, they came across a ferry, which agreed to take them across the Ashkini. The fees they were charged was within the range of what Divyaan had advised.

After crossing the Ashkini, they turned upriver, travelling north-northeast. For the next two days, they travelled upriver, until they came to the confluence of Vitasta. They turned northwards – upriver on the Vitasta. Whenever they came upon a town or village, or spotted any human settlement, they circled around these. They had decided that they would avoid unnecessary contact, until they came to Lakho. On the third night, the Akkadian and Pasher were suddenly awakened. While both of them were still wondering what had woken them up, they heard a blood-curdling howl.

They jumped up, checked on their animals, and then moved quickly but cautiously towards the sound. As it was a full moon, they could see everything clearly. They heard the howling a few more times and then finally came to a very strange sight. A man, with long, matted hair and beard, clad only in a loincloth, was howling towards the skies. Both the Akkadian and Pasher looked around, but could not find the reason for the howls. This man seemed to be howling at the moon.

"Can we help you?" the Akkadian asked as they came near this strange man.

"Who are you?" the man asked, "and how dare you disturb this most important dialogue between the Sun, the Moon, the Demons and I?"

"What in the name of Pashubar[56] are you talking about?" Pasher exclaimed.

The Akkadian was a little taken aback, as he had never heard Pasher curse before this. But he recovered quickly, and put his forefinger to his lips, indicating that Pasher be quiet.

---

[56] The main deity of the people of Wacha

"We are sorry, o revered one," the Akkadian said. "We, simple folks, do not understand such great things. So, we made the mistake of intruding."

"It is too late to be sorry," the man said, "now I will have to start my deliberations again next month."

"Why not tomorrow, Respected Sir?" the Akkadian asked, still humouring the half-naked man.

"You are really stupid, are you not?" the man answered. "You must be the person based on whom stupidity is defined. And your friend here must be the second most stupid person, as he is only a hundred times less stupid than you."

"Yes, Respected One," the Akkadian continued with the charade, "I am indeed stupid. I really hope you will enlighten me."

"I will have to do that, won't I?" the man answered. "I cannot forget my duties just because I am surrounded by people who don't understand it. It is only after full moon that the demons start eating away at the moon. The only way they would be scared away is if all the beings screamed at the demons. But, every full moon, it is only I who do this. So, they manage to eat away at the moon. I am getting weak with age, and soon, we will be without the moon."

"But, O wise one," the Akkadian continued in his flowery tone, "the moon is strong and is always able to grow back."

"I am sorry," the man answered, "your friend here; the second most stupid person cannot be a hundred times less stupid than you. No one could. He must be a thousand times less stupid than you. Do you really think that the Moon can recover by himself? He is back in full strength because I nurse him back. A few years ago, I was sick, and so the Moon completely disappeared on a full moon. I had to come out and fight the demons and give the Moon courage to come back. I do not have time even to rest when I am sick. The Moon grows back because I give him confidence that it is all right to do so."

"Of course, you do," the Akkadian said still humouring the stranger.

"Any which way, it is too late now," the stranger said, "I will have to make sure that the moon does not lose heart. I am sure I will finally defeat the demons in the next full moon. If not, then surely during the next. And if not that, I am sure I will definitely be victorious in the one after. Do you have anything to eat?"

"We do," the Akkadian answered, "but tell me, O Revered One, when did you start protecting the moon?"

"It was many springs back on a night exactly like this that the Gods came to me," the man answered.

"O Wise one, which God came to you," the Akkadian asked with interest.

"O Stupid One," the man said mimicking the Akkadian, "can you keep quiet or do you have to keep talking to show how stupid you are? Let me start again. No, let me eat first. And, then, let me sleep. Then, I will tell you."

"But …" the Akkadian started to protest, but realized this odd stranger may become a little more coherent after he had slept. "But, we will need a little time to warm up your food."

"I don't care. You can give it to me cold," the man said.

"Master," Pasher intervened, "I will find something that he can eat, without cooking or heating."

The stranger wolfed down everything that Pasher gave him. And immediately lay down, curled up and went to sleep.

"Master, shall we also sleep now?" Pasher asked.

"You go ahead," the Akkadian said. "I think I will make sure this man does not harm us or run away, while we are sleeping. I have a feeling that I may find his story of interest. But, I need at least one of us well rested. So, as I said, you can go ahead and sleep."

The Akkadian spent the rest of the night sitting next to the fire, keeping his attention focused on the strange man. His instincts told him that he needed to know more about this man. As the night passed and dawn was almost on them, the Akkadian was finding it more and more difficult to stay awake. He was almost dozing off when the stranger woke up. When he saw the Akkadian, he cringed away from him like a wounded animal. The Akkadian was careful not to make eye contact or any sudden movement, and spoke without looking directly at the stranger's direction.

"You were too hungry to wait for our food to be warmed yesterday night," the Akkadian said. "Instead, you decided to eat the food cold. The fire has not gone off, so if you are hungry, I can heat up some food."

"Who are you?" the stranger asked suspiciously. "Have they sent you from Ilpurjal[57]?"

By this time, Pasher had also woken up and had come and stood next to the fire. Bare-chested, with muscular figure, and with the fire reflecting off his body, he looked quite terrifying. The half-naked stranger cringed away, even further on seeing him. The Akkadian could see that the stranger was very close to taking flight. Very carefully, without moving or turning he spoke.

"This is Pasher," the Akkadian said, "or if you remember from last night, the second stupidest man in all the lands. I am of course the first." Then, the Akkadian laughed – as if at his own joke. He got the exact reaction he wanted from Pasher, a broad smile. And as always, Pasher's whole demeanour changed with his smile. Instead of the terrifying person of few moments ago, he looked extremely friendly and approachable. The stranger relaxed a little and the Akkadian continued, "We will be having breakfast soon. Would you like to share some of our hot food?"

"I am hungry. And when you are hungry, you eat," the stranger said, not giving a direct answer. "But first, I need some dhutura."

The Akkadian realized that some of the stranger's craziness must have come from chewing of dhutura leaves. He also knew that any chance of a sensible conversation with him would be gone if this man consumed dhutura again.

"You have to choose," the Akkadian said casually. "We plan to start on our journey soon after breakfast. And we will have our breakfast now. You can go in search of your dhutura or eat with us. If you go, then do not bother to come back looking for us, for we will be gone."

"All right, I will eat with you," the stranger considered. "I can always have the dhutura later."

As per the Akkadian's instructions, Pasher heated up a sumptuous breakfast. If the stranger was having any second thoughts, they disappeared with the aroma.

After breakfast was almost ready, the Akkadian turned to the stranger.

"Go wash up. Make sure your hands and face are clean. Rinse your mouth. In our camp, we eat like men, not gorge like animals."

The stranger licked his lips. The aroma of the food was too forceful an argument to challenge. When the stranger was gone, the Akkadian went to where Pasher was heating the food.

---

[57]A Town in Central Givenland/ Meluhha on banks of River Jhelum

"We will not be travelling today," the Akkadian said. "I will explain later, but can you please mix a strong portion of Kanuchara[58] into this man's soup, before he comes back. Make sure you put in enough herbs to mask any taste or smell of it."

After the stranger came back, they started eating. The stranger gulped down his portions with the soup, looking defiantly towards the Akkadian. The Akkadian did not say anything. The Akkadian ate slowly and when the stranger asked for more, he gave him his remaining portions. After they had finished eating, the stranger noisily licked his fingers.

"All right, I have eaten," the stranger said, barely able to keep his eyes open. "Now I will go and get my dhutura." He tried to get up, but sat down again. "I may have eaten too much. You all can continue on your journey. I will take a nap and then …" he curled up and fell asleep before he could finish what he was saying.

The Akkadian signalled Pasher to follow him.

"You must be wondering what I am up to" the Akkadian asked.

"I am sure you have your reasons and will tell me what I need to know," Pasher said. "But yes, I have no idea what your business is with this strange dirty man."

"I think he may know something that may be important to our quest," the Akkadian explained. "It may come to nothing, but I want to be sure. First, though, I need to get him a little more coherent. He may be almost mad, but I think dhutura is playing its part, as well. If he sleeps until evening, and we can talk before he goes and gets his dhutura, I think I can confirm whether there is anything to my thoughts."

Pasher went to the nearby banks of Vitasta to try to catch some fish. The Akkadian started thinking on the best approach to keep this strange man away from his dhutura. He also needed a way to get him talking, without seeming too inquisitive. After some time, Pasher was back.

"Master," Pasher said triumphantly holding up eight medium-sized fish. "I did not have your luck this time. I have gutted and cleaned these near the river, downwind from here. I think I will start grilling these now."

"Pasher, let us grill these after sunset," the Akkadian said. "I do not want our friend here to be stirred up by the aroma of grilling fish."

Pasher had been overly generous with the Kanuchara. The stranger, already tired and not in the best of health, was still asleep when the sunset.

---

[58]Valerian plant – the root of which is used as a sedative

After sunset, Pasher started grilling his fish. The stranger woke up, as the Akkadian had predicted, and immediately cringed away.

"Who are you?" he asked, but before anyone could answer continued, "I know you. You gave me food." Then, remembering more, he continued. "But, you lied. You said you will be starting on your journey after breakfast. But, it is dark again and you are still here. Why are you not gone?"

"Well, look who has come back to the land of the living," the Akkadian said. "And see how thankful and sorry he is. He is sorry that he has delayed us. And he is thankful that we stayed back to protect him."

"Thankful and sorry for what?" the stranger asked. "You must have stayed back for your own ill purpose. I have survived alone in this place. Why should I suddenly need your protection now? Any which way, I will bid farewell now and go look for my dhutura."

"Look for the big cat, you mean," the Akkadian said calmly. "Give him or her, our regards and please wish it a good appetite from us, as well."

The stranger looked at the Akkadian suspiciously.

"What big cat?" the stranger asked.

"Well, I did not ask its name now, did I?" the Akkadian answered. "I think that is what you should ask, first. Perhaps it will reply before taking the first mouthful."

"What do you mean?" the stranger asked. "Can you please speak plainly?"

"I surely can," the Akkadian said. "Soon after you had eaten our food, you fell asleep. You were sleeping like a dead man, when we had started to pack up to start our journey. That is when Pasher, with his sharp ears, first heard its chuffing. I still wanted to leave, but Pasher here is too kind hearted. He felt you will surely be killed if we were to leave you alone. Now, please go and look for your dhutura. Hopefully, the Chuffer will find you. However, whether you find your dhutura or Pasher's Chuffer, please do not bother coming back. You have already caused us enough delays."

The stranger looked at the Akkadian, not sure what to believe any more.

"I have never heard or seen any big cats near here," the stranger finally protested.

"Well, both of us must have made a mistake then and wasted a whole day," the Akkadian said sarcastically. "Or maybe even big cats do not like dhutura-spiced flesh. Why don't you go out and find out?"

The stranger gave the Akkadian an indignant look. Then, he walked to where Pasher was grilling the fish.

"I am really thankful to you for not leaving me at the mercy of this big cat," the stranger said to Pasher, "I am also sorry that I have delayed your journey. I am also sorry if I misbehaved yesterday night."

The Akkadian was happy that he was being ignored, for this meant that the stranger would be more open to Pasher. However, the Akkadian was not sure how well Pasher could take advantage of the situation. He need not have worried though, he soon realized.

"Forget about yesterday; you were not yourself," Pasher said in a very gentle and friendly voice. Then, he stopped and gave a reproachful look towards the Akkadian, leaving the stranger in no doubt that Pasher and the Akkadian were not in agreement. Turning back to the stranger, he continued, "Why don't we make a fresh start? Let me introduce myself, I am Pasher, I am a traveller from Pparaha." Being with the Akkadian had rubbed off on the man from Wacha, for he had learnt to become suspicious of everyone and was being thrifty with the truth.

"I am Kinjyaan," the stranger said joining his palms together, "and I am originally from Ilpurjal, which is south of here."

"It is nice to make your acquaintance," Pasher said, "I know my friend," then glaring again at the Akkadian continued, "told me not to care, but I would still like to know why you are living like this in the wild. My friend told me that it was none of my business, and even if I asked, you would most probably not share such things with a stranger."

"Shows how much your friend knows, doesn't it?" Kinjyaan sneered, and opened up to Pasher. "As I said, I am from Ilpurjal. I liked travelling since I was very young. I even travelled to places further than you can imagine, with my father who traded with Sumer. Just after I came of age, he died when his ship was wrecked by a storm. It was then that I started trading in Lapis Lazuli. I became quite successful. And I was to marry one of the prettiest girls in Ilpurjal. However, once after returning from Runaka, I found out that my betrothed had been chosen to be a Dasasa. It was then, that a friend informed me of some atrocious things that were happening at our Temple Sanctuary. I will not repeat these, as I do not think you will believe me. Any which way, I decided to run away from Ilpurjal. My betrothed agreed to run away with me, but she made the mistake of

180

mentioning this to one of the other Dasasas. One day before our planned getaway, the Chief High Priest declared that I was infected by some strange disease during my travels to Runaka. As this disease had no cure and was contagious, I was being banished from the town immediately, and if I were to be seen in Ilpurjal again, I would be sat on a stake. At first, I thought I would move to another town and plan on eloping with my betrothed at a later date. But, I soon found out that I was being naïve. I was not welcome in any human settlement. The Chief Priest made sure that everyone had heard about my disease. So, I started sleeping out in the open, eating what I could find. Finally, I came here. If you look around, you will see that there are many dhutura plants around here. That is why I started living in this area, spending my days chewing on dhutura and waiting for death."

The Akkadian was a little disappointed, as there was no mention of the Gods. He thought he might have to intervene, but then, found that he had underestimated his clever pupil, Pasher.

"That is sad, indeed," Pasher said. "Who can blame you for cursing the Moon? That was what you were doing yesterday, were you not? I know you said something about demons being fed or something, but as my friend explained to me, that was the dhutura talking."

"As I have said before, shows you how much he knows," Kinjyaan said, "I am really surprised that you tolerate such a person and call him your friend. I was not cursing at the Moon. Actually, it was quite the opposite. One night, when I was sleeping off the effects of dhutura, I was woken from my stupor by the bright light of the full moon. I felt that the Moon was mocking me and laughing at my fate. I jumped up and started throwing stones towards the Moon. Any stone that is thrown upwards must come down somewhere. One of my stones fell into a clump of trees, and there was a thump, followed by an eerie animal scream. Then, a strange animal ran out of the clump of trees. It looked like an ass, but bigger, its face longer and sharper. Anyway, soon after it ran past me, someone asked me why I was throwing stones. I looked around, but could not see anyone. For a moment, I wondered if it had been that strange animal that had spoken to me. But, I could hear the animal's faint gallop disappearing faraway, when I heard the voice again. It asked me why I was throwing stones. I answered that I was throwing stones at the Moon, as it was mocking me. Then, I asked whoever it was to come out and show himself. The voice ignored this. Instead, it told me that the Moon would never mock someone who was already down. It was shining on me to share my grief. Then, it told me that I should respect the amity the Moon had shown me and that I should stop chewing dhutura and help the Moon in fighting the demons of the night. He also said that the Moon needed many protectors to help it fight these demons. Stranger than these messages was the fact that this person seemed to be talking directly into my head. And, then, an even stranger thing happened. The animal that had run away returned with equal speed and went straight to the same clump of trees. And before it galloped away, I am sure I saw someone or something jump onto its back."

The Akkadian could not control himself any longer, but interfered with tact.

"And, of course, you did not go to the clump of trees to check the hoof marks," he said in a taunting tone. "Pasher, your new friend will soon tell you how this animal then sprouted wings and flew around."

"Of course, I did go and look for hoof marks," Kinjyaan said indignantly. Then, he turned to Pasher, "I looked and even found some hoofmarks. These looked like an ass's hoofmarks, only larger and less roundish. More oval shaped, and having longer and wider toes. Since then, I have tried a few times to stop taking the dhutura, but without any success, as you can see. However, I do shout at the demons that eat at the Moon on every full moon."

The Akkadian thanked whoever was guiding him again. Now, he was sure that he had not imagined either the voice or the conversation he had had on the night before reaching the Ashkini. He tried to recall the conversation, and the phrase that came to him again was the last thing the voice had said – "And the Gods, they are not all White". The voice had bid him to go in peace on his quest, the Akkadian was happy to note.

"Pasher," the Akkadian said, feeling more charitable towards Kinjyaan now. "Ask your new friend if he needs anything from us. That includes dhutura. If he really needs some, I will venture out and get him some. If he needs any food or clothing from us, and if you think we can spare it, give it to him."

"What new trickery is this?" Kinjyaan asked suspiciously.

"I do not think it is trickery," Pasher said quietly, "but let me ask you something. How long has it been since you were banished from Ilpurjal?"

"It was nine summers ago," Kinjyaan replied sadly, "that I lost my world."

"Do you like living like this, in the wild?" Pasher asked.

"One can get used to living like a wild animal," Kinjyaan smiled. "But, do you think he ever likes it?"

"I am not asking these questions without reason," Pasher said ever so gently. "Do you mind if I confer with my friend." And without waiting for his reply, he took the Akkadian aside.

"Master," Pasher whispered to the Akkadian, "do you really want to help this person?"

The Akkadian nodded but added, "Without jeopardizing the quest, of course."

"I know that, Master," Pasher said, "What if we provide him with some means to go back to Parroo? Perhaps, Viraan could give him some work there. You could send an introduction to Viraan. And am I right in believing that his story has helped your quest in some way?"

"You are becoming quite the debater, aren't you?" the Akkadian said with mock annoyance, but feeling quite proud. "All right, do what you need to. I don't think we need to send any message. Give him one of the special stones that light up under water, and once he takes it to Viraan, he will know for sure that we have sent him. Viraan will know what to do. That is, if Kinjyaan even tries to go to Parroo. If not, do not feel bad. You can only try to help him. It is up to Kinjyaan to take advantage of it. Don't tell him why the stone is special though, but merely ask him to take it to Viraan. Also, take this piece of jewellery. He can separate the stones and use it to pay for his trip to Parroo. Tell him to be careful with it. I know he will be all right. After all he will be travelling within Givenland. I know of places where he could be killed for the dirty loincloth he is wearing now. Anyway, I don't care. Why should I? I do not need anything from him anymore. I am going to walk around the camp a little."

As the Akkadian stood up to leave, Pasher stopped him.

"Master, I know you do care. You don't need to hide it from me. I know you can be very single-minded about something that has to do with your quest. People may perceive that as cruel, but I know that is not true. By nature, you are kinder than most people are. And I think finally, it is this inherent goodness, which will make you successful in your quest. But, you don't have to worry about Kinjyaan ever knowing of your kindness. I will take care of everything. You can go on your walk and leave the distribution of kindness to me."

For once, the Akkadian was speechless. He stood up, hugged Pasher, and walked away.

Kinjyaan and Pasher were still talking when the Akkadian returned. After some time, Kinjyaan came over to the Akkadian.

"You are very lucky to have a friend like Pasher," Kinjyaan said, tears flowing freely down his face. "Not many people can actually change the lives of others. I hope you appreciate this."

"Yes, I do," the Akkadian said seriously, but then continued in his previous derisive voice. "I assume now that you have seen me leave our camp and come back safe and sound, you want to go in search of your dhutura?"

"I have promised Pasher that from here on, I will not indulge myself in dhutura," Kinjyaan said solemnly, "and if not for my sake, but for the sake of the word I have given Pasher, I will never touch it."

The Akkadian realized that Kinjyaan meant every word he was saying. He knew this might change later, but for now he really meant it.

The next morning, Pasher bid farewell to Kinjyaan, as he started his southward journey. The Akkadian and Pasher soon broke camp and resumed their journey. They continued avoiding all the towns and villages. The same evening the Vitasta turned north-west, they made out the lights of Raisa[59] from their camp. The Akkadian decided to skip Raisa, and after breaking camp the next day, they turned away from the river, and started westward towards Lakho. They reached Lakho around noon the next day. Their arrival was uneventful, especially compared to the sights that had greeted them when they arrived at Pparaha.

Also unlike Divyaan, whom everyone in Pparaha seemed to know, it was only after enquiries to six different people, that they found his trading partner, Panjoo. Panjoo seemed to be Divyaan's opposite in every possible way. He was short and thin, his eyes were dull and his face without a smile. The only similarity between Divyaan and Panjoo was their resourcefulness.

"I hope you had a peaceful and enjoyable journey from Pparaha. How was Divyaan? Did you meet Kiraa? She is a real gem, isn't she?" Panjoo enquired in a flat and monotonous voice, devoid of emotions. "I have had the good fortune of visiting them a few times. Kiraa never lets me stay anywhere but their home."

"They are both fine," the Akkadian answered. "They asked us to convey their well wishes to you. And, yes, Kiraa and Divyaan are both gems."

"We have heard of some rumours of some strange happenings in Pparaha," Panjoo said, bringing his voice down in volume, but still in the

---

[59] A town in confluence of Rivers Jhelum and Korang

same monotone. "I hope it has not impacted them. I worry for them, especially as Kiraa always speaks her mind."

"From what I saw, she is quite intelligent," the Akkadian said evasively. "So, I am sure she will do what the situation requires."

"We will talk more about them later," Panjoo said, "now, tell me, how long would you like to stay in Lakho? My house is at your disposal. But, I cannot offer the same comforts as the lodging house down the street. Once you have rested for a few days, we will talk about what you need for your journey."

"We would love to stay longer," the Akkadian said, "but I would like to leave for Runaka within a day or two."

"That quickly?" Panjoo asked. "Well, I was hoping to spend some time with you, to learn about how things have been in Sumer. Don't worry, for Divyaan has already mentioned that you don't want anyone to know you are not Givenlander. But, Divyaan knows that I used do a lot of trade with your lands, and after meeting you, I would recognize where you were from. Akkadian, isn't it?"

"Yes, I am," the Akkadian said, "and I am really impressed that you could recognize that."

"Actually, one would not know by your accent," Panjoo said, "for based on only your accent, I would place you somewhere in the Eastern Givenland. But, your looks give you away, especially to people who have met Akkadians in the past."

"Well," the Akkadian said, taking advantage of the situation, "then you will understand why I cannot stay long. I want to cover as much of Givenland, as I can before the monsoons come in. But, I do need your help. I would like you to take care of my camels and asses while I am gone. I will need them when I head back south from here. I would like to acquire two asses from the general market. Not borrow them, but to acquire them for myself, for I might decide not to bring them back. We will need all the preserved food that was listed by Divyaan. I would also like to leave a few things behind in your care."

"Of course," Panjoo said, "whatever you need. I am sure, I can get everything by tomorrow and you can leave Lakho on the morning of the day after. But, why do you want to leave your camels behind? These would take you to Runaka much more comfortably."

"I know," the Akkadian replied, already prepared for this question, "but these animals have been travelling with me for some time now and I think I owe them some rest."

"That is true," Panjoo said. "I would ask you to dine with us, but my wife has just lost the uncle who brought her up. She is quite downcast. And that is why it is quite difficult for me to leave her alone for dinner."

"We will be fine and may even take a walk around the town tomorrow," the Akkadian said, "unless you think it would be an issue."

"That is a great idea," Panjoo replied. "If we meet tomorrow afternoon at your lodgings, I think I should have everything ready by then. I will take you and your companion to my stable to leave your animals and reassure yourselves that they will be well looked after. There is a room that I keep for storage next to the stables; you can leave anything you want to there."

Panjoo brought the preserved food and the two asses to their lodgings the next afternoon. They then went to the stable with Panjoo and left their camels and asses there. They had also packed everything they would not take on their onward journey into two big bundles. They left these in the room next to the stables.

They bade farewell to Panjoo that same evening.

The next morning, the Akkadian and Pasher started on their journey to Runaka.

Chapter 12

The Akkadian's Tale VI

"Master," Pasher said after they were a few mahahaths out of Lakho, "do you still plan to first visit the valley that Runggoo mentioned."

"Yes, Pasher, that is definitely still the plan. Why do you ask?"

"We have to pace our journey accordingly," Pasher said ponderously. "I mean, about the time of day."

"I like how you are thinking," the Akkadian said appreciatively. "I think we should cross the Mother River early morning on the day after tomorrow. But, I have been wondering about what we would gain by going to Runaka at all."

"Master," Pasher said, "I was thinking the same. We could come back from the circular valley and leave the asses and go back."

"Then, let us not go to Runaka," the Akkadian replied. "I am sure the lodge there will not do anything about it if we don't show up. Whereas, if Panjoo finds out that we started from Runaka, but did not make it to Lakho, he might organize a search for us. Yes, whichever way you look at it, not going to Runaka makes more sense. I will take care of the asses and be back at the valley before sunset. You can stay back and explore the mountains with your eyes, and also find us a good camping place for the night. I don't want to start a fire in the open for the first few days of our climb. I know I am being overcautious, but we are too close to our goal to take unnecessary risks."

"I understand, Master," Pasher said.

They came to the Mother River on the afternoon of the second day. They, then, turned northwards, travelling upriver along the Mother River. They soon came to the confluence of Kubha[60] and could, soon, see the ferries Panjoo had mentioned. They set camp a couple of Mahahaths away from the ferries. They broke camp before sunrise and were at the ferries first thing at dawn, before the first boatman had arrived. Thus, they were the first ones to cross the Mother River. After alighting from the ferry, they proceeded westwards towards Runaka. Soon, they could see the distinctive three-peaked hill that Runggoo had mentioned. They turned northwards after they were past the three-peaked hill, and soon came to a stream. Looking towards their left, they could see the waterfall, coming down in four long steps. They turned towards the waterfall. When they came to the base of the waterfall, they could see the natural staircase to the right. But, it was here that they came to the first flaw in their plan. It would be impossible for the asses to climb using these staircases.

"Master," Pasher said, "I think we should unload the asses here. You can then lead them away. I will start carrying our things into the valley."

"I don't think that is a good idea," the Akkadian said. "It is still some distance from the top of this waterfall to the cliffs. If we do come across someone and we are on our asses, we could say we have gotten lost. But, if you were carrying our things, it will look very suspicious. No, I would prefer to get our things to the valley on these asses."

Pasher looked around. He then moved to the middle of the stream, facing the waterfall, and started moving backwards. Then, he concentrated on the left of the waterfall and started walking towards a point about two hundred haths to the left of the waterfall. When he came back, he had a smile on his face.

"Master," Pasher said proudly, "I think I have found a place where the incline is a little less steep. Though we still cannot ride up with our asses, but with you pushing from the back, I can guide the asses to the top."

They managed to accomplish this without much difficulty. From the top of the waterfall, they had to lead the asses towards the cliffs onto the streambed, as the sides of the stream were too steep and rocky. However, the water only came up to the knees of the asses. They soon crossed in

---

[60]The River Kabul

between the cliffs and were inside the small circular valley. Everything was exactly as Runggoo had described. The valley was surrounded by sky scraping mountains on all sides. They immediately saw the six rocks jutting out of the ground, each about fourteen haths tall. They turned towards these rocks and after crossing these they came to the cliff, which seemed to go straight up. As they continued walking, after some time, the incline of the cliff started becoming gentler. They stopped and looked upwards. The Akkadian whistled out a deep breath.

"Pasher," the Akkadian said, "I think Runggoo was crazy to think I could climb this."

"No, Master," Pasher said, "I know you can. But, as you would have said by now, if the mountain was not distracting you, we need to hurry up and unload. Then, I will take you to the bottom of the waterfall. After which, I will see you when you come back after seeing to the asses."

The Akkadian snapped out of his despondency, and started helping Pasher with the unloading. After this was done, Pasher led the asses back to the bottom of the waterfall through the same path that they had come up. The Akkadian then rode off on one of the asses while leading the other. He soon came back to the three-peaked hill and turned left. The path was still deserted. After going about halfway to the ferries, the Akkadian alighted. He removed the saddle and reins from the asses, and smacked them on their buttocks with the back of his hand. The asses sauntered off to a nearby field and started chewing on some shrubs. The Akkadian looked around carefully, and once he was sure that there was no one in the vicinity, he threw the saddles and reins into the Kubha, and started back towards the circular valley. However, the sun was almost setting by the time he made it back to the valley. Pasher was waiting for him inside the doorway like cliffs.

"I am sorry it took longer than I thought," the Akkadian apologized. "Do you think we still have time to get to a higher place?"

"Actually, Master, it was good that you were late," Pasher said with a smile, "after you left, I went ahead and checked the start of the route Runggoo advised us to take. After that, I rebalanced all our things to make it more manageable for the initial part of our climb. I will, of course, have to rebalance these again when the slope gets steeper. But, after this was all done, and you were not yet back, I explored the valley a little more and found a cave. Whatever had used it for the winter has moved on, and by the spider webs on the entrance, nothing has entered it for at least a month. The best thing is that, though the cave looks quite shallow from outside, there is a passage to the left of the entrance, which leads you to a much larger cave. If we light a fire in this cave, I am sure it cannot be seen from outside. I have moved all our things into this cave for the night. We can start our ascent tomorrow morning."

"That is good news indeed," the Akkadian said with approval. "It will be nice to have a good night's rest before we start on our climb, which I still think is not possible."

"Yes, Master," Pasher replied, "and I am sure, that after a good night's rest you will feel more positive about the climb."

They lit a small fire inside the cave. Pasher fetched some water from the stream and made a thick stew.

"Master," Pasher said, "this stew is our special family recipe. Amongst other things, it contains the dried goat and sheep fat that Panjoo managed to find. The mushrooms you see in it are very special. They make your blood flow better. Even though we have prepared all the layers of clothing we will need, this will further ensure we do not have frostbite, which is the worst enemy of mountain climbers. Master, from today you are also the student. Whenever possible, I will try to explain why I am asking you to do something. But, many a time this will not be possible. I want you to follow what I say, and ask questions later."

"That goes without saying," the Akkadian said. "Why find an expert, if you are not going to use his expertise. So, please feel free to order me around. Until we finish this climb, you are the master." And the Akkadian meant every word he spoke.

"Thank you, Master," Pasher said. "Throughout our climb we will not start at dawn. We will wait for the sun to grow a little stronger, before we start our climb. If we start too early, the ground will be too slippery and our bones will be too cold and we will actually end up climbing less. We will start looking for a place protected from nature for the night much before sunset. We do not want to get caught in the open when night falls. This will be especially true at the higher altitudes."

"So, when should we start tomorrow?" the Akkadian asked.

"Tomorrow, we should start at day break," Pasher replied, "as we will not be affected by the mountain winds, yet, we should make as much ground as possible. I will decide every evening on how early or late we should start the next morning."

"If we are to start early tomorrow, let us turn in early tonight."

They made sure to put the fire out before going to sleep. Both of them woke up before sunrise. Pasher easily restarted the fire. After filling a sheepskin with his stew, they quickly ate their breakfast and dressed themselves based on Pasher's instructions.

"We have to make sure we are not cold," Pasher explained, "and yet, must also make sure we are not hot or sweaty. Both are equally dangerous to us."

Pasher had done a great job in balancing the loads, and their packs did not feel as heavy as they were. Both said a silent prayer, and started the climb.

For the first two days, the climb was not very strenuous. Pasher had the uncanny ability of finding the easiest way forward. He also managed to find caves, which were invisible to the Akkadian's untrained eyes.

From the third day, the climb became more difficult. But, Pasher's expertise and the Akkadian's determination still moved them forward at a good pace. But, even with this, the climb was taking longer than Runggoo had anticipated. By the fifth evening, they had not yet come to the snowline.

"Master, our luck has been a little mixed, don't you think? On one hand, we have been very lucky to find a cave to rest properly every evening. But, our progress has been a little slower than we had planned. I don't think we have a problem yet, as we are carrying about twice the provisions that we had thought we would need. However, we will need much longer than we planned on our return journey, and the problem is that we have no idea about how long we have to wait in the *offering cave* Runggoo had mentioned. I think if it is less than seven days, we should still be fine. But, if it is any longer, we will not make it back alive, at least not through this route."

"I believe in fate," the Akkadian said after much thought, "so, let us go on to the cave. If the people from Runggoo's valley come with their offerings by the seventh night – then we should be all right. If not, I will see that as a sign that I am allowed to help myself with what we need from the offerings. It will be my sin, not yours. I know you don't care, but that is how I want it."

"As you wish, Master," Pasher agreed, "we will proceed upwards then."

Late afternoon, on the eighth day, they crossed the snowline. The climb became more difficult, but Pasher continued to find ways to make their climb a little easier. It was two days later that they reached the ledge that Runggoo had mentioned. The ledge was flat but slippery with ice. They turned right and carefully proceeded towards the end of the ledge. And as

Runggoo had mentioned, there was an entrance to a large cave at the end of the ledge. They kept a little away from the entrance and made a lot of noise to make sure there were no animals lurking inside. When they entered the cave, it was shrouded with an eerie light. The Akkadian went and took a closer look at the moss growing on the walls of the cave that was emitting light. It looked like any ordinary moss. And though Runggoo had said the mosses were not poisonous, he decided against touching these. They then explored the whole cave and soon found the other mouth of the cave, nested high in the opposite wall. The Akkadian went to the end of the cave and easily found the footholds on the wall, that Runggoo had mentioned. Pasher climbed up to the ledge and could easily crawl to the other opening. The Akkadian followed him and came to this entrance. They went out to the outside ledge. Pasher went back and brought up a rope that measured exactly 575 haths. With the Akkadian holding one end to the cave entrance, Pasher went along the ledge to the right and as instructed by Runggoo marked the spot that was 575 haths from the entrance. As it was getting late, they went back to the cave and found a cranny to shield them from the crosswinds from both the entrances. While the Akkadian started working on a fire, Pasher checked and rechecked everything they would take with them the next day.

"Master," Pasher asked, "we have never discussed on how we are to proceed on the next part."

"What do you mean?" the Akkadian asked, looking up from his cooking.

"Master," Pasher said, "until we go down, we will not know whether it will be possible to climb up without someone helping from up here. I suggest that tomorrow morning I rappel down to the overhang over the cave first, and check everything out. Please stay on the ledge in case I need help to climb back. After that you can go down every day, and I will help you climb back up."

"That seems to be a good plan," Akkadian said, after giving it some thought. "Even if the people from Runggoo's valley start towards the cave at dawn, we will have enough time to go down and conceal ourselves on the overhang, before they arrive. But, let me ask you something. I understand that without someone helping from the ledge, climbing back will be difficult. But, if required, can it be done?"

"I can only be sure after I have gone down and climbed back once," Pasher replied, "but yes, I think it can be done."

"In that case, this is the plan," the Akkadian said, after thinking everything through. "As you suggested, early morning tomorrow, you will rappel down. After reaching the overhang, if you think you cannot climb back up without help, you will tug the rope only twice. If this happens, I will help you climb back up, and we will have to rethink our plan. But, if fate continues to be kind to us and you think you can climb up, you will signal with five tugs, and I will rappel down. Then you will lower me into the cave from the overhang. I have to check a few things in this cave. Then you will pull me up, back to the overhang. I just realized we will need some rope for you to lower me to the cave."

"I was planning to take a few short lengths of ropes with me, in any case."

"Good," the Akkadian said and continued, "then you will climb back to this ledge, making sure you are not observed, of course. By what Runggoo told us, the people with the offerings arrive at the cave around midday. So, if they are not there by mid-afternoon, it should be safe for you to climb back. Tomorrow, I will follow you back immediately after you are back to the ledge and signal me. Day after tomorrow and onwards, I will rappel down in the morning and wait for the people with the offerings. And if they do not come, you will help me come back up late afternoon. But, if they do, I will signal you with two tugs. You will first lower the bundle we will prepare. After lowering this, you will come down yourself. Then …"

"Master, sorry to interrupt," Pasher said, "but, why would you need me there, I want to make sure we minimize our unaided climbs back to this ledge."

"Pasher," the Akkadian said, "we might be close to something very wonderful. And trust me when I say that you do not want to miss it after coming so close. Now, coming back to the bundle I had mentioned. I want to make two packs, which should be light enough for us to carry easily. This should have all our warm clothes and also include a change of inner clothes, in case we have to be away for a few days."

"Do we need to pack any food?" Pasher asked.

"Even though I hope this will be provided to us," the Akkadian replied, "it might be a good idea to pack some dried food."

Both of them were quiet for a while. The silence was finally broken by Pasher.

"Master," Pasher asked, "do you really think that the Gods actually come and accept these offerings from Runggoo's people?"

"Well, we know that the offerings disappear from the caves," the Akkadian offered. "so, the first thing I should do tomorrow, is find out if some unscrupulous persons are making fools of the people of the Rungoo's valley to keep themselves fed. But whoever it is that is accepting these offerings, must have some divine help – if, as Runggoo says, there is no other way out of these caves."

"But, Master," Pasher asked after some more silence, "if it is the Gods who are taking the offerings, do you think we should be spying or interfering with them. How can that be a good thing?"

"I see it differently," the Akkadian replied without a pause. "If it is actually the Gods who are accepting the offerings, then I think it is they who have guided us here, as well. If they had not wanted us to be here, they would have put insurmountable obstacles in our paths. However, it has been just the opposite. Every time I thought I could not go forward, fate has seen fit to find me a new path. So, the way I see it, either it's the Gods who are taking the offerings or they have chosen me as the tool to discover this deceit."

"Master," Pasher said after some contemplation, "I think it would be very easy for you to fool me, considering you can convince anyone of anything, as I've observed. But, I think you really believe what you've just told me."

"Pasher," the Akkadian said, "I think we know each other too well for you to keep pretending that you are not intelligent. Others might see your brawn and assume that it cannot come with brains. I have never made that mistake. And you are right, for I do have the capability of convincing people. But, even I could not fool the Gods. Coming back to our plan, the only thing that I am worried about is the weather. In case it rains…"

"Master," Pasher stopped him, "perhaps, you are right and the Gods are easing your way, for I am sure we will not see any rain for the next few days. I am a mountain man, and know all these things," he confirmed. "We will have to decide upon the clothes to wear. On the day the offerings are made, I assume we will have to keep vigil until late at night. Though we are deep into spring, late night and early morning will still be very cold, especially as we will not have any protection from the wind. We will dress only in our warm inner clothes, and when you signal me to come down, I will bring down leather garments and blankets for both of us."

"I will leave that part of the planning to you," the Akkadian said, "and I will follow your instructions."

After that, they shared their food in silence. The Akkadian thought of all the people who had helped him get to where he was. He thought of Ishme and Vikoo, the caravan that brought him to Givenland, Tiraak and Runggoo, Viraan, the Teller and Nongru, Divyaan and Kiraa, Kinjyaan and Panjoo. He looked at Pasher and hoped that he would be able to go back to his people in Wacha. He wondered if he would see his wife again. Eventually, he pushed away all these thoughts out and instead thought about the initial conversation he had with Ishme, which had led him here.

The Akkadian smiled sheepishly to himself, as he remembered this conversation. Since he had come of age, he had possessed one ambition, to meet the White Gods of the Great Northern White Mountains. He had never forgotten his quest, but for a long time the means had become the end. He no longer cared about trading agreements, neither did he plan to scribe any messages on the walls of the cave of offerings, if he found out that the White Gods did not exist. He only wanted to find the White Gods – or the gods whom, since that evening near the Ashkini, he believed might not be all White. He did not want anything from them anymore. Instead, if they wanted him for some service, he was ready for it. The only thing he planned to ask from them is to help Runggoo's situation. And he had also decided that no matter how his quest ended, he would go back to Wacha. After that, he would go to visit Kurm to keep his promise to Ishme. But, he would then come back to Givenland. He would spend his time between Parroo and Wacha. He was sure that not only would his friends welcome him in both places, but he could make himself useful, as well. He was still thinking these thoughts when he fell asleep.

The Akkadian woke up before dawn and was happy to see that Pasher was already awake. When the Akkadian came back after his morning ablutions, Pasher was still engrossed in whatever he was doing.

"What are you doing, Pasher?" the Akkadian asked.

"Master," Pasher replied, "I am preparing the two bags that you had mentioned about yesterday. The ones that we would need after the offerings were delivered."

"Oh yes, of course," the Akkadian said. Then looking over Pasher's shoulder, he concluded, "you seem to have this one under control, so I will start heating up your soup."

"Already done and ready, Master," Pasher replied.

"So I see," the Akkadian said in mock exasperation upon reaching the fire, "is there anything at all that I need to do?"

"Master," Pasher said without joining in on the humour, "I am almost done with this. I have checked both the knotted and the plain ropes, and made sure they will not fail us. Next, we will have to start getting dressed."

After all this was done, they climbed to the higher entrance and proceeded to the ledge and then to the point that Pasher had marked out the previous day. As planned, Pasher first found a rock outcrop that was strong enough to hold twice the weight of the both of them put together. He then ensured the outcrop did not have any sharp edges. And then went on to push and pull it with all his strength. Once he was completely satisfied, he tied the long rope without the knots to this outcrop. This was the one they would be using for rappelling down. He used special knots that would not tear or loosen. He had learnt to make them as a child, and had become an expert by constant practice. He then did the same to the knotted rope that they would be using to climb up. Then, he threw the other end of both ropes down. After checking everything a few more times, he started rappelling down and soon disappeared from the Akkadian's view. The Akkadian waited, for what seemed to be an eternity. Finally, there was one tug on the rope. And then another. The rope did hear the Akkadian's plea, and the tugs did not stop at two, and was followed by three more tugs. The Akkadian said a silent prayer, and started his descent. Soon, he joined Pasher on the overhang. The Akkadian was a little disappointed at his first look at the cave. He knew he was not being logical, but he had expected something special, but looking down from the window-like aperture, it looked very ordinary. But, he did not ponder on it for long, and indicated to Pasher that he wanted to proceed to the cave. Pasher took out another small rope, which was also knotted and handed one end to the Akkadian, and tied the other to his own waist.

"Master," Pasher whispered, "after I lower you down, please go ahead with your explorations. I will spend the time in tying up the ends of both the ropes, so that from tomorrow, these will only fall up to this overhang, and not over the cave like now. When you want to leave the cave and join me here, please give a gentle tug on this rope, and I will pull you up. Please make sure that the tug is gentle, or we both will end up in the cave."

The Akkadian nodded, still a little out of breath from rappelling down. He then lowered himself into the cave with Pasher's help. After reaching the floor of the cave, he proceeded to the entrance of the cave. He took out a small wooden club that he had brought from Parroo for this purpose. Then starting from one side of the entrance, he started to check the cave for any hollow walls. He knew that he had limited time on his hands, but refused to be hurried by this. He wanted to be thorough instead of fast. After he had covered about one tenth of the wall, he went back to the spot that Pasher had lowered him to. He then gently tugged at the rope that was hanging there. Pasher soon pulled him up.

"Pasher," the Akkadian said, "I think this will take longer than I thought. Even though Runggoo had given us a general idea of the size of this cave, there are a lot of nooks and crannies that add to the surface area I need to check. Would we have enough time for you to pull me up if you kept a watch and warned me if you saw anyone approaching?"

"Not from here, Master. On the way down, I did see a rock jutting out, about a hundred haths higher than here." Then, pointing at this outcrop, he continued, "If I go up there, I will have a clear view of anyone approaching from the valley. I will see them much before they arrive. After seeing them, I can rappel down and still have time to call out to you, without having them see or hear anything. The only problem is you will not be able to come out of the cave until I come down. I have checked this overhang, but could not find a place where we can tie a rope to be lowered into the cave. And it would be too dangerous to use the ropes that we would need to rappel down and climb up to the ledge."

"I understand," the Akkadian said, and then continued after some thought. "I know what we shall do. After you are done with shortening these ropes, lower me into the cave. After that, climb up to the outcrop and keep watch. If you do not see anything until mid-afternoon, come down and help me out of the cave. But, make sure we will have enough time to get back to the ledge before sunset."

"Master, I am done with the ropes, and we can start with your plan now," Pasher said.

After lowering the Akkadian into the cave again, Pasher climbed to the outcrop he had mentioned.

The Akkadian again started checking the walls for any sign of hollowness from the point he had stopped earlier. He had just finished checking all the walls, when he heard Pasher call out.

"Master, I don't think anyone is coming today, so I decided to come down. I have some good news. I have found three other outcrops of rocks between here and the ledge. So, I can climb to the first outcrop, and then guide you to it. From there, we will proceed to the next outcrop. In this way, we will have an easier and faster climb back to the ledge. Are you almost done, Master?"

"I am done checking the walls," the Akkadian said. "There is one more thing that I need to do, which should not take long. Do you think we still have some time?"

"Yes, please do what you need to do. However, be as quick as possible. "

"I will not take long."

He then took out one of the stones that emitted light underwater and also retrieved the transparent bag that Divyaan had acquired for him, which now had attached to it a ten hath string reinforced by animal fat. After wetting the stone, he slipped it into the bag and lowered it into the circular pool of water. The water was about eight-haths deep. The Akkadian could clearly see the bottom of the pool, lit up by the stone, and observed that there did not seem to be any passage leading off from the pool.

He pulled up the stone and signalled to Pasher that he was done. Then they proceeded to climb up to the ledge, using the three outcrops that Pasher had mentioned. It worked exactly as Pasher had said it would. And they were back on the ledge a little before sunset. Pasher pulled up both the ropes and untied the ropes from where he had secured them.

"Pasher," the Akkadian said after they were back in their base cave, "now we can be sure there is something extraordinary going on in that cave. I have checked the whole cave, but could not find any other exit. What if the entrance is at a height? You might ask. But, considering the amount of offerings that Runggoo said were left behind in these caves, if the entrance was at a height, I would see drag marks, which I did not. No, I am now more convinced than ever that we will soon be discovering something supernatural and divine."

"But, Master," Pasher said with surprise, "I had thought that you always did believe in the Gods of the Great Northern White Mountains."

"Yes, I always did," the Akkadian said, "but there had been some doubt before. Not anymore, though."

The next day, the Akkadian rappelled down to the overhang above the cave and waited all day. But no one came. Around mid-afternoon, he signalled to Pasher, with five tugs on the rope, that he was ready to climb back to the ledge. It was the same story the day after.

Around mid-morning on the third day, the Akkadian thought he heard voices. The Akkadian was lying on his belly, and like other days, he had covered himself with a cloth that was grey like the rocks around him. He took his head out and listened carefully. There was no mistaking the voices, and as he continued to listen, the voices grew louder. He rearranged the grey cloth to cleverly camouflage himself. Then he waited, keeping as still as possible.

Finally, he saw two men enter the cave. They were not carrying anything. For a moment the Akkadian panicked. He was certain that they had discovered his presence. But, to his relief, they started cleaning the cave. After they had finished, they went out. The Akkadian was almost afraid to breathe as he waited.

After some time, many other men started trudging in. Most of them carried conical baskets on their backs, and the remaining either carried smaller baskets on their heads or sheepskin bags on their shoulders. There were twenty-three in all, the Akkadian counted them. They started laying out the offerings. He could see fruits, vegetables, barley, lentils, salt and spices amongst other things. The Akkadian assumed that the sheepskin bags contained raajaraas. However, it was the sight of raw fish and meat that excited him the most. Even in this altitude, the fish and the meat would go bad with time. So, whoever was accepting these offerings would have to come and take it tonight. After they were done, one of them, who was clearly the leader, checked everything. After that they left the cave, the leader bringing up the rear.

The Akkadian waited for a while to make sure that none of them was coming back. Then, he waited some more, to make sure they would not be able to see Pasher rappelling down. Finally, he signalled to Pasher, by giving the rope two sharp tugs. Soon, Pasher joined him on the overhang, with the two bundles that they had packed earlier. Before sunset, they pulled down their woollen headgear to their ears and put on leather ones over these. They also put on the leather outer garments and then sat close to the aperture into the cave, and started their vigil. They were silent and did not risk talking at all. Their anticipation and the cold made sure they did not nod off.

It was well past midnight when the Akkadian thought he heard a grinding sound coming from the direction of the cave. Even though the sound seemed to be coming from the cave, the sound seemed to be coming from much further away than the furthest walls of the cave. Pasher, too, must have heard something, for he turned his head sharply towards the Akkadian.

There was no mistaking the next sound they heard. And it was clearly coming from the cave. It was the gurgling sound of water being drained out. They peered into the cave, but could not see any movement. However, slowly, an eerie light started to engulf the cave. The Akkadian tried to remember if there were any of the light emitting mosses in this cave, but discarded the idea, as in that case the light would not suddenly appear. After some time, the gurgling stopped and the light lost its eeriness, and became steady. It was clearly coming from the direction of the circular pool. Then, they saw it. First, they saw the tip of a torch. It was clear that someone was coming up from where the pool of water had been, and was carrying a torch. The first thing that the Akkadian noticed was that the hand belonged to a woman and that it was adorned with gold ornaments.

Chapter 13

Ridhaan didn't think twice before shaking Riyaansh awake.

"Is everything all right?" Riyaansh came awake with a jump, "Has someone come?"

"No one else is here," Ridhaan answered. "Step out and we will talk." The twins stepped outside. "Everything is not all right!" Ridhaan exclaimed, shaking *The Akkadian's Tale* in front of his brother's face.

"You have finished reading," Riyaansh smiled. "In that case, I understand your frustration. But don't worry. That is not the end of the story."

"I may not have your memory," Ridhaan retorted, "but I clearly remember you telling me that you have finished scribing *The Akkadian's Tale.*"

"I did say that," Riyaansh replied, "but what I want to share with you now is *Ekur's Quest.* I have finished scribing that, as well." So saying, Riyaansh ducked into the sleeping quarters, and came back with a thinner collection of parchments.

"I have a few questions that you have to answer first," Ridhaan insisted taking the bound parchments from his brother. Then continued, his voice growing more and more frantic, "Why did you not scribe anything about The Akkadian's journey from Sumer? What was the route they took? What was the terrain like? Were there many hills or mountains? Were the valleys pretty? How many rivers did they have to cross? How did they cross these rivers? What about the local people they met on the way? How did they greet the caravan? Usually, whenever you have visited any place, you have always enlightened me with these details."

"I asked these questions and more, to Ekur," Riyaansh sighed knowingly. "And Ekur had asked the same questions to the Akkadian. The Akkadian got very irritated with Ekur for asking such unimportant questions. They were eating some type of grilled young lamb they call sila-nim[61], when Ekur brought this up. The Akkadian asked Ekur whether he knew anything about the lamb, like where it came from and who its parents were. When Ekur said that he did not, the Akkadian asked Ekur whether not knowing these things about the lamb made it any less tasty. And then the Akkadian walked out in a huff, and only got back to his tale the day after."

"So, that means I will not hear these details about any of the other journeys, as well," Ridhaan grumbled.

"You will only hear things that the Akkadian thought were significant for his tale," Riyaansh smiled.

"What about the dialogues?" Ridhaan asked, "He seems to remember and repeat these clearly. Too clearly, if one may say."

"Ekur felt that the Akkadian was so interested in the people around him," Riyaansh reminisced, "that he focused all his attention on this, and everything else faded in comparison. Also, as Ekur had heard some of these incidents, from both Ishme and the Akkadian, he was sure these were not made up for theatrical purposes. Why don't you read this and we can talk after that?"

"I hope for your sake," Ridhaan said with mock seriousness, "that I don't have to shake you awake, after I finish *Ekur's Quest.*"

---

[61]A spring lamb in Sumerian with no equivalent word in Givenland

Chapter 14

Ekur's Quest I

When the Akkadian came back to Kurm, it was for the sole purpose of meeting his Abgal and Ekur's namabba, Ishme. The day after arriving back in Kurm, the Akkadian went to Ekur's house. Ekur's uncle rudely threw him out. He did not even share the fact that Ishme was already dead. Ekur followed and caught up with the Akkadian. When he informed him about his Abgal's death, the Akkadian was devastated. He fell down to the street. When he recovered, he asked Ekur how he was being treated. At that time, Ekur had a tolerable, if not good life, and said as much. The Akkadian informed Ekur where he was staying, and also informed him that he would be in Kurm for two more weeks. A few days later, Ekur gave in his curiosity and went to see the Akkadian at his lodgings.

After arriving at the lodging, he found out that the Akkadian had been taken seriously ill, and as he had come back from travelling to strange lands, they had asked him to leave. They did share with Ekur the directions of the small house that the Akkadian was staying. Ekur went to this house and found the Akkadian delirious with fever, sleeping in his own filth. As Ekur had taken care of Ishme for a few months before he passed away, he decided that he could and would take care of the Akkadian. He stripped the Akkadian off all his clothes and burnt them. Then, he got some naña-si-è[62] leaves, and after grinding them, mixed it with kaš and water, and bathed the

---

[62]Soapwort – leaves of which were used as a disinfectant

Akkadian with the mixture, and then wrapped the Akkadian in clean blankets.

After that, Ekur left for home to fetch some of his things. At home, Ekur was greeted by his uncle and father. Upon learning where Ekur had been, he was told in unequivocal terms, to either stop seeing the Akkadian or leave home. As Ekur knew that without his care the Akkadian would surely die, he packed up his clothes and left home.

Ekur nursed the Akkadian back to health. But, while doing so, he realized that there was something seriously wrong with the Akkadian's left leg. By the time the fever subsided, the Akkadian had lost total use of his left leg, knee down.

"Why did you save me?" the Akkadian asked Ekur, "If I cannot go back to Meluhha, I don't want to go on living."

"I did my duty," Ekur said softly, "and from what my namabba taught me, the Meluhhans put even more value to life than us."

"I am sorry," the Akkadian quickly realized how unfair he was being. "However, you have put me in a quandary. Abgal had told me that if you were to ever come for my help, I should not give you anything for free. I know you saved my life, but your namabba would consider that as your duty."

"Please tell me about your journey," Ekur said, "and let me live here. In return, I will take care of you and do all your house chores." The Akkadian agreed.

The Akkadian and Ekur settled down in the small house that Ekur had found him. The Akkadian made arrangements for grains, vegetables, fish, meat, and all other things they needed to be delivered to their house. Ekur did the cooking, cleaning and all other household chores. Every morning, Ekur helped the Akkadian with his exercises. Though they had both realized that the Akkadian would never walk again, they still understood the importance to keep the rest of his body active. During late afternoons and evenings, the Akkadian told Ekur about his journey.

When he came to the part, where he saw the hand adorned in gold ornaments, he went quiet. His gaze was fixed into one corner of the room. At first, Ekur thought the Akkadian was reliving and savouring this most important moment in his life. He thought he saw the Akkadian smile. But then, he realized his lips were curved in pain. The Akkadian then clutched the left side of his chest and fell to the ground.

Ekur rushed to the Akkadian's side, lifted him up and made him as comfortable as possible then rushed out asking for help. As he was leaving the house, he came across the person who delivered meat and vegetables to their house. Usually, it was the Akkadian who dealt with him, but both Ekur and he knew each other by sight. They rushed back inside.

"I cannot help you," said the deliveryman. "You need a medicine-man, and a good one at that. I was making a delivery to one of the lodgings in the centre of the town. I heard that they have a very good medicine man staying there. But, if he can afford to stay in such a place, he must be expensive. I can give you the details of his lodgings. I don't think I can do anything else to help."

Ekur noticed that, unlike before, the Akkadian was not staring into nothingness any more. His eyes were moving and he seemed to be able to follow their conversation. After the deliveryman had left, the Akkadian signalled Ekur to bring him his outer garment. Then, from the lining of this garment, he produced a gold nugget. He handed it to Ekur. Ekur understood that this was the payment for the medicine man. Armed with the gold nugget, Ekur easily convinced the medicine man to visit the Akkadian. After checking the Akkadian, the medicine man took Ekur aside.

"I don't think there is much that we can do, except making sure that his passing on from this world is as comfortable as possible," the medicine man said. "To be honest, I don't understand how he is still alive. I will come and check on him every two days and try my best to make his last days as comfortable as possible. I think it is time for his near and dear ones to come and bid farewell to him."

Ekur thanked the medicine man. There was no one to inform, he realized. He knew all the Akkadian's near and dear ones were in faraway Meluhha. In Kurm, Ekur was the only one who could be called close to the Akkadian. In these last few months, the Akkadian's only visitors had been the people making the deliveries. Also, Ekur had no idea where the Akkadian's mother was, or for that matter whether she was at all still alive.

Ekur did his best to keep the Akkadian comfortable. There was not much change in the Akkadian's condition over the next two days. Ekur fed him as much as he could eat. Sometimes, the Akkadian signalled to Ekur that he needed to pass urine or stool, and Ekur would help him, by taking off his clothes, cleaning the Akkadian, and then cleaning up after him, as well. At times, the Akkadian was not able to signal Ekur, and Ekur would have to clean the Akkadian, his clothes and bed. On the third day, the medicine man came back. He told Ekur that the Akkadian's time was very near.

That night, Ekur was dozing near the foot of the Akkadian's bed, when he was awakened by something. Then, he heard it again.

"Ekur," the Akkadian was calling in a hoarse voice, "where are you, Ekur?"

"I am here," Ekur replied jumping up. "I knew you would get better. I knew you would prove the medicine man wrong."

"I wish that were true," the Akkadian whispered. "My end is nigh. Much like a lamp that burns brighter before going off completely, my strength has come back a little before it disappears forever."

"No, I do not believe that," Ekur said. "Let me go and fetch the medicine-man. I am sure we can …"

"Please, stop," the Akkadian whispered, "we do not have time for this. What I have to say to you now is more important than whether I live for a few more days or not. We always forget how fragile life is. When I came back here, I never thought I would end up not ever returning to Meluhha. Once I realized that I could not, I should have sent you there immediately. But, I felt, in order to succeed, you had to know the whole story, first. Now there is no time for that, either. But, you have to go there. You have to go soon. You have to go immediately."

"I promise you I will," Ekur replied, "but you know my situation. Now that my family has disowned me, I will have to work hard for a few years before I can afford such a journey." The Akkadian seemed to grimace. "Are you all right?" Ekur asked, "Are you in pain?"

"I was trying to smile, fool," the Akkadian said. "Now stop interrupting me and listen. I am rich – rich beyond the imagination of any person in Sumer or Meluhha. I could carry back only a tiny part of my wealth, but now in this room, there is wealth that can buy all of Kurm. I will give what I have here to you. You will keep one third. The other two-thirds you will deliver to my wife. I have also left you some gold. Use that gold to get to Meluhha. Don't let anyone know about the other wealth, or you will end up being killed for it." Ekur looked around in surprise. "But a lot more important than all this worldly wealth," the Akkadian continued, "is the wealth of knowledge that I have acquired. The Meluhhans will need this if they are to save themselves. They are being led towards their destruction by their arrogant, greedy, lecherous high priests; those ravagers of young women, those despoilers of society will cause the destruction of all of Meluhha. The Gods have already started preparing for this day. There is still time to avert it, though. But, we must act now."

"So, the White Gods of Great Northern White Mountains do exist?" Ekur asked unable to stop himself.

The Akkadian smiled again, and it still looked more like a grimace.

"Depends on what you mean by the Gods?" the Akkadian said, "Do they come from the skies? Yes, they certainly do. Are they supernatural? Yes, they are. Can they change the fate of humans? Yes, they can. Are they kind? Do they reward the virtuous? Yes, they are and they do. Are they wrathful? Do they punish the wrongdoers? Oh yes, they are and they do, and in ways you cannot even imagine, my young friend. You have been like a son to me. You have to go to Meluhha. You have to seek out Runggoo and Pasher. You will need their combined knowledge to seek out the Gods. Once you seek out the Gods, you will have to convince them that more time is required to bring back the Meluhhans to their original path of righteousness. Remember, that when they say they want to destroy all of Meluhha, they not only mean it, but also have the power and means to carry out this scheme, and they believe it is their responsibility to do that. They will not shirk from this responsibility of theirs. Meluhhans have to convince them that the situation is not beyond salvation."

"So, the White Gods do exist," Ekur whispered.

"Please pay attention," the Akkadian said. "Don't let your mind wander. This is too important. Bring me the club – you know the one I am talking about, the one that I brought back from Meluhha. And fetch me a hammer."

Ekur brought the club and a hammer.

"Most of my garments have a gold nugget or two stitched into them," the Akkadian said. "You will have to go through my clothes to find all of them. There will be fifty-six more left, after the one you gave to the medicine man. But, that is a small fraction to what is inside this club, which is hollow in the inside. As I was saying, most of it is still high up in a cave near a lake called Durshan[63]. You will need Pasher and Runggoo to help you to get there. But, they will only help you if … can you stop fiddling with that club? It does not have an opening; you will have to break it open. But, as I was saying and this is the most important, Runggoo and Pasher, or, for that matter, Tiraak, Viraan and any of my other friends in Meluhha will not even acknowledge that they knew me, unless you tell them the phrase. I…"

---

[63] A lake in a valley high up in the Hindu Kush Mountains

It was at this moment that Ekur could not control his curiosity anymore and struck the club with the hammer. He broke it, and many dazzling stones of different sizes fell out from it. For some time, Ekur was mesmerized by these. He had never owned any precious stones, but no one had to tell him that scattered in front of him was wealth beyond anyone's dream. Then he forced himself to look away from the stones, back towards the Akkadian.

"I am very sorry," Ekur said, "but could you please repeat the phrase. I know you asked me to stop fiddling with the club, but my attention was wandering. Now, however, you have my full attention."

But the Akkadian didn't seem to hear. His eyes, though focused on a point in the ceiling, seemed to be looking into the distance. He had a smile on his face – a real smile not the grimace he had given Ekur earlier.

"Can you hear me?" Ekur cried in a louder voice, "Please forgive me for not paying attention but you have my undivided attention now. Please repeat the phrase."

"A-na-poo-na," the Akkadian whispered.

"What was that?" Ekur said, "I was sure that the last time you were saying the phrase, it did not start with 'A-na' 'I'."

"A-na-poo-na," the Akkadian said, "are you sure that Dan-van-tree can fix Pasher's leg? And what did he mean by saying that he would fix the other problem, as well?"

Ekur realized that the Akkadian was not talking to him anymore. He was in some faraway place.

"Ka-lee, please believe me," the Akkadian whispered again. "The Givenlanders can be like Ma-noo and Ya-maa again. You cannot destroy a whole race for the fault of a few. You have to give them a chance. Listen to me, please don't walk away."

Then, the Akkadian was silent for a while. His breathing became rhythmic. It was clear that he was asleep. For some reason, Ekur decided that it was important to immediately scribe down what he thought the Akkadian had said, even though none of it made any sense to him. He silently thanked his namabba, for not only teaching him the Meluhhan tongue but to scribe, as well. He then did not move from the Akkadian's side, not even to examine the priceless stones that lay scattered on the floor. It was quite some time later that the Akkadian opened his eyes again. He looked more focused.

"Ekur," the Akkadian said, "I thank you for everything. And I trust you completely. I know you will deliver her inheritance to my wife. But, if she knew everything, even she would agree that it is more important that you get the Meluhhans to act now, to appease the Gods. I now understand what he meant, when he said that my son, who though not a Givenlander, will come as a Givenlander. You are the closest I have to a son. You are destined to go to them. So, be safe and try to keep the Meluhhans safe. Take help from Runggoo and Tiraak, and of course Pasher. Without Pasher's help, nothing will be achieved."

"I will strive to do my best," Ekur replied, "I am very sorry, but I did not catch the phrase; I will need to get help from your acquaintances in Meluhha. Without their help, I don't think I can achieve much."

"It is true," the Akkadian said, again with the faraway look, "the Gods, they are not all White. And even the ones who are White are not always White."

And then the Akkadian breathed his last.

Ekur did not cry or scream. Instead, he became extremely calm. He asked himself, 'What would the Akkadian want me to do next?' And it was clear to him what he needed to do. He, first, scribed down the final words of the Akkadian. Then, he got up quietly from the floor and fetched a leather bag. He collected all the precious stones from the floor and put them in the bag. He then swept the floor of the room to make sure he had not missed any of the stones. It was good that he did this, for he did find three more stones. After this was done, Ekur searched all the Akkadian's clothes for gold nuggets. It was almost dawn by the time he had found all fifty-six of them. He then put fifty of these in two other leather bags. He hid four of the other six in different parts of the house, kept two with him and hid the three leather bags in a bundle of his clothes. He then carried the Akkadian back to his bed. After that, he looked at the other things that he had found sewn into the Akkadian's clothes, in his pursuit of looking for the gold nuggets. Two were clearly maps, he saw. And he did not have to look at the maps for long to know that one of them was the map that the Akkadian had drawn with Viraan's instructions, while the other was the one that Runggoo had drawn for the Akkadian, to guide him on his quest. He carefully placed these in another leather bag. He could not be sure what the other few parchments were, but decided that if the Akkadian was carrying them in this concealed way, these must be important, so he put these in the bag containing the maps. After all this was done, he checked and rechecked the house to make sure he had not missed anything. He then let out a loud scream and followed it with cries of despair. As it was almost dawn, he soon had an audience of a few neighbours and some tradesmen, who were passing the house on their way to work. As he recognized the deliveryman amongst the crowd, Ekur thanked his luck. The deliveryman agreed to go and fetch the medicine man. He returned in a while with the medicine man. All the others had left by this time. The deliveryman then took leave to proceed with his daily chores.

"Are you sure that he has just died?" the medicine man asked after checking the Akkadian's body.

"I cannot be sure," Ekur replied. "I had fallen asleep. When I woke up, I found him here, unresponsive to my calls."

"Don't berate yourself," the medicine man said kindly. "You could not have done anything even if you were awake. As I had warned you, there was no chance that he would recover. I saw how you tried your best to keep him comfortable. Under the circumstances, that is all you could have done."

"I did what I could," Ekur continued in a sad voice. "But, I do not know what to do now."

"There is nothing for you to do now," the medicine man said. "His heart does not think anymore; his liver does not have any affection; his stomach is no longer cunning and neither can his eyes or ears be attentive anymore."

"But, this was a good man, a great man. How great! People will neither know nor understand."

"However great a person may be," the medicine-man said, "and however good or evil he may be, in death we all share the same fate. We are all fated to go to kur-nu-gi-a[64] and live in the darkness and eat dirt. If you can bear the expenses, I can arrange for his burial. If not, I think the city will take care of him."

Ekur thought quickly and replied, "He did give me a gold nugget to take care of his funeral expenses. I ..."

"I am sure I will be able to cover everything with that gold nugget."

The burial was carried out that same afternoon. Ekur came back to the Akkadian's house and pondered over the situation. He knew that in his old bundle of clothes, there lay riches, which until yesterday were beyond his wildest dreams. He was of course only thinking about the third that belonged to him. It had never crossed his mind not to deliver the other two-third to the Akkadian's wife. He started thinking about how he would

---

[64]The land of no return – The Sumerians believed that a person goes there after death

go about doing the other quest that the Akkadian had given him. He knew that the task was impossible for Ekur, unless Ekur started thinking and acting like the Akkadian. He knew that the first thing he needed to do was to find the fastest way to get to Meluhha. He wished his grandfather was still alive to guide him and even introduce him to someone like Vikoo, as he had done for the Akkadian. Then, he remembered that his grandfather used to keep a list of his friends and acquaintances with him. So he proceeded to the house that he had left a few months ago. His father was there when he arrived.

"So, you are back? You have come to beg for mercy, haven't you?" his father sneered. "We are looking for an urtud[65] and you are welcome to try and get that job."

"I do not have time for this," Ekur said commandingly. "I need to retrieve something from my grandfather's belongings."

"As you are no longer a son of this house, you have no right to those," his father retorted.

"Is my uncle home?" Ekur asked.

"Yes, he is," his father replied. "but, I know, he will tell you exactly what I have said."

"The reason I was looking for my uncle is slightly different," Ekur said. "I will be making an offer to buy his belongings. And I don't want you to cheat my uncle of his share."

"Oh, you want to buy them?" his father laughed and called out to his brother. After his brother joined him, he continued, "This beggar is offering to buy our father's belongings. I wanted you to share the pleasure of rejecting the offer with me. So, beggar, what are you offering us?"

"Well, I was planning to offer two of these," Ekur said taking out a gold nugget and placing it on his palm. "but, because you have called me a beggar, I think I will offer only one."

His uncle rushed to Ekur and took the nugget and bit on it.

"This is gold!" Ekur's uncle said in amazement.

Ekur's father took the nugget and bit on it, as well.

"Well, Ekur," his father said. "Stupid as ever, I see. As we are holding it now, what is stopping us from keeping the nugget and not giving you anything?"

---

[65]A domestic servant – which did not have an equivalent word in Givenland/ Meluhha

"I was hoping you would do something like that," Ekur said, and paused for effect. Then he continued with a smile, "I met the Master of the Levy before coming here and showed him that nugget," Ekur lied, "and if you steal it from me, I will get it back after having the pleasure of seeing you both flogged."

"And how do I know you are not lying?" his father asked defiantly.

Ekur ignored the question. "It will actually give me great pleasure to see you suffer. The circle will soon be complete and I will take pleasure at my father's suffering, as he did in his father's."

"I don't believe you," his father replied, a little less sure of himself now. "You are too weak to cause pain to others. That is why you went on caring for father, even after you did not need to. Go ahead ..."

"You are stupid as ever," Ekur's uncle cut in. "You have already caused us to lose one gold nugget. Now, you want us to lose the other one too, and along with it the skin of our backs. In any case, we were planning to throw the things Ekur wants. Just give it to him, and let him go."

"Fine, I will," Ekur's father said, "but I think it is you who is being stupid. I don't believe Ekur has the liver to cause us harm."

"But, why take the risk," his brother replied. "What would we gain by not giving away something we were planning to get rid of in any case?"

Then, before Ekur's father could say anything, Ekur's uncle went and fetched a trunk containing Ishme's belongings.

"Here, take it," Ekur's uncle said.

"And don't come back here ever again," Ekur's father added.

Ekur left without saying anything. Luckily, the trunk was light enough for him to carry by himself. Ekur walked out, his head held high, and his back straight, until he was out of the view of his father and uncle. He then sat down on the street, sweating with relief. He was amazed at how easily he had lied to and manipulated his father. He felt that the Akkadian would have been proud of him. He knew that the Akkadian might have handled the situation better. However, he thought proudly, it could not be that much better, as he had got the outcome he wanted at a cost that was less than he had set out to pay.

He then came back to the Akkadian's house – Ekur could not think of it as anything but the Akkadian's house. He opened Ishme's trunk and started going through Ishme's belongings. He found the bracelet, which Ishme had brought back from his first trip to Meluhha. He had worn it until the day he died. Ekur slid this onto his wrist. Then, he found what he was looking for: Ishme's list of all his friends and acquaintances, properly indexed by where they came from. Going through this, he found the name of a person who ran a lodging, which according to the notes was frequented by traders from Meluhha. He realized that the sun had already set that day, and by now most of the traders would be inebriated by intake of kaš[66]. He decided to leave this for the next day. He quickly put together a meal and ate it. Then he started sorting out his and the Akkadians things, focusing on the things that he would take with him to Meluhha. He wanted to travel light, but wanted to be ready for all weathers. He was glad to find some leather garments, which he immediately knew to be the ones that Pasher had chosen. He decisively put them into the pile of things that he would be taking with him. By the time he had sorted everything out, he realized that this pile had grown too large. He whittled it down to the absolute necessities, and by the time he was done, it was quite late. 'At this point, I think the Akkadian would sleep and get rejuvenated,' Ekur thought and decided to do the same.

He did not bother waking up early the next morning. He knew it would be useless to go to the Meluhhan traders' lodgings in the morning. They would be busy leaving for the day's chores. The best time would be to go there late in the afternoon and wait for them to come back. They would be more relaxed and more amenable to hear him out. As he had some time in his hands, he decided to tackle the next problem, which was finding a way to carry the Akkadian's wife's inheritance, without drawing too much attention. He thought of various options, but none were satisfactory. Finally, he decided to think about it later.

Around mid-afternoon, Ekur went to the lodging frequented by the Meluhhan traders, and found it quite deserted.

"What business do you have here?" an elderly man asked him gruffly.

"Sir, I came here to meet some of the guests from Meluhha," Ekur replied politely.

"The guests from Meluhha stay in my establishment, because I make sure that undesirables like you don't bother them," the man said, sounding even gruffer.

Ekur was taken aback for a moment. Then, he rebuked himself for trying to be Ekur and not the Akkadian.

---

[66]Sumerian Alcohol

"All right, I will leave," Ekur said in a tone that was definitely disrespectful. "My grandfather, Ishme, had led me to believe that I would always be welcome at the house of Ilsumalik. Perhaps this place belongs to someone else."

"I am Ilsumalik," the man said, "and tell me, why I would welcome any of Ishme's thieving relatives, especially after what they did to him? Hold on, what did you say your name was?"

"I should have introduced myself first," Ekur said. "I am sorry that I did not. My name is Ekur."

"Ekur," Ilsumalik repeated, his voice growing kinder. "You should have told me so. Yes, I know of you. Ishme told me that it was you who made his life liveable in that house that your parents stole from him. Tell me why you seek to meet my guests, and I will try to help you."

"I need to get to Meluhha as soon as possible," Ekur said, and then decided to embellish some more. "I have been commissioned by an acquaintance of my grandfather. He is very rich and powerful, and I am not allowed to disclose his name or my mission. However, I can say this, to my patron, who is very rich indeed, speed is more important than cost."

"That is interesting," Ilsumalik said, "but if I was not able to curb my curiosity, I would never be able to serve the Meluhhans. So, I will not ask you to divulge what you cannot. But, I do have to have an idea about how rich your patron is? I mean, how much can you spend? Is it as much as it would take to hire a whole crew?"

"He is ready to not only hire a crew," Ekur said conspiratorially, "but, if required, to buy the ship."

"It is like that, is it?" Ilsumalik smiled. "Then, it must be a woman. And as I promised, I will not ask any more. Let me find out who amongst my guests is planning to go back to Meluhha first. Then, I will negotiate for you. However, you would agree that your grandfather would not want me to do anything for free, as that would put you in my debt. And as Ishme must have taught you, you should avoid being in anyone's debt, especially to save a little for a rich patron. So, shall we say that my commission will be one tenth of the negotiated price?"

Ekur almost agreed. After all, for the first time in his life, he did not have to worry about the expenses. Then he stopped himself – that is not what the Akkadian would do.

"We shall say no such thing," Ekur said with a broad grin. "You are right in saying that Ishme would not want me to be in anyone's debt. But, even less than that, would he like me making a fool's deal. In your proposal, the higher the price, the more you benefit. No, let us fix the price. However, you will have to ensure that I start the journey within two weeks at most. If I can leave before the two-week period, I will increase your commission by one-tenth for everyday earlier that I commence my journey. Of course, there will be a similar reduction for every day's delay."

"By Bogu, you have got Ishme's heart and stomach[67]," Ilsumalik said, also with a smile. "I agree. It is indeed good doing business with you. In what form are you planning to make the payment?"

"Gold," then Ekur took out one of the nuggets.

Ilsumalik reverently took the nugget from Ekur, and bit it. "I think this is a fair value."

"Fair to whom?" Ekur laughed, "I will have this cut into eight pieces, and give you one."

Finally, they agreed on half of the nugget.

"Don't go anywhere," Ilsumalik said, after everything was agreed, "I will send one of my servers to you. Tell him what you would like to eat or drink. Don't worry about the cost, for it is all on me. I will be back later, when I have some more information to give you."

When the server arrived, Ekur asked him about every Meluhhan dish they were serving. Learn at every opportunity, his grandfather used to say after all.

Ilsumalik returned quite some time later.

"I have found someone who is planning to leave Kurm in ten days," Ilsumalik said proudly, "so, my commission will go up by four tenth."

"Yes, it will," Ekur said, "but why don't you double your commission by convincing him to leave in five days, instead. Find out what his losses would be by leaving earlier. If reasonable, these losses might be covered by my patron."

"I will try my best," Ilsumalik said. "And you do mean double, and not increase by nine-tenth for the nine days?"

"Yes, I do mean double," Ekur laughed.

Ilsumalik soon came back with an elderly Meluhhan.

---

[67] In ancient Sumer, it was believed that intelligence came from the heart and cunningness from the stomach

"This is Vaansh," Ilsumalik introduced, "and he is the trader who is leaving here for Thallo in Meluhha, by his own ship, ten days from now. He says that it would be impossible for him to leave in five days."

"Impossible?" Ekur said faking surprise, then continued in the Meluhhan tongue, "My grandfather was once told by his Meluhhan friend, Vikoo of Darromohe, that impossible is the least frequently used word in the Meluhhan language, as the Meluhhans think nothing is really impossible. Perhaps, my grandfather had misunderstood this friend."

"Your grandfather knew Vikoo, did he?" Vaansh said, also speaking in Meluhhan, "Sadly, he has moved on to his next life." He looked upwards and kissed his forefinger. "I think I did not make myself clear to Ilsumalik. It is not impossible for me to leave in five days, but quite improbable for anyone to cover the losses I would incur by doing that."

"But, how will we know this unless you tell me what the losses would be?" Ekur challenged.

Vaansh then gave him the figure. Ekur whistled through his teeth.

"Yes, that is improbable indeed," Ekur said, and then added. "Not just for someone to pay, but also be convinced that anyone could lose that much by leaving a few days earlier. Even losses amounting to a tenth of that would be difficult to understand."

The negotiations had commenced. Ilsumalik joined in from time to time to help Ekur, but not too obviously. Finally, they agreed on the price and the terms of payment to start their journey in five days.

"There is one last thing," Vaansh said. "When a person dies, in our custom, we do both burial and cremation. Whether a person is buried or cremated is decided based on who died, and the circumstances of his or her life and death. But, if a Meluhhan dies outside our realm, we always cremate the person. Then his ashes are carried back to where he lived in Meluhha, and the High Priests decide whether these ashes have to be buried or kept with the family. During this trip, one of my sailors died. And we will be carrying his ashes back with us in an urn. I know death is treated very differently here. So, I want to make sure that you do not have a problem sailing on a ship with a dead man's ashes."

"No, I don't have a problem," Ekur said. Then, he had a great idea, "actually, I will have an urn with another Meluhhan's ashes with me, as well. I hope you don't have a problem with this."

"Of course not," Vaansh said. "As both the departed souls will be in a hurry to get back to Meluhha, I think we will have fair winds. As we will start before sunrise, you should come back here a day before our departure. I will take your leave now."

After Vaansh was gone, Ilsumalik asked one of his servers to bring them some kaš.

"It was great doing business with you, O grandson of Ishme," Ilsumalik toasted by lowering his lips to the cup and both hands on his forehead. "I will not insult you by asking when you will pay me. I know you will do it before you leave. Is there anything else I can help you with?"

"There is one small thing," Ekur said. "Vaansh mentioned that he would take back his sailor's ashes in an urn."

"I heard that you are doing the same. If you want to keep this a secret, my lips are sealed."

"I wanted to ask where the Meluhhans get these urns to carry the ashes of their dead," Ekur said.

"Oh, your Meluhhan is not cremated, yet," Ilsumalik said, and then added conspiringly, "I hope he is dead already at least, or are you arranging that, as well." After laughing at his own joke, he continued, "Even if you are, it is not my business. Usually, they come to me and I acquire these urns for them. Some prefer the ones that a potter acquaintance of mine makes. But, most prefer the wooden ones made by a carpenter I know. The wooden ones, though not traditional for the Meluhhans, are more durable and less likely to break during a journey. I can get one for you. It will be my gift to you. Both types of urns come in three sizes and many designs. If you let me know your preference, I will have it here for you by the day after tomorrow."

"I would like two of the wooden ones. Please get me the largest size," Ekur replied. "As to the design and colour, as long as it does not stand out, I will let you decide."

The next two days elapsed slowly for Ekur. There was no one that he needed to bid farewell. After he had sorted out the things he would take with him, there was nothing much he could do at home, either. He spent most of his day either at the Marketplace, dreaming about Ishme and the Akkadian, or at Ilsumalik's lodge, surreptitiously listening in on the conversations between the Meluhhan traders. It was here that Ilsumalik found him early in the afternoon two days after they had their initial conversation.

"I have your urns," Ilsumalik informed Ekur.

Ekur looked around and was relieved to note that none of the Meluhhans had yet come back from their daily businesses.

"Thank you, Ilsumalik," Ekur said. "You have indeed been a good friend. If you fetch them now, I will take them with me. Also, in case you were wondering, I will pay you your commission day after tomorrow."

Ekur took the urns back to the Akkadian's home. He then opened one of the urns and was very pleased to see that two-thirds of the precious stones would easily fit inside it and the remaining one-third and the gold nuggets would fit into the other. But, after transferring these to the urns, he realized there was a flaw in his plan. The stones and gold rattled noisily in the urns.

Ekur went to a butcher in the other side of Kurm and bought a large amount of animal bones and entrails. After bringing these to the Akkadian's home, he took a large utensil and started a fire inside it and slowly burnt the bones and entrails. After this was done, he took out ten of the gold nuggets from the second urn and then topped up both urns with the ashes. He then retrieved the other four gold nuggets that he had secreted into various parts of the house. He needed one to pay off Ilsumalik's commission, and five more to pay Vaansh as down payment before their journey commenced. He would have to pay him four more after reaching Thallo in Meluhha. So, he would still have four left to get him to Parroo. He then sealed both the urns with wax. Of course, if the need was dire, he could always open the urn with the gold nuggets and retrieve some more.

The next afternoon, Ekur went to Ilsumalik and handed one gold nugget to him.

"I don't like the idea of charging you a commission," Ilsumalik said, "but, as I have told you, it is for your own good to not be in anyone's debt. Let me know if you need anything else, now or after you are back."

"I don't have many well-wishers here," Ekur said. "It is indeed nice to hear there is someone I can come for help when I come back."

Vaansh did not come back until quite late.

"I have been waiting for you since early afternoon," Ekur said, more as conversation than as a complaint.

"Well, you are the reason why I have to work late," Vaansh said, partly joking and partly complaining.

"We have already decided on the price for you to go back early," Ekur said with a chuckle. "Lucky for you that my grandfather is not here, or he would ask you to go and learn from a true Meluhhan, the value of one's words."

"I know," Vaansh said, "but I owe it to my profession to increase my profits as much as possible."

Ekur, along with the two urns and an assortment of clothes that belonged to the Akkadian and himself, accompanied Vaansh to his ship. Just before sunrise, they sailed for Thallo.

When Vaansh realized that Ekur had not taken permission from the Master of Levy to leave for Meluhha, he decided not to take any undue risk. So, Ekur was sent below to the bilges. As they passed towns of Larsa[68], Ur[69] and many others, Ekur had to bear the unearthly stench of a ship's bilges. Ekur consoled himself with the thought, that the towns he would have really liked to see like Babylon[70] and Sippar[71] were upriver from Kurm. As soon as they were out into the sea, Ekur was allowed to roam freely wherever he wanted. But, within hours of reaching the sea, Ekur was violently seasick, and never really recovered for the rest of the journey.

---

[68] A town downriver from Kurm in Sumer
[69] A town downriver from Kurm in Sumer
[70] A city upriver from Kurm in Sumer
[71] A town upriver from Kurm in Sumer

Chapter 15

Ekur's Quest II

When they reached Thallo, Ekur went to take leave of Vaansh.

"I have been meaning to talk to you since we left Sumer," Vaansh said, "but when you were not sleeping, your seasickness was not allowing you to keep your head out of the trough long enough to use your ears. I do not plan to visit Sumer for a few months. Most of my sailors will be taking this opportunity to visit their hometowns. As this is your first visit to our lands, I was thinking that in case you are headed in the same direction as any of them, you may want to travel with them."

Ekur quickly thought about it. He was yet to decide how to proceed to Purawanbhag. And he could not see any risk in taking up Vaansh on his offer.

"It is indeed very kind of you," Ekur said, "the first place I will be going to is Purawanbhag and if anyone proceeding towards there, I would really appreciate it if I could travel with him."

"You are in luck, indeed," Vaansh said. "The captain of my ship, Miraak, comes from Ankal, a small town in that general area. I know he plans to leave for Kdwar this very afternoon and then proceed by river to Ankal. He will be glad to help. Also, I wanted to let you know, when you are ready to go back to Sumer, come back here or to Kdwar, and seek me out. If you do not disrupt my plans, I will take you back for free. You see, my losses by preponing the trip were significantly lower than I had estimated. Wait here while I fetch Miraak. One more thing, Miraak is a very reclusive person. Please don't expect much conversation from him."

That is good news indeed, Ekur thought, as he did not want to talk about his trip either.

Vaansh came back with Miraak.

"I have told Miraak that you are planning to travel to Purawanbhag," Vaansh said, after the introductions. "He is fine with you tagging along."

"There is another ship that leaves here early tomorrow morning for Kdwar," Miraak said, getting straight to the point, "Vaansh will arrange for you to take this ship. I have already made arrangements for a boat to take me to Ankal from Kdwar. Even though Parroo is a little upriver, I will take you there, first. We will share the expenses equally. I think that is fair. Please tell me if you agree with this. From Parroo you can easily arrange to go on to Purawanbhag."

Ekur readily accepted.

The trip to Kdwar and, then, to Parroo was quite uneventful. Everything worked as Miraak had planned.

"Miraak, I am really grateful that you let me join you," Ekur said after the boat had docked. "I would really appreciate it if you could bear with me for a little more. I need to make a few quick enquiries and also make arrangements for a camel or ass to carry my belongings to Purawanbhag."

"Okay, but please hurry," Miraak replied. "I would like to be in Ankal by sunset. If you cannot make your arrangements on time, I suggest you come to Ankal with me. There is a suitable lodging near my place. I think the person who runs the lodging can help you acquire a camel, as well. However, it will then take you longer to get to Purawanbhag."

"I will try to be as quick as possible," Ekur said, "and I am very grateful for your offer."

Ekur then proceeded to a group of men who were standing near the docks.

"Excuse me," Ekur said politely, "I am looking for Viraan."

"There are many persons with that name. Which Viraan are you looking for?" one of the strangers asked.

"The Viraan I seek is a trader," Ekur said, "he is from Purawanbhag but his boats come to Parroo. He has a cousin called Tiraak, who is a prospector."

The stranger looked at Ekur suspiciously. "Why do you seek this Viraan?"

"I am sorry, but I think that business is between him and me," Ekur said politely but firmly, "however, I can tell you this, I come from Kurm in Sumer"

"Okay, come with me," the stranger said after a long pause.

Ekur followed the stranger into a nearby lodging, and was asked to wait in the inner courtyard.

"Why do you seek Viraan?" a voice called out from behind Ekur.

"That business is between him and me," Ekur insisted.

"Hmm," a man said entering the courtyard, "but I cannot figure out what business you can have with me, for I am Viraan from Purawanbhag. And I do have a cousin called Tiraak."

"You are Viraan?" Ekur said unable to hide his excitement.

"I am still waiting to hear about your business," Viraan asked, responding to Ekur's excitement with terseness.

"It is a long story," Ekur said. "I come from Kurm. And on hearing this, I am sure you are now at least inquisitive if not excited. But first, I need to relieve the person who has brought me to Parroo. He is waiting in the boat that brought us here, and would like to leave for Ankal as soon as possible."

Ekur quickly took a room in the same lodging. Ekur then went to the boat, thanked Miraak for all his help and came back to the lodge with his belongings and immediately went back to where he had left Viraan.

"As I said, I come from Kurm," Ekur began again.

"Is that supposed to mean something to me?" Viraan asked guardedly.

"If you are the Viraan I seek, it definitely should," Ekur replied impatiently. "I come from Kurm, and you did have a visitor from Kurm before. I know you helped him a lot, and so did he. I see that you're still having the boats pulled by animals, like he had suggested."

"Would this person have a name?" Viraan asked.

"The Akkadian," Ekur said.

"Like my name is the Givenlander and I assume you are the Sumerian," Viraan said wryly.

"No, of course not," Ekur said a little embarrassed, "I am sorry as I had always heard my grandfather mention him as the Akkadian. I sometimes forget that is not his name. His name was Ildùr."

"Is there anything you can say to remind me of him?" Viraan asked.

It was now Ekur's turn to be sceptical, even suspicious. There was no reason to believe that this person was the Viraan he was seeking. He decided to be a little more guarded in his conversation.

"The Akkadian came to Givenland seeking something very specific," Ekur replied without mentioning the White Gods or the Great Northern White Mountains. "He was helped in his search by you, your cousin Tiraak, and his partner Runggoo."

"Is there something more specific you could say that might remind me of him?" Viraan insisted.

"You all helped him, and another person called Pasher, go on a journey to the Great Northern White Mountains," Ekur tried again, not sure how much more he should share, especially as he still could not be sure of the stranger's identity.

"This Ildùr you speak of, is there something more specific you want to add?" Viraan repeated.

"I am being quite specific," Ekur replied, starting to get a little annoyed. "Without any acknowledgement or response from your end, I might add."

"Hmm, so you have nothing further to add," Viraan said after some thought. "Well, if you don't have a phrase that you would like to say here, I think …"

"Of course, the phrase," Ekur shouted out in excitement.

"Yes, yes. The phrase, please," Viraan asked expectantly.

"I am very sorry, I cannot remember the phrase," Ekur said.

Viraan was visibly disappointed. After some thought, he sighed and said, "Please stay in this lodge for a few more days. There are a couple of people I would like you to meet. They are presently not in Parroo, but I will send them a message and they should be here soon. We will talk once they arrive."

The next three days seemed really long to Ekur. He tried hard to remember the phrase the Akkadian had uttered, which Ekur had missed, because he had got distracted by the precious stones. He tried to go to sleep thinking about it, hoping it would come back to him in his dreams. He even tried thinking about it, while holding his breath. But, whatever he tried ended in failure. Then he started thinking of other ways to get the men's acceptance. Perhaps, he could tell them of the Akkadian's death or show them the precious stones.

By the third morning, he had made some decisions. Even if the Akkadian's friends did not acknowledge him, he would still try to go to Wacha and give the Akkadian's wife the urn, but he would not mention the jewels. And unless they acknowledged him, he would not share anything about what the Akkadian had told him the night he died.

Now, that he had left everything to fate, Ekur felt more at peace. And if he did have any doubts about the hand of fate, they were removed when soon after he had reached these decisions, Viraan came to invite him for dinner.

"Please join me for dinner tonight," Viraan said.

When Ekur arrived at Viraan's room, there were two more persons there with Viraan. Viraan got up to introduce them, but the older of the two stopped him.

"Before we talk of this Ildùr of yours," this stranger said to Ekur, "can our server, Shubhyaan, get you anything to drink?"

Both Viraan and the third man looked quizzically at the stranger who had spoken.

"I will only have water, thank you," Ekur replied.

"Are you sure?" the stranger asked again. "Once I send Shubhyaan away, he will not come back until we have concluded our discussions about this Ildùr of yours."

"Thank you very much," Ekur replied, "but I will be fine with water."

"Ok," the stranger said. "Viraan informs us that you have been seeking to meet us. I am Tiraak, and this is Runggoo. Please tell us why you seek us?"

"I am Ekur," Ekur said, "I come from Kurm in Sumer. Does that mean anything to any of you?"

"Should it?" Tiraak asked, faking disinterest.

"If you are who you claim to be, it should," Ekur retorted.

"Good point," Tiraak said. "I think it is important to establish who we are, first. Go with my cousin Viraan to either the town centre or the docks. Choose any three random persons. My cousin will convince them to come back here with you. Then you can ask them who we are."

Ekur was ready to protest, but realized that the stranger's words seemed to be logical and would at least ensure that Ekur was not trying to get grapes from an olive tree. So, he agreed and accompanied Viraan.

He chose two persons from the docks and one from the town centre. He made sure that Viraan did not have a chance to talk with them privately. The persons from the docks immediately agreed to accompany Viraan. The person from the town centre was initially reluctant, and had to be convinced by the promise of some raajaraas. After they were back, he asked Viraan to join Tiraak and Runggoo. Then, he asked one of the persons from the docks to accompany him, and instructed the person from the town centre to come in next, followed by the other person from the docks.

"Do you know anyone in this room?" Ekur asked the first person from the docks.

"This is Viraan of Purawanbhag. This is his cousin, Tiraak, who hails from Darromohe. And this is Runggoo, who I think comes from somewhere near the Great Northern White Mountains. He usually goes prospecting with Tiraak. I don't know who you are, though," the person answered without hesitation.

"Thank you for your help," Tiraak said to the person from the dock. "If you would wait in the room inside for short while, we will arrange for some refreshments."

"Do you know anyone in this room?" Ekur repeated to the person from the town centre.

"I know this man who came with you to the town centre," the person from the town centre said. "He is Viraan of Purawanbhag. I have seen both of these other gentlemen town, and I might have heard that they are prospectors. But I don't really know who they are. I hope I will still get my raajaraas."

"Yes, you will get your raajaraas," Viraan said, "but, first, please wait in the other room for a short while."

"Do you know anyone in this room?" Ekur repeated to the second person from the docks.

"Why do you ask such a question?" the person asked.

Ekur had not expected this, but before he could compose an answer, Tiraak interrupted.

"Please, humour us," Tiraak said. "As you are already here, we would really appreciate it if you would be kind enough to answer our question."

"Okay," the person said, "I hope that this is not some kind of a trick. This is Viraan, the trader from Purawanbhag. This is Runggoo, the prospector. You are Tiraak, the prospector. This is a person who arrived a few days back, and seeing his dark skin and hearing his strange accent, I am guessing he is from somewhere near the Great Unending Waters."

Viraan then led the three witnesses out of the room and came back after arranging refreshments and raajaraas for them.

"Now that it is established that we are, who we say we are," Tiraak said, "let us talk about who you are. You told Viraan that we are supposed to know someone called Ildùr. Is there any other thing you would like to add?"

"As I told Viraan, there was a phrase, which I was supposed to repeat, but I have forgotten how it goes. I ..." Ekur started to say.

"Sorry, I am forgetting my manners," Tiraak said. "Before we talk about this Ildùr of yours, I wanted to ask you again whether Shubhyaan can get you anything else."

"Again with your Shubhyaan," Ekur said impatiently. "I have been asked enough times whether Shubhyaan can bring me something, and as I said before, I am fine. Can we get back to Ildùr?"

"Let us do that," Tiraak said with steel in his voice. "You say that this Akkadian of yours taught you a phrase. He said that none of us would acknowledge knowing him unless you repeat this phrase. You have come all the way from Kurm in Sumer to seek us out, but you forgot the phrase. So, assuming this phrase exists, are you sure that you ever knew this phrase?"

"Are you all not listening?" Ekur said in exasperation. "Yes, the Akkadian did share the phrase with me, but I have forgotten it. Can we move on now?"

"Well, I am not sure where we can move on to?" Tiraak now said with equal frustration. "I think it is best that you go back to Kurm. Re-learn this phrase from Ildùr, scribe it down if required, and come back."

"I wish I could," Ekur said with genuine despondency, "sadly, the Akkadian is dead."

"Ildùr is dead?" Runggoo exclaimed. It was as if he had been struck physically. He leaned against the wall and continued, "When did this happen? How did this happen? Do the people in Wacha know?"

"So, you do know Ildùr?" Ekur asked Runggoo accusingly.

"I always feel bad when people die," Runggoo trying to recover. "Death is an important part of life in Givenland. So, when I hear someone had died, I always want to know the how and when of their death."

"And why did you mention Wacha?"

"You must have said something to Viraan," Runggoo said unconvincingly, "and he must have repeated this to us."

"All of you know that is not true," Ekur said close to tears with frustration. "Please believe me when I say that the Akkadian wanted me to come here and seek you all out. It was very important to him. I don't understand why you are behaving the way you are."

"That is because you are not hearing yourself," Tiraak said. "We either know Ildùr, or we don't. If we do know him, and we promised him that we would not acknowledge his existence beyond a select circle, unless the person came to us with a phrase, then why would we acknowledge knowing him without hearing the phrase? And if we don't know him, why should we acknowledge any knowledge of him? So, whichever way you look at it, we are doing the right thing."

"If you put it that way," Ekur said. "So, if you don't know the Akkadian, you cannot help me get his ashes to his wife, either."

"His what?!" Runggoo exclaimed with genuine surprise.

"His wife in Wacha," Ekur said, "and please don't act surprised. As Tiraak said before, you either knew the Akkadian or you did not. If you did know him, you would also know that he had a wife, and if you did not know him, you would not care that he had a wife." Then, it dawned on him. "No, actually, you might not know that he had got married in Wacha. He never told you about his wife before leaving on his quest."

"Let us stop talking about Ildùr for a moment," Tiraak started, "but can Shubhyaan …"

"Please, enough of that," Ekur said finally raising his voice. "Let us continue to talk about Ildùr, and not about Shubhyaan."

"In that case, I think we are done here," Tiraak said.

"No, I don't think we are," Runggoo said, and stayed Tiraak with his hand, "I agree with you, Tiraak. If we knew Ildùr and made an agreement with him, we should honour that and if we did not know him, we did not know him. But, that should not stop us from helping a person from faraway lands, who is trying to get a husband's ashes to his wife, who does not even know that she has been widowed. Tell us, Ekur, what is the name of this Akkadian's wife?"

"I am sorry, he never mentioned her name," Ekur said, starting to despair again. "But, if someone can guide me to Wacha, I can meet Pasher. I am sure he will help me."

"I was forgetting," Runggoo said, "Pasher will be …"

"If you don't know the phrase, I don't think Pasher will help you, either," Tiraak cut in, not allowing Runggoo to finish.

"How would you know?" Ekur asked. "As I assume, much like Ildùr, you don't know Pasher, either. In any case, whether he acknowledges knowing the Akkadian or not, or whether he introduces me to the Akkadian's wife or not, I have to go to Wacha and find out for myself."

"I will guide you there," Runggoo said.

"Are you sure about this?" Tiraak asked.

"Yes, I am very sure," Runggoo said. "See me tomorrow after sunset to finalize all the arrangements. I do have a question, and trust me when I say that your answer, or even your refusal to answer me, will not change my mind about taking you to Wacha. What is your relationship with this Akkadian called, Ildùr?"

Not wanting to antagonize the only person ready to help him, Ekur replied, "My grandfather, Ishme, taught the Akkadian your tongue."

"I think we are done here now," Tiraak said. "And Ekur, I think it does not make sense for us to sit down for dinner. It is best you bid farewell now."

"I agree," Ekur said and left, seething in anger and frustration. After reaching his room, he realized Runggoo had not told him where they would meet the next day, so he started back towards Viraan's rooms. As he approached, he heard the men speaking amongst themselves.

"You heard him," Tiraak was saying. "He is Ishme's grandson. If memory serves me right, Ildùr's Abgal had everything he had stolen through lying and trickery by his family. I am sure this Ekur is up to no good. Runggoo, after hearing who he is, are you still sure you want to take him to Wacha?"

At first, Ekur wanted to rush in and tell them the truth about his relationship with Ishme and how he opposed his parents' behaviour towards Ishme. But, he knew none of this would help. Ekur continued his eavesdropping.

"He does not come across as someone with bad intentions," now Runggoo was saying, "in any case, my word is my bond. I have to take him to Wacha. But, I would like you to take a guide and proceed to Wacha first thing tomorrow. Meet Pasher and tell him everything. I still cannot believe that Ildùr is dead. I can't imagine what this news will do to Pasher."

"Okay, I will do as you say," Tiraak said. "You know, I usually trust your instincts. But, I also believe in basing everything on hard facts. And facts do say something different about Ekur. We know for a fact that he is a liar. You will agree that if Ekur had heard the key phrase from Ildùr, even if he had forgotten it, he would have remembered it during our conversation. I all but told him the phrase."

Ekur wondered what Tiraak meant by the last statement. But, as he heard some other voices approaching, he decided it would be best to go back to his room and ask the lodge-keeper about Runggoo's whereabouts the next day.

Trying to go back and talk to Runggoo and instead overhearing Tiraak and Runggoo's conversation had been beneficial for Ekur. But, he need not have bothered to go back, for much before sunset the next day, Runggoo came over to inform him that all the arrangements for their trip to Wacha had been completed and they would leave the lodge at sunrise the next day.

"I am sorry if I lost my temper yesterday," Ekur said. And then knowing fully where Tiraak was, innocently added, "Before we leave for Wacha, I wanted to apologize to Tiraak as well. Do you know where I can find him now?"

"I was too busy making the preparations for our journey," Runggoo said with discomfort, his eyes shifty. "So, I have no idea. I don't think I will be seeing him before we leave tomorrow. Maybe you can see him on your way back from Wacha."

The next morning, Runggoo was already waiting with two asses when Ekur came down. One of these asses was already laden, so Ekur lifted his travelling bags on to the other. Then, they headed out towards Wacha. Initially they rode in silence.

"Ekur," Runggoo said finally breaking the silence, "what was your purpose in seeking us out?"

"As I have said before," Ekur replied, "it is because the Akkadian wanted me to do so."

"And Ildùr told you this phrase that would be required to get us to acknowledge his existence?" Runggoo asked.

"Yes, he did," Ekur replied, "but I have forgotten it. Why is this so difficult to believe? Haven't any of you ever forgotten something important in your lives? Why don't you all ask yourselves a different question? Why would someone travel all the way from Sumer without a reason?"

"I hear you," Runggoo said, "and I think it is best if we don't talk about this anymore, as neither of us will understand the frustrations of the other."

Chapter 16

Ekur's Quest III

Runggoo and Ekur reached Wacha, a little before sunset, and the first thing that struck Ekur there was the stench. He was not sure where it originated, but it was really overbearing. Interestingly, there had been no mention of this when the Akkadian had told him about Wacha. Then Ekur smiled at the realization that with the Akkadian's steadfast and single-minded determination to achieve his goal, he might have not even noticed the stench.

Runggoo mistaking Ekur's smile for a sneer said, "I see you are sneering at these people. You are wondering why the people here prefer to live with this smell. Perhaps, you are even thinking that someone should give them a lesson on cleanliness. Well, trust me if you had come here from late spring to early autumn, you would not be greeted by this smell. In summer, this place would have welcomed you with the sweet smell of flowers and fruits. This is true for most of the mountain valleys. What you smell now is caused by a combination of things. First, is the burning of animal fat for cooking, then, there is the burning of dried animal manure for heating. And the daily fog from the cold fronts stops the smell from dissipating away. People, who live here, hate it even more than you do. As it gets colder, making it impossible to clean yourself, it actually gets worse. But, they accept all this as a price to pay to live in these valleys, a price they are willing to pay, as given a choice they would not desire to be anywhere else."

"Thank you for enlightening me," Ekur said mockingly, "but my smile, which you misunderstood for something else, was for an altogether different reason. The Akkadian had told me about his stay in Wacha in great detail. He had told me many things, but had never mentioned this overbearing smell. I was smiling at how remarkable a person he was, as most probably he did not even notice the smell, and that is why he never mentioned it."

"Yes, he was indeed a remarkable person," Runggoo said. "I mean he must have been if he did not notice a stench like this." Then, looking at Ekur almost pleadingly, he continued, "Can I ask you something? Please hear all the questions carefully before answering any of them. First, did Ildùr really ask you to come here? Second, in Parroo, why did you not accept Tiraak's offer to let Shubhyaan get you some refreshments? Third, are you very sure that Ildùr mentioned this supposed key phrase to you?"

For a moment, Ekur came close to telling Runggoo about why he was unable to hear the phrase, and how the Akkadian had died before he could repeat it. But, Ekur could not bring himself to admit that he had lied, for he remembered the conversation that he had overheard between Runggoo and Tiraak, in which Tiraak had called Ekur a liar, to which Runggoo had not objected.

"There you go again with your Shubhyaan," Ekur said, "I really appreciate the fact that you have guided me here. You are as big hearted as the Akkadian had said you were. But, if I remember correctly, in the beginning of the journey you said that it would be best not to talk about this anymore, as we will not understand each other's frustrations."

"Yes, I did," Runggoo said. "And I am sorry that I brought it up. But, as a great man who I was lucky enough to call a friend had once told me, hope is something that is not bound by agreements or laws. Maybe that is why I was continuing to hope."

The phrase sounded exactly like something the Akkadian would say, followed by an anecdote, of course.

"You acknowledge knowing this great man," Ekur blurted out, unable to stop himself. "I am sorry, for we did decide that we would not talk about him."

"I don't understand what you mean," Runggoo said playing along. "As it is getting late, we need to hurry and go to the chief's hut and pay our respects. We will not be welcome in anyone's hut before we have done this."

"Please lead the way," Ekur said sincerely. "From what I have heard, Nongru is a very kind and worldly person."

"First thing you need to learn is that once someone becomes a chief, he is not called by his name by anyone, from inside or outside this valley," Runggoo said.

They soon came to the chief's hut. There was a strikingly good-looking couple sitting on the entranceway of the hut. Ekur immediately knew them to be Nongru and his wife Khongrem. There were two male toddlers, both around the same age, playing in front of the hut. It was clear that Nongru and Khongrem were expecting someone. This in itself was not unusual, though, he knew the chief would be informed the moment an outsider arrived in the valley. However, Ekur also knew that Tiraak must have arrived and warned them to expect Ekur's arrival.

When they saw Runggoo and Ekur approaching, the woman Khongrem, called out, "Someone please take Bugyel and Bujang inside to Khongmu."

A slightly older but very well-built man came out and effortlessly swung both kids onto his shoulders and took them inside.

"O Respected Chief and O Divine Wife of Chief," Runggoo said, "I am Runggoo of Swastu valley. Please accept our humble greetings and this humble gift." He then took out a leather headgear and some jewellery beads and laid them in front of Nongru and Khongrem.

"O Respected Chief and O Divine Wife of Chief. I am Ekur of Kurm in Sumer. Please accept our humble greetings," Ekur followed, bowing to the ground, and quickly took out one of his gold nuggets, and placed it in front of Nongru and Khongrem. "And please accept our humble gift."

"Welcome to our valley O strangers to our land, if you come in peace, you will beget peace. If …" Khongrem started, but stopped and looked expectantly towards Nongru.

It was clear that Nongru had decided not to play out whatever charade that was planned. He got up and embraced Runggoo.

"Well met, Runggoo. Finally fate has brought us together. You are a brother of another brother of mine. That makes you my brother," Nongru said. "And brothers do not bow down to each other, but embrace each other, with their hearts held as close to each other as possible. Especially in this time of grief, at the loss of our brother, this is how we share and reduce our sorrow."

Both Runggoo and Khongrem were trying to signal Nongru to stop, but he would have none of it.

"Runggoo," Nongru continued, "you will sleep in our house during your stay, and please, I will not hear any arguments on this. Another brother of mine tried recently, without any success, as well."

It was clear from Khongrem and Runggoo's expressions that they had resigned to the situation and they did not make any more efforts to stop him.

"So, Ekur of Kurm," Nongru said, turning to Ekur, "what business brings you to this valley far, far away from your lands?"

Ekur bowed low very slowly and came back upright, even more slowly. He was giving himself time to collect his thoughts. He knew this was different from conversing with Tiraak or Runggoo. He knew that within this valley, Nongru was the master of life and death. If there was even a hint of insult or accusation in what Ekur said to Nongru, he might never live to see the outside world ever again. But, if he came across as too weak, Nongru would not take him seriously.

"O respected Chief," Ekur said, "I have come to your valley for a few reasons. First and foremost, someone dear to me died recently. His name was Ildùr. He informed me, while on his death bed, to bring this news along with," Ekur paused, as if saddened by the memories of the loss, but in reality trying to decide whether to lie about the contents of the urn, and then continued, "an urn containing his last remains, to be given to his wife who lives in this valley of yours. I am very sorry, but he died before he could tell me her name. My next reason …"

"Wait!" Nongru interrupted, "I am a simple man and prefer to solve one problem at a time. If this Ildùr came to this valley and married someone here, he would need the permission of the chief. So you would agree that I would know who his wife was. Why don't you leave this urn containing his ashes with me, and I will make sure that she gets the news of her husband's death and this urn. Do you have a problem with this proposition of mine?"

"Who am I to question your judgment, O respected Chief," Ekur said, but ventured to add, "I would have very much liked to have made acquaintance of the wife of someone who was really important to me."

"I hear you," Nongru said, "but we are talking about what you need to do, not what you would like to do. Now, let us talk about your next reason."

"While on his death bed, Ildùr made me promise another thing," Ekur said embellishing the truth. "He asked that I deliver the news of his death to you and a man who was very close to him called Pasher. He also asked me to personally make sure that Pasher is all right and does not get too emotional about this news."

"Interesting," Nongru said plainly. "I want to believe you, but anyone who knows Pasher would never believe that he could get too emotional. And you did say that Ildùr was close to Pasher. You seem to want to add something?"

"Yes, O respected Chief," Ekur said, falling further into the quicksand of lies, "Ildùr did not say that Pasher was emotional. But as Pasher never showed his emotions, Ildùr was more worried that …"

"Ekur," Nongru commanded, "stop this nonsense before I lose my patience. I will ensure that you get to meet Pasher before you leave this valley. Was there any other reason for your visit?"

Ekur silently scolded himself. He was sure that the Akkadian would have never set foot on Wacha, before deciding what to say and more importantly what not to say. He realized this was his last chance, and quickly decided to be more open.

"Yes, O Respected Chief," Ekur started, "the last reason is more complicated. Ildùr was narrating his quest to me." And to prove his genuineness, Ekur told them in some detail about the Akkadian's journey. Coming to the night at the cave, Ekur continued, "As he was telling me what happened at the cave, he fell sick again. When he briefly came out of his delirium, he told me that Givenland was in grave danger and that I should come to Givenland to find you all. He told me that with your help, this destruction could be averted. He then told me this phrase that I would have to repeat, in order for you to acknowledge that you knew Ildùr. I am very sorry, but I have forgotten this phrase."

"Interesting," Nongru said, "very interesting, indeed. I see you have managed to successfully seek out Runggoo. Did you have any luck with Viraan or Tiraak?"

"Yes," Ekur said, "Initially fate was kind to me, I found Viraan quite easily. But, that was the last act of kindness I received from fate. As I have forgotten the phrase that Ildùr had told me, none of them acknowledged knowing him."

"Of course, when you first met Viraan, you told him that you had forgotten this phrase," Nongru asked.

"No," Ekur said. "I had totally forgotten about the phrase. It was only when Viraan mentioned the phrase, that I informed him that I had forgotten it."

"Even more interesting," Nongru said. "Of course, you then told them about this Ildùr's journey and the dangers Givenland faced."

"No," Ekur said, "I could not talk about something that important, until I was sure."

"So, you wanted to be sure of their identity, but were not able to. And now that you know I am Nongru, the Chief of Wacha, and there can be no doubt about my identity, you decided to talk about it. Is that what you are saying?" Nongru asked.

Ekur realized how big a hole he had dug for himself. But, he also knew that if he accepted now that he had lied earlier, his future would only become bleaker.

"I know how this may sound," Ekur started.

"In Wacha, I judge what sounds like what," Nongru said imperiously. "So, please stick to the facts."

"They did prove their identity to me," Ekur said sheepishly.

"I have one more question before we get to what should be done next," Nongru said. He paused. He looked at Runggoo and then at Khongrem. Then he looked towards his doorway. It was clear to Ekur that there were at least two people inside the doorway listening to their conversation. Suddenly turning to Ekur, Nongru asked, "Have you ever heard of Durshan Lake?" then noticing Ekur's start, continued, "You don't have to answer, I can clearly see from your face that you have."

"Yes, I have," Ekur said, realizing all was lost, "but I was not supposed to mention Durshan to anyone but Pasher."

"Of course," Nongru said. "Isn't that a little convenient? You were supposed to tell that to the only person you are yet to meet."

"Please believe me," Ekur started, "If you hear me out …"

"Believe you? That would indeed be a very difficult thing to do," Nongru said with feeling. "I think you are done talking. It is my turn now. Unlike the others, I will not tell you that I have never heard of Ildùr. Instead, I will tell you with pride, that I was lucky to not only have made his acquaintance, but to have been befriended by him. I owe him this chiefdom, my wife and my life. We are going to celebrate his life and mourn his death. And we are not going to do these in secret. "

"Then you help me do Ildùr's bidding?" Ekur asked hopefully.

"Refrain from talking, unless I give you permission to do so," Nongru said again reverting to his imperious tone, "next time you disobey me, one of your fingers will be broken. And when I do grant you permission, please make sure that you not only speak the truth but that I can believe it, as well. Or you will face the same consequences as disobeying me. I know that Ishme, who you claim to be your grandfather, was someone Ildùr really respected. But, I also know that Ishme's children lied and stole from him. Do you disagree that they did?"

Ekur shook his head.

"Perhaps, Ishme's grandson Ekur was not corrupt like his parents, uncles and aunts," Nongru continued. "But, I cannot confirm that for a fact. This Ekur comes to Givenland, but forgets a phrase that Ildùr told him he would need to be acknowledged. And you've just confirmed that you had not even mentioned this phrase, until Viraan brought it up. Therefore, I don't think I would be reaching, if from this I deduced that maybe you did not even know such a phrase existed until you heard of it from Viraan. And then when Tiraak, Runggoo and Viraan refused to acknowledge you, you kept quiet about your reason for seeking them out. But, suddenly you decide to tell this to me. Then I find out that you have heard about Durshan Lake, but did not mention it until I brought it up. These lead me to believe that the truth is very different from what you are saying. Would you like to hear what I think the truth is? You are permitted to answer my question."

"Yes, please," Ekur said. He was now sure that he would not leave Wacha alive.

"I think you are as bad as your parents," Nongru said, "or probably worse. I think you found out that Ildùr had come across something beyond anyone's dreams up there, near the Durshan Lake. And you must have tortured Ildùr for more information. No, that cannot be, as I don't think you could make Ildùr talk in that way. No, I think you took Ildùr captive and tortured your grandfather Ishme in front of him. That would make Ildùr talk. You must have got all the information, but some locations even Ildùr could not take you to or tell you how to reach. You would need Pasher and Runggoo for this. Then, you came to Givenland, thinking that you could trick Ildùr's friends and acquaintances in helping you get to your destination near Durshan Lake. But, you did not realize that if you ever played a game of Goats and Lion with Ildùr, you would lose on your best day while he was having his worst. Even as you were extracting information from him, he was already laying his traps, by not mentioning the phrase. That would explain your memory lapse, would it not? Then again, everything I said is my conjecture of what might have happened. But, I cannot be sure. And that is the reason you are still alive and will leave this valley alive."

At this, Ekur released an audible sigh of relief.

Nongru continued, "Yes, because there is an infinitesimally small chance that you are telling the truth. And I cannot take the chance to harm someone who might have been close to Ildùr. Therefore, this is what is going to happen now. You will first tell us why Ildùr never came back from Kurm. On this, I don't care if you lie, as long as what you say pleases a grieving widow's ears, you will not be punished. Then you will tell us how he died. Tomorrow, you will get to meet Pasher, if you still would like to. But, I would suggest that you meet him in my presence. If you are indeed telling the truth, then you must know that if Pasher meets the person he thinks has harmed his master, he would tear him apart, limb to limb. And he can do so with his bare arms, too. After you have done these things, you will leave Wacha forever. Do we have an understanding? You may speak now."

"I will do as you say," Ekur said and could not help adding, "and I do not have to resort to lies to please a widow's ears. The Akkadian, I mean Ildùr, led a life that would make anyone who knew him proud. I do not have any regrets that you all do not believe me. The regret I will leave with is that in all probability I will fail in what the Akkadian tasked me with, now that I know I will not have the help of any of you. But, that does not mean I will stop trying."

"If what you say is indeed true," Nongru said sadly, "and if you really knew and understood Ildùr, you will also understand why we cannot do anything without the phrase."

Ekur then turned towards Nongru's doorway and assuming the Akkadian's wife was listening from inside, he started his narration.

"The Akkadian's only reason for coming back to Kurm was to meet his Abgal …" Ekur started his narration.

Ekur went on to narrate all the events that happened between the day that the Akkadian came to see Ishme after returning from Givenland and the day the Akkadian became sick again, thus needing the medicine-man.

But, when it came to the events after that, including the night the Akkadian had died, Ekur kept it short. "When he came to the part about what happened in the Offerings Cave either through excitement or exertion, he fell ill again. After that, even though I got him the best medicine man I could find, he faded in and out of consciousness. It was then he told me about Givenland being in danger and asked me to come here and seek the help of his friends and acquaintances. He died soon after telling me this."

Everyone was silent for some time.

"I think you might be telling the truth," Nongru said, "but how can I be sure? And even if I were, I am not sure what I could do. I am bound by the promise I made to Ildùr, and thus unable to help you, without hearing the phrase."

"I also think you are telling the truth," Runggoo said, "but, like Nongru I am bound by my promise made to your Akkadian. But, more than that, Ildùr got me to start believing in fate again. And I think the reason you have forgotten the phrase but remembered everything else, is because that is what was fated. I don't know why, but I am sure there is a reason for it. And if it is so fated, perhaps you will remember the phrase someday."

After that, everything happened very fast. Nongru invited Ekur to eat dinner with him and Runggoo, which Ekur accepted. Ekur requested Nongru to be given permission to meet the Teller. Nongru politely refused without giving any reason. The dinner was a very quiet affair.

The next morning, Ekur did get to meet both Pasher and the Akkadian's wife. Both meetings were held under the watchful eyes of Nongru and Runggoo. Both meetings were very short, and only involved an exchange of commiserations at the death of a person they all loved.

After this was done, Ekur realized he still did not know the name of the Akkadian's wife.

"We will be leaving Wacha now," Runggoo said taking Ekur aside. "I will ride with you to Ankal. From there, you have to go where fate leads you. I will gift you the ass that you rode to Wacha. If you want, I can also give you a camel. But, after that you are on your own."

"Thank you very much for everything," Ekur said. "I wish my fate had been different and had allowed me to be called your friend, but whatever shall not be, will not be."

"No one knows the ways of fate," Runggoo said, looking towards the mountain peaks. Then running his fingers through his hair and skilfully wiping away his tears, he said, "please be ready to leave the moment I have taken leave from Nongru."

While Ekur was waiting for Runggoo, Tiraak appeared.

"I am really surprised to see you here," Ekur said, his voice laden with sarcasm.

"I know you are not at all surprised," Tiraak said. "I know whatever you may be, you are not a fool. I will always wonder who Ekur was. Was he really on a quest from Ildùr but was crossed by fate? Or was he a fiend on a mission of his own with deep ulterior motives? Whatever you might be, I needed to thank you for bringing the news of Ildùr's death to us, and especially for ensuring that his ashes reached his widow. Hopefully, this might give her some closure." Then shaking his head chuckled, "you know what I just realized? How can I be sure that Ildùr is dead? I don't even know if that urn contains anything, let alone Ildùr's ashes. To Ekur's surprise, Tiraak started laughing. "This is a conundrum that Ildùr would have appreciated or may still appreciate. Who knows?"

Before Ekur could add anything, Runggoo came out of Nongru's hut and Tiraak walked away laughing.

Runggoo and Ekur left Wacha. The return journey was spent as silently as the onward. Runggoo accompanied Ekur to Ankal and bid his farewell.

Chapter 17

After Ridhaan had finished reading, this time, he waited for Riyaansh to wake up next morning.

"Do you believe this tale of the Akkadian and Ekur?" Ridhaan asked.

"Yes, I do," Riyaansh said, "I think it is more plausible that it happened than of Ekur making it up." Then, Riyaansh paused. "Why do you ask?"

"Well everything seems to be too precise and prearranged," Ridhaan said thoughtfully. "When the Akkadian needs help, Vikoo arrives. When he is about to be thrown out of Wacha, the Teller tells him just the story that would help him most. When…"

"When Ekur needs to meet Riyaansh," Riyaansh interrupted said softly, "he ends up in an out of the way street in Kdwar, just when Zayaa is playing outside. When people are conspiring about killing Zayaa and in a Raakanaa, Ridhaan is there to hear them, even though he has not gone to the Raakanaa in days. But, we know these things did happen. When Riyaansh decides not to do anything, his wife gets killed and his town destroyed. That happened, as well. No, I have stopped questioning the ways of fate. There is another thing." Then he paused again.

"Come on," Ridhaan said impatiently, "out with it. Tell me what is it?"

"I can do more than tell," Riyaansh said, "Ekur gave me these on the last evening before he left for Sumer." Then he produced three maps, two of them without markings.

"Well, this is convincing indeed," then examining the maps, Ridhaan asked, "if everything in Ekur's tale is true, then is Pparaha the right destination for us?"

"Well," Riyaansh said. "I think the voice talking in Zayaa's head has made the choice for us, but don't worry. Ekur was there a few years after the Akkadian. And according to him, Divyaan and Kiraa must have been exaggerating. He actually mentioned that if he were to ever live in Givenland, he would choose Pparaha."

"I had seen Ekur always kept his hands and feet covered, and you said that some of his fingers and toes were fleshy stumps. Why was that?" Ridhaan asked. "After all, he had Ildùr's climbing clothes."

"It seems he did not have all the inner and outer layers."

"And what is your plan after we get there?" Ridhaan asked after some more thought.

"First, we need to see whether this woman who speaks to animals really exists," Riyaansh said. "If she does not, I will know that whatever was guiding us to Pparaha was wrong. Then I will let you choose whether Parroo or Lakho should be our next destination. But, if she does exist," Riyaansh paused, "we will discuss what to do after talking with her."

"Well, if she does not exist," Ridhaan said, "then we go to Lakho. In the tale of the Akkadian and Ekur, Parroo is where the words are, and Lakho is where the action is." Then after a pause he asked his twin, "What are you planning to tell Shyaan?"

"Well," Riyaansh said, stroking his chin, "since the day we met him, when his two loaders had left him in a lurch, I have been upfront with him. He needed us to load and unload his boats, and we needed the work. And we have always told him that we will part ways in spring."

By the time spring came, Shyaan had not only come to depend on the twins, but had also taken a liking for them. But, he had also realized that Riyaansh was serious about not going back on his words. Two weeks into spring, Shyaan got a consignment to be delivered to Parroo. On the way back, Shyaan stopped at Ankal. At the request of Riyaansh, Shyaan acquired two camels. With the rest of the twins' share of profits, he acquired jewellery that could be easily tradable.

Riyaansh, Ridhaan and Zayaa bid farewell to Shyaan and started off towards Pparaha.

As they were coming from Ankal, they travelled directly west and after coming to Airavati, turned south. In this way, they ensured that they would arrive at Pparaha from the north instead of northeast. As they were coming close to Pparaha, they came across a herd of goats. On looking around, they saw a young boy sitting under a tree.

"We seek the one who talks to animals," Riyaansh said, dismounting and walking up to the boy.

"How do I know that you have come without reason to cause ill?" the boy asked.

"Other than my word," Riyaansh said, "which is also my bond, I don't know how to convince you that I come with good intentions."

"Someone with reason to cause ill would say exactly what you have just said," the boy countered.

"But, what can the great one who talks to animals have to fear from someone like me?" Riyaansh said. "And if I indeed had an ill purpose, would I come here with my daughter?"

It was then that the boy noticed Zayaa sitting on the other camel.

"That last argument is more convincing," the boy said. "Come, I will take you to her."

They soon came to a hut. And a woman came out at the boy's knock.

"What is it now?" the woman scolded, "don't you know this is the busiest time of my day?"

Before the herder could answer Riyaansh said, "We have travelled from far seeking you, and we don't mind waiting for a time when you are less busy."

"Quite the orator, I see," then she saw Zayaa hiding behind Riyaansh and peeking at her from his side, "and who do we have here?"

"I am sorry that I am forgetting my manners," Riyaansh said. "I am Riyaansh of Darromohe, this is my brother, Ridhaan, and hiding behind me is my daughter, Zayaa."

"Well, Riyaansh from somewhere much further south than Darromohe," the woman said, "I am Tanaa. And it is none of your business where I am from. I am fine if you do not want to share something. However, if you plan on more lying, we are done here."

"I am really sorry," Riyaansh said, "but for reasons that I cannot share, I have become a little miserly with the truth. But, with you, from here on, I will either tell the truth or say nothing."

"That sounds fair," Tanaa said. "I have not given you any reason to trust me, yet. What brings you here?"

"The reason is not very easy to explain," Riyaansh started, "I mean it is," then coming to a decision, "no I think it is best if you hear it directly from my daughter. As she managed to repeat it yesterday, I am sure she still remembers it. Zayaa please tell Tanaa about your dream that was not a dream."

"Well, we were in this hill," Zayaa started, giving Riyaansh a knowing look, "it was near this magic place." Shaking her head, "I cannot tell you where, or it will disappear. Anyway, I had this dream. Well, actually, it was not really a dream, because I was awake. There was this person, very white, like me. And yes, it was early morning. The person was wearing something yellow and shiny on his head." Going close to Tanaa, Zayaa continued in a conspiratorial tone, "I think he was magic. He can talk without opening his mouth. He told me," then with pride added, "not Appi or Sikkappa, but me. He said, go to Pparaha. He said go from the north side, and first spend a few days with the special woman, the one who can talk to animals. Can you really talk to animals?"

Tanaa went very quiet.

"I know it is not easy to believe," Riyaansh said, "but Zayaa usually …"

"I cannot talk to animals," Tanaa smiled, "but the animals know how to hear me." Then turning to Riyaansh, she said with seriousness, "It is more believable than you think, but if you all are going to stay with me for a few days, let us go in," then turning to the boy-herder she said, "Sanj, please see to the camels. You can take them for a saunter if you like. I am sure our guests will not mind."

The next evening, after Zayaa had gone to sleep, Riyaansh signalled that Ridhaan come out and join him outside.

"Well, seems like the woman who talks to animals does exist?" Riyaansh said.

"I have not seen her talk to an animal, yet," Ridhaan said.

"Well, whether she really talks to animals or not is not important, at least, we know that people believe she does," Riyaansh said. "But, we now need to talk about what we do from here. I think Ekur coming to me, and us being twins was fated. We shall become one and be in two different places at the same time. While one stays with Zayaa in Pparaha, the other tries to succeed where Ekur failed. As fate brought Ekur to me, I think I am fated to take Ekur's place. That means you will have to go and live in Pparaha as Zayaa's father, Riyaansh. When either of us gets tired, we will switch places. But, of course we will do that, only if you agree."

"You know my weakness," Ridhaan said. "I would love to be Zayaa's father even for a short while."

"Then it is settled," Riyaansh said. "We will have to bring Tanaa into our confidence. She already knows that the two of us exist. I think we should tell her about the Akkadian's quest. Perhaps, we should leave out names of people and the exact locations for the time being. And we will not mention anything about the Durshan Lake."

For the next few days, Zayaa was sent out in the care of one of the many herders and Riyaansh told Tanaa about the Akkadian's quest and what happened to Ekur after that. After the tale was told, Riyaansh told Tanaa about their plans of becoming one person but being in two places.

"Are you sure you are comfortable with bringing up your brother's daughter?" Tanaa asked Ridhaan.

"It will only be for a short while," Ridhaan said, "As Riyaansh said, if we get tired of our roles, we can always switch places. I promise to him in your presence that I will be there for her no matter what. That is a covenant I make with my brother."

"I understand why you all are doing this," Tanaa finally said, "and I will help you. But, I still feel that you are tempting fate."

"If we are indeed tempting fate," Riyaansh said, "then it has been fated that we shall tempt fate."

"That is a very dangerous logic," Tanaa observed, "but as I said, I will help you. From what you told me, unless Ekur left some of his gold nuggets, you will not be able to acquire proper accommodation in Pparaha. However, don't worry; I will arrange one for you. It will be done in two to three days. It will be through so many middlemen that no one will know that I am involved in any way. Please do not object, as this will be my gift to Zayaa. If your male pride still has a problem, you can pay me back when you can."

Riyaansh smiled and said, "I have forsaken pride. Ekur had predicted that I will be a player in the game that the Akkadian started. I have finally realized the importance of this quest. And to be successful, I cannot afford things like pride and shame, and maybe even honesty and guilt."

"You want to embark on something good and holy, by forsaking qualities that make us who we are?" Tanaa asked with disbelief.

"I want to embark on something good," Riyaansh said, "but not necessarily holy. If I believe everything that Ekur told me, the Gods have decided to destroy Givenland as we know it. And I am embarking on a quest to somehow dissuade them. So, in a way, I am going against the will of Gods. That cannot be holy. Ekur failed, because he was not ready to compromise his decency and virtuousness. To succeed I have to become like the Akkadian, so I will remind you not to expect to eat chicken without killing a hen — ends always justify the means," he quoted the Akkadian.

"I still cannot agree with you," Tanaa said. "And I know we will not see eye to eye on this, so let us not discuss this any further. What do we do next?"

"Ridhaan and I," Riyaansh began, "will have our falling out during dinner tomorrow. I, acting as Ridhaan, will say that spending every moment with my brother and my niece is getting extremely tiring. I, continuing to act as Ridhaan, will add that if I wanted to live with children, I would have got married and had my own. And even though I wish them well, I am not settling down with them in Pparaha. At this Ridhaan, acting as me, will say that if I leave him when he needs me the most, I need not ever come back. Then I will storm out from our dinner. After that Ridhaan, acting as me, will tell Zayaa that from then on he does not want any mention of her Sikkappa. Zayaa, being very good at keeping secrets, will never tell anyone that her father has a twin brother."

"Why do we have to complicate it so much?" Ridhaan asked, "Why can't you just go on a trip?"

"Because, in that case Ridhaan will have to visit Riyaansh from time to time," Riyaansh said, "which means we will run the risk of being seen together."

"You are indeed not Riyaansh anymore," Ridhaan said at last, "I don't know what you have become, but I liked the old Riyaansh better. Have you decided where you are going first?"

"Lakho, of course," Riyaansh said, "I thought you had chosen that for me."

Later that evening, after Zayaa had gone to sleep, Riyaansh and Ridhaan were alone outside Tanaa's hut.

"I want to ask you something," Ridhaan said. "What did you mean when you said that Ekur was not ready to compromise his decency and virtuousness, and that is why he did not succeed?"

"When I was scribing out Ekur's visit to Parroo," Riyaansh said, "I realized that he had missed a trick. Once he realized that the friends of the Akkadian were expecting the key phrase, which of course he did not have, he should have kidnapped Viraan, tortured the phrase out of him and presented it to Tiraak and Runggoo. He should have realized that the one should always be sacrificed for the good of many."

Ridhaan peered at his brother, hardly recognizing him. "You really mean that, don't you? I don't know what part I am supposed to play in all this, but I will tell you now that I don't think I can be that ruthless, even if I wanted to."

"Couldn't you?" Riyaansh said, "Think what you were ready to do to Tikoo to save Zayaa and me. No, my brother, for the right incentives, we can all be ruthless. The difference is that Ekur thought because his cause was a just one, he needed to uphold his morality. I think differently. Since my cause is just, I don't care what I have to do to achieve my goal."

"As I said brother, I don't think I know you anymore," Ridhaan said and then after some thought added. "But in that case, why are you not proceeding to Parroo and doing what you feel Ekur should have done?"

"Because I cannot be sure who I will meet first," Riyaansh said without needing to think about it. "If I meet Runggoo first, I don't think I can torture any information out of him. And there is also the chance that Tiraak, with his cunningness, has already considered this weakness and instructed the others that on torture they are to give out a different phrase. No, brother, I cannot risk this. Ekur has closed those doors by going first."

They had their falling out exactly as planned, during dinner next evening. Zayaa pleaded to no avail, but her father and uncle refused to forgive each other. Finally Ridhaan, as Riyaansh, asked Zayaa to bid farewell to her uncle forever, and never mention about his existence ever again.

Chapter 18

Riyaansh left the next morning with one of the camels and half of the jewellery that Shyaan had exchanged for them. He proceeded towards Lakho, following the Akkadian's path as closely as he could. When he reached the Ashkini, he backtracked about a mahahath and looked around near all clumps of trees to see any sign of strange hoofmarks. He did come across some, but could not be sure whether they were footmarks of asses, which had been left distorted by weather and time. He stayed in the general neighbourhood for a few days, hoping to see or hear something. Then he moved on and crossed the Ashkini and travelled upriver along it. His journey was slower, as he kept searching for something out of the ordinary, but not knowing what it was that he was looking for. It took him five days to travel to the confluence of the Vitasta. The Akkadian had done it in two, he thought to himself. He then calculated the pace at which the Akkadian and Pasher were traveling. Once he turned upriver on the Vitasta, he stopped searching for the unknown and started travelling at the Akkadian's pace. Like the Akkadian, whenever he came upon a town or village, or spotted any human settlement, he circled around those. He covered each day the distance he had calculated the Akkadian and Pasher would have covered daily. On the third night, he reached the place where the Akkadian and Pasher must have encountered Kinjyaan.

He set up camp and started exploring the area for any signs of the place that the voice spoke to Kinjyaan. It was around twilight on the third day that Riyaansh thought he heard a loud snort. He looked around but could not see anything. He laughed and thought to himself, '*The Akkadian had difficulty scaring Kinjyaan, but somehow he has put the fear of the chuffer in me. But*

Kinjyaan lived here for a long time, and he was sure there were no big cats near here.' But, he still walked around the place, to make sure there was nothing. As he did not hear or see anything else, he ate his dinner and fell asleep. It was almost dawn when he was brought awake by a snarl. A spotted cat, about five times the size of the ones people kept in their homes, but much smaller than a Lion, suddenly appeared and jumped towards him. The cat had its claws extended and would have taken out his right eye, but just before contact, he jerked his head away. However, the main claw did hook into the skin near his eye and ripped his face open, down to his left chin. But then, a very strange thing happened. He heard a much louder snort, and the cat that had attacked him jumped off him at this. Riyaansh's first thought was that the cat that had attacked him must have been a youngling and now the parent cat had arrived. Riyaansh prepared himself for the inevitable. But, nothing happened. He heard a lot of growling and snorting, but it seemed to be moving further and further away. Riyaansh sat up, and holding his cut up face, looked towards the snorting and growling. He was amazed to see that the cat that had attacked him was fighting a losing battle with a big black bear. Riyaansh did not wait around to see the result of the fight. He looked around and saw that his camel, though agitated, had been unable to free itself and take flight. He did stop to pick up his most important possessions, and then mounting his camel, rode away. It was after some time that he realized he was riding southwards instead of north. But, he kept on riding. He soon came to the outskirts of some town. There were some herders already out with their herds. He stopped near them, almost falling off his camel. Riyaansh was unable to talk, but had the presence of mind to utter Tanaa's name a few times before losing consciousness. When he next came to his senses, he was in a hut. As he tried to sit up, someone pushed him to the ground again.

"What did I say about tempting fate?" Tanaa said.

"Tanaa," Riyaansh said with evident pleasure, but immediately winced with pain. After blinking away tears of pain, he continued, speaking through the corner of his mouth, "I hoped they would recognize your name and bring me to you. But, this does not look like your home." He realized that talking was getting easier.

"You are lucky that the herders you met had more common sense than you do," Tanaa mocked. "In your condition, if they had tried to bring you to my place, you would not have survived the journey. They have done a very good job at not only dressing your wound, but also sedating you to limit your movement, and drip feeding you gruel to keep you hydrated and ensure you do not starve. I have to say that I could not have done better. But, of course, Ridhaan and you will no longer be identical. Your scar will ensure that. You both can no longer change places at will. That is why I spoke about tempting fate. Oh yes, another thing – the herders are all curious to know what happened. They say that by the look of your cheek, it has been ripped open by a wild cat of some kind."

"That is exactly what happened," Riyaansh said and told Tanaa about the attack and, then, his rescue by a bear.

"You do know how to make your life more interesting than it needs to be," Tanaa chuckled.

"You may laugh now, but for a moment there I thought my life was ending," Riyaansh said reproachfully.

Tanaa went out and came back a little later with one of the herders.

"Riyaansh, if you don't mind, can you please repeat your ordeal to this man." Tanaa said.

"You got someone to share your mirth," Riyaansh complained, but repeated his story.

"That is strange indeed," the man said seriously, "we have not heard of any leopards roaming about this area for a long time. But more interesting is the seemingly unprovoked attack on the leopard by the bear. That is, unless the leopard had previously harmed the bear or its children. Unlike other animals, a bear can hold grudges, much like humans. Whatever it was, you are very lucky to be alive. The Gods must have been watching over you to keep you safe."

"Or to stop me from going north," Riyaansh muttered under his breath.

In two more days, Riyaansh was well enough to travel, and after thanking the herders, Tanaa and Riyaansh came back to Tanaa's home in the outskirts of Pparaha.

A few days later, Ridhaan, who was now Riyaansh, came with Zayaa to visit Tanaa. One of the herders informed Tanaa of their approach long before they actually arrived. So Riyaansh was shipped off to Sanj's hut. After Zayaa had gone to sleep, Riyaansh came to Tanaa's home. He saw Zayaa from afar, not daring to get closer, in case she wakes up and sees his scar. He felt real physical pain at not being able to go and stroke her hair, as he would usually do when she was sleeping.

"You know it is not too late," Ridhaan said, after Riyaansh had joined him outside. "We can still tell her who you are and that it was all a trick we were playing on her."

"No, Ridhaan," Riyaansh said firmly. "Fate has decided that you shall be Zayaa's father, while I follow in the footsteps of the Akkadian and Ekur. But, remember our covenant. Whatever happens, you shall never forsake her. You will ensure so, even if you get married and have children of your own."

"I had not planned on getting married even before I had this responsibility," Ridhaan said. "So, I don't think I will change my mind, when things are more complicated. Go in peace brother, and do not worry about Zayaa. She will be in safe hands."

"I know," Riyaansh said, growing tearful. "Our world would be a much better place, if everyone had a brother like you."

"Don't get emotional on me," Ridhaan laughed, "it does not become the new you. And to be entirely honest, I don't mind my fate of a long and safe life in Pparaha, and I definitely do not envy you of your dangerous adventures. So, where will you go from here?" Ridhaan asked deftly, changing the subject, for he knew it was embarrassing his brother.

"Not Lakho," Riyaansh said. "Fate has let me know that I was on the wrong track. And I think it has also told me what to do next. I was attacked in the same spot that the Akkadian had met Kinjyaan. Thus, I think I need to seek out Kinjyaan before I do anything else."

Riyaansh stayed with Tanaa a few more days and then headed out to Ankal, planning on proceeding to Parroo from there. But, fate intervened again.

Riyaansh was feeling a little desolate, since the day he had not been able to stroke Zayaa's hair or even be in the room she was sleeping. He, therefore, decided to visit the Raakanaa. As he was quietly drinking raajaraas in one corner, he noticed a group of five very noisy men.

Then he heard one of them shout out. "I think Kinjyaan is drunk. One more cup and he will go out and howl at the moon."

Riyaansh turned and looked more closely at the group, but realized that none of them could be described as skinny. He continued to watch them and saw that after they had imbibed another round of raajaraas, the stoutest member of the group, stood up and staggered out of the hut and started howling at the moon.

One of the other members of the group went after him and said, "Quiet Kinjyaan! Stop or they will not serve us any more raajaraas."

But, he was too late, for the group was indeed ordered to leave. Riyaansh quickly got a jug of raajaraas and followed the group at a safe distance. They all proceeded to the same lodgings. After they had noisily disappeared inside, Riyaansh approached the lodge-keeper.

"Do you have any room in your lodge?" Riyaansh asked.

The lodge-keeper looked suspiciously at Riyaansh and the jug of raajaraas.

"You know you can drink that in the raajaraas hut itself," the lodge-keeper said. "You don't need a room for that."

Riyaansh realized how stupid and suspicious he must have looked, trying to get a room at this late hour, arriving with only a jug of raajaraas.

"I see why you think it is strange," Riyaansh quickly recovered. "I need a room, and I also need my camel stabled. You see, I have put up in a different lodge, where I am sharing a room with my companion. My companion, however, snores louder than a bull might roar, especially when he's drunk. And my lodge has no more rooms available," Spoken like the Akkadian would, Riyaansh thought.

The lodge-keeper guffawed and said, "I know what you mean. But, in my case, it is my wife who snores like that after imbibing raajaraas, so I have no escape. Yes, I have a room. But, I am not sure if it will be any quieter, as it is next to the two rooms of those noisy men who came in just before you are lodged."

"Believe me, no one can be worse than my companion," Riyaansh said and laughed out loud. "If you do not mind, I will quickly fetch my things and of course my camel."

"Please hurry. Now that the last room is taken, I can turn in. Come down to the courtyard for breakfast. We do not serve food in our rooms."

Riyaansh quickly went to the lodge he had put up at, and woke up the lodge-keeper. And after quickly retrieving his things and taking possession of his camel he went back to the lodge where Kinjyaan was putting up.

The next morning, Riyaansh went down to the inner courtyard soon after dawn. He was happy to see none of the other guests were down, yet. And his day was made, when Kinjyaan was the next person to come down. He thanked his fate and sat down very near where Kinjyaan was sitting.

"I am Riyaansh of Darromohe," Riyaansh introduced himself politely.

"I am Kinjyaan of Parroo," Kinjyaan replied.

After the introductions, Riyaansh turned and looked intently at Kinjyaan, and then smiled, as if recognition had just set in.

"Hey, were you not the person who was howling at the moon outside the raajaraas hut yesterday evening," Riyaansh said and then laughed out loud. "It is really funny what people do when they have had a little too much to drink."

"I think you are making a mistake …" Kinjyaan started denying.

"No use denying it," Riyaansh almost shouted. "I never forget a face. It was you that I saw, just yesterday, howling at the moon."

"Okay," Kinjyaan quietly said, "Maybe it was me. But, I am really embarrassed by what I did, so it would be nice if you stopped talking about it."

"Why are you embarrassed now?" Riyaansh asked in a quieter voice. "You know it is very funny that we are never embarrassed by the things we do after imbibing raajaraas, until the next morning. It would be so much better if we were embarrassed while doing it, and stopped."

"Could we please talk about something else?" Kinjyaan pleaded.

"I was planning to," Riyaansh asked. "When I saw you yesterday, I was reminded of a story an Akkadian friend named Ildùr once told me." He stopped for effect, but grew a little disappointed at not getting any reaction at the name Ildùr. "He was travelling somewhere north of Ilpurjal," he continued, and saw Kinjyaan stiffen at the mention of Ilpurjal. Riyaansh spoke now with renewed confidence, "He was travelling upriver on the west bank of the Vitasta, when he came across this moon howler. But, unlike you, he did so after chewing dhutura."

Kinjyaan was getting visibly uncomfortable as Riyaansh went on. He started eating faster, to finish his meal quickly and leave the place.

"Come to think of it," Riyaansh went, louder, "Ildùr did say the name of this moon-howler was Kinjyaan. Didn't you introduce yourself as Kinjyaan?"

"Who are you?" Kinjyaan asked in desperation. "Have you come from Ilpurjal? Well, whatever you have come for, you are not getting it. They may have punished me for no fault of mine before. But now, I too have powerful patrons, who will not allow me to be punished for things I have not done."

At the mention of friends, Riyaansh realized that he did not have much time, as Kinjyaan's friends from last night could be there at any moment. So, he decided to stop beating about the bush.

"No, I am not from Ilpurjal," Riyaansh said, "and the only thing I want is some recognition for my friend Ildùr from Sumer, without whose help you would still be howling at the moon in the wilderness. And don't try to deny it. You have already acknowledged that you are Kinjyaan, and that you are from Ilpurjal. I just want to hear you acknowledge that you did know Ildùr."

"I don't know what your game is?" Kinjyaan whispered standing up. "But, I have never met or heard of anyone called Ildùr."

"Go ahead," Riyaansh hissed standing up, "come on, go ahead and deny that you have not heard of or met Pasher, either."

Kinjyaan sat down again. Then, very quietly, he said, "I cannot do that. I cannot deny knowing Pasher. If it was not for Pasher, I would have surely been dead in the wilderness by now."

"So, you do know Pasher?" Riyaansh sat down and sneered. "Why are you not ready to acknowledge Ildùr? Yes, you were granted your new life by Pasher, but it was with Ildùr's sanction. He may have seemed unkind to you, but Ildùr allowed Pasher to be kind to you. So, why don't you acknowledge that you met Ildùr at the same time as you met Pasher?"

"Because I did not," Kinjyaan said.

"You want to tell me that Pasher was alone when you met him," Riyaansh said, panicking as he realized that he too was coming to a dead end like Ekur.

"No, Pasher was not alone," Kinjyaan was saying. "But, he was not with any Akkadian or Sumerian either. He was with someone called Shubhyaan. I don't know what your game is or why you want me to be acquainted with this Ildùr. But, I hope I never see you again. Please tell your masters in Ilpurjal to leave me alone." Saying this, Kinjyaan left.

At first, Riyaansh was confused at why Kinjyaan was ready to accept everything else, but until the end, he did not acknowledge Ildùr. He was deep in thought and did not notice that many other guests had joined him in the inner courtyard for their breakfasts.

Then, suddenly, the truth dawned on him and before he could stop himself, Riyaansh blurted out quite loudly, "Of course. Ildùr is Shubhyaan and Shubhyaan is Ildùr."

Then, noticing that he was surrounded by other guests, who now curiously were looking at him; he quickly got up and went back to his room.

He was still contemplating his next move, when his door flung open and Kinjyaan and the companions from the previous evening rushed in, followed by an elderly man, who was better dressed than the others. As Kinjyaan and his companions pinned Riyaansh down to the floor, the elderly man closed the door and walked over and put his foot on Riyaansh's head.

"Can you please repeat to me what you said in the courtyard?" the man commanded.

"I am very sorry," Riyaansh said, realizing he may have pushed Kinjyaan too far. "I did not mean Kinjyaan any harm. I was …"

"Stop babbling," the man said sternly, "I don't care what you said to Kinjyaan. Repeat what you said, just before coming up from the courtyard."

Riyaansh knew he could not lie. But he could not give in too easily.

"First, you have to tell me who you are," Riyaansh said in a voice that sounded much more confident than he was feeling.

"I am Viraan of Purawanbhag," the man said, "and if you do not answer me immediately, I will ask my men to start breaking your limbs."

Riyaansh knew that fate had decided to intervene yet again, but was it to help or hinder. But, he could not see any harm repeating something Viraan already knew.

"Ildùr is Shubhyaan and Shubhyaan is Ildùr."

Viraan signalled his men to let Riyaansh go. Riyaansh stood up dusting his clothes.

"Go and keep guard outside this door," Viraan instructed his men. After they were gone, he asked Riyaansh, "Who are you?"

"I am Riyaansh," Riyaansh said simply.

"Repeat the phrase again and tell me who taught you the phrase," Viraan said.

"Ildùr is Shubhyaan and Shubhyaan is Ildùr," Riyaansh said, "I …" he was about to say that he had just found this out, but then realized that Viraan had called it 'the phrase'.

Then, he remembered where he had heard the name Shubhyaan before. During his discussion with Ekur, Tiraak had asked Ekur many times whether Shubhyaan could fetch them something. And, Riyaansh remembered, he had always mentioned it before asking Ekur for the phrase. When Ekur had narrated his tale, the name 'Shubhyaan' had not seemed important. Now, everything was clear to Riyaansh.

As realization hit him, he started laughing and said, "Oh Ekur! You stupid, stupid Ekur, if you only knew how close you were."

"Again with your babbling," Viraan started angrily, but then stopped, "did you say 'Ekur'?"

"I think you are bound by your word and your honour to help me," Riyaansh said with confidence. "Now that you have heard the key phrase from me, do remember your word. Or is Ildùr a forgotten memory and promises made to him no longer matters?"

"Our words are our bonds," Viraan said, "if I were given a choice between giving up my life and going back on my words, I would choose to give up my life every time. And a word given to someone like Ildùr is even more important. But, please tell me who taught you that phrase?"

Riyaansh almost blurted out everything, but he stopped. "All in good time, but Runggoo, Tiraak and you need to be together to hear my tale. I …"

"Okay," Viraan said. "I can arrange for my cousin and Runggoo to be in Parroo by day after tomorrow. I will also arrange for your journey there."

"Please let me finish," Riyaansh said and hesitated for a moment. "I want us all to meet in Wacha. And yes, I want you to make the arrangements for me to get there."

"All right," Viraan said. "Please be ready to travel with me at the break of dawn tomorrow. And I will also ensure that the others come to Wacha. I don't think we can take your camel, so I will arrange it to be stabled somewhere safe."

"How do you know I have a camel?" Riyaansh asked in surprise.

"My reaction to your commands comes out of respect for a friend," Viraan said, "but please, do not interpret that as a weakness. There is nothing much that goes on in these parts that I cannot find out about."

Viraan said this to put Riyaansh in his place, but Riyaansh was actually pleased, for he knew that powerful friends were exactly what he needed now.

When Riyaansh came down at dawn the next day, Viraan led him to waiting asses. They immediately started for Wacha. Riyaansh tried to start a conversation, but was told by Viraan that the first conversation he wanted to have with Riyaansh was how Riyaansh had come to know the phrase. As Riyaansh did not want to divulge this until they were all together, they rode on in silence.

Chapter 19

They reached Wacha on an afternoon and when they reached Nongru's hut, Nongru and Khongrem were sitting outside, as Ekur had found them. But, there were two more persons sitting with them. Riyaansh immediately knew them to be Tiraak and Runggoo.

"O respected Chief and O divine Wife of Chief," Viraan said, "I am Viraan of Purawanbhag. Please accept our humble greetings and this humble gift." He took out a leather garment and a silver tiara, and laid them in front of the Nongru and Khongrem.

Before Riyaansh could say anything, Nongru cut in, "Well met, Viraan." Then, looking at Tiraak, Runggoo and again at Viraan he said, "So, finally, I meet every one of the trinity." Then he turned to Riyaansh.

"O respected Chief and O divine Wife of Chief," Riyaansh said, "I am Riyaansh of Kdwar. The only gift I bear you is the news that Ekur has safely returned to Sumer. And please believe me, when I say that Ildùr would not have wanted his death on the conscience of any of you."

Runggoo took a sharp intake of breath. Tiraak's eyes almost popped out. Viraan shook his head. Nongru shot up from his seat. Riyaansh looked around and saw that Khongrem was actually smiling.

"You are a brave man," Nongru finally said, "I will give you that. Foolish yes, but brave too. So, Riyaansh of Kdwar, tell me what is stopping me from ordering your head to be separated from your body?"

"Ildùr is Shubhyaan. And Shubhyaan is Ildùr," Riyaansh said.

"Never give a knife to a monkey," Nongru said, "for you don't know what he will cut with it. You have somehow learned the phrase, but did you take time to find out its uses?"

Riyaansh knew it was best not to reply.

"At least, you know when to keep quiet," Nongru continued. "You see, Riyaansh of Kdwar, I have not given my word to anyone about extending my unconditional loyalty, if I hear a certain phrase."

Now, Riyaansh was a little taken aback. He definitely remembered that Nongru had said something different to Ekur.

"So, Riyaansh of Kdwar," Nongru continued, "what do you have to say in your defence for the foolish effrontery of insulting me, the Chief of Wacha?"

Riyaansh was not sure of how to answer this. He was considering grovelling for his life in front of Nongru. Then, Nongru started laughing aloud. Everyone else, except for Khongrem, joined in. She just shook her head and smiled.

"Well, I was told that you talk and behave like our Ildùr," Nongru finally said. "Perhaps, you will get there someday, but as of now, you are not even close."

Then, Nongru came up to Riyaansh and said, "But, I think you will still do. Well met, Riyaansh of Kdwar, and welcome to our valley. Now, tell us, how you know of this phrase."

"I managed to guess it, with Viraan's help of course," Riyaansh said mysteriously.

Now, it was Nongru and the others, who were taken aback. But, he laughed and said, "Let us all go in for our dinner, during which Riyaansh can tell us how Viraan helped him to guess the phrase."

As most of the tale was already known to everyone in the room, Riyaansh managed to finish Ekur's tale by the end of the dinner. He told them everything that Ekur had told him about what happened on the night Ildùr had died, including the club with the precious stones, and how it distracted Ekur from hearing the phrase. And he read out the exact conversation between the Akkadian and Ekur. But, for some reason, he hesitated in informing them about what Ekur had done with the precious stones. He also explained about why he had not divulged anything to Viraan and had also insulted him after arriving in Wacha. It was a small revenge on Ekur's behalf, for their mistreatment of Ekur.

"I see what you mean," Runggoo said, "but, Ildùr would have wanted us to behave exactly as we did."

"I agree," Tiraak said, "but I still feel a little guilty about Ekur losing his toes and fingers."

"Riyaansh, what is your plan, now that you have found us?" Nongru asked.

"As you said earlier," Riyaansh humbly said, "I am not Ildùr. I was not really sure that I would get this far, at least not this quickly. I had always imagined playing it as fate dictated. And I had expected that, at some point, fate would guide me to hand over the oars to someone more deft and able at steering this boat than me. I have some thoughts on what needs to be done, but I have no idea on how to achieve it."

"Well, I think you are not giving yourself enough credit," Nongru said. "You managed to get here and also managed to secure our support. So, let us hear your thoughts."

"I think our journey will be guided more by fate than by our actions," Riyaansh said, "but may I ask you some questions first?"

Nongru looked around, and after getting nods of agreement from the other three men, said, "Go ahead. Of course, we may not have all the answers, or may even choose not to answer these questions – at least not yet."

Riyaansh took out a parchment from inside his loincloth.

"I hope we don't have to read from that?" Tiraak asked, wrinkling his nose.

"No," Riyaansh replied with a straight face, "but if someone could hold it for me while I read, that would be really appreciated." After the laughter had subsided, he continued, "Please do not worry. I plan to wash my hands thoroughly before I touch anything else. You see, I could not think of a better hiding place. My first question is for you, O Respected Chief …"

"Please," Nongru protested, "in such company, Nongru will do."

"Okay, Nongru, is Bugyel your son?"

"Yes," Nongru said with surprise. "He is my first born. How do you know that name?"

"Well," Riyaansh started, but Runggoo stopped him.

"I think we should hold off our questions to him," Khongrem said putting her hand on her husband's arms, "I am sure that a lot of things will become clear as we go along."

Everyone nodded their agreement.

"Okay," Riyaansh continued, "is Khongmu Ildùr's wife?"

Nongru kept quiet. Then, he finally said, "Go ahead and ask your next question, before I answer this one."

"Okay," Riyaansh continued, "is Bujang the son that the Akkadian never knew of?"

"I know we agreed not to ask any questions," Nongru said angrily, "but I cannot adhere to that any longer. This man is asking questions about things that should not even have been heard outside this valley. Tell me, Tiraak, do you know who Khongmu is, or tell me Runggoo, who Bujang is? You do not know, do you? So, how is this man, who has come to Wacha for the first time today, asking about them?" then turning to Riyaansh, he said accusingly, "Tell me how long have you been spying on us? Who is your spy in this valley?"

"Nongru," Runggoo intervened, "please calm down. I am sure there is a logical explanation. Let us give Riyaansh a chance to explain before we start losing our temper."

"Okay," Riyaansh said, almost starting his explanation. But something inside him rebelled at the unfairness. Even though he realized that he was taking a big risk, perhaps even risking his life, he decided to say what he wanted to say, not what the people around him wanted to hear. "Yes, I have an explanation, but why should I be required to give you one. When the Akkadian described you all to Ekur, each of you had many different qualities, but one common trait you all shared was your fairness. If Ildùr was still alive, I would have told him that he was indeed a very bad judge of character. You all threw Ekur out because he did not know the key phrase, even though by the time he had left, each of you were sure that he was telling the truth. You led him to believe that if only he could have repeated the key phrase, he would have had your unconditional help and support. Well, I have given you your key phrase, so where is your unconditional help? Where is your unconditional support?" As all the others started to speak at once, Riyaansh raised his hand to stop them, "Please wait, I am not done, yet. Let me finish and then you can do whatever you want with me. I think whatever it is that the Akkadian learnt up there, it is momentous. I did not have the good fortune of meeting the Akkadian, but you all were close to him. From what I learnt from Ekur, the Akkadian may have had penchant for melodrama and exaggeration, but not for blatant untruths. In his final conversation with Ekur, he talked about the destruction of Givenland. This is something bigger than any of us. I have abdicated my rights of being my daughter's father for this cause. So, I feel I have earned the right to confirm some facts. And, O Respected Chief, there you sit, trying to decide what punishment I should get, forgetting that I am doing this for the cause of a man that I did not even know, and also forgetting that without that man, you would not have the ability to punish anyone anywhere. Now, I am done. Now, do whatever you please, O Respected Chief."

All the others knew that Riyaansh had gone too far. Even Khongrem was afraid to intervene. They all looked at Nongru who had sat down, with his hands pressed into his face. They could see he was angry, by the shaking of his head and the trembling of his shoulders.

Finally, Nongru spoke, still not looking up. "How do you do that?"

Riyaansh looked around confused, "Do what?"

"Make an address like O Respected Chief sound insulting," Nongru said. It was then that the others realized that Nongru was shaking not with anger, but because he was trying to control his laughter. Everyone including Riyaansh joined in. The laughter went on for some time, and relaxed everyone.

Finally, Nongru said, "Riyaansh, what I am about to say now, I say from the bottom of my heart. You mentioned that you did not have the good fortune of meeting Ildùr. But, I am sure it is as much his loss as it is yours. I have been the Chief of Wacha for some time now. And yes, I would never have become the chief, but for Ildùr. However good our intentions, power always goes to our heads. Thank you for bringing me back down to earth. Please feel free to ask me whatever you want. From here on, my help and support is truly unconditional. But, at some point of time, you will have to satiate my curiosity. You are asking me the truths about Bujang that very few people in Wacha know, and I was sure no one outside Wacha including this trinity knew. So, I would really like to know how you came to this conclusion."

"Since you put it that way," Riyaansh said, "I will explain it to you before we get into anything else. You see, I am a scribe, as my father was. After I realized how important the Akkadian and Ekur's tale was, I immediately scribed everything down. And as everything I had scribed was lost in a flood, I scribed it all again. It is always easier to connect things, when you are scribing them down. What I mean is, when I scribed it all down, the conversation between you and the Akkadian immediately after you became chief, and especially your promise of taking care of his offspring, stuck to my mind. Later when Ekur came here, two boys were playing in your courtyard. I had assumed that Bugyel, because of the gyel, meaning royal, must be your son. You confirmed it, as well. Then your wife called out for someone to take them to Khongmu. When I put these observations together with your promise, and the fact that your wife did not ask Khongmu to come out to take the children in, I came to these conclusions."

"You said you wanted fate to put this quest into the hands of someone deft and able," Nongru said with admiration. "I think fate already has. What other questions do you have?"

"This has nothing to do with what we have to do next," Riyaansh said, "but considering that my introduction to this tale was through Ekur, and we all now know how he suffered because of the key phrase, I would really like to know how the key phrase came to be," Riyaansh asked.

"First, tell us how I helped you guess it," Viraan insisted.

"Well, when I first blurted it out during breakfast," Riyaansh said, "I had no idea that was the key phrase. I was talking to Kinjyaan, who told me that he had not met Ildùr, or for that matter any Akkadian or Sumerian, but the only person he had met, along with Pasher, was a Givenlander called Shubhyaan. When I realized they were one and the same, I blurted it out. Then, when you asked me to repeat it in my room, you mentioned 'The Phrase'. And then I remembered, that Tiraak had repeated the name Shubhyaan, many times during conversations with Ekur. That is when I realized that I had stumbled upon the key phrase."

"I like how your mind works," Runggoo said, "Ildùr would have really liked you. Now, let me tell you about the origin of the key phrase. It was during dinner the night before Ildùr was leaving Parroo for Ankal that we came up with it. Tiraak asked me how people in Lakho or Runaka would react to a name like Ildùr. I said that unless you wanted everyone to know that you were not from Givenland – you would not go with such a name. It was then that Tiraak decided on the name Shubhyaan. He said that he had always liked that name. It was then that Ildùr came up with the idea of the key phrase. As you said, he did like his theatrics. So, if you have no more questions, tell us what needs to be done next. Or are we leaving that to fate, as well?"

"In my mind, this is still a continuation of the Akkadian's quest," Riyaansh said and then asked his companions, "are you familiar with the Torch Running that is done every seven years?"

All except Khongrem nodded.

Khongrem said, "I have heard of it, but I cannot honestly say that I am familiar with it."

"It is not really important that you know everything about it," Riyaansh said. "But, let me quickly explain. Every seven years, on the day of the Winter Solstice, a torch is lit in either Lakho or Thallo. It alternates between the two. The year it starts from Lakho, it ends in Thallo, and the year it starts from Thallo, it ends in Lakho. The torch is then carried by runners through all the original 108 main cities and towns. So, some small towns like Ankal are in the route, but towns like Parroo, which grew bigger much later, is not on the route. About five hundred people are involved in the whole run, as it moves either east to west or west to east, but slowly meandering either southwards or northwards. There is a bigger than normal ceremony for the Summer Solstice, in the town the Torch Run culminates in. In this ceremony, only two of the runners are felicitated: the one who started it and the one who finishes it. People forget hundreds of the other runners the moment they hand over the torch to the next runner. But, as I was saying, these details does not have anything to do with what I was about to say."

"But like Ildùr, you don't want to give up the chance of telling a good tale either," Tiraak said to everyone's laughter.

"The reason I mentioned it was to say that, in our case, I am one of the in-between runners." Riyaansh continued, "The Akkadian started it. And it is fated for someone else to finish it. We all know how much the Akkadian believed in fate. But, he also believed in planning and action. He planned on coming to Givenland and then made it happen despite many hindrances. He did not wait in his house, listening to his father's stories, while fate did something to get him here. I believe that it will be fate that will guide us, but with help from us in doing our part of planning and actions. The first thing we need to do is analyse what little the Akkadian told Ekur in his deathbed. We also need to find out what Pasher may have heard or seen. We need …"

"Sorry for interrupting your flow," Nongru said, "but I am not sure when conferring with Pasher will be possible. After Ekur brought the news of Ildùr's death, Pasher informed me that he needs to deliberate with his mind and soul, or something like that."

"Now, I am sorry for interrupting you," Riyaansh said, "but can you remember what Pasher said, I mean what words did he use?"

"Hmm," Nongru pondered, "in that case, let us hear it from Khongrem."

"After Runggoo left Wacha with Ekur," Khongrem said, "Pasher was very restless for the next few days. We all knew how close he was to Ildùr. And we assumed that this was his way of grieving. Then ten days later, he came to us, and informed us that he would like to go away from our valley for a while. Pasher told us that he had made peace with his master's death. But there are some dilemmas that it has created, which he now needed to resolve. He then said that his mind and soul were in conflict and he had to contemplate on the journey he took with his master. And that he could not share anything else, at least for the time being."

"Have you heard such nonsense ever?" Nongru grumbled, "and this from one of the strongest and bravest men I have ever met".

But Khongrem held his hand to calm him down, "Then my husband asked Pasher, how long he would be gone. To which Pasher replied that he was very sorry, but he had to decide which was more important, to be true to one's words or to do the right thing. At least that is how I remember it."

"And then that was what was talked," Nongru said. "I wish sometimes that her memory of words were not as good. But, she never lets you forget anything you have ever said."

"I know I am the only person here who did not know Ildùr," Riyaansh said, "but I can almost hear him say – whatever cannot be cured has to be endured." Then, seeing the look on the faces around him, he realized how what he had said could be totally misconstrued. He quickly added, "I think that was very bad timing on my part. I meant that about Pasher not being here, and not your memory, O Divine Wife of Chief." And seeing Khongrem's smile and wave her hand continued, "And somehow I also have this feeling that we will come across many of these, obstacles – no, the word I am looking for is annoyances. So let us take it step by step."

Riyaansh referred back to the parchment that he had extracted from within his loincloth.

"Let us analyse each of the uttering of Ildùr to Ekur on his death bed," Riyaansh said, "and see what we can learn."

"As you seem to have already put some thought to this, please take the lead my friend," Nongru said on behalf of everyone.

"Let us first make sure we know what was being said," Riyaansh said, "then, let us discuss the why. The place I would like to start with something he said – A-na-poo-na, are you sure that Dan-van-tree can fix Pasher's leg?' And what did he mean by fixing the other problem, as well? Now, I think he is calling out to Annapurna. As some of you may know, in Darromohe, Thallo, Purawanbhag and some other places, Goddess Annapurna is considered to be one of the many forms of the Goddess, the form who provides nourishment to all. In his next sentence, he is questioning whether Dan-van-tree can fix Pasher's leg. And I think what Ekur heard as Dan-van-tree is really Dhanvantari. Again, as some of you might know, he is another form of the God of Life, and, interestingly enough, he is the form who cures all living things of their illnesses and ailments. Now, if we put all of this together, I think we can safely conclude that he was not calling out the names as an invocation, but, and I know this might be considered blasphemy, Ildùr was having a real conversation with Annapurna. If you think about it, the Chief High Priests have been claiming to be in communication with the Gods, and we believe that. Therefore, we should not have a problem believing Ildùr had a conversation with Goddess Annapurna. But, there are a few things that I cannot explain. All of you know that Ildùr was a believer. He believed in fate, in his own Gods, in the Gods of Wacha, and he believed in the Gods of the Great Northern White Mountains. Why is he calling her 'Annapurna', rather than 'Goddess Annapurna'? And again why does he say 'Dhanvantari,' instead of 'Lord Dhanvantari'? This question, I was hoping, Pasher could answer. However, as Pasher is not here to do so, do any of you know if something happened to Pasher's leg while he was with Ildùr on his quest?"

No one spoke for a few moments. They sat looking at each other.

Then, finally, Nongru said, "This is the last time that I will be praising you on your intelligence and powers of deduction. I will not insult you by mentioning this again. It is clear that you are remarkable indeed. I don't think I will ever really understand how the brains of people like Ildùr and yours work. Sorry, I am digressing. Yes, Pasher did have an accident up there in the mountains. But, his leg was completely healed by the time he came back, except a scar on his right leg, going straight down from his outer thigh to the ankle. I had asked Pasher about it in Ildùr's presence, but the latter had said that I will know in good time, after he was back from Kurm. Something about a promise he needed to keep. When he did not come back, I never asked Pasher."

"Then, unless anyone else has a better explanation, let us assume for the time being that my interpretation is right," Riyaansh said, and as no one objected continued. "Now, before we go to the next sentences, Nongru brought up something, which reminded me of a question I needed to ask you all. Am I right in assuming that neither the Akkadian nor Pasher shared anything about what happened up there with any of you?"

"Yes, you are right," Nongru said. The others nodded.

"I think this is because of his promise to Ishme," Riyaansh said, "the one about Ishme being the first one to know about the Akkadian's discovery of the White Gods. He also repeated this promise to Khongmu before leaving on his quest. So now, I know that many of the questions I was expecting answers to today, will have to wait. So, let us go to the next sentence: 'Ka-lee, please believe me. The Givenlanders can be like Ma-noo and Ya-maa again. You cannot destroy a whole race for the fault of a few. You have to give them a chance. Listen to me, please don't walk away.' Ka-lee has to be Kali, another form of the Goddess. And Goddess Kali, being the form for Time, Change and Continuity, is also therefore associated with destruction. This connects well with the part about causing the destruction of a whole race; I will come back to the part about the faults of a few later. Also, again, the fact that the Akkadian does not call her Goddess Kali is interesting, but the more interesting part is where he asks her not to walk away. I have not had the good fortune of seeing a vision of any God, but I am sure that if someone calls out after a vision, it will be something like *don't go* or at most *don't go away*. I think walk away also definitely points to an actual physical presence. Coming to the sentence I skipped over, Ma-noo, I assume, is the Manu, the fabled founder of our Race. Now, Ya-maa must be Yama, the God of Death and Learning. I am still confused with the fact that Manu and Yama have not only been mentioned together, but are referred to almost as a related pair. But ..."

"It feels nice to be able to add value," Tiraak cut in excitedly, "for I think I might know the connection. When I was younger, I used to go deep into the valleys in the Mountain that Touches the Sky for my prospecting. There, once, I met an old man who lived in a cave and spent most of his days in meditation. As he had not seen any other human being for a long time, he liked for us to go and talk to him after sunset. All the others avoided going up to him, especially as his unwashed, matted hair and unwashed body was offensive to the nose. But, I felt bad for him, and went to see him every other day. He was considerate and always tried to sit downwind from me. He claimed to have been a High Priest in the Temple Sanctuary of Rahira. According to him, the original teachings of the Gods were being corrupted by the Temple Sanctuaries, and that is the reason why he had left, choosing, instead, the life of a hermit. He once told me that Manu and Yama were the first upholders of Dharma, which is what keeps order amongst everything. He mentioned that they were brothers, and he did clarify that he meant real brothers, not just brothers in the upholding of the Dharma. He also mentioned that Manu and Yama together founded our Race, not Manu alone, and it is by the virtue of being the first to die that Yama became the God of Death, basically by precedence. Of course, I have no way of knowing how much of this the old man was making up, but I believe that there can be no smoke without fire. I think it is safe to assume that at the very least there is some relationship between Manu and Yama."

Riyaansh thought about this a little while and said, "Thank you, Tiraak. That really makes sense. Now, if we come back to the other thing that we had skipped over, the part about the 'fault of a few.' I think the Akkadian had already made it very clear who these few were – the arrogant, greedy, lecherous High Priests, is what he called them. The next part is where another mystery lies: When Ekur asked the Akkadian if the White Gods of Great Northern White Mountains really do exist, the Akkadian did not answer the question directly. He listed a set of characteristics, and said if these were the qualities that defined the Gods, then they did exist. I think the Akkadian was not being evasive, but was just unsure himself. Or, perhaps, he knew the exact truth, but did not think he could explain it to Ekur in the limited time that he had. Then, the last part – 'The Gods, they are not all White. And even the ones who are White are not always White.' The first part is self-explanatory, especially as he specifically mentioned Kali, and in our teachings, though Kali has been described of being coloured different hues, she is always of some dark shade. I cannot understand the part about the Gods not being always white. At first, I thought the Akkadian might have been talking about them not always being peaceful, if by 'white' he meant peace. But the more I think about it, the surer I get that if we can solve this particular clue, we will come much closer to the whole truth. I know you all may have many questions, I will try to answer them now."

There was a long silence. No one asked any questions.

Finally, Runggoo broke the silence, "I am sure I will have questions later. But, I am still trying to think through the implications of what I have just heard. Even though I had known that Ildùr was seeking the White Gods of the Great Northern White Mountains, I was sure that once he got there, he would find a logical and worldly answer to the whole thing. After he came back, I could tell from Ildùr's demeanour that something significant had happened up there. But as you all know, he refused to discuss it. He told me that he needed to think it through, before he would be ready to talk. The only thing he told me is that he was sorry that he could not keep his promise to me, as everything had turned to be much bigger than any of us. Pasher did say something interesting once. He said that the impact of their discovery on Pasher himself was much greater, as he was influenced in not only his heart and soul, but his body, as well. When I asked him to explain, he said he had already said too much, and I should wait for his Master to explain. The only other discussion I had on this was with Ildùr, just before he left for Kurm. He asked me if I could find a way to get to Durshan Lake by travelling directly west from the Mother River. I told him that this should not be difficult. I even offered to go there and find out, while he was still visiting Kurm. But, Ildùr said that we still had time. And it would be best if I went with Pasher and him. If I knew the destruction of Givenland was involved, I would have pestered them for more."

"This only makes it more mysterious," Riyaansh said. Then after some thought added, "I feel we should stop worrying about what we don't know, and start working with what we do know. For though the Akkadian mentioned that the calamity is years away, he did also say that we should act now."

"What do you suggest?" Nongru asked, "It is clear that you already have some thoughts."

"Please remember that this is bigger than all of us," Riyaansh said tentatively, trying to find the right words, "and remember, he said that the Givenlanders have to convince the Gods. I think Bujang has to leave this valley. He has to grow up in Givenland as a Givenlander."

"But, Riyaansh, I don't see how what you are asking is even possible. Khongmu has never even left this valley," Khongrem objected.

"My son, who though not a Givenlander, will come as a Givenlander," Riyaansh said quietly, "that is what Ildùr said. So, please bear in mind, it is his decision not mine. For Bujang to go as a Givenlander, he has to be brought up in Givenland, by a Givenlander. So I am sorry, but Khongmu cannot accompany Bujang. The person, who will complete the Akkadian's quest, will be Shubhyaan's son and not the son of Ildùr and Khongmu."

"Who will explain that to Khongmu?" Khongrem said. "Good luck trying to snatch away from her the only thing that is dear to her."

"After hearing the whole story, being Ildùr's wife, she will insist that we make her husband's wish come true, and she will hand over the thing that is most dear to her, to the predestined guardian."

"And are you going to be the predestined guardian?" Khongrem asked.

"I don't think my role in this tale is that of a guardian," Riyaansh said sadly, "or why did fate conspire to take away my right to be a father? No, my role is different. But, the fated guardian is with us in this room and knows that this is his fate."

The others all looked at each other.

"Somehow, I think he means me," finally Tiraak said. "I am not sure why though, as I think everyone else in this room would do a better job. But, if you really think I have been fated for this role, I will do it."

"Thank you," Riyaansh said.

"Would you mind telling us why it should be Tiraak?" Runggoo said.

"I know you would like the role more than anyone else in this room," Riyaansh said, "but each of us has very different roles to play. As I go through my other requests, I think you will agree with me. But, before we get into those, I think it is important that we talk to Khongmu. After all, even though I think she will understand and agree, we have to hear this from her."

"It is getting late," Khongrem said, "I don't think this is the right time to start talking to Khongmu."

"You are right," Riyaansh said. "The journey we are embarking on will be a long and strenuous one. So, neglecting our rest and thereby health would not be the smart thing to do. We can convene again after breakfast. Viraan had told me that I will need the chief's permission to get lodgings in Wacha. I hope it is not too late."

"All of you will be staying here," Khongrem said. "I know my husband likes to have some changa before turning in. I will bring you all a jug. But please, no more serious discussions. Those can wait until tomorrow."

After Khongrem left, Nongru started pouring changa for his companions and said, "As I said before, without Ildùr, I would not be chief. Even so, I am more thankful to Ildùr for helping me get married to Khongrem. In spite of the fact that he had literally risked getting me killed during that affair."

"And I am glad that Runggoo no longer considers me a stranger, but a friend," Riyaansh said sipping his changa.

"What do you mean?" Nongru asked.

But before Riyaansh could say anything, Tiraak asked Riyaansh with a chuckle, "Don't you ever forget anything that you have heard?"

"Usually not after I have scribed it," Riyaansh answered.

"Well, the first time I introduced Runggoo to Ildùr," Tiraak explained to Nongru, "Runggoo informed Ildùr that he does not drink alcohol. But the next day, when Ildùr saw him imbibing raajaraas, he thought that we were involved in some no good scheme. It was then that Runggoo explained to him that he only drank alcohol with friends, not with strangers."

"I have to think of you as a friend," Runggoo joked, "as I don't want someone with your memory as an enemy."

Everyone laughed. But on Viraan's insistence, they all went to sleep soon after.

Next morning during breakfast, Nongru mentioned that he needed to sit down with the Elders. So, it was decided that Khongrem would first talk to Khongmu, and inform her that the others knew about her and Bujang. Then during the day, Riyaansh would share with Khongmu, everything he had shared with the others. All except Nongru and Khongrem would join them. Then over dinner they would continue their discussions.

When they sat down for dinner, after the initial pleasantries had been fulfilled, Nongru turned to Riyaansh. "What did Khongmu have to say about your request?" Nongru asked.

"We have told her everything, including my interpretations of the Akkadian's last conversation with Ekur," Riyaansh said, "but we have not discussed my request, yet. I thought we would discuss all my requests over dinner."

"Well, let us get started then," Nongru said. "But, the only person that can grant you your first request is Khongmu."

"Khongmu," Riyaansh started, "believe me, for I know how attached you get to a child, especially when you are bringing him or her up alone, without a spouse. But, you will agree that what we are talking here is bigger than the emotions of any of us. But I think ..."

"Riyaansh," Khongmu said, "from your unnecessarily long and meandering sentences, I assume you are going to ask for something really unreasonable. And as you have mentioned a child being brought up without a spouse, I think this has something to do with Bujang. So, please come to the point and speak plainly. For how long do you want to take Bujang away from me?"

"I don't know," Riyaansh said, caught unawares at Khongmu's words, "but I know it will be a very long time, if not forever."

"I cannot give up Bujang forever," Khongmu plainly stated. "How long I am willing to live without him depends on how convinced I am about the necessity of it."

"Okay, I will not beat about the bush this time," Riyaansh said. "Ildùr's son needs to be brought up as a Givenlander. Bujang will have to move to Givenland, and be brought up by a Givenlander. "

"I still don't see why I can't be the one who brings him up," Khongmu said. "I can go to Givenland and bring him up as a Givenlander."

"Even you cannot believe that. You don't look like a Givenlander, neither do you talk like one. So, why do you think Bujang will think that you are a Givenlander? No, you know, as well as me that that will not work."

"Yes I do," Khongmu finally said, "but I have to see Bujang at least once a year."

"I think that is fair," Riyaansh said. "But only from afar."

"We will talk about what afar means later," Khongmu said coldly. "But, even though I would like to argue against it, I think you are right. Besides, you have convinced me that my husband would have wanted this."

"Then, let us not have any more discussions about it," Riyaansh said with relief, "and I would like to move on to my next request. We have to find the westward route to Durshan Lake. As Pasher is not here, I think Runggoo will have to work alone in finding this route."

Runggoo nodded.

"In case you were wondering what I will be doing," Riyaansh said, "Viraan and I will be working on finding ways to get some control over as many of the High Priests and Chief High Priests as possible. We know that many of them do not care about what is good for their people, but only about what is best for their own selves. I have already told you what fate they had planned for my daughter and me. You also know what was done to Kinjyaan. And I am sure, these are not isolated events. And, of course, we have Ildùr's words for it – the arrogant, greedy, lecherous High Priests, he called them. So, we are going to use their arrogance, greed and lechery and any other flaw or for that matter even their good qualities to start getting them to do our bidding. And I am sure that those faults will include avarice; so if required we will have to buy some of their allegiances."

"Buy them with what?" Tiraak said. "We all know the Temple Sanctuaries are very well off. No offense, but you have already told us that you could not even afford to acquire a proper house in Pparaha. I know Nongru is the Chief of Wacha. Runggoo and I have done quite well with our prospecting. My cousin here is a very successful trader and is most probably the most prosperous of us all. But in spite of this, everything we own will not be enough for us to buy the support of any one High Priest, let alone a Chief High Priest, especially if we want them to work against the Temple Sanctuaries."

"You did not cover everyone in this room," Riyaansh said quietly.

"Whom did I miss?" Tiraak said looking around, "If you mean Khongrem and Khongmu, I assumed that I was covering them with the mention of Nongru as the Chief of Wacha."

"I am sorry," Riyaansh said, "but I don't think we have time to talk in riddles, so I will directly come to the point. I should have been more straightforward. Maybe as it is not my decision to make, I was not being very direct. If you remember Ildùr's last words …"

"I thought I heard you say you will directly come to the point," Runggoo interrupted, "but if you are referring to the cave near Durshan Lake that Ildùr mentioned, you can forget about it for the time being. Without knowing the exact location, I don't think we will ever find this cave."

"I was not referring to what the Akkadian had left behind in the cave," Riyaansh said, "but to what he had brought out of it."

"Of course," Tiraak said. "But, do you think Ekur will still be willing to share that?"

"Why not?" Nongru asked. "After all, that was a promise he made to Ildùr, not to us."

"I think I know Ekur better than any of you," Riyaansh said, "and I can vouch that he would never keep someone else's inheritance. More importantly, the person who has to decide whether this fortune should be used in this endeavour is Khongmu, and not Ekur or anyone else."

"I want for nothing in Wacha," Khongmu said. "Nongru has kept his promise to my husband well. I am sorry I should not have said that, for I truly believe that both Khongrem and Nongru would have done the same even without the promise. So, yes, I not only agree to share this fortune, but insist that it be used to achieve my husband's last wishes. If you think it would help, I am willing to travel to Kurm to convince Ekur to give me my inheritance."

"But Ekur did leave you something," Riyaansh said. "Remember the urn he left behind for you? Would you mind fetching it now?"

"You want me to fetch my husband's ashes?" Khongmu asked incredulously.

"As dictated by Sumerian tradition," Riyaansh replied gently, "your husband was buried and not cremated. The ashes in that urn belong to animals from a butcher's shop."

"So, every night I have been talking to an urn containing nothing of my husband. Why would Ekur play such a cruel trick on me?" Khongmu wept. "Now that I know the truth, I don't want to see it again for the rest of my life. I will fetch it now." After coming back with the urn, and handing it to Riyaansh, she said, "The urn is all yours. Do what you want with it."

"Never give away something without knowing its value," Riyaansh smiled, "or you will live to regret it."

"What value can the remains of animals have?" Viraan asked.

Riyaansh took the urn. He took it close to the stove where water was being boiled. From the fire, he took a log and broke a splinter off it, and after holding it to the fire, he used the burning splinter to melt the wax off the lid of the urn. As he was doing it, he saw that everyone's attention was riveted on him. He smiled at the realization that he had also picked up a penchant for theatrics, much like the Akkadian. And then with a flourish, he poured out the contents. But, he did not get the reaction he had expected, for the stones were all covered with ashes, thus not shining.

"Can I please have a big pail of water?" Riyaansh asked Khongrem.

"Don't worry," Khongrem said irritably, "I will clean it up. But why you would do such a thing is beyond …"

But by this time, Riyaansh had picked up one of the larger stones and was cleaning and polishing it on his sleeves.

Seeing this, Nongru stopped Khongrem and said with mounting excitement, "Wife, please bring him his pail of water."

By now, everyone including Khongrem had seen the stone Riyaansh was holding between his thumb and forefinger. Khongrem rushed to bring him a pail of water. Riyaansh carefully gathered all the ash-covered stones and dropped them into the bucket. Then, one by one, he took out the stones and laid them in front of Khongmu.

"More than half of these are blue diamonds," Viraan said after picking up one of the larger stones and studying it against the light, "and they are almost flawless in colour and shape. Honestly speaking, I have only seen very small stones like this, and even those were not of the same quality. I don't know how these could be polished like this. From what I have heard, in the lands of Misr[72], for even four of these small ones, you can name your price, and not expect any bargaining. In Dilmun[73] and Makkan[74], if you take an ornament made of three, five or seven of these stones, they will open up the town granary for you. I don't think anyone has ever possessed these many stones, definitely not of these sizes and quality. And I am sorry, Riyaansh, but I have to advice Khongmu to think again before giving these up. I know she said that she gets everything she wants in Wacha. But with these, she can own Wacha and more."

"And with these, we can afford to do what Riyaansh was planning?" Khongmu asked.

"That and some more," Viraan replied without hesitation.

"In that case, Riyaansh, you can have them," said Khongmu simply.

"I have heard of people getting corrupted for much less," Riyaansh said after some thought. "I propose that we keep aside a third for Bujang's future. And we create a council to decide how the remaining fortune will be used. I think by virtue of being the inheritor, Khongmu should be in this council and have a say on its membership."

"And of course Riyaansh," Nongru said, "as without him we would not have known what Khongmu had in the urn. Of course if Khongmu agrees."

"If you all really think that I am capable of deciding on such important things," Khongmu said, "I think the Council should be all of us in this room. At present, the only person who should be added if and when we even get an opportunity to do so is Ekur. Also, we should try to let Ekur know that we now understand that he came here with the best of intentions. And that his intuition in putting his faith in Riyaansh has been vindicated. In future, if we add members to this council, which I would like to call Ildùr's Council of Protectors, it will be with the agreement of

---

[72]Egypt
[73]Basra, Iraq
[74]Oman

everyone in the council. Now, before we go into any other business, I have a request – no, a demand of my own. At the first opportunity that Bujang can be informed of the truth of his parentage, it should be done. And unless I am dead, I want myself and only myself to be the one to tell him. I want to explain to him why I am taking the decision I am taking today. I don't want him to think even for a moment that I had forsaken him. And if he hates me for it, I don't want it to be anyone else's fault."

"I don't see a problem with that," Riyaansh said. "I think we can make that promise."

The others nodded their agreement.

"Also, before I forget," Viraan said, "if Khongmu really wants to reach Ekur to give him the news, I might have a way. I can arrange for the message to be delivered to Kurm, by some trusted trader."

"That would be nice, indeed," Riyaansh said, "but one cannot be too careful in these things. So, I propose that the message simply says – we met your friend from Kdwar, everything is clear now. And it should only be signed Viraan."

"Won't that be too mysterious and make people more suspicious?" Runggoo asked.

"I don't think so," Viraan said. "People will assume that it has something to do with trading and is being sent in a code."

"Then, it is all decided," Khongrem said, "and I insist that we stop talking and eat. From tomorrow, I am not serving hot meals any longer, as we are ending up eating it cold every day."

"As usual, my wife is right," Nongru said. "I think you all should plan on staying in Wacha for the next few days, as we discuss further details of what we all will need to do. This will also give Khongmu some more time with Bujang."

"And before Riyaansh warns me," Khongmu said with a sad smile, "I promise I will not do anything to make Bujang suspicious about his impending indefinite departure."

Chapter 20

It was dinnertime at Riyaansh's house, too.

"Since that day, we have been planning and preparing to do Ildùr's bidding to Ekur on his death bed. Like everything else, we have had our share of failures and successes. For some of the failures, I will never be able to forgive myself. Having said that, I still can't see how we could have done anything differently," Riyaansh said and picked up his notes again. Tiraa whispered in Zayaa's ear that she needed to relieve herself, and left the room. When Tiraa was gone, the elderly gentleman put down his notes again.

"I know I have not finished my tale completely. There are gaps, some deliberate and others not. Also I am sure you must have many questions. But before everything else, may I spend some time in private with my daughter?" Riyaansh entreated.

"I am sorry," Zayaa said, "but we all make our choices. And these choices have consequences. You made yours to abandon me. The consequence is that you have lost any right for any alone time with me."

"I understand," Riyaansh said. "Could I perhaps have some private time with Vyaan and you?"

"Yes," Zayaa said, "but only to spare my daughter the displeasure of listening to the conversation. You see, having a father like Vyaan, she would never understand how a person's self-aggrandizement can be more important than his daughter's wellbeing."

"If you all don't mind," Tanaa said, "I would like to quietly observe you all, and stop anyone from saying or doing anything that they will regret for the rest of their lives. So, why don't we stop now and continue later, once Tiraa has gone to sleep."

After Tiraa had gone to bed, the four of them went to the other end of the house.

"What is it that you wanted to talk about?" Zayaa asked, still angry.

"Zaa," Riyaansh said, "This is not how I wanted it to be. I know you want me to regret my decision of switching places with Ridhaan. But, my question to you is this – in what way did Ridhaan fail you as a father?"

"And my question to you is this – how could any father have the heart to do what you did to me? And when I arrived here, you told me that I should tell Tiraa about everything that has happened to me. That means you know what happened to me at the Temple Sanctuary. But, you still only cared about this quest of yours, and did not care enough about your daughter, to come and see how she was? I think it is because Mother Tanaa knew what a pathetic father I had, that she took pity on me and decided to help me."

"Enough Zayaa," Tanaa said, "don't say things, that after knowing the truth you will never forgive yourself for uttering. Riyaansh might have done many things that I don't agree with. But I can't see what he could have done to protect you that Ridhaan did not do. Or what more Riyaansh could have done afterwards, that he did not do."

"Is there anything at all that he did do for me?" Zayaa mocked.

"Who do you think came up with the idea of scaring the other High Priests away from even touching you? I did not even know about those leaves that look like dhutura but are of a different nature. Why do you think the Chief High Priest of Parroo suddenly came to Pparaha and tried to take you away? Yes, my dear, he is on our side. The Council of Protectors sent him there at your father's behest. And don't forget what he has to live through every day – the guilt he feels about what happened to you, along with the guilt of having his twin brother take his place, the twin brother who got murdered in his place."

"Murdered?" Zayaa asked, "What do you mean?"

"Remember, when Ridhaan died, his body was brought to my home?" Tanaa said, "The reason he died is not from shock, but because he was poisoned. That is why he was frothing from his mouth."

"Why didn't you tell me?" Zayaa asked and, then remembering, added, "and you knew what Sikkappa was saying when he talked about me not being his daughter. You could see how hurt I was by being disowned by him. But you still did not say anything. Why Mother Tanaa, did you not care for me, whom you called the daughter you never had?"

"And negate the sacrifices that your father and uncle made?" Tanaa asked. "Please, Zayaa, stop thinking about yourself, and start understanding the greater good."

"No, Tanaa," Riyaansh said, "she has every right to say what she is saying now. I think I should have explained everything to her, about what I was doing and why. Ridhaan had asked me to do exactly that. But, I ignored him. I thought as I was the chosen one, therefore my decisions must be the right ones. Today, I know I was wrong, and that Ridhaan was right. I assumed that she was too young to understand, but that was not my assumption to make. But Zayaa, can we keep aside your anger against me for some time. Let us instead concentrate on ensuring Tiraa's safety. We also need to see that Ildùr's bidding gets done, or all the sacrifices that people like Ridhaan has made will be in vain."

"Please tell me, how we can make sure that Tiraa avoids my fate. Have you already found some way?"

"Not yet," Riyaansh said. "But, first, can I ask you something else"? How much are you planning to tell Tiraa about your story?"

"I don't know," Zayaa said, "but I am not ready to divulge anything that will make her think that she is not Vyaan's daughter."

"I think we have agreed that she is my daughter," Vyaan said. "I shall suffer no more discussion on this."

"Do you think Tiraa is not Vyaan's daughter?" Tanaa asked Zayaa.

"As Vyaan has said, Tiraa will always be his daughter," Zayaa answered, "But, we all know ..."

"All this is my fault," Tanaa said with a faraway look. "When Vyaan picked up Tiraa for the first time, I thought you all knew. Whatever the circumstances, I could not imagine that anyone could have such unquestioned love for the offspring of his wife, conceived by the seed of another. Sorry, I am babbling. Tiraa is Vyaan's daughter. You were already with child the night you were taken to the Temple Sanctuary. Actually, you almost lost her with that night's activities. But, I managed to ensure her survival."

"Did you hear that, Vyaan," Zayaa said excitedly. "Tiraa *is* indeed your daughter."

"But she always was," Vyaan simply said.

"In that case, I am going to tell her everything," Zayaa said. "I think there have been too many secrets."

"Good. Now let us discuss about how we can ensure Tiraa's safety," Vyaan said.

"As I was saying, I have not been able to come up with a solution yet," Riyaansh said. "With Apaan as our opponent, it will be very difficult for us to predict his moves. Everyone tells me that you are a great Goats and Lion player. This means you must be good at planning and executing traps. So, we were hoping you could help in coming up with a plan that will save Tiraa and neutralize Apaan. Of course, we will give you any help you need."

"If the safety of my daughter and Givenland is at stake, I am ready to take on any foe," Vyaan said calmly, "but I need time to think."

"Of course," Riyaansh said, "If you need to be alone, we will give you space and make sure you are not disturbed."

"No, I think better with people around me," Vyaan said. "But what will be a distraction, are all these unanswered questions that are still remaining in your story. If we could answer these, it will help my mind concentrate better."

"Why don't you ask your questions?" Riyaansh asked.

"Ok," Vyaan said. "Which city in Givenland did Tiraak take Bujang to? He must have come of age, and if he has a fraction of his father's cunning, he could really help us in this crisis. I think if he was helping us, or, even better, was taking the lead, we would definitely find a way to protect Tiraa. Sorry, I am digressing. My questions, in no particular order, are as follows: where did Tiraak take Bujang? What has since happened to each of the Council of Protectors? How successful were you in penetrating the Temple Sanctuaries? Did Runggoo find the other route to Durshan Lake? Was he lucky enough to find Ildùr's cave? Also, how do I know that scar of yours? Where have I seen it before? There are many more, of course. I would also like to know about what happened to my Sikkappa. The reason I ask is that you have said that you were keeping Zayaa in close observation, so I was hoping you might know something."

"Hmm," Riyaansh stroked his chin, "all very good questions. I think it is quite late now, so let me ponder over them. I hope to answer them all, if not by tomorrow, then at the latest by the day after tomorrow. I don't want any more deceptions. But, I will be able to give you better answers after I hear about something else."

"I can guess what," Vyaan said, "Bujang is coming here, isn't he? But even if he does, how can you be direct and honest without breaking your promise to Khongmu?"

"Good question," Riyaansh answered, then keeping it vague, said, "Everything does not happen as we hope they will, so all we can do is keep trying."

"You mean you will break your word?" Vyaan asked. "Sorry, I forgot our promise. I can wait until tomorrow or the day after for the answers to my other questions."

"Vyaan," Zayaa said, "I think it best that you and I don't plan for anything tomorrow. I would like to talk to Tiraa. If we are to inform her everything, I don't want to procrastinate any longer. I will do it alone, but Tiraa, me or perhaps both of us might need you to keep us sane."

"Of course," Vyaan immediately said. "That has to come, first. And maybe the three of us may decide to run away from it all. In that case, we will not need any of those answers."

"If you would like privacy," Riyaansh said, "I will ask Sanj to take you to my other hut. We will make sure the three of you are not disturbed there. All your food will be provided there and either Sanj or someone else will fetch you from there on the day after tomorrow morning."

Zayaa and Vyaan spent their whole day with Tiraa in Riyaansh's other hut. Even though Zayaa had the mother-daughter talk with Tiraa before they had left Pparaha, these discussions were more directed on how a woman's body matures and how children are conceived. Tiraa still did not comprehend the concepts of rape or even sex under duress. But, what she did understand was that Apaan was a monster who had caused inexpressible suffering to her mother. And she wanted Vyaan to avenge her mother's pain. Both Zayaa and Vyaan decided to wait until Riyaansh had answered Vyaan's questions, before they could think about what would be best for Tiraa.

The next morning, Tanaa came to fetch them to Riyaansh's main hut. When the main hut came into view, they could see that there were quite a few camels and asses stabled outside. They walked in, expecting a lot of company, but were surprised to find Riyaansh sitting alone in the front room.

"I think we are ready to discuss all your queries," Riyaansh spoke as soon as they walked in, "and I think it is time to introduce you to some of the others. Your first question first: where did Tiraak take Bujang? The answer needs to be handled a little delicately. So, if I could request Tiraa and Zayaa to go out to the courtyard with Tanaa for a while." Then sensing some disagreement, he said, "If for nothing else, to oblige an old man. Believe me you will soon know why this is necessary."

After Zayaa and Tiraa had gone out with Tanaa, Riyaansh signalled to Vyaan, "Please wait here," and went inside.

Soon after Riyaansh had left, an elderly woman came into the room from inside. Though she looked familiar, Vyaan did not recognize her. However, he felt irresistibly drawn to her.

"Well met," Vyaan said guardedly. "I think I know you, but I am unable to recall from where."

"I never expected recognition, so I never thought you not knowing me will cause me pain," the elderly woman said, "but it does. However, that is my fault, not yours. Since the last time I held you to my bosom, I have always hoped and craved for your forgiveness, for what I had allowed to happen, whatever the reasons or intentions. So, tell me son, will you ever be able to forgive your mother."

"But my parents died in a ship wreck, that is why Sikkappa brought me up," Vyaan protested.

"I know what you were told, what you had to be told. But I wanted to explain to you, why I did, what I did, for I knew that my son might not understand the importance of what had to be done, but I was sure that Ildùr's son would understand why this could not be any other way. So Bujang, my son, will you ever be able to forgive me?" And Khongmu turned away her face to hide her tears.

"What are you saying?" Vyaan asked. "This cannot be true. I heard Ildùr's tale from Riyaansh. He was a giant amongst men. He changed the course of history in Wacha to get his way. I cannot be his son, I am someone who was unable to protect his wife and who is now wondering who will help him protect his daughter. Please, if you are indeed Khongmu, tell me what new trick is Riyaansh playing?"

"It is no trickery, my son," Khongmu said, "and from what I have heard of you, I should be as proud to have you as a son, as I was to have Ildùr as my husband. As I said, the only thing I crave from you is your forgiveness, and if it is not too much to hold you once more to my bosom.

If I can get these, I would happily start my journey to join your father in the after-world."

"If I am really Bujang," Vyaan said finally, "then mother, I cannot forgive you. You can only forgive someone's wrongdoing. From what I hear, you sacrificed your right to be close to your son, so that your husband's bidding could be achieved. Yes, this made me miss a mother's affection, but I did not even know that I was missing it. Instead, by doing what you did, you ensured that I met Zayaa, without whom I cannot imagine being alive. But, please, if this is a trick, I promise to do whatever you all want, but beg of you not to play with a poor man's feelings."

"I understand why it is difficult for you to believe," Khongmu said sadly. "So, I will call another, whom you will have to believe. But, I need your word that you will not judge this person, until you hear him out."

"You have my word," Vyaan said.

"Riyaansh," Khongmu called out towards the inner door, "could you please come in with Tiraak?"

And to Vyaan's amazement, Riyaansh entered the room with his uncle, Shubhyaan. Then, he realized the reason Khongmu had taken the promise.

"Sikkappa," Vyaan said, "I have given my word. And it is from you that I have learnt that a man's word is his bond. So, I will not judge what you did by making me think that you were dead for these many years. I will not judge you, until you have explained why you saw fit to abandon me when I needed you the most."

"You have heard the entire story from Riyaansh," Tiraak said, "after we left Wacha, we stayed in Parroo for a few weeks. At first, I looked at it as a job that Riyaansh had proposed and the Council had concurred. But within days, you changed all that. As Riyaansh might have mentioned, I had become extremely fond of Ildùr. And I saw much of your father in you. The more time I spent with you, the more I liked you. And finally I started thinking of you as a nephew, who was as close as a son. When Riyaansh took us both to Pparaha and with Tanaa's help, settled us down in the house next door to his brother and daughter, I decided to take Ildùr's Givenlander name, Shubhyaan. By the time you brought up the subject of going to Sumer, I had become your Sikkappa. Not only did I try to dissuade you, but also did not inform the Council about this. However, when Ridhaan mentioned it to Riyaansh, the Council felt this was fated. By this time Viraan had already made contact with Ekur. So, Viraan and Ekur through their trading contacts, and by using many middlemen, ensured you joined a caravan to Kurm. Then …"

"I am sorry, Sikkappa," Vyaan said, "but I don't think the Ekur I knew in Sumer had any missing toes and fingers."

"That is because he hides it well," Riyaansh answered. "Try and think back, have you ever seen him without his loose and unshapely robes?"

"Now that you say it, I think I did not," Vyaan said thoughtfully.

"Well, I think you can work out the rest of it," Tiraak said, "so, let me come to why I had to leave. When that incident with Zayaa happened, the council decided that I was to do nothing about it for the time being. But, I could not reconcile with this decision. Instead, I made my own plans for revenge. But, I did not want to risk doing anything before you were back. But Runggoo had guessed what I was up to, and the day before you were to arrive back in Pparaha, which was also the day before I had planned on attacking Apaan, he and some others came to Pparaha, and after putting something in my raajaraas, which made me unconscious, spirited me away. The council again explained to me that we were not strong enough yet, and that trying to exact our revenge on Apaan at that point of time would be futile. I did agree. But, I was honest with the rest of the council and informed them that if I went back to Pparaha, I was not sure I would continue to feel the same. I could not go on seeing the person that had hurt and was continuing to hurt your Zayaa, and not do anything about it. The council decided that I should never return to Pparaha. I am sorry; it was my weakness that kept me away from you. I hope someday you can forgive me."

"Oh, Sikkappa," Vyaan said, "and I do hope you don't mind me continuing to call you that. There is nothing to forgive, now that I understand why you could not be there." Then turning to Khongmu, he said with tears in his eyes, "Ayei, I doubted your motherhood. So, any punishment you decide will be too little for me. But before you decide on my punishment, please take me to your bosom."

Khongmu hugged Vyaan, and mother and son cried into each other's cheeks. When finally they came back to this world, Vyaan looked around.

"Would you like someone to fetch Zayaa and Tiraa?" Riyaansh asked.

Vyaan, still overwhelmed, nodded.

Riyaansh went out and came back with Tanaa, Zayaa and Tiraa.

For Zayaa, seeing Tiraak was like seeing a ghost for the second time too and within days.

Vyaan, between tears and smiles explained everything to Zayaa and Tiraa. Khongmu hugged Zayaa and Tiraa, and would not let go of either of them.

"As we are doing introductions," Riyaansh said, "there are some more people who are in the next room, people whom you have heard about but have not yet met." So saying, he went in, and came back with three elderly gentlemen, an elderly woman and a young man of Vyaan's age.

"As you may have guessed," Riyaansh said, "these are Runggoo, Viraan, Nongru and Khongrem. And this young man is ..."

"Bugyel," Vyaan completed his sentence. It was again time for tears and smiles. Except for Riyaansh, who stood aside and observed how Tiraa's grandmother was totally forgiven and how even his daughter was totally engrossed in what her mother-in-law was saying. But, he did not envy Khongmu any of this, even though everyone had seemed to have forgotten his fatherhood and grand-fatherhood. Tanaa came over to the corner he was standing in and squeezed his hand.

"There's nothing one can do," Riyaansh said with a wan smile. "As Zayaa said, we make our own choices. And therefore should not complain about the outcome. And as you once told me, you cannot tempt fate and not expect to pay the penalty. I think I should let these people enjoy what they perceive as good fortune until at least lunch is over. After that, I will have to bring them back to the reality of harder times still ahead of us. I will go and check with Sanj if anything untoward or unusual has happened. I think I will skip the joyful lunch, and be back by mid-afternoon. I would appreciate it if you took care of everything until then."

"You don't fool me with your cynical outer shell, Riyaansh," Tanaa said, "why don't you take some time and try to win Zayaa over?"

"Time," Riyaansh said. "That is what we are most short of. And I will be honest with you, I will die satisfied if not a happy man if we can save Tiraa and also come up with a way to convince the Gods to let Givenland survive, even if Zayaa does not forgive me. It is more important that she is convinced to be a part of this endeavour than to be a part of my life."

So saying, he quietly opened the front door and left. Even though no one was paying him any attention, while he was there, everyone immediately noticed that he had left.

"What is with Riyaansh?" Runggoo asked Tanaa.

"I think he has gone to check the perimeter for any untoward happenings," Tanaa said unconvincingly.

285

"If you ask me, Riyaansh cannot tolerate happiness anymore," Tiraak said. "He thrives in melancholy, perhaps even thinks that is the best way to keep people from forgetting about the impending doom."

"Or, perhaps, there is nothing for him to be happy about," was Tanaa's rejoinder.

"What do you mean?" Tiraak asked. "He used to say that he would give up everything if he could just stroke his daughter's hair once more, as she slept. Well, he has got his daughter back now. Why couldn't he forget about this quest of his for a little while?"

"Has he got his daughter back?" Tanaa asked looking at Zayaa. "I think we all have forgotten that this is not his quest, after all. If you all had accepted Ekur for who he was, Riyaansh would not even be a part of this. If Zayaa's skin did not make Ekur think of the White Gods, Riyaansh would have been living somewhere else, oblivious of the impending doom. If his face had not been scarred by fate sending a leopard where none was supposed to be, Riyaansh might have been peacefully dead by now, poisoned by Apaan or his men. Remember that he did not even know your Ildùr. When Ildùr was breathing his last, he asked Ekur to do something, and get help from all of you to achieve this. That was Ildùr's bidding not to Riyaansh, but to you all. In your council, it is Riyaansh who is the outsider. And yet, he has sacrificed more than each and every one of you, hasn't he? And by what he told me before he left, he might not be happy, but he is satisfied with his lot and more than ready to leave the happiness to you all. The least you all can do for him is to let him be."

"I am really sorry," Tiraak said. "For the last many years, in my mind, this has become Riyaansh's quest. Though he was neither chosen nor nominated as the leader, if I were to ask anyone in the council who our leader was, I think each and every one would spontaneously answer that it was Riyaansh. We are so used to him instructing us, taking control of us that we sometimes forget to think about him. Do you think someone should go and make sure that he is all right?"

"I don't think that is necessary," Tanaa said. "He is not someone who likes to show or share his tears. I think if we let him be, he should snap out of whatever is bothering him by the time he is back after lunch."

"I don't think it should always be his choice," Zayaa said quietly. "Mother Tanaa, could you please take me to my father?"

Tanaa took Zayaa outside, and they soon spotted Riyaansh sitting on a boulder and looking into the horizon, focusing alternately on the west and the northwest. Zayaa signalled Tanaa to wait and approached Riyaansh alone. Hearing the footsteps, Riyaansh assumed it was Tanaa, coming to make sure he was all right.

"Tanaa," Riyaansh said without looking back, "I hope everyone is still enjoying their well-deserved happiness. I was sitting here and wondering the mysterious ways of life. Ildùr came from a place far away to the west. He wanted to go to a place that, even if not as far, is some distance to the northwest from here. If you drew a map from Kurm to Runaka, none of the roads would cross Pparaha, Wacha or for that matter where Kdwar used to be. So how did we all get entwined in this? I sometimes think about what would have happened if fate had not brought Ekur to Kdwar? Or his path had not crossed Zayaa's and mine? But then again, how can I complain about Fate. It was fate that ensured that after my wife's death, when I was dysfunctional with grief, Ridhaan overheard Tikoo and his companions discussing what the Chief High Priest of Kdwar had planned. If that had not happened, we could not have saved Zayaa. If it was only me being sat on the stake, I would have chosen that fate to what happened to Zayaa, later. But it would have been her fate as well, to die on the stakes."

Then, focusing on the North-eastern horizon, he continued, "For the last few days, especially after seeing Zayaa up close again and also meeting Tiraa, I have really been thinking. What if we run away to Wacha? No one would dare follow us there. And we could all be safe. But then, what if Givenland is indeed destroyed because Vyaan was forced away from his fated destiny? Will Tiraa forgive us when she realizes that we took a decision to save her and sacrifice Givenland? No, she will not. Zayaa and Tiraa's fate is now entwined with Vyaan's destiny. I think it is best that they know all the choices and then make their own decisions. Please do not misunderstand me; I am not shirking my responsibility. I just think that from here on, it is Vyaan and Zayaa's destiny to lead this quest. If they allow me to be useful and go on playing a small part, I will. If not, I have decided to walk south and see where the land ends."

"But that would be shirking your responsibility to your granddaughter, wouldn't it?" Zayaa said quietly, trying unsuccessfully to hold back her tears. Riyaansh's head snapped in surprise, and he looked embarrassed to find Zayaa there. "I am sorry but I still cannot say that I can forgive and forget the implications of the choice you made for me. I will need time to understand why you did, what you did. Maybe someday we will have time for you to explain it better to me. But, even I understand that you did not have the choice of taking responsibility for your daughter and Givenland, at the same time. You had to choose one. But, if you walk away now, you will be shirking your responsibility to Tiraa and all of Givenland at the same time. If you walk away now and something happens to Tiraa, will you be able to forgive yourself?"

"I hear you," Riyaansh said in a melancholic voice. But then he stood up and wiped off his tears, "I don't think any of us have the time or luxury for brooding. This is a time for planning and action. Let us go back and get to it. I think everyone has had a long enough break. Let us bring them back to the hard realities of life that we are all facing."

And then, he took a step towards the hut. But Zayaa stopped him.

"I know everything is urgent," Zayaa said, "but a few moments will not hurt. Please hold me and let us think of Sikkappa and Ayei for a while in silence. Let us imagine that fate has not taken everything away from us and none of this has ever happened and we are still in Kdwar and they are with us."

Riyaansh held Zayaa for a while and then quietly said, "My daughter, you can blame me as much as you want, but don't complain about fate. Yes, it does test us but while it is taking from us with one hand, it is giving to us with the other. I know it is an unfair question to ask, and you will in all probability hate me even more for asking this. Would you rather have us happily back in Kdwar, having, thereby, never met Vyaan nor had Tiraa as your daughter?"

Zayaa jerked her head off her shoulder. For a moment, Riyaansh thought he had gone too far and lost her forever. Then Zayaa said, "You know when I said I cannot forgive and forget the implications of the choices you made. I think I will still never be able to forget. But I have to forgive, for I just realized that it was you who chose Vyaan to come and live next door to me. And if there is one thing I am sure of in my heart, as much as I hate Apaan for what he did, I love Vyaan more."

"And in those thoughts lie the salvation of Givenland," Riyaansh finally smiled. Then father and daughter held each other for a while and then walked back to the hut. Tanaa happily noted that Riyaansh's arms were around his daughter. But, when they came back and sat down for lunch, it was back to business for Riyaansh.

"Vyaan," Riyaansh said, "as promised, let's answer your remaining questions. You have met every one of the original council. The only person who is not here is Ekur. But amongst us, you were the last person to meet him. To the question whether Runggoo found a westward route to Durshan Lake or not, for the time being let it suffice that if required he can get us there. We have no idea, yet about Ildùr's cave, having said that we are still very well-off and will not have a problem planning and executing a journey to the Great Northern White Mountains. Are there any more questions that need to be answered before you can give your undivided attention to the two issues?"

"Not at present," Vyaan said, "but why do you say two issues? The last time we talked about it, you had said that we needed to find a way to save Tiraa."

"You are right," Riyaansh said. "I will stop making assumptions that are not mine to make. The way I see it, if we think about saving Tiraa in isolation, we can solve it easily. You can flee to Wacha with Zayaa and Tiraa. Nongru here would provide you his protection without hesitation, won't you Nongru?" Nongru nodded. "Or you can flee to Ekur in Kurm. I am sure Viraan can arrange your safe passage. Viraan, do you think you could do that?" Viraan bowed his head. "So, you see, we already have two fail-safe alternatives. But, that would also mean not doing your father's bidding, and also may ultimately mean the destruction of Givenland. And I think Tiraa here should be the one making that choice. Because if Givenland was indeed to be destroyed, the rest of us can always blame it on fate, which gave us no choice as we had to save Tiraa."

"That is neither fair nor factual," Vyaan protested, "I don't think you have thought through all the possible options. Why can't I leave Tiraa with my mother in Wacha and then start on the quest to fulfil my father's bidding?"

For a long time, the council members had got used to deferring to Riyaansh to lay out the choices. They now found it refreshing to see someone attack Riyaansh's logic. However, this was short-lived.

"I think it is you who is not thinking," Riyaansh said. "No, that is an unfair thing to say, for I have been thinking about this for years, while you have only heard about it in the last few days. The moment Tiraa disappears, both Zayaa and you will become fugitives. This will make it very difficult if not impossible for you to travel through Givenland. And …"

"I don't know about what the others feel about this," Vyaan interrupted, "but I think this is a risk worth taking, especially as it guarantees Tiraa's safety. Riyaansh, are you forgetting that it is your granddaughter's wellbeing that we are discussing?"

"Vyaan," Riyaansh said, "you are not the first person to think I am heartless. I would love to be a nice and kind grandfather, but I don't have the luxury. And please don't misunderstand me, I like the way you are challenging my logic. This will ensure we do not make a mistake. Coming back to your suggestion, let us assume that you are able to overcome all the hurdles being a fugitive would create, and still reach the Gods in the Great Northern White Mountains. What then? How will you convince them not to destroy a whole race for the fault of a few, when you could not keep your own daughter safe within that race? How will you ask for trust, when you could not trust them yourself? No Vyaan, I think you know as well as me, if we are to save both Tiraa and Givenland, there can be no hiding or running away involved."

Vyaan kept silent for a while. Everyone waited with bated breaths for his next argument. But, he surprised everyone with what he said next.

"I need a little time alone with my wife and daughter," Vyaan said. "I know that it is bad manners to get up from an unfinished meal and I also know many of you may feel excluded by my doing this. But I agree with Riyaansh, we don't have the time or luxury for niceties. So, I hope you all don't mind, but don't really care if you do."

There was a bemused silence after they left.

"Well, if I had any doubt before, now I am sure that Vyaan is destined to lead this quest," Runggoo broke the silence with a chuckle. "He does share a common trait with his predecessors, who also happen to be his father and father-in-law. Like them, he also does not really care what anyone else thinks. But at least he is a little more polite than his predecessors – until now, that is."

Everyone including Riyaansh joined in on the laughter that followed.

"As we do not know how long they will take," Riyaansh said, "I think it best we continue eating, as otherwise the food will go wasted. They can catch up when they come back. Or if they take too long, I will make sure I can get some simple hot meal ready for them."

It turned out to be a good suggestion, as it was quite some time before Vyaan, Zayaa and Tiraa returned to the gathering. When they came in, Vyaan started to speak but was stopped by Riyaansh.

"I think you all should eat first," Riyaansh said, "Tanaa is boiling you some gruel. We will talk after that."

Zayaa started to protest, but Vyaan stopped her by squeezing her shoulder.

"I agree," Vyaan said, "to succeed we need to stay healthy, and that means eating and resting well." Then, turning to the others, he added, "We will be back momentarily."

They were back soon and, before Riyaansh could get everyone back to business, Vyaan took charge of the discussions.

"Appi," Vyaan said, to everyone's surprise, addressing Riyaansh, "and don't look so surprised, for after all you are my wife's father, and I think if I ever knew my father, I would address him by the Akkadian synonym of Abba. So, if you have no objections, I will call you Appi." Riyaansh nodded. "We, that is, Zayaa, Tiraa and I, have had a long talk and come to some decisions. First of all, we have agreed that the decision on how to proceed is something that Zayaa and I need to take, not Tiraa. We know that we may take a decision that leads to an unpleasant outcome, but that is a risk parents take in different measures every day. And Appi, we all now understand, to some extent at least, why you did what you did. When you unilaterally took the decision to leave Zayaa with your brother and investigate Ekur's story, you were not shirking, but actually taking on a bigger responsibility. Zayaa wanted to talk to you privately first, but I told her that you of all people would appreciate getting to business first and take care of emotions later."

Riyaansh had no answer to this and just nodded.

"Zayaa and I both agree that running away is not the solution," Vyaan continued. "If we cannot keep our daughter safe in Givenland, then indeed Givenland would not be worth saving. But I, I mean we, believe that there may be a way to not only ensure Tiraa's safety, but have the best wishes of the people of Pparaha, when we proceed to meet the Gods to do my father's bidding. But before I get into the details of my, our plans, we do have some questions. The first one is to Riya... I mean Appi and Tanaa. You remember the herb that Zayaa used to trick the other High Priests. How long can the effects of that herb be made to last? To be more specific, can it last a whole evening?"

"I don't think it can last all evening," Riyaansh said after some thought. "I am sure it will last for at least a third of the evening. The amount she will have to ingest for it to last for the whole evening will make the effects less predictable. In all probability, she will fall asleep halfway through the evening."

"Oh," Vyaan said with disappointment, then pondered aloud, "but we need it for later that evening, and it will be dangerous to try to chew it in front ..."

"So, you do not really want the effect to last the whole evening, but be in effect towards the end of it," Tanaa said with interest. "Is my understanding correct? If it is, I may have a solution."

"Yes, that is what we will need," Vyaan said with renewed hope. "We need the effect to start halfway through the evening and, from then on, a third of the evening is more than what we would need for it to last."

"Do you remember the screaming cow disease?" Tanaa asked. "It was caused by a certain worm that infected the entrails of cattle. Many knew the herb that could kill these worms. But, the problem was getting it untouched to the entrails, as the stomach juices rendered them useless by the time these got to the entrails. Some people tried putting it through the other way, but also without success. It was then that I hit upon a solution that saved most of our cattle. I wrapped the herbs with a paste of rice. After some trial and error, I arrived on exactly how much covering of the rice paste would ensure that the stomach juices would melt away the rice paste but not touch the herbs, or at least not all of it, before the herbs got to the entrails. We can make a paste of the leaves and enclose it in the rice paste. In this way, we can make sure that the effect will set in at a later time. Of course, I will need some experimentation on the actual person before coming to the exact amount of the rice paste."

"Good, good," Vyaan said. "My next question is again to you two. Do you know of any herb that would help reducing pain? What I need is for a person to not even flinch once she has consumed it, even if she is hurt."

"The same herb does exactly that and more," Riyaansh said. "You will still be hurt but your brain will not know you are feeling this and you will not flinch."

"Okay," Vyaan said and then asked, "what about something that could alter one's voice?"

"There are many such herbs and animal products," Tanaa said. "Could you be more specific?"

"What if I wanted a woman to sound like a man?" Vyaan asked.

"Most of the herbs that can achieve this," Tanaa said, "have side effects. But, the same thing can be achieved by practicing for less than ten days."

"Do you think you can train Zayaa to change her voice?" Vyaan asked.

"Definitely," Tanaa said. "With Zayaa as my student, I think it can be achieved in five days. But, she will have to continue practicing until the day she needs to do this."

"She will do that, won't you, Zayaa?" Vyaan said, and Zayaa nodded in agreement. "Next, do you know of any herb that will help to stop or significantly reduce bleeding? Not something like the bark and leaf buds of the Banyan tree, which needs to be applied, but something that can be ingested and will work the instant the bleeding starts."

"I am sorry," Riyaansh replied, "but I do not. Tanaa have you ever come across anything like that?"

"No, I have never heard of any herb that will do that," Tanaa said after giving it some thought.

"But I have," Khongrem offered. "As you know, in some of the valleys further east from us, they speak a different tongue. I have heard that the tongue they speak is spoken by the people who live north of the Mountain that Touches the Sky. I have also heard of people who have travelled there through the mountain passes, many mahahaths to the east of our valleys. One such traveller brought back a tree they call the tree of life[75]. This tree has many uses and almost all its parts have medicinal values. The inner bark of this tree, if applied or ingested helps the coagulation of blood. I cannot confirm the other uses, but I know this works, as many people in our valleys drink a soup made from the inner bark before wrestling and other activities that can cause cuts and bruises."

"How easy will it be to acquire some?" Vyaan asked, relieved and excited, "and how long will it take?"

"If needed urgently," Nongru said, "we could get it within ten days."

"Now, for my last question," Vyaan said. "What type of control do we have over the Chief High Priest of Parroo? And do we have any other such people in our control."

"I will let Viraan answer that," Riyaansh said.

"The Chief High Priest of Parroo is special," Viraan said and then added. "We don't control him. He is one of us by choice. I will tell how this came to be some other time. We do have varying degrees of influence on another three Chief High Priests, in Ankal, Lakho and Ganbanlika[76]. We do have influence, again in varying degrees on the High Priests of many other cities and towns. But, there are many other big centres where we do not have any influence at all. Riyaansh convinced us to stay away from Pparaha. We had efforts ongoing in Darromohe, Thallo and Runaka. But, when Riyaansh sent out the word about this meeting, he also advised us to temporarily suspend all such activities. The Chief High Priest of Parroo had already reached Darromohe to execute a plan that he himself had plotted.

---

[75]Sichuan Thuja – one of the evergreen coniferous trees of the Thuja family
[76]A town in Central-Western Givenland/ Meluhha

But, he has agreed to do nothing for the moment. But, he has had to stay back for the originally planned duration, as otherwise it would look suspicious."

"Does that mean I cannot talk to him?" Vyaan asked.

"Let us first speak about what you need to convey to him," Viraan said noncommittally. "Then we can decide on whether we must send a messenger or have me go and see him in Darromohe. If not, we will think of some way to get you to meet him."

"Good," Vyaan said. Then he remained silent for a while and then looked around the room. "In that case, I think we have a plan that should work. I think this plan should work as it is based on exploiting Apaan's overconfidence from all his successes, which has become his biggest weakness."

Then Vyaan laid out his plan. The others, especially Riyaansh, had many questions and required many clarifications. By the time they had discussed all these to everyone's satisfaction, it was almost dinnertime.

"I think it will work," Riyaansh finally said. "Of course after we sleep over it, we might come up with new questions and risks. But, I think in principle this should work. We will, of course, have to make sure that our preparations are perfect, in order to reduce risks. Before Vyaan, Zayaa and Tiraa returns to Pparaha, we will need to go over the plan over and over again. Sorry, I think we can discuss these tomorrow morning. I think we need to celebrate Vyaan and Zayaa's plan over some raajaraas and then have dinner. Everything can wait until tomorrow."

"Except for starting Zayaa's voice training," Tanaa said, taking Zayaa's hand and leading her away. "We will be back soon."

Starting the next day, Tanaa started checking, through trial and error, how much rice paste would be required to delay the effect of Riyaansh's mysterious herbs by half an evening.

Khongrem sent Bugyel along with two other Wacha people who had accompanied them to Riyaansh's place, to one of the eastern valleys of the Mountain that Touches the Sky to fetch the inner bark of the Tree of Life.

The day before Vyaan, Zayaa and Tiraa were to leave for Pparaha, Zayaa asked Riyaansh to go out for a walk with her.

"Appi," Zayaa said, addressing Riyaansh as Appi for the first time since Ridhaan had taken his place, "I am sorry that I judged you earlier, before trying to understand why you had to do what you did. You see ..."

"Zaa," Riyaansh interrupted, "you have every right to be angry at me for the choices I've made. It is not important what my intentions were, but I did not fulfil my duties towards you. For that, I will never forgive myself. I am glad that you now understand why I had to do what I did. That is enough for me."

"I wanted to tell you that I am proud of you," Zayaa said, "yes, I did need Vyaan's help, but now I understand how difficult it must have been for you to leave me. And I also wanted you to know that Vyaan has taken a real liking for you. According to him, with you on our side we cannot fail. Tiraa said that she would love to spend time with you, but is still in too much awe, seeing how everyone else defers to you. She asked me to tell you that she hopes to get to know you better during our journey to the Great Northern White Mountains."

Riyaansh, the scribe, could not find words to express his feelings. Instead, he took his daughter in his arms and cried unashamedly.

Chapter 21

Based on Tanaa's advice, Vyaan, Zayaa and Tiraa started their journey from Riyaansh's hut around mid-afternoon, so as to reach their home at dusk. Tanaa rode with them to the place, where they had met a little more than a week back. From there they proceeded on foot. They were dressed as herders, in the same clothes that they had left home, and carried similar baskets on their backs.

When they reached home, they were not surprised to find that the three herders who had taken their place were already expecting them. Though they were still impressed with Tanaa's network, they were no longer surprised. Soon after they arrived, the herders left with the baskets.

Two days after coming back, Zayaa resumed her duties. As the Winter Solstice neared, things got very busy at the Temple Sanctuary, and Zayaa started going there before dawn and only coming back home late in the evening.

Five days later, just after midnight, when the Temple Sanctuary was quiet, Apaan walked out of the main doorway of the Temple Sanctuary. Sensing rather than seeing some movement in the shadows underneath the parapet awning, he moved towards it.

"Greetings, O Chief High Priest," a voice floated towards him.

"Greetings, Sanj," Apaan said. "Why did you want us to meet in this secret manner?"

"O Chief High Priest," Sanj said, "I know you are fearless, but you know that I am not. I have to be careful, as Tanaa still thinks that I am her spy. I have come to report to you about some strange happenings. But you know how it is; my conscience can bear my sins better when there is some gain involved."

"You rascal," Apaan chuckled, "you will never change. But, why should you? I am sure you are making Tanaa pay you for betraying her, as well." Then, he handed a small rectangle seal and said, "This will give you enough grains from the granary for your woman and her family to eat for a week and also make enough raajaraas to keep her husband drunk and not disturb you when you are with her."

"O Chief High Priest," Sanj said, "believe me, what I am about to tell you now is worth not a week's grain but at least a couple of months. It will be very difficult to break Tanaa's trust for anything less."

"Okay, one more week's grain it is then," Apaan said handing him another seal. "And you will get nothing more from me, you rascal. You do remember that the punishment for lying down with the wife of another is still the stake."

"Except if you are a High Priest, of course," Sanj whispered.

"What did you say?" Apaan retorted.

"Nothing, O Chief High Priest," Sanj said quickly retreating. "You are indeed kind to indulge me. Now, let me tell you what has been happening. Tanaa had a lot of visitors a couple of weeks ago. I wanted to come earlier, but was sent off on errands, which were impossible to avoid without raising Tanaa's suspicions. The first to arrive was from here, the one they call Dreamer of Truths and she came with her husband and daughter. Then …"

"Stop your lies, you scamp," Apaan said. "I would have been informed, if Zayaa had left Pparaha."

"Indeed you would have," Sanj said, "if she had left as herself. They left as herders, with the Dreamer wearing the clothes of an animal singer to hide her skin."

"Clever," Apaan said with open admiration, "very clever. But why not clever enough to stay away?" Apaan wondered aloud.

"I was planning to come to that later," Sanj said, "I heard them discuss that. They were near a large cowshed and could not see me snoozing on the hay roof. The Dreamer wanted to run away. But, another voice said that it would be impossible to run from you. So, instead they have a plan, which will get her and her daughter to the Temple Sanctuary of Parroo, under your nose and with your reluctant permission. I did not understand what that meant. But, I thought it must be significant, so I started checking on who were these visitors and also eavesdropping on as many of their conversations as I could. Amongst the visitors there was the Chief High Priest of Parroo, the Dreamer's uncle-in-law Shubhyaan, some more people whose names I could not catch. I heard the Chief High Priest of Parroo say that he was concerned that the Chief High Priest of Darromohe was onto him and was out to get him."

"So Shubhyaan lives." Apaan whispered. "Were Parroo and Zayaa ever together? Who else did you observe with Parroo?"

"Now that you mention it," Sanj said thoughtfully, "I heard the Chief High Priest of Parroo only talk to this voice that I could not recognize. As I could not understand what they were talking about, I may have misheard some of the words. He then said something about preponing the plan and being here on the Winter Solstice. Then, there was this other person's voice again, the one that had talked about the plan to take the Dreamer and her daughter away from here to Parroo. He asked the Chief High Priest of Parroo whether this would not look suspicious. Especially given his previous visit was also on a Solstice. To which the Chief High Priest said something about this being a very auspicious year for the Temple Sanctuary here in Pparaha. And if he could convince a couple of other Chief High Priests to come to Pparaha, as well, it may still look suspicious but would have to be accepted."

"Interesting," Apaan said, stroking his chin, "very interesting."

"You will stop them from coming here uninvited?" Sanj asked.

"Yes, the Chief Priest of Parroo will not come here uninvited," Apaan said with a sinister smile and then started speaking, as if Sanj was not even present. "I will invite him here, first thing tomorrow morning. This will keep him guessing what I suspect, and how much I know. A guessing man is a nervous man. And if you are nervous, you cannot think straight. Of course, he may become too nervous and decide not to come. No, he will come. Of course, he will. There is something about our Dreamer that keeps bringing him back. If he has the same red blood as mine, it is the skin colour, or maybe it is her hair. Even when I am with someone half her age, I sometimes think of her. The High Priests still doesn't seem to get enough of her, yet she has somehow remained fresh. So Parroo, is it her skin colour that attracts you? Whatever it is, I will make it the cause of your downfall."

Then, he looked first towards the east and said, "Parroo," and then looking towards the southwest he said, "Darromohe," and then he leaned against the wall with a grin.

"Tomorrow," Apaan continued with his grin, "another invitation will go out. But, this will not be carried by any common messenger. I will have one of my High Priests take it to Darromohe. The Chief High Priest there is nothing like me. He really believes in the purity of the High Priests. We will exploit this problem between Darromohe and Parroo. My High Priest will tell him that I would like him to come as the chief guest and that Parroo will also be in attendance. If Darromohe is out to get Parroo, I think he will not be able to give up the opportunity. Especially as the High Priest I send will volunteer to stay back at the Temple Sanctuary in Darromohe, thus making the required seven High Priests for the Winter Solstice ceremony. No, I think if I play it right, this will work splendidly and both Parroo and Darromohe will be here. But then again, I can't remember when the last time I played it wrong. Do you?"

Sanj shook his head not sure whether an answer was expected.

"I actually do," Apaan continued, "that was when Parroo twisted my hand into making Zayaa the Dreamer. But, isn't life interesting, now that it has arranged for me to destroy Parroo and devour Zayaa's daughter to celebrate that. I cannot wait for the Winter Solstice. I wish it were tomorrow. No, I do not. I shall relish the anticipation. But, I do need something to dissipate my excitement tonight. Why did I let all the Dasasas go home? I am in dire need of company tonight. Perhaps, I should have asked Zayaa to stay back. Perhaps, I will ask her to stay back tomorrow. No, I will not. On the night after the Winter Solstice, I shall have her for desert, while I describe my main course, her daughter, to her. I wish I had some way of getting her husband as a starter. He might be old, but still looks like a tasty dish."

And then he started laughing aloud. That was when Sanj realized that Apaan was indeed a madman.

Four days before the Winter Solstice, Riyaansh and Tanaa entered Pparaha, also disguised as herders. As they approached from the gates and were still a few streets away from Zayaa's house, a quarrel broke out between two herders near Zayaa's doorway. Soon, many other herders came to the spot and started taking sides, forming a large and chattering crowd of people. But, there was one man who seemed to have no interest in the commotion. His eyes remained glued at Zayaa's door. This aloofness, made him stand out, and he was easily spotted. A young female herder went next to this man, lifted her clothes to above her knees, squatted down and started urinating.

"You animals," the man shouted, standing up. "Where do you think you are? What do you think you are doing? Go back to your cattle. Pparaha has no need for the likes of you. Animals! Hey, can't you hear what I am saying? Get out. This is a place for humans, not animals."

The female herder did not seem to be paying any attention to him and went about her business, but from between her long hair, she was looking past him towards Zayaa's door, and observed Riyaansh and Tanaa dodge through Zayaa's doorway.

"Well, sir," she said standing up and straightening her clothes, "when one has to go, one has to go."

"That is true only for animals," the man spat.

Then moving to a different spot on the street, he sat down to observe Zayaa's doorway.

Once inside, Riyaansh and Tanaa gave each other a look of satisfaction.

"Well, Appi, Tanaa," Vyaan said, "I assume that commotion was for your benefit."

Riyaansh smiled. "How are you three holding up? Is Zayaa still up for it?"

"Yes," Vyaan said after a little hesitation. "But I think she has some moral dilemma over the whole thing. Last time we talked, she said she would like to discuss it after you get here."

As was the case for the last few days, Zayaa returned late from the Temple Sanctuary. Even though she was visibly tired, her eyes at first lit up at seeing Riyaansh and Tanaa.

Then Zayaa smiled wanly and said, "Appi, we need to talk."

"Why don't you wash up?" Vyaan said. "Then, let us sit down over some raajaraas and talk."

Zayaa nodded and came back after having washed up.

"You all have the raajaraas, while I bring you up to date," Riyaansh said. "Everything is going according to plan. Bugyel came back a week ago, with the inner bark of the Tree of Life. It does stop bleeding, if you apply it to a cut. One of the herders volunteered for the more painful trial of ingesting it daily, to figure out how long it takes for the coagulation effects to start working. We now know it takes two to three days. So Zayaa, you will have to start the day after. Tanaa will create the rice-paste enclosures for the other herb by the day after tomorrow. The others will be arriving according to the plan. By now, they know their roles very well. Now, it is all up to fate."

"There is a land beyond Sumer," Vyaan said. "This land has thousands of fighting men. But many years ago they were once defeated by a small band of desert nomads. When the nomad chief was asked what weapons he had used to achieve this seemingly impossible task, he said that his weapons were planning, preparation and practice. As we have used these same weapons, victory will be ours. Now, I know Zayaa is anxious to discuss something, so I will keep quiet."

"For the last few days, one thing is bothering me," Zayaa said. "I know I have used something similar to protect myself from the High Priests. And I don't care whether the act is morally right or even outright sinful. To save Tiraa from my fate, I am willing to become immoral and a sinner. However, this time we are claiming that the Gods are speaking through me. Won't this create a problem when we face the Gods themselves?"

"I see it differently," Riyaansh said. "If our goal is moral and intentions pure, I don't think the Gods will hold it against us. If they have not struck down these people who exploit young girls in their name, how can they hold it against someone who is trying to save her daughter? No, I am sure. And if the Gods are truly omnipresent and are listening to us now, I hereby declare that if they do find any fault with what we are about to do, I take that sin onto myself. And neither Zayaa nor Vyaan should be answerable for these, when they see you in the Great Northern White Mountains."

"What did you just do?" Zayaa said with alarm. "I was convinced by your arguments. Why did you have to invoke the Gods?"

"If I expect others to believe in what I am saying, I need to trust my own words first," Riyaansh said. "So, in my mind, I did not take any risk at all. Now, if no one has an objection, I would like to talk to Zayaa. Alone."

Before Zayaa could speak, Vyaan said, "Tiraa, in any case, it is past your bedtime. And Tanaa has not heard any of my stories, yet. So, let us go upstairs and see what she thinks of them."

"Okay, Appi," Tiraa said. "Please tell her the pancake one. You know the one with all of the animals."

"You know how I feel about keeping secrets from Vyaan and Tiraa," Zayaa said after they had left.

"Zaa," Riyaansh said, "when you hear my question, you will understand why I could not ask it in front of Vyaan. You had once told me that you love Vyaan more than you hate Apaan. Is this how you still feel?"

"Yes, I do," Zayaa said without hesitation.

"Good," Riyaansh said. "If you were given a chance of wreaking vengeance on Apaan, but in doing so, you will also be choosing to harm Vyaan or Tiraa. In such circumstances, would you choose to exact or forgo your revenge?"

"What type of harm?"

"Never mind that question," Riyaansh sighed. "Let me ask you another. If forgiving Apaan meant protecting Vyaan from a risk to his wellbeing, could you forgive Apaan?"

"Again what type of harm?" Zayaa repeated.

"Zaa," Riyaansh said patiently, "don't answer me now, but think about these questions. The future of Givenland depends upon you being able to answer these questions unconditionally. Please promise me you will ponder over these in the coming few days."

The next day, Tiraak arrived in Pparaha. And like everything else, since his meeting with Sanj, Apaan got reports of Shubhyaan's return to Pparaha the same day.

"Why are you here?" Apaan pondered, "and where were you all these years? I am surprised that you are still alive." Then he laughed aloud, "don't worry, I will change that very soon."

The next morning, Tanaa made a paste of the inner bark of the Tree of Life and mixed it with cow milk to make it palatable. After all Zayaa would have to consume it twice a day.

The evening of the same day, Runggoo arrived with Viraan. Apaan could not figure out what their role in the plot was, but pushed away the thought as unimportant. After all, his enemies did not know that Sanj had already forewarned him.

The next morning, the Chief High Priest of Darromohe arrived to a lot of pomp and show. Apaan had decided not to meet him until the ceremony next evening. He knew that Darromohe, though old, was still very sharp. Apaan had come up with a plausible reason for getting both the Chief High Priests of Darromohe and Parroo to Pparaha, but he was not keen on putting its believability to test.

Late afternoon that same day, Runggoo and Viraan arrived at Zayaa's house. They came in openly, without any attempt at concealment. Vyaan and Tiraa sat down for an early dinner with all their guests. Over dinner, the discussions were all about happy or funny events from the past. After dinner, on Riyaansh and Vyaan's insistence the others agreed to go over next day's plan for one final time. Zayaa came home quite late from the Temple Sanctuary, and Runggoo and Viraan left soon after her arrival.

After the Dasasas had all left, Apaan was updated about Runggoo and Viraan's activities.

"So Sanj was right," Apaan thought. He knew Sanj was too greedy to betray him, but it was always good to have a confirmation. "My little white dove, what are you up to? Have I misjudged something?" Then he smiled and dismissed the thought, "No, I think it is you who have misjudged me. Tomorrow, you all will be taken care of. And I will have Tiraa on the night after. Perhaps, I will make you watch. You said she might be my daughter. I wish there was some way to confirm this. If I knew she was my daughter, it would spice up the session, at least for me. However, we cannot have everything, can we? I will have to be content by making you watch us."

Next day, everyone at Zayaa's house was up before sunrise. Actually most of them had barely slept. Zayaa gulped down the Tree of Life paste. Tanaa checked again to ensure Zayaa remembered exactly when she was supposed to swallow the rice-paste pellets that contained the mysterious leaves. Zayaa left for the Temple Sanctuary just before sunrise. Riyaansh insisted that the others lie down and take some more rest, even if they could not sleep.

Around midmorning the Chief High Priests of Parroo and Ankal arrived in Pparaha. This time though, there was no welcome party, nor were there any dancers to usher them through the streets with showering of petals, as had been done for the Chief High Priest of Darromohe. Even though runners had come ahead to inform the Temple Sanctuary of their imminent arrival, no one was there at the city's gates to welcome them. They were met by one of the High Priests at the Temple's main doorway. Apaan had instructed the High Priest on what he had to say to the arriving Chief High Priests, in front of their entourage. The High priest had thought that he had misheard Apaan, and consequently asked the latter to repeat his instructions. Apaan told him to go and do what he had been told. The High Priest was, therefore, following Apaan's instructions as he walked up to the Chief High Priest of Parroo.

"O Chief High Priest of Parroo," Apaan's High Priest said, "I am sorry, but as you know, you are not the Chief Guest for tonight's ceremony.

All seven of our main guest rooms have been taken by the Chief Guest and his people. We, however, have a room for you in the outer perimeter. But, the rest of your party has to make their own arrangements. O Chief High Priest of Ankal, we were not expecting you here today. We are very sorry, but we cannot accommodate you in our Temple Sanctuary. You and your party will also have to find your own accommodations. If you could let us know where you are staying, we will inform you on whether you may attend tonight's ceremony."

Then, the High Priest waited for the inevitable outbursts from both the Chief High Priests.

"Please do not worry," the Chief High Priest of Parroo said, much to the surprise of Apaan's High Priest. "As I knew that I was not the Chief Guest, I had assumed that the accommodation will be an issue. So, I have made my own arrangements."

"And, also, please do not put yourselves out on my account," the Chief High Priest of Ankal said. "I was born in Pparaha and therefore have a birth-right to attend any Temple Sanctuary ceremony. If I cannot get a seat as a Chief High Priest, I will stand with the rest of Pparaha. We will go now to our lodgings, and come back later for the ceremony."

As they were turning, a parchment seemed to drop from the Chief High Priest of Ankal's robes.

"O Chief High Priest," the Pparaha High Priest said, "you seem to have dropped something."

"No, I did not," the Chief High Priest of Ankal protested. Picking up the parchment he added, "It seems to be addressed to the Chief High Priest of Pparaha."

At this, the Chief High Priest of Parroo turned around to take possession of the parchment. "May I take a look at that?"

But, before he could get to it, the High Priest had quickly taken possession of the parchment. He knew how Apaan valued his privacy, and was not going to risk having something addressed to him read out in public.

After the two Chief High Priests left, the High Priest went inside and gave the parchment to Apaan.

It simply said, "*Apaan's wellbeing lies in making new alliances. An enemy's enemy is usually the best friend one can wish for.*"

"Are you sure that this was dropped by Ankal?" Apaan asked his High Priest.

"Well, I think so," the High Priest replied. "But when I tried giving it back to him, he denied it was his."

"Of course, he did," Apaan scoffed. "Sometimes, I think if I could replace all of you with asses, and gain on the deal. I am sure Ankal must have been shocked to see that I have Pparaha's prized idiot as a High Priest. It is clear that Ankal was trying to send me a secret message, and I am sure Parroo must be suspicious now. It will not help him though. And that is why I am sparing you. Now, go and arrange for a small fire to be started at the lodge that Parroo and Ankal are staying. But, before the lodge is set on fire, get rid of the occupants from one of the houses near it. I will wait in that house. When people start rushing out of the lodgings, grab hold of Ankal and bring him to this house. Make sure that Parroo or his people don't know what you are up to. With the confusion created by the fire, this should not be difficult – even for an idiot like you."

Properly chastised, the High Priest made all the arrangements to perfection. And around noon, the Chief High Priest of Ankal found himself face to face with Apaan.

"I got your message," Apaan said without any ceremony, "I assume you want to talk to me."

"O Chief High ..." the Chief High Priest of Ankal started.

"I don't think you have the time for such formalities," Apaan cut him short. "Just get to the point."

"Well, I am here under duress," the Chief High Priest of Ankal said. "The Chief High Priest of Parroo knows some secrets about me, which puts me under his control. He came to Ankal and forced me to accompany him here. He is planning to do something in today's ceremony and wants me there to support him. He plans to take the Dasasa called Dreamer and, more importantly, her daughter back to Parroo. He has somehow convinced their well-wishers that this would be in the interest of Dreamer and her daughter. He, however, has some ulterior motive. I know this because of his sneer and wicked chuckle, when he talks about either of them. It would leave no one in any doubt of his nefarious purpose."

"Why are you telling me this?" Apaan asked.

"I will speak plainly," the Chief High Priest of Ankal said. "I don't really like the idea of having any dealings with you. You see, I was born here. Seeing what you did after becoming the Chief High Priest, I did not want to continue living in Pparaha. I moved to Ankal, where my mother came from. As her family has very influential patrons, I was soon nominated as a High Priest and after some time became the Chief High Priest. But now, I find myself trapped in the control of the Chief High Priest of Parroo. And from what I hear, along with being evil, you are also very cunning and intelligent. So the way I see it, with prior knowledge of what is going to happen, you will be able to destroy the Chief High Priest of Parroo. And, hence, here I am, talking to you."

"I believe you," Apaan said after some thought. "If you had tried to sell me a story about how nice I was and would therefore help you, it would have indeed been difficult to digest. Is there anything else you can tell me?"

The Chief High Priest of Ankal shook his head. Apaan then signalled to his High Priest to take him away.

Apaan sat there for a while, pondering. "Are you sure that Parroo did not realize that Ankal was gone?" he asked his High Priest, when the latter returned.

"I am sure," the High Priest said. "The fire was set somewhere in between their rooms. Thus, they came out on to the streets from different exits. And as your discussion was very short, I am sure no one would have missed him."

"Good," Apaan said. Then, more to himself than the High Priest, he said, "now that I know what Parroo wants, I will pre-empt him. By the time we are done, even the people he has brought along will abandon him, not wanting to be a part of his disgrace. The only thing I would like to know is why he wants Tiraa. Zayaa, I understand. But, what is special about Tiraa? I am sure there are young girls in Parroo who are just as pretty and capable of making a man's loins burn in anticipation. So, why do you want Tiraa? Should I play it safe and let things roll, before doing anything? But it might become too late. Luckily, it is happening today evening. And there is no night in between to cause me to lose sleep."

This year, the decorations for the Winter Solstice had been out done. There were many different types of flowers, decorated all through the façade and inner courtyard. All the walls were decorated with sandalwood paste drawings and jasmine water was being sprinkled all around the courtyard. There were ropes tied between the pillars, creating pathways and standing areas.

Runggoo, Tiraak and Viraan arrived early, but they did not stand near the Ceremonial Platform, but instead took up position towards the centre of three different common areas. These exact positions had been designated for them by Vyaan.

Zayaa's family had never used the honour of using the privileged enclosure. But, today would be different. Vyaan, Tiraa, Riyaansh and Tanaa had come as the ceremony was about to start and proceeded towards the privileged enclosure.

"This area is for the family of main Dasasas only," one of the High Priests said, barring their way, his full and contemptuous attention on Tanaa. "And in any case, you are not even allowed inside Pparaha, let alone the Temple Sanctuary. Go back to your animals. And leave without creating any disturbance. Vyaan and his daughter may enter."

"Since when are parents not family?" Riyaansh said quietly removing the hood of his cloak that was covering most of his face, "I am Zayaa's father, or did you not recognize that. And I say with all honesty that here stands her mother," he then followed this claim with the word 'incarnate', in his mind.

It was then that the High Priest turned to Riyaansh. His face went white as if he had seen a ghost, which, in fact, he thought he was seeing.

"But how can that be?" the High Priest said, and then as much as confessed, "It can't be. I personally saw you being forced to drink the … I mean everyone knows Zayaa's father is dead."

"Especially the ones who killed him," Riyaansh smirked. "Next time make sure you finish the job you have started. Now, if you really don't want me to discuss aloud what was done to me, you will stand aside."

Thus saying, he pushed the High Priest out of his way and took Tanaa by the hand and proceeded to the privileged enclosure.

The High Priest took a little time to recover and then rushed inside. At that moment, Apaan was overseeing the final preparations. He first placed the Chief High Priest of Darromohe in the front of the small procession that was forming. Then he placed the Chief High Priest of Parroo behind Darromohe. He happily noted the look of open hostility that the Chief High Priest of Darromohe gave the latter. It was at this moment that the High Priest bearing news of Riyaansh and Tanaa arrived.

"Apaan," the High Priest called, "we need to talk."

Apaan turned around angrily.

"My dear son," the Chief High Priest of Darromohe, known for being a proponent of correct behaviour and attitude, said before Apaan could

307

react, "you are a High Priest, are you not? You cannot behave like a child any more. If your Chief High Priest has given you some liberties, you should show your maturity by not taking advantage of it. What you just did would be inappropriate even in private, but in public and on such an auspicious day and moment, it is downright sacrilegious."

"I apologize," the High Priest said, but in his anxiety did not stop to be given permission to speak and continued, "but we have to talk now …"

"No, we do not," Apaan growled. Even though it was not directed at him, he was still smarting from the other Chief High Priest's remarks about giving liberties. "As you can see, you have already delayed us. Now go back to your position and contemplate on what you have done."

"But …" the High Priest started.

"There is nothing else to discuss," Apaan said. "I have more than enough High Priests present in this Temple Sanctuary today, so I don't really need you for the ceremony. Don't force me to do something you will regret."

The High Priest still wanted to finish what he had come to say, but one look at Apaan's eyes stopped him. He meekly bowed his head and left.

"You are too kind," the Chief High Priest of Parroo said, to Apaan's added chagrin. "If a dog won't learn, the best thing to do is to get rid of him and get a new dog."

"Well," Apaan could not help replying, "it is important for people in our positions to know the difference between dogs and people." And then, he again went over the entire procession to make sure everyone was in the right position.

As the ceremony was about to start, Zayaa swallowed the rice-paste pellets that contained the mysterious leaves.

Even though it was Apaan's right to be the first to enter the Ceremonial Platform, he bent with his right hand outstretched to signal the High Priest of Darromohe to enter first. After refusing to do so twice out of politeness, the High Priest of Darromohe started entering the platform. And before Apaan could even straighten himself, the Chief High Priest of Parroo started following. Apaan, wanting to ensure that he was the second to enter, side stepped him and started entering the platform. The Chief High Priest of Parroo, instead of giving ground, pushed Apaan forward. Apaan crashed headlong into the High Priest of Darromohe and they both stumbled and fell. The crowd burst out with laughter. As they stood up,

Apaan looked accusingly at the Chief High Priest of Parroo, who by this time had already taken a step back and was looking concerned but innocent.

"Is this some juvenile prank?" the Chief High Priest of Darromohe asked rubbing his hips. "If so, I am not sure that I see the humour in this. I can see that the crowd enjoyed it. But next time, start with a joke instead of pushing an old man down."

"I am sorry," Apaan said, "I think I got pushed from behind," and then looking accusingly at the Chief High Priest of Parroo continued, "you know how Parroo can be. And now he stands there with that innocent look. You are not falling for it, are you?"

"I don't like this new way of addressing Chief High Priests," the Chief High Priest of Darromohe expressed his displeasure. "And I don't see how anyone could have pushed you from such a distance. As for the Chief High Priest of Parroo, he will have to answer for many things, but this is not one of them."

Apaan, growing despondent by the initial part of the Chief High Priest's answer, perked up at the last statement, but decided it would be best not to speak anymore. The first part of the ceremony involved invoking the various Gods by name, through incantations and hymns sung towards their praise. Apaan's incantations were famous throughout Givenland. His voice was famous for both its timbre and devoutness, and having heard him call out to the Gods, one could never imagine his true nature.

After the invoking of the Gods was done, Apaan stood up.

"People of Pparaha," Apaan's voice boomed. "I, Apaan, the son on Dhanaan, Keeper of the North-eastern Granaries, Controller of Airavati, Member of the Eastern Council of High Priests and the Chief High Priest of Pparaha stand before you on this very proud day for Pparaha. It was on this day many …"

"O Chief High Priest of Pparaha," the Chief High Priest of Parroo cut in, "let me tell the people of Pparaha …"

"O Chief High Priest of Parroo," Apaan called out, "you of all people should know that a Chief High Priest's opening declaration should never be interrupted." He then turned towards the crowd continued, "As I was saying …"

"O High Priest of Pparaha," the Chief High Priest of Parroo burst in again, "I would never have interrupted you unless I thought it was important. I wanted …"

"O Chief High Priest of Parroo," Apaan boomed, "shame on you for repeating your mistake again. And, that too, in front of the Chief High Priest of Darromohe, who is also the Keeper of Protocols." Then again turning towards the crowd continued, "As I was saying, this is indeed a very proud day for us, for it was on this day, 273[77] years ago, that our city was born. There are many present here, who are descendants of those first twenty-one[78] families that came here to start this town. I envy them the pride they must feel, knowing that without the fortitude of their forward-thinking ancestors, there would be no Pparaha. We will talk more about them and our blessed Pparaha momentarily. But first, I would like to request our Chief Guest, the Chief High Priest of Darromohe to address the good people of Pparaha."

"O Chief High Priest of Pparaha," the Chief High Priest of Darromohe said, "it is indeed an honour to be the Chief Guest at such an auspicious occasion. In all my years as a Chief High Priest, I have never been to a Winter Solstice celebration," and then paused, leaving the people wondering what was coming next, "where there were four Chief High Priests present. And that reminds me, we all saw the Chief High Priest of Parroo interrupting our host's opening declaration. I am sure many of you are curious, like me, to understand why he did this. So, O Chief High Priest of Pparaha, with your leave, I would like to ask the Chief High Priest of Parroo for his reasons."

If protocol had allowed it, Apaan would not even have interrupted earlier. Since his meeting with the Chief High Priest of Ankal, he was impatiently waiting to confront the Chief High Priest of Parroo.

"O Chief High Priest of Darromohe," Apaan said, "you are my senior in age, experience and wisdom. So who am I to question your decision? O Chief High Priest of Parroo, please, enlighten us what was so important that you interrupted the opening declaration."

"O Chief High Priest of Pparaha," the Chief High Priest of Parroo said, "I thank you. And O Chief High Priest of Darromohe, I really appreciate your kindness. I would first of all like to apologize to everyone for what may have seemed to be an inopportune interruption. But …"

Runggoo, keeping his head down, shouted out from his position, "Come to the point." Everyone in the Ceremonial Platform immediately tried spotting Runggoo, to find out who had spoken.

---

[77]100010001 in binary and therefore very significant
[78]10101 in binary

Apaan smiled, happy that the crowd was heckling the Chief High Priest of Parroo.

Viraan had positioned himself in the crowd directly behind where Tanaa and Riyaansh had taken their seats. Immediately after Runggoo, he called out in an extremely loud voice, "Stop procrastinating. Come to the point." The crowd immediately turned towards the direction from which Viraan's voice had rung out.

At exactly that moment, Tanaa, who was sitting with her head bowed, stood up to face the platform. Apaan immediately saw her.

"Who has allowed that She-animal into my Temple Sanctuary?" Apaan shouted before he could control himself. But, he quickly calmed himself. "My good people of Pparaha, please be patient and let the Chief High Priest of Parroo complete his explanation."

"As I was saying," the Chief High Priest of Parroo started.

But, Apaan was barely listening. He was still looking towards Tanaa and wondering how she had got in the Temple Sanctuary and made it into the privileged enclosure. It was then that Riyaansh brought his head up and looked directly at Apaan. Apaan was shocked. He had ordered Riyaansh's death on the same night he had used Zayaa for the first time. He had ordered not one, but three High Priests to take care of this. They had reported back with the news of Riyaansh's death. So how could he be sitting here? Because despite his scar, there was no mistaking that it was Riyaansh. It was then that he realized that he had missed most of the Chief High Priest of Parroo's explanation.

"… but the honour is not just Pparaha's but also Parroo's, and I am sure the Chief High Priest of Pparaha will accept this honour," the Chief High Priest of Parroo concluded. But Apaan knew what he was talking about, so it did not matter that he had not heard most of the explanation.

"O Chief High Priest of Parroo," Apaan said, "I don't think this honour shall ever be Parroo's. Please perish that thought from your mind. Zayaa and Tiraa belong to Pparaha. I can …"

Then, seeing the bewildered look on the faces of everyone around him and the laughter that was ringing out across the crowd, he stopped.

The Chief High Priest of Darromohe took Apaan aside and whispered to him, "O Chief High Priest of Pparaha, is this another attempt at humour? There is a time and place for everything. I cannot fathom your reason for doing what you just did, especially on such an important day for Pparaha. A day made even more propitious with the announcement that the

Chief High Priest of Parroo just made. With this new honour, you need to bring more dignity to your countenance, and not such levity. With the behaviour you are demonstrating this evening, one has to wonder whether you have the maturity to do justice to this honour."

Even though the crowd could not hear what was being said, Apaan was sure they could make out the fact that he was being told off. For the first time, Apaan was a little worried, but he quickly shrugged it off.

"O Good people of Pparaha," Apaan said first to ensure the crowd did not get too impatient, "please bear with us. We have some gifts to distribute, but first we need to confer and agree on some protocols. So, please be patient."

Riyaansh was getting a little nervous as Apaan seemed to have quickly recovered full control of his faculties.

"O Chief High Priest of Darromohe, please accept my heartfelt apologies," Apaan whispered. "I hope you will look more kindly at my mistakes when I explain the situation. The Chief High Priest of Parroo has been conspiring against me for quite some time. As you know, if anyone of our holy order has some grievances against another, the protocols of getting relief are quite clear. I would have no complaints, if he had sought to avail of these, but the depravity of his purposes is evident through his actions. Instead of taking his complaints to the Grand Council of High Priests, after the last Harvest Festival, he met with his co-conspirators in a place near here. They were there for weeks coming up with their evil plan to further their despicable purposes."

Then, misreading Darromohe's look of disbelief, he ploughed on.

"I know it is hard to believe," he continued in a whisper, "but one person, who was present there, was appalled that a holy person like the Chief High Priest of Parroo was involved in such an unholy congregation. This person found it to be his moral and ethical duty to come and inform me about it. As I was looking towards the crowd, I spotted one of the Chief High Priest of Parroo's co-conspirators. I was so exasperated by this audacity that momentarily I lost my faculties."

"O Chief High Priest of Pparaha," the Chief High Priest of Darromohe said patiently, "I am old-fashioned and traditional in my ways. There are many things that have become acceptable now that we could not even imagine in our younger days. I have learnt to condone these practices. I know that some of you use hallucinogens to give a better performance, and yes, I also know that these occasions have become more about your performance rather than the reverential invocation of the Gods. But what I cannot condone is the overuse of these. Because when you do that, you lose your senses."

Then raising his hand to stop Apaan from interrupting, he continued. "Let me finish. Immediately after the Harvest Festival, the Chief High Priest of Parroo had come to Darromohe. He was there for almost a month, conducting research in our libraries. How could he have been conspiring against you, without being in two places at the same time? This year the Grand Council of High Priests had their annual retreat in Darromohe. A vacancy has been created in the Council by the death of the Chief High Priest of Dijikot[79]. The Chief High Priest of Parroo asked the Grand Council of High Priests for an audience. During this, he asked us to consider the fact that the Northeast was not represented in the Council, and therefore fill the vacancy with someone from the Northeast. Quite a few of the council members, including myself, were against this, as the nomination to the council has always been based on capability and nothing else. At this, the Chief High Priest of Parroo made an impassioned plea, in which he convinced a majority of the council on the suitability of your candidature to fill the position based also on your capability."

Then Darromohe looked around, as if to say 'what capability?'

"My anger with the Chief High Priest of Parroo," the Chief High Priest of Darromohe continued, "is because of this unconventional way that he got you nominated to the council. If you had been listening to him, you would have heard him explain that the only reason he interrupted you was to add this new title in your address. As you know, even before the confirmation, which for the Grand Council of High Priests sometimes takes years, a person can start using the title of 'Nominated to the Grand Council of High Priests'. So, you have to be either out of your mind on some hallucinogen to imagine that the Chief High Priest of Parroo was conspiring against you. Unless, of course, those members in the council who thought you were mad were actually right."

By now, both Vyaan and Riyaansh were getting really worried. First of all, Apaan still seemed to be keeping his cool. And Zayaa had not started playing her role, yet. They would be more at ease if they knew that Apaan was indeed very confused. Apaan was not sure whether to believe what Darromohe was saying. His instinct told him that Darromohe was being honest, but his cunningness was telling him to be suspicious of everything and not forget the probability of Darromohe being one of the conspirators. An enemy's friend was an enemy; it was telling him, especially one who is praising your enemy and claiming to dislike him at the same time. It was his

---

[79]A town in Western Givenland/ Meluhha

instincts and cunningness working together that had made him so successful. And he trusted both. But, as they were telling him two different things, he was not sure how to proceed. Even though he was used to manipulating others, it was yet to cross his mind that someone could have made a plan to manipulate both Darromohe and him at the same time. But then he realized there was an easy way to prove the Chief High Priest of Parroo's complicity. He just needed Ankal to tell Darromohe what he had told him.

"O Chief High Priest of Ankal," he called, still keeping his voice low to make sure it could not be heard outside the Ceremonial Platform. "Please come here for a moment." Then, he continued in a whisper, "O Chief High Priest of Darromohe, I am not sure what the Chief High Priest of Parroo is playing at, but please hear what the Chief High Priest of Ankal has to say and then you will understand the situation better."

But even before Ankal had reached where they were, Viraan called out from the crowd.

"Is this a gathering of the Chief High Priests, or will be addressed at some point of time?"

Runggoo followed, "It would be better if we had one instead of four Chief High Priests in that platform, maybe then we would get some attention."

Emboldened by these remarks, many others started shouting out similar things to the Chief High Priests.

"O Chief High Priest of Pparaha," the Chief High Priest of Darromohe said, "I will listen to the Chief High Priest of Ankal. But, please go and control your people. I have seen enough excitement today, and can do without seeing four Chief High Priests being heckled out of a Ceremonial Platform."

Apaan knew what Darromohe was saying was true. It was never a wise thing to let a crowd be directionless for too long. It was for this very reason that these large gatherings were never allowed outside the Temple Sanctuary. But, he was no longer sure whether it would be wise to leave Ankal alone with Darromohe.

"Someone get on the platform and tell us some jokes, until these jokers get their acts together," a voice rang out, followed by many statements agreeing to the sentiments of the first speaker.

Apaan decided he had to do something to pacify the crowds, first.

At that moment someone from the crowd shouted, "Or maybe we can see some dancing."

'Of course,' Apaan thought with relief, 'I need to change the schedule and have the dancing now.'

"O Good people of Pparaha," Apaan said, raising both his hands to calm the crowd, "we are indeed sorry for keeping you all waiting. But, we still need to discuss some protocols. So, instead we will first have something you all have been waiting for. The Dreamer-of-Truths-Yet-to-Come will lead ten other Dasasas in a prayer to the Gods. And as you all know, when our Dreamer leads a dance adulating the Gods, the Gods themselves do sit up in adulation. So, I give you the Dreamer."

Zayaa had been feeling the effects of the leaves just as Apaan had spotted Riyaansh and had stopped listening to the Chief High Priest of Parroo. Being on the Ceremonial Platform and her other senses having become more acute with the loss of the senses of touch and pain, she could hear parts of the discussion between Darromohe and Apaan. She knew the plan was to confuse Apaan by the appearance of Tanaa and then Riyaansh, but she realized their plan was working even better than expected. So, she had decided to postpone her part for a while. But then, Apaan had himself gifted them an even bigger advantage. What she was going to do would be dramatic even from the corner of the Ceremonial Platform she was standing in, but from the centre, and after Apaan's grand announcement the impact would be many times more. She led off her dance troupe to the centre of the Platform and started giving the performance of her life.

As Apaan started turning away from the crowd, suddenly someone caught his eye. He was surprised to see that Sanj was sitting with a big grin in the common area, quite close to the Ceremonial Platform. Apaan realized that the reason he had noticed Sanj, was because the latter was waving both arms to get his attention. After a few attempts, Apaan got the attention of the High Priest nearest to Sanj and beckoned him to come nearer to the Ceremonial Platform. The High Priest needed some time to get there through the crowd.

"I need that man detained," Apaan told the High Priest pointing at Sanj. "I know what I said before about having no disturbances, while our visitors are here. I do not care about that anymore. That person does not leave the Temple Sanctuary before I have talked with him. Then I shall decide whether he leaves at all."

Then realizing he had kept Ankal and Darromohe with each other for longer than desired, he quickly hurried there.

"Has Ankal explained everything?" Apaan asked.

"Yes, he has," the Chief High Priest of Darromohe said, looking at Apaan in a strange way, "and I think I will have to ask the Chief High Priest of Parroo for an explanation. And I still can't see what logical explanation he can have for doing what he has done. I …"

It was at that moment that Zayaa, nearing a climax of her performance, in a very sensuous position, with everyone in the crowd fully focused on her, suddenly stopped. She came to a standstill with her hands by her side. The musicians stopped, not sure what to do next. Then Zayaa lifted her head and gazed unseeingly into the distance. Then she raised her hands, as if in supplication.

And Viraan's voice rang out. "Quiet, everyone! I think the Dreamer is having a revelation."

Everyone looked towards Zayaa with different emotions.

Those involved in Vyaan's plan had been getting more and more anxious and nervous, as time passed without Zayaa playing her part. Finally, they sighed in relief and watched with anticipation for their plan to unfold.

For Apaan, it was trepidation and apprehension. He finally understood that these were too many coincidences. It was clear that it was someone's plan that was being executed to perfection. But, he was still confident he would come out as the winner. He knew he would have to play hard and without fear. After all, it was his Temple Sanctuary and his town.

The six High Priests of Pparaha were worried as usual. Whenever the Dreamer had these visions, they were always apprehensive that she would talk about their first contact with her.

The Chief High Priest of Darromohe was looking with disbelief and eagerness. He had been in the Temple Sanctuary of Darromohe for a very long time, but had never had any direct proof of the existence of the Gods. This did not in any way shake his belief in the Gods, but over time, he had become sceptical about the many claims from all over Givenland about direct or indirect revelations by the Gods. He was not sure what, but he felt something was different about this. First, he tried to push it away as an influence by the tensions of the already strange evening. Then he thought he was being influenced by Zayaa's skin colour and countenance. Finally, he looked at the other Chief High Priests and decided to keep an open mind.

"O people of Givenland," Zayaa said using the male voice that Tanaa had trained her for, "hear well and in my voice recognize the bidding of all your Gods. Hear well and do our bidding, or be ready to face our Wrath.

Hear us well for we have decided to bestow on you some great honour indeed. We have chosen one of you to be a Dasasa. But, she will not be an ordinary Dasasa, for she will not be a Dasasa in one of your Temples Sanctuaries. She has been chosen to be a Dasasa in our Abode in the Great Northern White Mountains, beyond the Valleys of Swastu, above the Lake of Durshan. Now, hear us, you High Priests of Pparaha, and hear well all six of you. Your sins have not gone unnoticed by us. But you have done one good deed in your lives. You paid heed to our message and stayed away from defiling our messenger, Zayaa of Kdwar. For this deed, as long as from here on you stay away from sinning any more, you shall be forgiven. But hear our bidding now – you shall make arrangements for our Dasasa to be brought to us. Hear well, people of Givenland, good and bad; people of Givenland old and young; people of Givenland of plains and hills; people of Givenland from all cities, towns and villages. Hear well, O people of Givenland, by doing our bidding is your only path to salvation. O people of Givenland, you will send Tiraa, the daughter of Zayaa of Kdwar and Vyaan of Parroo to our Abode to be our Dasasa. And make no mistake, for if you don't start on these arrangements before three full moons have passed, be ready to face our wrath. We have spoken. Let our words be carved in your Temple walls. And let our bidding be done."

Zayaa continued to stand in her position, hands outstretched, looking into the distance.

The people immediately bowed and started holding their palms together in supplication and appreciation for being allowed to be present at this divine event.

The High Priests of Pparaha started entreating the people to keep calm and assuring them that the Gods' bidding will definitely be done.

Apaan first tried to get the attention of his High Priests, but when this failed, he decided to use his voice famous for captivating crowds.

"O Good People of Pparaha," Apaan's voice boomed, "please remain calm. This is of course some hoax being perpetrated on all of us. I will not deny that it has been very well planned and very well performed, but it is still a hoax."

"You mean you have been lying to us for all these years," Tiraak's voice rang out, with many immediately repeating the question towards the Ceremonial Platform.

"Are you telling us this Dasasa is indeed not the Dreamer-of-Truths-Yet-to-Come, like you have been proclaiming for years?" Runggoo shouted out, immediately being joined by others who threw the same question at the Ceremonial Platform.

"O Chief High Priest, are you telling us that it was a hoax for all these years?" Viraan asked. And this time, along with the question, much footwear was also thrown at the Platform. One of these, very well directed by Sanj, hit Zayaa. Zayaa did not even feel it, but started bleeding. However, as the effects of the Tree of Life took over, the blood congealed and the bleeding stopped. Everyone who saw this gasped and bowed their heads in prayer.

"O People of Givenland," Zayaa started speaking again in the same masculine voice, "hear us well and …"

"Enough of that Zayaa," Apaan shouted. "You cannot fool me and I will not allow you to fool the people of Pparaha. All of you High Priests of Pparaha put a stop to this nonsense. Take her inside and gag her if required, but make her shut up. I …"

"Stop, you puny human," Zayaa rebuked in the same voice, "do not talk while your betters are not yet done talking. Do not bring down our wrath on all humanity by angering us thus. And do not worry, we have not forgotten you. You will get your just deserts. O High Priests of Pparaha, will you allow this man to stand between you and your salvation, decide now. Shall you continue on your paths of depravity or are you going to lead a path of purity and without sin from here on. Decide now. Whether you want salvation or eternal suffering?"

"You do not scare me," Apaan said, "nor do you scare my High Priests." Then quickly thinking on his feet, he added, "O Chief High Priest of Ankal, tell the good people of Pparaha what you told me this afternoon. Or even better let the holiest of holies amongst us, the Chief High Priest of Darromohe share what the Chief High Priest of Ankal shared with him."

"Are you sure you want me to do this?" the Chief High Priest of Darromohe asked. The lack of proper address would normally have made Apaan wary, but he was too preoccupied to notice now.

"Of course, I do," Apaan said impatiently, "why would I ask otherwise? But repeat only what you have heard from Ankal. Remember, he is here to refute any untruths."

"O Good People of Pparaha," Darromohe started and having become a full believer quickly added, "and, of course, with your permission, O Dreamer-of-Truths-Yet-to-Come. The Chief High Priest of Ankal has made some very serious allegations. I still cannot believe this of a Chief

High Priest of our order. And I have to add that none of this has been confirmed, yet. But according to the Chief High Priests of Ankal, one of the Dasasas has been treated with sinful depravity in this very Temple Sanctuary. I am …"

"What are you talking about, you old fool?" Apaan said, "I thought as much. You must be a part of this conspiracy. Shut up, shut up now. Let the Chief High Priest of Ankal speak instead. I had warned you he is here to refute any untruths from you. Tell them the truth Ankal."

"The Chief High Priest of Darromohe has indeed not told you the truth," the Chief High Priest of Ankal began, much to Apaan's relief. "As you all know, the Chief High Priest of Darromohe is very traditional and is known for his strictness. He is also very well known for presiding over one of the most moral and unsoiled Temple Sanctuaries in our land. So, I dared not share the whole truth with him. We have found out that this Temple Sanctuary of yours has become an illustration of immorality and depravity. And it is not one, but many Dasasas who have been treated with decadence and debauchery. It is sad indeed …"

"You two faced jackal," Apaan cried out, "I will rip your tongue out. Tell them what you told me only this afternoon."

"O Good People of Pparaha," the Chief High Priest of Ankal said, "this afternoon I warned your Chief High Priest to fear the consequences of his sins. But, he replied that you were his cattle to do with as he pleased. I warned …"

"Shut up, you dog," Apaan cried out, now almost out of his mind, "people of Pparaha, I will yet prove to you that this is a hoax. The Gods are omniscient. They would definitely know that Tiraa is indeed not the daughter of Vyaan. I can tell you with …"

"That may be what you believe Apaan," Tanaa called out in a voice loud enough to drown Apaan's words, "O People of Pparaha, you know that I am a worshipper of truth. And having taken care of Zayaa before and after Tiraa's birth, I can tell you with certainty that Tiraa is indeed Vyaan's daughter."

"Don't listen to this she-animal that belongs in sheds and not in this Temple Sanctuary," Apaan said now with desperation. Then seeing three of the High Priests already on the Ceremonial Platform, he addressed them, "O High Priests of Pparaha, you heard the voice supposedly of the Gods proclaiming that you have never defiled Zayaa. Having taken your turns with her on innumerable occasions, you cannot really believe in the prophecy of that voice. Take her inside and wait for me. I will come in once I have calmed down our good people."

"No, Apaan," the High Priest who was chastised earlier in the evening said, "I have indeed done many sinful things. Some I did at your behest and some out of my own depravity. But, I have never touched the Dreamer. The Gods had warned me not to, and I ensured that I did not."

"And for that very reason, neither did I," said the second High Priest.

The third High Priest nodded and said, "And I do not know about the others, but now that I have been given a chance of salvation, I am going to try to do the bidding of the Gods or die trying."

Apaan now looked like a cornered animal. He looked around and his eyes fell on a knife. He jumped and picked it up, then lunged at Zayaa. But, one of the High Priests reacted quickly and tried to stop Apaan. He was not entirely successful, though. Instead of Zayaa's body, the knife struck her outstretched hand, which started bleeding. But, all the people looked in wonder as Zayaa did not even flinch and continued to stand exactly, as she was, as blood dripped from her wound.

"He has stabbed the Dreamer," the third High Priest shouted.

By this time, the other two High Priests had joined the first three. One of them twisted Apaan's arms until he dropped the knife. They quickly got some ropes and tied Apaan's hands behind him.

"O Dreamer," the High Priest who had been chastised earlier said, "please tell us what Apaan's punishment should be?"

"We do not need to ask that, do we?" the third High Priest said. "We know that he is a rapist and a murderer, and therefore, he shall be sat on a stake."

Zayaa could not believe how well the evening was going. It was beyond what they had planned, beyond even their wildest expectations. And now, she could finally have the vengeance that over the years she had almost given up on. Then she remembered what her father had asked her, about Apaan and Vyaan, and finally understood why he had asked her to ponder over his questions. The knowledge that she had Apaan at her mercy to do as she pleased would have to be revenge enough for her. She decided that the salvation of Givenland, which was directly linked to the future of Tiraa, was more important to her than Apaan's punishment.

"O People of Givenland," Zayaa said, continuing in the masculine voice but more gently, and to the crowds amazement, her hand stopped bleeding, the crowd started ululating and bowing their heads in prayer, but immediately went quiet when Zayaa continued, "you have forgotten that when we gave you this land to live in and prosper, you promised to live with the codes that we laid down for you. We taught you to be humans and distinguish yourselves from animals, but you all have taught yourselves to be animals again. Neither did we teach you to make stakes, nor did we tell you to punish others by sitting them on these. Now you shall start taking the first steps back towards humanity. From this day on, we shall not condone the use of stakes any more. There shall be punishment for all sins and all crimes, but not without relief. O Chief High Priest of Darromohe, this is a message for your Grand Council of High Priests. You shall ensure that not only are the laws upheld, but also that justice is meted out fairly. You shall ensure that another Chief High Priest like Apaan shall not happen. You shall also decide Apaan's punishment. We have spoken. If the journey of our chosen Dasasa to our abode does not start by the third full moon, you shall hear from us again, but not so kindly." Then Zayaa put her head down and immediately cried out in pain holding her wounded hand with the other and said in her normal voice, "Where am I?"

"What did she do?" Tanaa asked Riyaansh in despair. "She just spared that animal. What happened to her vengeance? You know she could have run away to Wacha, after that night at the Temple Sanctuary. But, she stayed back to exact her revenge. And now that she got her chance, she let it go. And it is not only her; she owed it to all the others. Some of whom are not lucky enough to be alive today. What has she done?"

"She just took the first but enormous step towards the salvation of Givenland," Riyaansh said with a smile. "For when she stands before the Gods, with Vyaan on behalf of all Givenland, and ask them not to punish the many for the sins of a few, if they truly are Gods, how can they refuse this forgiveness to Zayaa who could forgive Apaan? No Tanaa, I am not wrong when I say, that indeed she did it because she was thinking of the others, not herself. But please do not misunderstand me – Apaan sitting on a stake is something that got fated, the day he despoiled Zayaa and caused Ridhaan's death. And I will make sure that it happens, but for Givenland's sake I also needed Zayaa to forgive him, first."

"That makes more sense," Tanaa said, "she forgave him in public, knowing that you would still arrange for his punishment."

"No Tanaa," Riyaansh smiled. "That would not work, would it? After all, the Gods are supposed to be omniscient. No, she does not know it. If I could use her, I would have arranged for a full pardon and release. I will have to do it the harder way. However, my instincts tell me the Chief High Priest of Parroo will help us on this, as well."

"What about you? Are you not afraid of tricking the Gods?" Tanaa asked.

"I am close to completing what I have been living for," Riyaansh said. "Once, I see Apaan sitting on a stake, I will die peacefully, hopefully with blessings from the Gods, but without it if so fated."

Riyaansh's instinct was right.

"May I say something with everyone's permission?" the Chief High Priest of Parroo said. "It seems that the Gods want even an animal like Apaan to receive fair justice. Who are we to question their judgment? We should just do their bidding. But I also understand why, for many in Pparaha, it might be impossible to adhere to this bidding. So, I think it would be best for everyone, if Apaan was moved to somewhere else, till his fate has been decided by the Grand Council of High Priests. If all of you are willing, I shall arrange for guards to take him to Parroo and keep him there for the duration."

"I think that is a good idea," the Chief High Priest of Darromohe agreed and then turned to the crowd, "O Good people of Pparaha, we are all blessed indeed to have been present in this truly auspicious and divine occasion, for how many people can truly claim to have heard the voice of God. I also stand here, my head hanging in shame that someone of our order has done you all such unspeakable harms. We will ensure that the next Chief High Priest and the High Priests you will have shall be true men of God. I also promise you that even they shall be kept under close observation. But, now I would request all of you to kindly proceed to your homes. I promise you that all the actions that I have promised will be open and you shall be kept informed about everything that is being done."

The people knew that it would have to be a very brave man, indeed, who would disregard the command of the Gods. So, they started leaving, but not before many of them came and touched Zayaa's feet and asked for her blessings. Zayaa sat surrounded by the others who had suffered like her, the other Dasasas, and begged that people not touch her feet, for she was only the messenger, and otherwise a commoner like any of them.

Voices in the Night

Tiraa woke up. It was still dark outside. She could hear voices floating in from outside. Then she remembered she was in her grandfather's hut. At first, she thought it was the voices that had woke her up. Almost immediately as her stomach cramps came back, she realized that it wasn't. This went on for some time. Finally, when it stopped, she could still feel her upper thighs and back aching. She got up and realized the bleeding that her mother had talked to her about had started.

"Ayei," Tiraa shrieked.

Zayaa came running in. Tiraa told her what had happened.

"My baby daughter has become a woman," Zayaa said with a warm smile. "Now, I am truly feeling old."

Meanwhile, Vyaan and Riyaansh were still outside speaking to each other.

"Have you decided what you will do?" Vyaan asked Riyaansh.

"Well, your wife refuses to be convinced," Riyaansh said, "so I shall have to be a part of your quest, at least until the terrain becomes too tough for these old legs."

"Uncle Nongru asked me to talk to you about some message."

"Oh yes, about that," Riyaansh was reminded. "Your uncle Runggoo had a visit from someone from a different valley. It seems Pasher has been living somewhere in the mountains near this valley, but somehow found out about what is happening. His message was 'Master's son shall have a guide who has been to Durshan'. So, we assumed that Pasher wants to join your quest. But remember, the quest is more important than anyone's emotions, so even Pasher shall go only if he does not become a burden. And only if he shows up before you all leave on your mission."

"What do you mean by before you all leave?" Vyaan said, "I thought you were coming with us."

"And I will," Riyaansh said, "but, I will join up with you in Lakho. I have some things to take care of before that."

"What things?" Vyaan asked, and then, looking at Riyaansh, he decided he did not want to know. "No, do not tell me, for even if I lie, Zayaa always knows."

Soon Zayaa came out.

"So, Appi," Zayaa said, "you have decided to come with us I hope."

"Yes," Riyaansh said, "but I need to take care of some unfinished business, first. I promise that I will catch up with you soon."

"It is Mother Tanaa, is it not?" Zayaa teased. "That is your unfinished business, isn't it? You can tell me. You know she is already like a mother to me."

"Go and sleep," Riyaansh said admonishingly. "From tomorrow, you shall have to start your preparations. Anyway I am off to bed now."

After Riyaansh had left, Zayaa kept on looking sorrowfully after him. "He is planning something terrible, isn't he?" Zayaa said. "No, don't answer that. Just take me in your arms." Then snuggled up against him, she said, "Tomorrow, we shall start planning the quest your father wanted you to go on. But today, let us enjoy the end of the previous one. Your plan worked. Our daughter is safe. For today, only that matters, and, of course the fact that she is a woman now. Don't look so surprised, we both knew this day would come."

Glossary

Abgal	Literally meaning great elder – abba gal – but also used to address elderly wise men
Airavati	River Ravi
Ankal	Town in Eastern Givenland/ Meluhha on banks of River Sutlej
Ashkini	River Chenab
Ašša	Horse in Sumerian, as horses were not indigenous to Givenland, they were still quite rare
Babylon	City upriver from Kurm in Sumer
Banyan tree	the leaves and buds of which helps stop bleeding
Bogu	Sumerian God of wealth
Changa	Alcohol brewed in the Himalayan valleys by fermenting barley stuffed inside cucurbits
Darromohe	City in Southern Givenland/ Meluhha on the banks of River Indus
Dijikot	Town in Western Givenland/ Meluhha
Dilmun	Basra, Iraq
Dishta	grinder usually made of stone
Durshan	A lake in a valley high up in the Hindu Kush Mountains
Ea	The Akkadian name for Enki - God of intelligence and mischief amongst other things
Enki	Sumerian God of intelligence and mischief amongst other things
Énsi	City governor or city lord originally coming from the term 'lord of the plow land'
Ganbanlika	Town in Central-Western Givenland/ Meluhha
Givenland	What the people living in Meluhha called their own land (explanation in Chapter 7: The Akkadian's Tale I)
Great Northern White Mountains	Hindu Kush Mountains
Great Unending Waters	Arabian Sea
Haths	Measure for length used in Givenland (measuring approximately fourteen inches)
Ilpurjal	Town in Central Givenland/ Meluhha on banks of River Jhelum

Kaigavas	Type of leather glove
Kanuchara	Valerian plant – the root of which is used as a sedative
Kaš	Sumerian Alcohol
Kdwar	Town in Givenland/ Meluhha, a little upriver from the mouth of the Indus River
Keenjhar	Lake Kalri
Ki-en-ĝir	Sumer in Sumerian – this was the form used in formal speeches
Kù	Money or wealth in Sumerian
Kubha	River Kabul
Kurm	Town in central Sumer on the banks of River Euphrates
Kur-nu-gi-a	The land of no return – Sumerians believed that a person went there after death
Lakho	Town in Northern Givenland/ Meluhha near where River Kabul meets River Indus
Larsa	Town downriver from Kurm in Sumer
Limak	Town in Southern Givenland/ Meluhha south of Lake Kalri
Mahahaths	1025 haths – or in binary 10000000001 haths
Makkan	Oman
Meluhha	What the Sumerians called Givenland
Misr	Egypt
Mother River	Indus River
Mountain That Touches the Sky	Himalayan Mountains
Namabba	Grandfather
Naña-si-è	Soapwort – leaves of which were used as a disinfectant
Ñizzalkalamma	Very intelligent person
Panj	Panjnad – Beas, Chenab, Jhelum, Ravi and Sutlej coming together before joining the Indus
Parroo	Town in North-Eastern Givenland/ Meluhha on the banks of River Sutlej
Pashubar	The main deity of the people of Wacha
Pparaha	City in East-Central Meluhha near River Ravi
Purattu	River Euphrates
Purawanbhag	Town in North-Eastern Givenland/ Meluhha south of Parroo
Raajaraas	Givenland/ Meluhha's staple alcohol brewed from Barley
Raakanaa	Place where one could buy and drink raajaraas
Rahira	Town in South-Western Meluhha/ Givenland
Raisa	Town in confluence of Rivers Jhelum and Korang
River Swastu	River Swat

Runaka	Town in Northern Givenland/ Meluhha on the banks of River Kabul
Sat on a stake	A heinous form of death sentence – described in detail Chapter 7: The Akkadian's Tale I
Shatadru	River Sutlej
Sikkappa	Paternal uncle
Sila-nim	Spring lamb in Sumerian with no equivalent word in Givenland
Sippar	Town upriver from Kurm in Sumer
Šumeru	Sumer in Akkadian
Swastu	Swat valley
Thallo	Port City in South-Eastern Givenland/ Meluhha
Tree of life	Sichuan Thuja –One of the evergreen coniferous trees of the Thuja family
Ur	Town downriver from Kurm in Sumer
Urtud	Domestic servant – which did not have an equivalent word in Givenland/ Meluhha
Vipasa	River Beas
Vitasta	River Jhelum
Wacha	A valley in the Himalayas somewhere in Western Nepal

The Author, I.J. Roy, lives in Chappaqua, NY with his enduring wife and two overactive sons, trying to balance between his bread earning job at the Big Apple and finding ways to channel his hyper-imaginative mind. Being a history buff and geography enthusiast from early childhood, IJ uses his analytical nature and imagination, to bring to life for his readers, ancient places that time has forgotten.

www.ingramcontent.com/pod-product-compliance
Lightning Source LLC
Chambersburg PA
CBHW020334180626
46812CB00001B/207